SISTERS IN LOVE

The Atkinson Saga
Book Two

Mollie Hardwick

SAPERE
BOOKS

Also in the Atkinson Family Saga
The Atkinson Heritage
Dove's Nest

SISTERS IN LOVE

Published by Sapere Books.

24 Trafalgar Road, Ilkley, LS29 8HH

saperebooks.com

ISBN: 978-0-85495-559-6

For my mother, Frances Atkinson, of Lancaster

In June there's a red rosebud, and that's the flower for me;
But oft have I pluck'd at the red rosebud, till I gain'd the willow-tree.
The willow-tree will twist, and the willow-tree will twine —
Oh, I wish I was in the dear youth's arms that once had this heart of mine.

OLD LANCASHIRE BALLAD

CHAPTER ONE

Joe Atkinson stood in the hall of his uncle Ephraim's house in St Leonard's Gate, Lancaster, and surveyed his surroundings. There had been no one to welcome him but Aggie Noon, the servant who had been with the family since he had joined it nine years ago in 1818, for he had arrived in the middle of Sunday morning when his aunt, uncle and cousins and the other servants were at church.

'You picked a funny sort of time, Joe,' she told him roundly. No master-ing or mistress-ing of youngsters for Aggie, nor yet sir-ing and madam-ing for her employers. Sister to Miss Noon who kept the Royal Oak and was a highly respected personage in Lancaster, Aggie prided herself on speaking to others as she thought fit, be they the highest in the land.

'I'm sorry, Aggie,' Joe said meekly. 'I couldn't help it — the coach only took me as far as Preston yesterday, and I had to stay the night and hire a horse after breakfast.'

She looked him up and down: six feet of slender manhood, with his father's red-gold hair and hazel eyes, a high clever forehead and a sort of dreaming look to his face. Her grim expression softened and she unconsciously straightened her severe cap. She had always had a weakness for Joe. A good boy from the start, who'd more than made up to Mr and Mrs Atkinson for the son they'd never had.

'Aye, well. I've a lot to do. You know your way round, or if you don't by now, you never will. D'you want a sup of summat? It'll be a good hour to dinner.'

'I'm not hungry, thank you, Aggie.' He was, but it was not his way to interfere with the work of the kitchen or make a nuisance of himself.

'Please yourself. Where's your luggage?' Her sharp tone suggested that it was not quite respectable of him to arrive without any.

'I had to leave it in Preston at the inn. They're sending it on tomorrow.'

'Let's hope they do, that's all. You can't trust nobody nowadays. I'll get on, then.'

She bustled down to the kitchen, leaving Joe standing somewhat forlornly in the middle of the hall. How small everything looked, compared with his childhood memories of the house that had once seemed very grand to him, even beside his parents' beautiful old house in Kendal. Now the wallpaper's design of formal leaves and flowers looked less impressive than it had done, the marble floor less grand, the tall clock in the corner shrunk from the size it had once seemed to him, when he had hardly dared to pass close to it in case it fell on him and crushed him. There was the graceful table still bearing its silver tray with the Atkinson arms engraved on it, and above it, in a place of honour, the portrait in oils of his beloved grandfather, Old John: teller of strange, fascinating tales, giver of the sort of gifts a boy really wanted, singer of jolly songs.

Joe looked up at the broad, rosy face above the old-fashioned cravat with the fox-head pin in it, which Joe himself owned now. 'Grandfather,' he said softly. He had stood by the old man's deathbed, crying, and at the graveside in the churchyard of the Priory Church high on the hill beside the frowning castle. But it seemed to him that Old John lived on here, in this house, to comfort and sustain his grandson when in need, even now that the boy had become a man.

His reverie was broken by the sound of wheels on the cobbles and the chatter of voices. They were home from church early. The door opened and he was suddenly surrounded by his family, being kissed and hugged by Aunt Mary and his cousins and warmly slapped on the back by Uncle Ephraim.

'Joe, lad! We thought you'd given us a miss. Come along in.' He was being propelled into the parlour, a cousin on each arm; his aunt sailing in front like a large comely merchant vessel. Then pelisses and bonnets were being taken off and handed to Aggie, his uncle's tall hat sent out to its peg in the cloakroom off the hall, Aunt Mary's plain-ish cap, flattened by her flower-trimmed bonnet, exchanged for a finer one with bows on it. Joe remembered from the past her taste for elaborate caps. But the once-rich brown hair under this one had grown grey-streaked, and the lady, once buxom, was now undeniably stout. She was very like her mother, Joe's grandmother Bateman, but had a placid expression that the farmer's wife had lacked.

A lifetime of legal problems and family worries had turned Ephraim's hair, too, to grey, and thinned it, even though he was not yet fifty, seven years younger than his wife. The dark blue Atkinson eyes had paled a little, and there were furrows above the high-bridged nose. Ephraim needed spectacles all the time these days. He had worn them in church, taken them off, and now put them on again — narrow gold-rimmed things that aged him, though he gave no thought to that. He was still slim and active from all the walking he did up and down the streets of the hilly grey town where he had so many clients and friends, for he would never ride when he could walk. In all Lancaster there were few more respected than he. *Integer vitae, scelerisque purus*, a legal colleague had called him in public at some dinner, bringing a flush to his pale cheeks — Horace's 'man of life upright, from all guilt free'. It sounded priggish, but Ephraim Atkinson was not so, only oblivious to self-interest and the attractions of high office. Many a female client had wept on his shoulder without shame, and many who had stood in the dock now went free because of his persuasive arguments to the jury. Other, more hard-bitten lawyers frankly called him soft, saying that with a few less scruples and a bit more concern for the letter of the law, Atkinson might have worn a judge's wig by now.

Joe moved a little closer to the man he had thought of as his father since he was eight and a half. No one could really take the place of his own young father, the master carpenter tragically killed by a fall of timber in his own workshop on the night when the town of Kendal rejoiced in the victory of Waterloo, but Uncle Ephraim had done everything in human power to make his brother Francis only a happy shade in the boy's mind, a gentle ghost standing beside that of the young wife who had grieved herself to death for him a year after the accident. There were other things to efface: the dreadful life Joe had led with his father's partner, Will Raven, and with the cruel, bitter woman Raven had married out of infatuation. To escape them the child had walked from Kendal, up by the pass to the Lakes, almost twenty miles on the road to Lancaster and the safety of St Leonard's Gate.

As though the thought had gone out in words, a girl's voice said, 'Joe! You're gigantic. Do you remember Adam? Gracious me, he wouldn't know you now!'

'Of course,' he answered at once. 'How could I forget him, dear old fellow?'

'Some people,' said a softer, slightly lower voice, 'thought it was not Christian to bury a dog in the garden with a proper headstone. But we thought it quite right, did we not, Belle?'

And we put a bunch of flowers on his grave every year on the anniversary.'

'Thank you, Dove.' Joe turned to the twin sisters. He had not seen them during the year he had spent at university and travelling. Something astonishing seemed to have happened to them in his absence. Had they really been schoolgirls when he saw them last? Now they were young ladies who had reached the advanced age of sixteen. They sat together on a sofa, two roses on one branch, smiling at their boy cousin — Belle's smile brightly coquettish, Dove's gentler. Their dresses differed, for Mary had never followed the silly custom of making identical twins dress alike; Belle's was primrose-pale yellow, Dove's white. Both were ankle-length with flounces at the hem and neat waists where waists ought to be, not under the bosom as had been the fashion in their mother's young womanhood. Their long sleeves were *à la gigot,* leg-of-mutton shaped — full at the shoulder and narrow at the wrists — and trimmed with fine lace, and their bodices came discreetly up to the point of their collarbones because they had been to church.

Joe noticed nothing of this, for he was too busy staring at their faces. Whimsical nature had chosen to ignore their parents' looks, the traditional English brown hair and blue eyes, and had instead bestowed on them a sensational colouring unknown in their part of the world. Shining hair of the palest gold, dressed with a centre parting and grape-cluster ringlets on each side, and skin like that of white peaches, touched with the most delicate of healthy pink on rounded cheeks, made all the more startling their large dark eyes: soft, deer-like eyes, fringed with dark lashes. Examined closer (as they had already been by impassioned admirers) the eyes proved to be not brown, but a very deep hazel. Belle, who considered herself quite a dabster at history, had informed one of the admirers that her eyes were exactly the same shade of those of Mary Queen of Scots; a piece of information which left the youth gaping, but still more interested in the eyes than in her erudition.

To these charms were added distracting mouths, rose pink, of a softness that made their outlines prettily blurred, like the mouths of very young children. Joe, staring from one to the other, remembered, very vaguely, the night he first came to St Leonard's Gate after his fearful walk from Kendal, and a small creature who had appeared at his bedside, so fair that in his sleepiness he had taken her for an angel, but she had only been his cousin Dove.

His vision cleared. The two lovely creatures on the couch were once more the little girls with whom he had been reared as a brother, seeing them in all their stages of development. The crimson blotches of scarlatina had disfigured them, their whoops had rung round the house during a whooping cough epidemic, they had lost their milk teeth and gone about lisping, with toothless smiles. He had mended their dolls, acted as clergyman when their kittens were christened or mangled birds and mice were buried. They had attended, with him, grown-up funerals: first of their grandmother Bateman, then of her husband the farmer, and Belle had been inclined, most disgracefully, to giggle, while Dove's soft mouth trembled and drooped with sorrow, and her small hand clung to his. They had really changed very little — Belle the mischievous, Dove the quiet and sympathetic one. He smiled shyly at them, and was annoyed to feel his neck turn slightly red. But he failed entirely to notice the look in Dove's jasper eyes, a look that was only for him, and had always been there.

'Well?' said Ephraim.

The substantial Sunday dinner was over. Mary, who had been nodding off over the tea that followed, had gone upstairs for her afternoon sleep; the girls were off to see friends in Dalton Square. Somewhere in the house the servants took their ease, and Joe and his uncle confronted each other across the fire in the study lined with law books. All their serious talks had taken place there; this was going to be another one.

'So you've done it, after all. Given up university and all that lay before you, to go into cotton. I hope you know what you're doing.'

'You said I might when I was twenty-one, Uncle. And I am — almost.'

Ephraim pulled on his pipe. 'Trinity term was up in July. It's the middle of August now. Where have you been since?'

'Travelling. You said I should see a little of the world.'

'I did. So you took ship to France — saw the sights of Paris, maybe?'

Joe shook his head, blushing, to his uncle's grim amusement.

'Ah. You contented yourself with London, I suppose. Always a lot going on there.'

'I — I've visited London often. I was there in June, when we beat Cambridge in the rowing match. We — some of us went to town afterwards to celebrate.' Joe remembered with an inward shudder the head he had endured next morning, after a night on strong ale with fellow students.

'So. You didn't go abroad, or to London. Would you favour me with an account of where you *did* go?'

Joe swallowed. 'I came up here. I ... went round some of the towns.'

'Such as?'

13

'Oh, Stockport, Bolton, Blackburn … and Derbyshire, a place called Cromford, right in the country. Richard Arkwright owns it now — that's the son of the man who built it. There's a fine factory and a settlement for the workers —'

'I know all about Cromford, and the Arkwrights. How did you find the settlement, then?'

'I was disappointed, Uncle. It's a good design — the cottages all in tiers so that each has an outlook, and all hard by the mill — but it had got as dirty as a town, and the people were poor and miserable. As bad as Bradhope, or worse. It shouldn't be so, in my opinion. Arkwright's rich — all the owners are. Can't they pay better wages, or get someone in to improve on the machinery so that these wretched folk don't have to work like slaves?' Joe was growing heated. 'There are little children working there, at Cromford and in all the other factories: tiny children no more than seven years old. Some come from the cottages and some are parish apprentices brought in from the towns. They work from five in the morning till eight at night, with an hour off to eat in, standing every minute of the day —'

Ephraim held up his hand. 'All right, Joe. I know about these things, believe me. I gather you want to abandon the law and enter the cotton industry? Is this your reason, then — the poor conditions in the mills? Is this why you've thrown away Oxford and all the money I've spent on you?'

Joe shook his head vigorously. 'No, Uncle. Not quite that. I've tried to tell you before, but you wouldn't understand.'

'I *am* notably stupid,' Ephraim murmured to his pipe.

'It's not so much that I wish to be a reformer, as such,' Joe rushed on, 'though I've talked a great deal with a Christ Church man, Lord Ashley. He was before my time but he's been back to Gaudies and someone introduced us. He's in Parliament now and has tremendous ideas for bettering things.

I'll never have the power he has in high places, but what I want to do is improve conditions in the mills by improving the machinery. Do you know how old-fashioned it is, Uncle? I've studied it and I *know*. I met —' his voice was hushed with reverence — 'I met Samuel Crompton himself, two years ago, in Bolton. He was very old and ill, dying, but he was good enough to see me. He told me how he came to invent the spinning mule, all those years since, and how he improved on Hargreaves' spinning jenny with a twenty-spindle carriage that could weave muslin — and what notions he had for new machines, if he was spared. I — I ventured to tell him some thoughts of my own, and showed him a few sketches, and he said I was a promising lad and he wished he'd had such a son. Then he grew tired and I had to leave him.'

Ephraim pondered, his face grave. At last he asked, 'And do you know much about machinery, Joe?'

'Yes. A lot.'

'How — apart from these visits to mills?'

'I've studied. Books and designs, and the history of machinery.'

'Yes. I suppose Oxford affords plenty of access to such things, though in my time we were more frivolous-minded, I recall... How are your mathematics?'

'Very fair.'

That meant excellent, Ephraim thought. He knew Joe's modesty. 'And you're good with your hands.' He looked at them, the long strong workman's hands Joe had inherited from his father: Francis's hands. The skill which in Francis had been used to create furniture had in Joe been transmuted: both practical men, not the stuff of lawyers. Ephraim sighed, glancing round the study, with its tier upon tier of ponderous volumes, bound in sombre brown calf. Once he had imagined them all coming into Joe's possession, the office premises housing Joe — the attorney Joseph Atkinson carrying on the family tradition. Well, it was not to be. He fired a parting shot before abandoning the argument.

'You've actually handled machinery, I suppose, not just looked at it and drawn pictures?'

'Oh, yes. Often.'

'And made a fair nuisance of yourself in the process, I suppose, hanging round mills?' Joe blushed hotly. He had, indeed. 'Very well. We'll see.'

In Joe's boyhood this phrase had meant anything from temporising to ultimate refusal, and it rang ominously in his ears as he left Ephraim's study. He felt anxious, restless, more uncertain of himself than he had done since he left Oxford. For a time he wandered about the house, opening doors here and there, inspecting the familiar rooms which had all unaccountably dwindled, like the hall. Out in the garden, under the heavy-laden apple trees, he found among the windfalls in the grass a small headstone, crudely engraved with what seemed to be a cherub's head, and under it an inscription cut in wavering letters of various sizes:

Here lies ADAM,
faithful friend of Joseph, Belle
and Dove Atkinson 1816-1827.
He was a very lovely dog
But here he lieth like a log.

Joe smiled, then felt his eyes sting with tears. Adam, the puppy of his last happy year in Kendal, before the deaths of his father and mother; companion to him in the dreadful time that followed, which he preferred not to remember, when crazy

Aunt Jane had tried to kill Adam, and Joe and he had run away by night to take refuge with Uncle Ephraim. He shook his head, casting the memories away, and breathed with enjoyment the sweet wood smoke-scented air of autumn. He had missed this exhilarating freshness in Oxford and in the industrial towns where he had been in the past weeks.

Suddenly he decided to go for one of the long walks he had always taken to dispel dark moods, and, with a word to Aggie in the kitchen, set out north-east, across Skerton Bridge and up the Caton Road that would bring him to his favourite walk along the banks of the silver Lune.

Ephraim relayed to Mary what had passed between him and their nephew, and waited for her judgment. She sat at a games table, a pot of glue before her, painstakingly pasting items from the papers which struck her as quaintly interesting into her 'snippets book'. It had grown steadily since the children were little, and now consisted of several fat volumes. Ephraim considered it bad for her eyes, but she always countered that it made good light reading for the long evenings, and was so much more entertaining than silly novels.

'*A man in livery,*' she read out, '*called at the White Mill public house, in Bowland, and ordered a bridal dinner to be prepared forthwith. The dinner was duly prepared, but the wedding party never arrived. It was a mischievous joke.*'

'But not a very amusing one,' Ephraim said, an edge of impatience to his voice. 'A disgraceful waste of food in these hard times.'

'Oh, I expect it got eaten.'

'Come now, Mary, put your mind to what I've been telling you. Shall we let Joe go his own way, or not, do you think?'

'I don't see we've a great deal of choice, seeing he's twenty-one in less than a month.'

'You know what I mean. Joe's head's as full of noble ideals as an egg's full of meat, but he's not a fool. Today I've listened to him. It's his turn to listen to me, and if I can't reason him out of these daft ideas I'm not the advocate I used to be. A bit of good sense from both of us, and he'll think again and realise he's on the edge of making a hash of his life.'

Mary pasted an edge down firmly and gave it a little tap with her fist. 'And what will he do then?' she enquired.

'Return to Oxford, I hope. I wrote to them when I got his letter about the step he proposed to take, asking that a place be kept open for him for Michaelmas term. They're perfectly agreeable to it.'

Mary closed the scrapbook, took off her glasses, and lifted her eyes to Ephraim's. 'My dear, it may seem simple to you, but we must think most carefully about this. Joe's almost a man now. It may be he'll refuse to go back to university, and then take some path that will be more mistaken than the one he plans now. And yet … would we be right to let him follow his own way, without a warning? We've had enthusiasts before in our family, God knows, and look where it took them. Your Francis *would* become a carpenter, and one of his own planks killed him. Then there was —' She stopped, her face set in angry lines that spoiled its usual pleasant calm.

Ephraim finished for her. 'Eleanor. I know you won't speak of her if you can help it.'

'No, I won't. I hope I'm a good Christian woman, but I can't forgive her, my own sister though she is.'

Ephraim made no comment. It was little wonder that his kindly Mary could not bring herself to forgive the family upheaval caused by her pretty younger sister's elopement with a handsome Scotsman, her dramatic disillusionment with the marriage, the flirtation that had ended in a duel between her husband and her new lover, and her second elopement which had led to the premature death of her mother. Now Eleanor was living in London in high style with the man she had chosen, Jesse Bradshaw. The sisters had not met since her flight, and never would again if Mary had her way.

'And, of course, there was that awful business of Margaret,' Mary went on. 'Even younger than Eleanor, no more than a child, running off with a troupe of actors to Lord knows what fate. She may well be dead by now; best, perhaps, if she is. That's what comes of children following their own bent, my dear. We'd best talk to Joe, for his own good.'

'Aye. Happen.'

Mary could not help a smile. The once-pedantic Ephraim was becoming more and more infected with the local speech, mixing as he did with broad-spoken clients. She liked it; it made him sound like Old John.

'It's not that I grudge the money I've spent on Joe,' Ephraim said. 'A sound education's never wasted, and he's had that. Besides, we could well afford it.'

Mary nodded. When her father had died of an apoplexy, not long after her mother's death, she had come into money, his capital and the proceeds from the sale of Highriggs Farm, being the only sister whose existence he recognised. Poor Father. He had wanted a farmer son-in-law so much, a good sturdy man to inherit Highriggs and bring him fine grandchildren to carry on the line. And instead — two daughters lost to him — one vanished, one living in sin — and herself, Mary, with only girls. It was hard that a man should see his fondest hopes decay, as the song said. She knew how Ephraim felt, he who had dreamed of passing on his experience and wisdom to the boy he thought of as a son.

Well, such was life, and it was not her way to worry uselessly. 'We must pray for guidance,' she said, beginning carefully to cut out an item entitled RUMOURED APPEARANCE OF SEA-SERPENT IN MORECAMBE BAY.

When the rest of the household had retired candles were still burning in the sisters' bedroom, strictly against orders. Their twin tent beds took up much of the floor space in the large, cheerful room with its flower-striped wallpaper and the graceful Chippendale-style clothes press that had come from their dead uncle Francis's workshop.

Mary thought it eccentric for twin sisters to occupy separate beds — had she not had to share, in her girlhood at Highriggs? But wilful Belle complained that Dove disturbed her, so she must have a bed of her own. She was possessive over all her belongings, and ever covetous for more.

'Dove? Are you asleep?'

'No. You know I can't sleep with a light burning. Do go to bed.'

'I must wash with elderflower water first. I swear I saw a freckle today. Dove? What do you think of him?'

There was a silence. Then, 'Very well grown and handsome.'

'Oh, indeed?' Belle's tone was affectedly careless. 'But you always did dote on him, so I suppose you'll become quite unbearably sentimental now. Myself, I can't see what charms he could have for any girl. I don't care at all for carroty hair and a figure like a … a curtain pole.' She giggled. 'I'll tell you something, though.'

'What?'

'I could make him fall in love with me as easy as winking.' She mopped her fair, damp face, and made eyes at it in the mirror. 'What will you bet me I don't — your lilac gloves? Oh, do say you will, it would be such a joke!'

Dove's voice was muffled by the lavender-scented sheet she had drawn almost over her head. 'I hope you won't think of such a thing. How can you be so silly, Belle? Joe is our own dear cousin. Let him be.'

Oho, thought naughty Belle, *is* that *how the wind blows?*

Aloud she said, 'Goodnight, Dovekin,' and pinched out the candles.

In the darkness behind the snowy muslin curtains that draped her bed Dove's eyes were wide and sleepless, her tender heart beating alarmingly beneath her hand. *Our own dear cousin, always: now dearer than ever, dearer far.*

CHAPTER TWO

In the three weeks that passed before Joe's twenty-first birthday both Ephraim and Mary tried to talk him out of his resolve, she with gentle reproaches, he with cogent arguments, with warnings, even with bribes. But Joe proved quietly adamant against all suggestions that he was too delicate for factory life, too unworldly to stand up to the hard men he would encounter, too young to make his own way. Just before the birthday Ephraim unexpectedly lost his temper.

'Go on, then! Go down to Bradhope and see what sort of reception you'll get there when old Bradshaw hears you want to join his firm. He'll kick you from there to hell before you can say knife.'

'Why should he, Uncle?'

'Because he hates us Atkinsons like poison, that's why. I once refused to speak for the prosecution against some of his hands that had thrown a few bricks through a window. He turned against me then and he's never changed. I hear he's taken a vow to injure any of our family that comes his way. And we've no cause to love him on another count, I may tell you. It was his son Jesse that seduced your Aunt Eleanor and took her from her lawful husband, and now, I'm told, Bradshaw's promised to hound them down if they set foot in the north again. If you go to him you'll be putting your head in the lion's cage.'

Joe had heard the story of wicked Aunt Eleanor and her lover many times from various sources, and had visited her husband, the old soldier Roderick Mackenzie, now crippled and ailing in his pensioner's cottage. It seemed to him that Aunt Eleanor had been at least as much to blame as young Bradshaw, but he was not prepared to argue with Ephraim on the point.

'I wasn't thinking of going to Bradshaw's, Uncle. I thought of Mr Whittingham.'

Ephraim exploded. 'Whittingham! The man's a fool — and something of a twister, even though he *is* a client of mine. I could show you papers piled a yard high from cases I've fought for him when I've known him to be in the wrong and been half-ashamed to take my fee. I beg you'll think twice about any alliance with him.'

Joe met Ephraim's gaze calmly. 'I've approached him already, Uncle, and we came to provisional terms. He's managing the mill on his own at present and needs a partner. If I buy myself in he'll be pleased to have me.'

Ephraim stared, then laughed shortly. 'You'll not buy yourself any partnership with Whittingham with my money, lad — I'll see to that.'

'No,' returned Joe quietly, 'but I can with my own. The money Grandfather Bateman left to me in trust until I was twenty-one. I can claim it on Thursday.'

Ephraim gave him a long look that held anger, frustration and disappointment, before turning on his heel and striding out of his own study. Joe remained, moving the brass paperweight on the desk into different positions, staring at it unseeingly. He felt rebuked and sore, and uncertain of himself.

He had not taken overmuch to Walter Whittingham, a talkative, vague man who did not inspire confidence. The Bateman legacy seemed a great deal of money to him, who had never owned a penny on his own account. Was he about to throw it away? For a moment he hesitated on the verge of going after Ephraim and offering to try another term reading law at Oxford. Then pride drew him back, as though the shade of Samuel Crompton had laid a ghostly hand on his shoulder. He would not change his mind, and time would prove him right.

His birthday dawned as if specially bestowed by some kindly god of weather. The September air was of champagne freshness, the sun shone with a golden brilliance brighter than summer's, the rich garden scents pervaded the house, for it was warm enough to leave doors and windows open. The hero of the day came down to a breakfast table surrounded by beaming faces, Ephraim restored to his usual benevolent self, Mary and the girls rosy with excitement, the servants assembled in the dining room to greet him: the men, Isaac Mason and William Robinson, with a handshake (for in this house servants were friends), Mary's maid Ellen Casson and the two girls who cleaned with a bobbing curtsey. Only Aggie maintained her own stiff-backed stance, saying with a sharp nod, 'At least it's kept fine for you.'

Their eyes strayed from his pink glowing face to the pile of wrapped be-ribboned presents in front of his plate. He glanced bashfully at them, fearing to hold up proceedings, but forced on by cries of 'Open them! You must see them, Joel!' and, from the normally silent Isaac, 'Aye, let's 'ave a luke.'

One by one the contents of the lovingly wrapped packages were revealed. A gold half hunter watch from Ephraim, a chain and handsome fob from Mary, the engraved porphyry acting as a seal, with the family arms cut in it; a fine cambric handkerchief worked with flowers in an exuberantly careless design from Belle, a pretty purse more simply embroidered. He held it up, examining it closely.

'What's this? A little bird, inside a posy. A dove. Isn't that so? A dove for the maker's name.'

Dove blushed the colour of a sunset cloud, then paled again, raised her eyes to his and dropped them. For some reason he felt embarrassed, as though something far too rich had been thrust upon him, though it was a very simple gift. But Belle's arms were round his neck, Belle's sweet-violet perfume in his nostrils.

'Do you like my handkerchief? Don't you think it beautiful? The others are all very fine, but I put *so* much work into mine. Say you like it best!'

'Belle.' Her mother's quiet voice sent her back to her chair, but not before Joe had felt the impact of her extraordinary prettiness in the bright morning light, her daintiness in the ruffled morning wrapper that she had been forbidden to wear for breakfast because it was far too informal. This morning she had got away with it, and sat like the Queen of the Fairies clothed in lace cobwebs. She gave Joe the full benefit of her eyes, so he never noticed that Dove's were still cast down.

From the servants there was a snuff box of papier-mâché, lacquer-red in colour with a fashionable design of Chinese birds and foliage, and from friends and relations a whole pile of smaller gifts.

'Thank you,' he said, bowing. 'Thank you, everybody.'

There were more gifts at the birthday dinner that afternoon at two o'clock; the table had been set with the best linen and silver, vases were full of the jewel colours of plain and shaggy dahlias, fiery autumn leaves, late roses and blue Michaelmas daisies. Apart from the immediate family, there were many Atkinsons present whom Joe hardly knew. His godfather James had died, but James's brother Richard, now mayor of the town, was there in all his glory, and Thomas Dilworth, the wealthy sail-maker, who had stood by Ephraim's side as best man, with his wife Alice, Joe's godmother, a faded beauty fully confident of the charms she had revived with a set of splendid false teeth and a brown rinse for her ringlets. There, too, was the Dilworths' daughter-in-law, Arabella, Belle's godmother after whom she had been called. Dove's, alas, was dead long since, poor Aunt Ann, and so was her godfather, General Doveton. In babyhood she had been 'Doveton's lass', and so had grown to be called Dove, though her given name was Maria.

And there sat stout innkeeper Atkinson of the Spink Bull, beaming redly in the corner upon the crate of ale that he had himself provided. Beside him, transferred with much pain from a bath chair, was a bowed figure that had once been tall, with white hair still tinged here and there with red: Roderick Mackenzie, husband of the disgraced Eleanor, bereft of one arm in the Peninsular wars and now racked with pain and illness. He had been brought here under protest but was enduring stoically the jollity that was so foreign to his everyday life in the lonely cottage with only his Bible for company. Joe saw Ephraim summon Isaac and point to the sideboard. Isaac then conveyed a small decanter containing dark golden liquid, the fine malt whisky which was the only drink Roderick deigned to touch.

So many faces, growing redder and more cheerful as the food went down: the game soup, rich Lune salmon dressed with shrimps from Heysham, a mighty piece of roast beef delicately pink at the centre, brown and crisp outside, young vegetables and roast potatoes, salmis of quail shot over the Bowland moors, jellies, blancmanges and puddings, wines red and white in which at last the health of the new-made man was proposed by Ephraim, gravely enough:

'We know not what his path in life may be. All our paths have their stumbling-rocks, their stiles which seem, perhaps, insurmountable, their long weary miles which we fear our feet may never traverse to the end; sometimes we descend into the Valley of Humiliation, as did Bunyan's Pilgrim, sometimes, it may be, even into the Valley of the Shadow of Death.' He caught Mary's eye, and read rightly in it the message, *You're making them all miserable. This is a birthday party, not a funeral.* With a twitch of a smile at her he went on, 'But then, if we are favoured, come the Delectable Mountains, the House Beautiful. And if our young traveller should pause — as which of us has not? — awhile in Vanity Fair, are we to blame him? Let us send our fondest wishes after him, that he may come safely through all the perils of the road. Friends, neighbours, I give you — my nephew Joseph.'

'Joseph! Joe! God bless him! Speech, speech!'

Joe was scarlet, his cravat choking him, as he rose to his feet, all too conscious that he had drunk more wine than he was used to and that his mind was a perfect blank. He cleared his throat and began to stammer something — he knew not what — about being honoured and grateful, and hoping to carry out the wishes of those dearest to him, who ... who... He brought his halting remarks to an abrupt end and sat down to cheers as hearty as if he had been Lancaster's most eloquent orator.

A little hand was clasping his wrist. 'Well done!' whispered Belle, her eyes sparkling all kinds of messages.

'Was it all right? It sounded a lot of rubbish to me,' he murmured.

'Oh, no, it was perfect. You're so clever. But boys *are,* aren't they? — I mean men. Now, I could *never* make a speech like that.'

The hand was very warm, and now nestled within his own. He was conscious of the sweet warmth that was so close to him (though the dining chairs were wide-seated and should have kept them well apart) and quite unconscious of his own susceptibility to flattery. So Belle wooed him, darting glances round from time to time to see whether they were being noticed. They were.

'The puss,' Alice Dilworth murmured to her husband. 'And that lad hardly out of diapers.'

Mary saw the by-play, but, mother-like, thought it only cousinly affection. She wondered why Dove was not equally lively, and why her cheeks had faded to a white-rose paleness. Perhaps the child was feeling sick after all that rich food.

Under the thick dark lashes and the delicate scimitars of brows, Dove's eyes were brimming with tears. Joe, the serious, was laughing at some sally of her sister's, taking a flower from the posy in her low-cut bodice and bestowing on it a courtly kiss. Belle leant across her neighbour when Joe's attention was distracted for a moment.

'I'll thank you for the lilac gloves,' she hissed.

The tears broke away and rolled down Dove's cheeks. She pushed back her chair and hurried from the room.

'Poor child, she *is* taken sick,' Mary murmured aside to Ephraim.

Belle looked after her sister, something like dismay on her face. *I didn't mean it, not truly,* she thought. *He's a great booby and I don't care for him at all. But she does ... oh dear. Oh, well. It will pass, it's all a nonsense. What a goose she is, for sure.* She shrugged white shoulders above huge puffed sleeves and turned to Joe, laughing.

Walter Whittingham's office in the mill at Bleasdale, between Bradhope and Garstang some miles south of Lancaster, impressed Ephraim no more favourably than did the man himself. He looked round with disapproval at the papers that littered the desk in no visible sort of order, the shabby furniture, uncleaned windows, and general state of dusty disarray. Fastidiously he flicked the seat of a rickety chair before occupying it. He was glad he had insisted on accompanying Joe to see his future partner. Perhaps the unprepossessing look of the place would put him off. But Joe, who had already seen it, and in any case took no notice of such things, was looking round in eager excitement.

'That's right, that's right, make yourselves at home.' Whittingham was effusive, delighted to have persuaded a reputable person to put money into the business. He subsided heavily into his own chair, a shapeless, untidy bulk of a man, in his sixties but looking older. Grey hairs straggled over a balding crown, his rheumy colourless eyes were perpetually running, a dirty handkerchief was brought out to mop them. Ephraim's nose wrinkled in distaste.

'Well, Mr Atkinson, we meet again, eh, and in happier circumstances than t'last time.' Last time had seen Ephraim defending Whittingham on one of the occasions when faulty judgment combined with shiftiness had got the man into legal trouble. He had lost the case, unable for the first time to cover up for his client.

'Yes,' Ephraim answered shortly. 'We hope so.'

'Very good of you to come all this way. Only too pleased to see you. You'll take a drop of…?' He fumbled in the false drawer of his desk, and the top of a bottle appeared.

'Thank you, we won't trouble you. My time is limited, and I'd like to get down to business as soon as possible. You have the papers ready, I take it.'

Nothing seemed less likely, in view of the confusion reigning on Whittingham's desk. After scuffling among them in vain, he rang the bell for a depressed-looking clerk, who silently imposed some sort of order and produced a sheaf of documents which he handed to Whittingham.

'Aye, that's better. If you'll be kind enough to draw up your chair we can look through 'em together.'

Ephraim did so, though reluctantly. Whittingham seemed as careless about personal cleanliness as about the state of his office.

Joe watched his uncle admiringly, listened to him sharply checking points of the agreement, querying some, crossing out others, to Whittingham's querulous dismay. Joe had read law for two years, but with such lack of interest that very little of it had impressed itself on his brain; now he realised just how unfitted he had been to practise it, and how right was his decision to choose another profession.

Ephraim paused, making a legal lip. 'It's very unusual for a mill owner to appoint a partner outside his family or associates — and one completely unused to the business.'

Whittingham smirked. 'I've faith in the young man, that's why.'

'And his premium — if we may so regard it, as the arrangement seems to partake of the nature of an apprenticeship — that will be particularly welcome to you?'

'Money's always welcome.'

'And no small amount of money is involved here, I think you'd agree?'

'I'll see he gets value for it. Any knowledge I can pass on to him, I will.'

'I trust you will, indeed. And he will gain practical experience in your mill, in all branches?'

'Aye, and outside it. He'll go to Liverpool to buy for me on 'Change, and to Manchester, even, to see the finished yarn sold, though he'll not be buying there, seeing as we spin our own. There won't be much he doesn't know about cotton by t'time he's finished.'

'And there's another point.' Ephraim put the tips of his fingers together. 'This contract operates for a period of five years, after which the partnership may be dissolved at the wish of one or both partners. I would like to see a clause permitting my nephew to ask for an earlier termination should the arrangement not have worked to his satisfaction.'

'Nay, that's not fair. Me having spent much time and trouble on him, to have to thresh around for someone else, and start all over again? I'm an old man, Mr Atkinson, I've no time for that. We'll stick to what's on paper, if you please.'

No reasoning of Ephraim's would move him, and at last Ephraim abandoned the question. It was up to Joe to make the best of the situation he had forced. Repressing a sigh, he called Joe over to the desk. 'You've heard all that was said, and you're satisfied with it?'

'Yes, quite, Uncle.' Joe's eyes were bright, his hand trembling on the pen.

'Then sign here.'

The depressed clerk was called in to be the second witness to the two signatures. The deed was done.

The next question was where Joe was to lodge. Ephraim, anxious to keep closely in touch with the boy's progress, suggested that he remain at St Leonard's Gate and ride to the mill and back daily. Joe was happy with the idea, but Mary demurred on the grounds that he would be tired out after a week. In private she told Ephraim her real objection.

'You may not have noticed, Ephraim, but I have. There's something going on between the girls about our Joe. I don't know what it is, and I'd be the last person they'd come to. In my opinion Dove's taken a great kindness to him, and either Belle has too or she's putting it on, the little madam.'

Ephraim was startled. 'Kindness? You mean affection, fondness? Well, of course. Joe's always been a brother to them both.'

'I don't mean sisters' fondness. Joe's a man now, and a well-favoured one.'

'But — they're only children. Far too young for such thoughts, surely,' said Ephraim with a father's refusal to credit that his beloved daughters could ever grow up. 'Come now, you're imagining what can't be there.'

Mary raised her eyebrows. 'Can't it? If you spent as much time in this house as I do you'd sing another song, my dear. Every lad in the neighbourhood's made sheep's eyes at them, one time or another — and got some back, too, at least from Belle. Dove's not the coming-on kind, which is why I don't want her upset by spites and jealousies, and I think it far better for Joe to lodge near his work where he can't do any harm.'

'Dear me. And Joe? Do you think his heart is involved — if I may use such a phrase?'

'Heart? I should say his heart was in Whittingham's mill at present. But there's no saying what may happen with three young people under one roof. Believe me, I know these things.' She laid her hand on his, the plump matronly hand where the broad wedding ring gleamed despite the wear and scratches of twenty-one years. Ephraim raised and kissed it, with unaccustomed emotion.

'I'm sure you do, my dear. I would trust you on any point, however knotty. It shall be as you say.'

And so Joe went, happily enough, to lodge in Whittingham's house next to the mill. It was dark and not very clean, inhabited only by Whittingham and his deaf old housekeeper (his wife had died years before), and neither bed nor board was as good as it would have been at his uncle's. But he was too young to notice or care, only glad to be where he was, and at night the sound of the purling river lulled him to sleep.

His Aunt Mary's mind was easier. In her daughter Belle she discerned what she had always feared to see in a daughter of hers — a likeness to the flighty sister she would not name.

That sister, Eleanor, sat in London, in the window of her drawing room in Bryanston Street, Marylebone. Across the gardens she could see where the west end of Oxford Street joined Park Lane, the steady procession of carriages and riders from west to east, and the eye-resting stretch of autumn-red trees and faded grass that was Hyde Park.

She and Jesse had been lucky to rent a house here, in so fashionable a quarter, on the edge of Marylebone and Bayswater. The rich and great lived in palatial houses in Park Lane, facing the almost-rural park. Such splendid dwellings — Elgin House, Dudley House, Gloucester House, Grosvenor House, Dorchester House (all calling themselves residents of Mayfair), and, at the southern end where Hyde Park Corner gave way to Piccadilly, Apsley House, home of the great Duke of Wellington who had conquered at Waterloo. There he was, no longer commander-in-chief of the army, but Prime Minister of England, a reluctant politician of the same embattled nature as ever. Only a few months ago, in March 1829, he had defied the law by fighting a duel with Lord Winchilsea about his supposed backing of the return of Roman Catholicism to the country. Sometimes Eleanor and Jesse saw him out riding his old charger Copenhagen: a proud, stiff figure with his great eagle nose rivalling the point of his cocked hat, viewed by Londoners with awe but no longer with the same affection as when he had been England's saviour from the devils of France and Spain.

Eleanor had her own horse, Rowan, and Jesse his, the mare Lucetta, called after that old, old lady in Lancashire, his grandmother Madam Bradshaw of Eagle Hall. It was she, quaint romantic old creature, who had financed them for their journey south, when Eleanor had run away from her marriage and her family, and Jesse from his tyrannical father. Even now they received tiny scribbled notes from her on fragile paper, wishing them well, or giving them some item of news, sometimes of a highly improper character that would make them laugh.

'She must be more than a hundred by now,' said Jesse, regarding one of these scraps of correspondence. 'When we saw her last I expected her to crumble to pieces before our eyes. I only hope we may be the same, at her age.'

Or even live to see our children grow up, Eleanor thought. Children were often in her mind, as the possibility of having them grew more and more remote. She remembered vividly attending the wedding of her sister Mary and pitying her because she was too old to expect babies, but Mary had been so much younger than she herself now. How cruel it was to be called Mrs Jesse Bradshaw yet have no right to the name, for her husband Roderick Mackenzie still lived on, so she heard from a woman friend, the only correspondent she had in Lancaster. She and

Jesse had brazened it out in London, as he, with a combination of charm, tact and drive, had risen from being a mere private gentleman to taking his place in Parliament as member for a small Kentish constituency.

A fine house, everything she wanted in the way of clothes and jewels, a barouche, servants, a Chinese bowl in the hall full of calling cards with coronets on them, a handsome, affectionate partner, rising towards fame; yet she was still only Eleanor Mackenzie, neither maid, wife nor widow, with no status in her own right, and no child in the nursery.

She had never thought of herself as particularly maternal until her thirtieth year had come and gone, and strange urgings had arisen in her, pangs of painful envy at the sight of bonneted, beribboned infants being pushed in their painted go-carts through the park; even poverty-stricken mothers nursing their ragged babes on doorsteps sent the knife into her heart. *Spoilt,* she told herself; *you were always spoilt, Eleanor.* Now Jesse spoiled her, his beautiful 'wife' whose country complexion and natural ringlets put town ladies in the shade, but he would not grant her the child she wanted.

'What difference would it make?' she had demanded, again and again. 'Nobody in town knows our situation, nobody is likely to come from the north and give us away. General Doveton's dead, or he might have betrayed us — he was such a friend of Mary's, and I know she hates me. So why not?'

'Life, my love,' said Jesse, lightly flicking one of her crystal earrings and making it swing, 'is a house of cards. One touch, and the whole comes toppling down, bringing the inhabitants with it. Now I am responsible for my actions and so are you — both grown people. Would you have an innocent involved, one who never did any harm? The word *bastard* is a harsh one still, Nell. Do you remember a girl brought before the Mayor of

Lancaster and sent to the house of correction for three months' hard labour? I recall my father bringing home news of her case. All she had done was to bear a child out of wedlock.'

Eleanor flung away from him. 'That was quite different. In her station in life —'

'In any station in life. Not a lady in all Mayfair dare admit openly to such a thing. If she did, every door would be slammed against her. You know that's true.'

'Yes, but —'

'No buts about it. Come, be reasonable and see it as I do, there's a dear girl.'

That she could not do, but she reluctantly accepted the precaution on which Jesse insisted: the brandy-soaked sponge that had originated in raffish post-Revolutionary France, never mentioned but frequently employed in fashionable English society. Religious prejudice about the limitation of families had outlasted the Age of Reason; any reformer rash enough to publish a pamphlet about it was like to find himself behind bars. Jesse had strong views on the subject which he aired only to trustworthy and like-minded colleagues.

'I saw plenty of poverty in the north, God knows, but nothing like London's. Do those bigots imagine the poor breed like rabbits because they want to? What can a beggar-woman do with ten or twelve children but sell them for prostitution, or dispose of 'em at birth? I've seen infants floating in the Thames like drowned kittens, or lying in the gutters broken by carriage wheels. Is *that* obeying God's holy ordinance to increase and multiply, or is it brutish ignorance and stupidity? Where's the sin of showing such folks how to limit their families to a decent number? Aye, and I'd include the highest in the land and parsons living on a wretched stipend in houses bursting their sides with children they can barely keep in shoes.

Well, we must wait, I suppose, or be clapped in Horsemonger jail for treason — or whatever name they put to the crime of telling the truth.'

He entered his own house on this late autumn, almost winter day, elated by an afternoon session at the House in which he had drawn some cheers from Opposition frontbenchers by his frank remarks about reform, and shouted invitations to cross the floor. Sometimes he had strong suspicions that he belonged to the wrong party, particularly with the old duke looking down his nose (if such a feat were possible, with such a nose) at any suggestion which smacked of change. Recalling the afternoon with pleasure, he went up to the drawing room.

Eleanor was still sitting in the window seat, her arm along the sill, her feet up, in an attitude of Récamier-like grace. She looked up languidly at his entrance, and he saw that she had been brooding again. She made a charming picture seated there, the late light catching her pale hair dressed in elaborate puffs and curls, owing something now to the camomile rinse her maid used on it, but still lovely. Her figure was as slender still as when she had dressed as a country boy to rescue Jesse from the house imprisonment his father had imposed on him; long legs, tiny waist, small bosom almost obscured by the wide, ugly balloon sleeves of her dress.

Her face, too, had kept its girlish fairness, thanks to a leisured life and the aid of costly creams and lotions. But there were little pettish lines of discontent round her mouth, and others marking her brow, as though she were always about to frown. Jesse dropped a kiss on them, and was rewarded with a smile.

'Well, my love. What have you been doing with yourself today?'

She yawned. 'Oh … I don't know. Caroline called and took breakfast with me. Then — oh yes. We went for a drive in the park. Nobody remarkable to be seen — except us. By the way, Yates said I was to tell you that Blazon's gone lame in the left hind foot. He's keeping him to the stables till it mends.'

'Poor fellow. At least it's not with overwork. How was Caroline?'

'Much the same as ever. Talk, talk, talk, all about Percival's being asked to shoot at Lord Allbury's in Berkshire, and she doesn't want to go because William's teething and Georgiana's being hateful to her governess so that she doesn't like to leave them alone. Very tedious.'

Why did he ask about Caroline? she was wondering, angry with herself for letting the thought come into her mind. Well, the truth was there to be faced — she was jealous of Caroline, her pretty ladyship, Caro Thrale. A personable husband, two fine children and a third on the way. Jesse's eyes had beamed with pleasure at the sight of her across the dinner table. They had taken wine with each other, danced together. Percival Thrale's mind was on other things: horse-racing, shooting. Why should not Caro have taken Jesse's fancy?

Eleanor twisted, compulsively, her own thin delicate 'wedding ring': a fraud, only a fraud, though made of the best gold, and guarded by a heavier ring of turquoise and pearl. Caroline was *married*: to a stick, a superannuated dandy, but married. This was her grievance and preoccupation, almost as much as her childlessness. And, worse than Caro — who was, on the face of it, an honest enough woman and a devoted mother — there were the Roamers: the ladies who took lovers, some of them unmarried, even. Might not the day come when one of them, single, rich, beautiful, eligible, caught Jesse's fancy?

She saw in her mind's eye the scene, much as it had happened in the old king's time to the faithful, ageing mistresses of his sons. Dolly Jordan, mother of Clarence's brood, suddenly informed that her services were no longer required. Julie de St Laurent, reading at the breakfast table that the Duke of Kent was to be married to Victoria of Saxe-Saalfeld-Coburg. Maria Fitzherbert, deposed from acknowledged morganatic wifehood to the Prince Regent for a dirty, vulgar princess from Germany. If it could happen to them, why not to her? Then all would be gone — her position in society, her hopes that some day the true ring might go on her finger — and Jesse would be legally wedded. To someone else.

He read her thoughts, he who knew her so well. He had fancied Caro Thrale, indeed — though she was slightly too rabbit-toothed for his taste — had fancied others, and followed his fancy to their charming beds. Sometimes it was merely pleasant, more often expedient. Bored parliamentary wives liked to be entertained during their husbands' absences at the House. They would never blab a lover's name, only, very casually, hint that So-and-So was a very civil young man and seemed to have sound ideas. What about a word to Lord This, a hint to the Marquis of That, or even the P.M.? It was all so easy, the boudoir door locked during the lady's rest-time, the servants strictly forbidden to try the door-knob — and, oh rapture, and no 'little consequences'.

To Jesse it was all in the game, no recriminations, no regrets. He cared deeply only for politics, and for Eleanor. They had come together in such a romantic fashion, quite ridiculously so, yet it seemed that Fate had matched them to each other, the harum-scarum girl and the solid, aspiring young man. He was sorry for her, but there was nothing for it: old Mackenzie lived on. Jesse would never let her know of his infidelities, but they would continue while his career demanded them.

'What about tea?' he said. 'I seem to have talked myself dry this afternoon. The most extraordinary thing, my dear: Grey said —'

'Tea. What a good idea. Do ring the bell.'

He pulled the ornate bell-rope by the fireplace. The fire wanted mending, but a servant would do that. He thought how pleasant it was to have reached the point of being reasonably well-off and to be accepted by Society. In this horribly snobbish time a cotton manufacturer's son, if known for such, might be frozen out of a drawing room, his remarks greeted by titters, by faces hidden behind fans, by silences and brusque replies. He had endured a little of it, and in his northern pride intended to endure no more. So Eleanor — will she, nill she — must follow where he led.

'Oh,' she said, watching the maid pour tea from a silver urn, 'there was one person we met in the park. Caro seemed to know him, though he was only accompanied by some doctor or other, with a northern kind of name. Preston, was it? No, Bolton, Doctor Bolton. Do have one of these little cakes. The new cook is really very clever with pastry.'

Jesse looked ruefully down at his substantial figure. He tried not to eat as grossly as so many men did. But the cakes were good indeed. His mouth inelegantly full, he asked, 'This person, with a Doctor Preston or Bolton. Describe him.'

Eleanor's face became animated. 'Oh, so quaint and unusual — a Jew, of all things, but very handsome in a melancholy sort of way — black curls, big black eyes, an Eastern sort of complexion but pale rather than sallow, and dressed very fancifully. He made me the most beautiful bow and said something I didn't quite understand — I think it was in poetry.

Do you remember how Margaret and I used to rave about Lord Byron? Well, Caroline said this young man adored Byron too and altogether modelled himself on Byron, though I would say he was a much softer character...'

Smiling, Jesse stemmed the flood. 'And what was this paragon's name, pray?'

'Oh,' said Eleanor, her eyes sparkling. 'It was Disraeli, Ben Disraeli. I thought it so picturesque, just like himself.'

Jesse said nothing, stirring his cup of tea round and round. So his dissatisfied wife had her fancies, too. Fair enough, sauce for the goose. But for some reason the cake he was eating had turned tasteless, and he had a strong feeling that if he ever met Mr Ben Disraeli he would dislike him very much.

CHAPTER THREE

In fact, it was several months before he had that pleasure. Parliamentary zeal kept him away from home for much of the time, not only at the House but in his constituency, a day's drive from London, where he had friends among the local squires. He enjoyed spending nights in the quiet of the country, talking to straightforward people; they were not as straightforward as northern folk, but they were restful after the cut and thrust of London social life. From one of these excursions, in the early March of 1830, he returned home to find a gentleman's hat and cane in the hall. The hat was exceedingly elegant, of silk beaver, as worn by all the dandies; the cane ebony with an ivory handle of intricate design banded with silver.

The owner of these things sat at ease in the drawing room, on a chair placed not too far from Eleanor's. At Jesse's entrance he looked up with a dazzling smile which, for some reason, made Jesse think of a persuasive street hawker. He was a vision of exotic elegance from his shining black-ringleted head to his equally shining pointed silver-buckled pumps. The tight-fitting trousers above them were of rich green velvet, the waistcoat girding his slim figure was a blinding shade of canary yellow; from the sleeves of his dark blue surtout peeped out lace frills that would have done credit to a buck of the last century. Jesse, used to sober-suited Members of Parliament and country gentlemen in homespun, blinked uncontrollably, but managed to extend his hand. The vision rose to take it in long white fingers blazing with rings.

'Mr Disraeli, may I present my husband.'

Eleanor's tone was bright and excited, like her face. By George, the fellow's company had taken ten years off her, thought Jesse. There were smiles and bows, obligatory remarks about the excessively windy weather, some unusually solicitous enquiries (or so they sounded to him) from Eleanor about his journey and the state in which he had left his friends in Kent, through all of which he was acutely conscious of tactful interjections, sympathetic smiles, and darting looks of comprehension from the most extraordinary pair of eyes Jesse had ever seen. He was the last man in the world to be impressed by other men's physical charms, yet again and again he felt his own eyes stealing back to those long, languorous orbs, as near black as ever eyes were, the whites very faintly yellow-tinged, a golden look to the lids; in their looks were smiles and dreams, and star-sparks of amusement, though nothing very amusing was being said. *Good God,* thought Jesse, *I must be going soft in the head.*

'Mr Disraeli,' Eleanor was saying, 'is shortly to make the Grand Tour. Isn't that thrilling! Oh, how much I envy you, sir. Paris, Rome, Venice ... such places to see, so different from this dreary London.'

'The modern Babylon,' sighed her guest. 'But you, dearest lady,' picking up her hand and kissing it as casually as another might pick up a glove, 'have surely graced all these yourself.'

'Oh, well, we did travel a little, when we were first married. But Mr Bradshaw has been so very occupied since he went into politics, haven't you, my dear?'

'Yes,' said Jesse lamely. 'Yes, yes, of course.'

'Ah,' breathed Disraeli, directing those eyes to the moulded ceiling as though he saw visions opening up in it, 'Paris, Rome, Venice. I never was so struck with anything in the whole course of my life as with Paris.' He proceeded to describe it in terms which made Jesse wonder whether he could possibly be talking about the same city as the one he and Eleanor had visited. Lyrical, even gushing, he took them on a verbal tour of the Continent. 'The whole range of the High Alps, with Mont Blanc in the centre, without a cloud ... I stood so entranced that I scarcely observed the spreading and shining scene which opened far beneath me. On Lac Léman I was privileged beyond dreams — dear lady, think of the felicity, to be rowed by that very boatman who performed the same office for Lord Byron!'

Eleanor's eyes widened as she listened raptly to her guest's account of the sublime electric storm, exactly as described in the third canto of *Childe Harold*. Then they were with him at Venice, among marble palaces, in Florence, viewing masterpieces of art... Jesse ceased to hear the soft, musical voice lazily winding itself round rolling phrases. He was puzzled by the foreignness of this young man, in spite of his obviously native English speech. Italian? Spanish? Not quite. Disraeli ... D'Israeli ... how *did* he spell his name?

Suddenly he remembered what Eleanor had told him. Jewish, that was it. Jews, after centuries of existing as underdog in England, were now tolerated, even individually respected, but were still not permitted to enter Parliament, even though a year earlier Roman Catholics and Dissenters, who had been banned along with them, had been allowed entrance. Jesse included among his burning enthusiasms the conviction that offices of State should be open to all, whatever race or creed. He could not have told why: perhaps he was reacting against his father's oppression of his mill-hands.

When Disraeli had left, with bows, smiles and compliments, and was but an elegant shape retreating up the street, Jesse said, 'What an extraordinary young man.'

'Yes, he is. But so interesting, and different from all those bores.'

'I should like him to come to dinner.'

Eleanor was surprised, but pleased. A week later Disraeli was of the company round their table, a small, select company of seven. The odd number was caused by Disraeli's having arrived without a lady on his arm. He smilingly apologised. 'Would that I could have presented to you my sister Sarah, my other self, but she is at present at home with our parents in Buckinghamshire.'

The news delighted Eleanor; she would have him more or less to herself, for he was placed at her right hand at dinner. She was very conscious of him at her side, of his delicate attentions to her, and, with a pang of jealousy, of his smiles and soft words to Caro Thrale, prettily pregnant and all the more receptive to compliments. Eliza Amesbury, the other lady present, looked and was something of a bluestocking, and addressed Disraeli in loud pedantic tones on topics too serious for the light civilised conversation that should prevail at a dinner table. Eleanor tried to catch her eye with a *Be quiet!* expression, but it seemed that this versatile young man was perfectly capable of dealing briefly but wittily with rumours of commercial distress in New South Wales, the new police force, or anything else. Eleanor perceived that he actually seemed to enjoy fielding Eliza's ponderous remarks, even making her laugh. He had a wonderful way with women; she sensed that he preferred their conversation, however silly, to men's. When the moment came for the ladies to withdraw she could not help a wistful backward glance at the glittering ringlets turning attentively from one to the other of the gentlemen who remained in the dining room to smoke cigars and drink port.

In fact it was Jesse who monopolised Disraeli, fascinated by his conversation and by a curious sense that his destiny was to be influenced by this exotic creature. He had discovered that the young man's claim to fame was that he wrote novels. Jesse pressed him on the subject.

'Then to write is your ambition — to reflect the world as you see it?'

Disraeli blew a plume of smoke towards the chandelier. 'No. I have so far written to amuse — and succeeded, I hope. And I have written to — as it were — reflect myself in my own eyes. By that image, I may be guided on my life's path.'

'Which leads towards...?'

The long eyes were inscrutable. 'Power? Fame? Admiration? Anything but failure and obscurity. I have already become something of a *succès de scandale,* it appears; it is my desire to become in another sense a *succès de mérite.*'

'And what — if I may ask — is your chosen *métier?*'

A slow smile, anticipatory of his hearer's astonishment. 'Politics.'

He was rewarded by three surprised faces, Jesse's most of all, for though he had had no notion of Disraeli's aims something in his subconscious mind had linked the young man with his own. This, then, was the link.

Delicately he said, 'Would there not — forgive me — be an impediment to your entering Parliament?'

Quite unoffended, Disraeli replied, 'The fact of my race, you imply? Not at all, sir. I am, in fact, a baptised Christian, and as such may sincerely take the oath.'

'By Gad!' John Thrale was leaning forward eagerly. 'You mean you're — well, I congratulate you, I do indeed. A most sensible step.'

'It is my good old father you should congratulate, Sir John. He quarrelled with his synagogue and marched us children up to St Andrew's, Holborn, to be marked on the forehead with the holy sign and to have the world, the flesh and the devil formally abjured on our behalf by our godparents; even though they may have been a shade embarrassed at our maturity, which may well have allowed us a preference for all three, given the choice.'

As the gentlemen moved to join the ladies John Thrale murmured to his neighbour, Percy Amesbury, 'A queer card, what? D'you think Bradshaw's wise to take him up?'

Amesbury shrugged. 'Who knows? Not quite a gentleman, clearly. But what does that mean nowadays, with changes in the air?'

Jesse had few more opportunities to cultivate his *protégé* (if such was the right way round of the situation) at that time, for in May Disraeli was to make the Grand Tour, including an inspection of the East, that 'great Asian mystery' which he felt held clues to his own enigmatic personality.

Fortunately for all concerned, Jesse was detained at the House all that day when, coming to call her mistress to dress for an early, solitary dinner, her maid Cobbs turned the handle of the drawing-room door and found it resisted her pressure. She paused, listened, and with a grimace almost breaking into a snigger, softly retreated down the back stairs to the servants' hall, where, very commendably, she kept her own counsel.

Eleanor pushed her young lover gently away from her. On the broad day-bed he lay, his head propped up on his hand, his spaniel curls cascading over her face, dropping gentle kisses on her eyes, cheeks, nose and mouth.

'My angel, you are not to feel regrets. That is to deny experience, and to deny experience is to be as good as dead.'

'I don't feel regret — exactly, Benjamin. I don't know what I feel. It was wonderful. I shall never know anyone like you again.'

'True, very true,' he murmured against her hair. She was pleasantly conscious of the sweet pomade he used, and a cologne with a lemon tinge to its essence, and the soft gentle languor that had won her to his wooing with almost no resistance, despite her fear of becoming disreputable. Jesse had never wooed her like this — indeed, it was rather she who had wooed Jesse. From the first she had known that Benjamin's siege to her was destined to triumph, though she had fought it half-heartedly.

'I am twice your age,' she had told him.

'Nonsense. Pray don't soil that charming mouth with a manifest lie.'

'Well, at least I'm much older. I know you're twenty-six, and I'm certainly a lot more than *that.*'

His melting gaze had brought a girlish blush to her bosom, neck and face. He surveyed its progress with affectionate amusement. 'So is the Venus de Milo, yet it makes her no less lovely. Indeed, to me maturity has a more powerful charm than callow youth, when it takes such a form as hers — and yours.'

'What a shocking flatterer you are! Where did you learn to say such things?'

With a comical sideways look he laid his finger across his lips first, then hers. 'Silence is the better part of candour.'

The clock chimed, and Eleanor started to her feet, pulling up the low-cut bodice of her dress to cover her shoulders as she ran to the wall mirror to straighten her hair. 'What a fright I look, good heavens!' When she turned Benjamin was putting the finishing touches to the arrangement of his lace neckcloth, before fastidiously pulling out the wrist frills which so becomingly set off his white hands. He really was the coolest of customers, and wickedly experienced; yet under the conceit and facile charm such a dear boy, for whom she felt something Jesse had never roused in her — though of course she loved Jesse, and it was dreadful to think she had just betrayed him.

Benjamin took her hands and kissed them, palms upwards, sending a delightful shiver through her. As he left, as gracefully and discreetly as he had arrived — even contriving to shut the heavy front door without a sound — she knew that it would not be his last visit, and despite the scolding of her conscience she felt happy, and young, and released; the false wedding ring on her finger for once did not trouble her at all.

But within two months he had left England to taste 'the great Asian mystery' with his friend Meredith, his sister's fiancé. Eleanor took a regretful private farewell of him, and treasured in her locked jewel box the verse he had sent her, with a bunch of primroses.

Bright beauty, modest, wise, witty yet kind,
Where in one goddess may one so much find?
Accept, sweet lady of the primrose hair,
These simple blossoms, though they be not fair
As those soft ringlets which my heart entwine;
From him who signs himself — thy Lover, thine!

Eleanor laughed and sighed, and put the cool flowers against her cheek. Dear Ben, how many ladies had he written such lines to? It was to be hoped he was a better novelist than he was a poet; according to Jesse, he would one day be a better politician than either. So young, so young…

An even younger man with none of Disraeli's assurance and poise, the nephew Eleanor scarcely remembered, took stock of his own surroundings, and felt his spirits plunge into the deepest dejection he had ever known. The long, high spinning room in which Joe stood was not Whittingham's. He had been sent on an errand to a mill in Blackburn, and after carrying it out had asked if he might take a look round.

His request was met with deep suspicion. Again and again he reassured the owner that he was not any kind of inspector and had no motive other than interest in manufacture before he was allowed, under escort, to go from room to room in the mill. What he saw depressed him beyond measure, the more because he had seen it all before. Looms operated by creatures who might themselves have been mechanical objects, not flesh and blood: skeletal men and women, haggard and toothless, wizened children whose looks bore no resemblance to normal childhood. Dull-eyed, brutish of expression — if such sullen faces could be said to hold any expression at all — they might have been imps from an inferno greyer and uglier than Dante could have conceived. Some had obviously been deformed from birth, some lacked an arm or a hand, torn off in the machinery. Joe knew that he must not speak to any of them, for an answer would earn them blows from the overseer who strode up and down the room.

Cotton detritus filled the air, choked the nostrils, lay like snow on the clothes and hair and faces of the operatives, causing coughs and sneezes which were drowned in the roar and clack of the machines. Its only virtue was that it helped to mask the smell of filthy humanity that had neither time, inclination nor the means to wash.

As Joe and his escort moved along, a child slipped suddenly to the floor and lay inert. The overseer marched up to it and gave it a kick in the ribs. Joe broke away from the man beside him.

'Stop him! Can't he see the poor creature's swooned?'

'Nowt o' t'soart,' replied his companion laconically. 'It's nobbut gone asleep. They're allus at it. I'll wakken it up soon enow.'

A few more kicks with the toe of a large boot had this beneficial effect. The child dragged itself to its feet, then to its knees, and went back to work, eyes still closed. Joe could not tell whether it was a girl or a boy, though its rags gaped like open wounds.

Feeling sick, he indicated that he wanted to leave. Out in the air, he was almost dizzied by the change from the atmosphere inside. He wandered along through mean cobbled streets, past rows of slum dwellings, over gutters which ran with filth. He knew what he would find inside those terrace cottages were he to walk in — for as often as not there would be no answer to a knock. Infants, too young to go out to work, drugged with one variety or another of the 'sleeping-stuff' used to keep them quiet while their parents or brothers and sisters were at the factory. It might be a substance called 'Godfrey', brewed up locally by the gallon, or laudanum, or paregoric; even pure opium. The children usually died in the end. Best for them if they did.

He passed a woman tumbled across the two steps of a house, her head back at a broken angle, her tattered shawl flung wide.

She looked dead, but he knew from experience that, like the child in the factory, she was only sleeping. Too much Godfrey, the loss of a day's work, and her life was virtually over. He knew better than to touch her.

He was out of the worst of the town now, on the edge of the country, where black smuts gave place to green grass and trees in fresh bud. High overhead a skylark trilled, the 'layrock' to which Lancashire poets wrote simple odes. How long would the lark survive, as the horrible town spread? It was May, the sweetest month of the year, its hedges bright with blossom and its scents intoxicating. He sat down on a grass tussock, under a tree, and took out of his pocket a newspaper, folded with one item uppermost. He read it, even though he knew it almost by heart.

Statement to the Right Hon. Robert Peel, by the Hand-loom weavers of Blackburn.

Our dwellings are wholly destitute of every comfort.

Every article of value has disappeared, either to satisfy the cravings of hunger, or to appease the clamourings of relentless creditors.

Were the humane man to visit the dwellings of four-fifths of the weavers, and see the miserable pittance which sixteen hours' hard labour can procure, even of those who are fully employed, divided between the wretched parents and their starving little ones, he would sicken at the sight.

And so on and so on. The statement had been put out by some good clergyman — the Reverend Fletcher, that was he — trying, like so many others, to help, and as ineffectually. Joe felt the most ineffectual of the lot. He had gone into cotton with his eyes open, as he thought, the scene illuminated by a blaze of idealism, and what had he found? The designs he had worked on for improved machinery had been looked at with casual patronage by mill owners, and passed off as commendable, interesting, not bad for a young 'un. But any suggestion of his that they might be put into practice had been met with stares.

'You've your own workshop, then?'

'No.'

'Well, we've none, either. We'll make do with t'machines we've got till summat better comes along.'

'But if my ideas could be put into practice they *would* be better — more yarn could be spun in less time, and the operatives could work shorter hours...'

He might as well have talked to the moon. Nobody listened or cared.

He was glad to be back in Lancaster, where at least the black curse of industry had not taken over the town, and where the factory conditions were less loathsome, though capable of much improvement. That night he rode to his Uncle Ephraim's, to be received with the usual warm welcome. Mary was quick to notice his changed looks.

'You've lost weight, Joe.'

'Have I, Aunt? I feel all right.'

'Does that woman at Whittingham's feed you?' she enquired suspiciously.

'Oh — yes. I get plenty.' He did not add that much of it was stodge, porridge, watery stews, heavy plum duffs, the sort of stuff the housekeeper had been feeding to Whittingham for the best part of twenty years. He hardly noticed such things, though he did notice that the beef on which they were dining was very fine, and that he felt better for it.

Belle had been looking him up and down. 'You don't look very clean,' she said. 'Don't they wash your linen?'

'Belle!' Her mother glared across the table. 'How dare you say such rude things to your cousin? Leave the table at once.'

Belle pouted, but slipped out of her chair and flung off towards the door, turning at it to say defiantly, 'Well, it's true.'

'It is,' Joe told them shamefacedly. 'Don't punish Belle, she's quite right. It's the — places I go to. I shouldn't have come here without putting myself under the pump in the yard. I'm sorry, I'll leave if you want me to.'

Mary looked censorious, but answered, 'Of course we don't want you to. Stay where you are. Have some more, go on.' She ladled more vegetables on to his plate, and Ephraim cut another tender pink slice of beef for him.

When the meal was done, a nod from Ephraim drew Joe after him to the study, where his uncle settled himself in the comfortable wing chair, leaving Joe to take an upright one that gave him an unpleasant feeling of being on trial.

Ephraim lowered his glasses and surveyed him. 'Well, then. How goes it?'

'Not well, Uncle.'

'So, only six months' trial, and not well. Elucidate.'

Joe did so, his words gaining momentum as he went on: the lack of interest in his notions, the conditions he found in the mills, his disillusionment with the world of industry. Ephraim listened with patient attention.

'But,' he said at last, 'you told me, in this very room, that you knew all about the workers and their conditions. I could quote you on oath in court, if I had to. Where, then, is the surprise in all this? What new has happened?'

Joe started a sentence, stuttered, and began it again. 'I — it — I don't know how to put it. But it seems all to have got worse. Or else it is that I thought when I was part of it myself it would be better … I could talk to people, and they'd take notice of me because I was one of them…'

'*The glorious company of the Apostles,*' Ephraim murmured. 'So you thought your very presence would bring about reforms?'

Joe flushed. 'I'd hardly put it like that, sir. I merely felt I might make them see reason. But I'm nothing to them — just a sort of apprentice to Mr Whittingham, and they'll go their own way whatever I say. And I'm not dreaming it — things do seem worse, truly. Today in Blackburn — it was sickening. The same in Oldham last week. There's poverty in the Liverpool streets when I go over there, but not the sort I see in the mills. You've no idea…'

'I have, Joe, I have. And, if it's any comfort to you, I would agree that conditions are getting worse. Every day children are born and children die; every day hearts grow harder and filth piles thicker. We are moving down to hell, unless changes come. *Facilis descensus Averno*, Joe, all too *facilis*. Now it appears to me — and I have been listening to you very carefully — that your disillusionment with your chosen way of life is something you must bear with, override, and use to your own advantage as well as that of others.'

'But how?' Joe's face was a mask of despair.

'By accepting that it *is* your chosen way of life, and that to wriggle out of it, even supposing that you could, would be a coward's way. Forget your visions of sweeping reforms. Charity begins at home — and what you feel for these wretched operatives is charity in the truest Biblical sense — *caritas,* loving concern. Isn't that so?'

Joe had not thought of it that way, but he nodded.

'Very well,' his uncle pursued. 'Is all well at home — at Whittingham's? Are conditions ideal? Are the workers happy, clean, sufficiently rested?'

'No. He's not a hard master, like some. But they work too long and the children suffer. And the houses are dirty, even though they're on the edge of Bowland.'

'Exactly. Then take action on it. I see you're going to ask me how, and I can't tell you. But I would throw out a few suggestions, things I would do in your place. I would find out what good women of means and influence there are in the neighbourhood. Seek them out and try to turn their charitable impulses away from the sewing of text-embroidered loincloths for naked savages to the rescue of Christian children. Persuade some pious young lady to start a school, or a crèche, or both — or start one yourself. Use your mathematical wits to convince Whittingham that his workers needn't work such long hours, and set up before him a picture of himself as a paragon among millowners. Get him to install a rest place where his people can sleep and eat during the working day. Hint that a friend of yours with parliamentary influence is very interested in conditions among factory apprentices, and particularly in the fact that they're known to sleep on the mill floor, and to run away and be found dead, just to spite their masters. That sort of thing.'

He leaned back and surveyed his nephew's mobile face, on which doubt, consideration, and possibly a gleam of hope appeared in turn. At last Joe said, 'It sounds a tall order. But if you think it's best, Uncle, then I know I must do it. Or at least try.'

Ephraim nodded. 'Good lad.' He swung round towards his desk, took from it a sheaf of papers and began to study them. The interview was at an end. Even so did he conduct himself in court, dropping the argument at exactly the right moment.

In the hall Joe found Dove lurking in the shadows by the grandfather clock, a small figure in a pale-coloured bedgown.

Her hair was stuffed under a floppy cap; she looked like a servant rather than one of the young ladies of the house. He had not noticed her at all at supper, possibly because she hardly spoke, having her eyes intent on him and her mind working out what ailed him, for she could tell that something did. Belle, on the other hand, had chattered a lot, and had seemed unusually animated. He had thought in passing how pretty she was, a positive raving beauty compared with the poor caricatures of girls he had seen that day.

He was faintly irritated to find Dove so obviously waiting for him. Now that he had left his uncle's authoritative presence he was beginning to feel ashamed of running to him like a child with a cut knee after so little time out in the world, and irrationally resentful of Ephraim's sensible advice. He only wanted to say a swift goodnight to the household and be on his way back, to ride off his anger and frustration in a sharp canter down the quiet lanes. So he said sharply to Dove, 'Were you looking for me?'

She knew at once that he was displeased, and said softly with her head down, 'I'm sorry. I only wanted to give you this.' A small wrapped package was put into his hand.

'What is it?'

'A cake. Martha was baking today and I saved this for you. In case they were not feeding you very well at Mr Whittingham's. It's very good. It has almond paste and walnuts in it — you always used to like them.'

Touched in spite of himself, he said more kindly, 'Yes, I did and I do. But I get plenty to eat, Dove, indeed — you've no need to fret yourself about me.'

She raised her eyes to his. The old house had seen few such looks as they held, and another man would have kissed her. But Joe was eager to be gone, and not particularly pleased to be treated like a schoolboy being given a special morsel for his tuck box. He gave her a comradely clap on the shoulder.

'Your cake will get eaten, never fear. Where's Aunt Mary?'

She nodded towards the parlour, and with a careless 'Goodnight' called over his shoulder, he left her looking wistfully after him, paler than before in the subdued light from the hanging lamp.

He left the house briskly and went round to the stables where his uncle's horses dozed in their stalls. His own whickered as he called out to it. He took the blanket from its back and led it out into the sweet air of the May night. Just as he was about to mount a sound came from the darkness below the great oak tree that overhung the stables. The soft, indistinguishable murmur of voices, then a feminine giggle, and a man's deeper laugh. Joe made a wry face. One of the maids entertaining a lover, though he would have thought them all either too old or too plain to attract any.

Then he heard an unmistakable 'Sssh!', followed by silence.

He turned towards the spot the sounds had come from; in the light from an upper back window there was the gleam of a face, as suddenly withdrawn or covered. *Silly besom,* thought Joe, *as if I'd spy on her amours.* Idly he wondered which of the women it could be, but it was really no business of his. A cluck to the horse, a shake of the reins, and he was off southwards, the hoofbeats ringing on the cobbles until they died away altogether and only the whispering of the trees and the stirring of the stabled horses could be heard.

Under the oak a male voice said, 'That was close. Would he have told?'

A giggle. 'I don't know. Best take no chances, though.'

Then a sigh, and a kiss.

CHAPTER FOUR

The King was dead.

'One knew it was coming, of course,' said Jesse. 'No man could have lived in his state. Yet now he's gone, there's a strange feeling in the air.'

'Relief?' Eleanor suggested.

'No ... no, not quite that. I don't think people in general hated him; it was the firebrands who exaggerated his extravagance and voluptuousness, or whatever it was they damned him with. If he'd pawned his crown and put on the red cap of Liberty they'd have danced the *'Ça Ira'* in the streets with him — and chopped his head off the first time he refused to sign a paper.'

'I think it was the affair of the Queen that did it,' Eleanor reflected. 'To put aside one's wife and refuse her a place at the coronation takes some explaining away.'

'Not to me. I was presented to her, when she was still at court, and believe me, a coarser creature never turned a mangle. Poor George! I pitied him. Well, he's gone to his reward now, whatever that may be, and better luck to him in the next world than in this.'

The funeral was to be at Windsor, too far to go for whatever spectacle there might be, as they had no invitation to the interment in St George's Chapel. But on the day when it took place they drove out through streets of shops firmly closed, and private houses with the shutters up. Church bells were tolling a melancholy *dong-dong-dong,* one taking up from the other until they had tolled far beyond the sixty-seven years of the King's age. As Jesse and Eleanor drove along the Mall, the boom of minute-guns sounded across St James's Park.

'Yet not one person is in mourning,' Eleanor marvelled, 'except those who usually wear black, I suppose.' She glanced down at her own becoming dress of black moiré trimmed with small ruffles, and, approvingly, at Jesse's sober attire. One must set an example. 'How sad. Do you think... I wonder if Mrs Fitzherbert is grieving for him? Poor woman; if things had been otherwise she might have been *there* now.' They were approaching Buckingham Palace, that expensive monstrous folly which the late King had insisted on having built on the site of modest old Buckingham House, though he was too far gone in health to enjoy living there or anywhere.

Eleanor had a particular sympathy for the King's dignified, Roman Catholic morganatic wife, long estranged from him; she knew what it was like to be married and yet not married, to wonder if one morning your husband-by-courtesy was going to break the news over the teacups of his forthcoming wedding to somebody else. Suddenly her spirits sank. The July air was heavy and dank, the strolling people had the faces of Cruikshank's caricatures, Jesse had fallen silent. And she was missing Ben Disraeli.

In Lancaster, too, the shops were shut, but a greater air of decorum prevailed. In the Priory Church a very long funeral sermon was being preached by the vicar, while his congregation dozed, gazed round the monuments, or — if seated far enough back —furtively played noughts and crosses. The choirboys, almost eclipsed in their glorious mediaeval stalls, indulged in the popular and intricate game of paper cricket, in which a prayer book and a pin were used to pick out at random letters of the alphabet which represented scores or ways of being out. During that sermon many imaginary bails were removed with the batsman's feet over the popping-crease, or because he had *put his Legs before the Wicket, with a Design to stop the ball,* as the rules they all knew well put it. Merely to sit still and listen to that prosy old bore going on about someone who was only a fattish profile on a coin to them was more than boyish natures could endure.

The Atkinson pews were filled with family and servants. The women felt aggrieved that Ephraim had insisted on mourning being worn; of course it was only right and proper, but such a nuisance. For the servants there was no choice but whatever black garment they possessed, and all the women owned at least one. The Atkinson ladies had not been forced into mourning since the death of Farmer Bateman years before, when the twins had been children. Now they had ludicrously outgrown those clothes which had been taken out of the store-chest, inspected with laughter, and hastily distributed among the poor. Mary had owned a singularly handsome dress in the newest mode — now it was out of fashion, and she was too fat for it in any case. In the three weeks that had passed since the King's death new dresses, pelisses and bonnets had been made for her and the girls. At least they would come in if (heaven forbid) there were another loss in the family.

The girls looked charming, like peaches nested on black velvet. Belle's colour was far too bright and her expression too lively for a funeral service. Dove's pensive face maddened her, and she began to entertain herself by trying to make her sister laugh. In her reticule was an engagement card left over from a dance, with the little gilt pencil still attached to it. On the back she drew a succession of grotesque faces, each more awful than the last. It was the portrait of the new King William, with pineapple-shaped head and popping eyes surmounting the body of a plump frog, that broke down Dove's resistance and caused her to give a splutter of laughter which she immediately turned into a theatrical and unconvincing cough. Mary and Ephraim turned to glare at them both, Dove scarlet with embarrassment, Belle with her face in her handkerchief as if suddenly overcome by the pathos of the vicar's words.

Recovering, Dove felt justifiably cross. True, she had not been thinking of the late King, but of the beauty of the old church, of her parents' wedding there, and of the dream she dreamed every Sunday: that one day she would stand at the altar with Joe, and hear them pronounced man and wife.

She had lived in a dream since the day Joe had come down from university. His image came between herself and everything she saw; his voice was in her head, causing her unconsciously to imitate his way of speaking, a purer English than their speech at home. His displeased look, the night she had pressed that wretched cake into his hands, haunted her. Fool that she was to behave like a soft-headed little schoolgirl. Belle would never behave so. Indeed, on the all too rare occasions when Joe rode over, Belle was always in the highest flirts, teasing him, coquetting, drawing compliments from him. Their mother noticed it, Dove knew — everybody must notice.

And she knew something else, because she and her sister had grown from the same cell and were really one person split into two — though with differences of character. From a giggly little girl, always merrier than Dove, Belle had recently changed, no longer a chit prinking at the mirror and flapping her dark lashes at all men, but a woman, grown conscious of her own power, expressing it in every look and movement. And there was a strange excitement in her which communicated itself to Dove, sending shivers through her, like presages of a storm.

The service was over. The last prayer for the departed had been intoned, the last amen echoed by the congregation. And before leaving the church they had sung 'God Save the King', which, oddly, had been more moving than anything else.

Outside they moved in sober procession among neighbours and friends down the church path. They were almost at the gate when Belle, who was walking behind with Dove, exclaimed, 'Drat! My sandal!'

'What's the matter?'

'The ribbon's broken — look.' She displayed it. The cut she had made with embroidery scissors during the service, under the cover of her skirt, looked very convincing since she had pulled and frayed the edges a bit. 'I'll have to sit down in the churchyard and tie it. You go on — I'll catch you up.'

She ran back, on one sandalled and one stockinged foot, along the stony path back towards the church, followed by some disapproving looks. At that moment her mother looked back and summoned Dove. 'Where is Belle going?'

Dove told her, and Mary sniffed. 'Careless girl. A new pair, too. What am I to do with you two, always having to buy new shoes? Well, come along, and if she's late for dinner we shall start without her. I'm surprised the vicar went on so long, knowing how difficult it is for servants to keep food waiting...'

Belle was indeed late, arriving with scarlet cheeks and a slight limp from walking all the way with an improvised fastening to her sandal. Mary looked at her long and hard, but said no more. Dove ate little at the meal. The feverish excitement emanating from her sister was affecting her again, more strongly than ever.

Weeks passed, Dove growing steadily more uneasy about Belle's behaviour. She was aware of notes secretly written and hastily put away on her entrance, of other notes received by unknown means — possibly when Belle made an excuse to go off on her own during shopping expeditions conducted under Ellen Casson's escort. And, in later weeks, of Belle's unusual silences and brooding looks. At last, in their room, she forced a discussion.

'What is it? What's the matter? Something is, I know. Why won't you tell me?'

Belle did not meet her eyes. 'Why should I? There's nothing to tell.'

'Oh yes, there is. Belle, it's very hurtful that you keep it from me, when we've always told each other everything.'

Belle went to the chest of drawers and began to take out garments, fold them and put them back, quite unnecessarily, for Ellen took meticulous care of them. Dove followed and stood facing her, willing her to look up. At last she did, dropped the garments, and flew to Dove, hiding her face against her neck.

'Oh, yes, there *is* something wrong, there is! And I couldn't tell you because … I can't explain now.'

She was crying, her tears wet on Dove's face. Dove wiped them gently away. 'You must. What have things come to if you and I can't help each other? Sit down. I'll do anything I can — anything, Belle.'

After a moment, Belle said solemnly, 'Will you help me to run away?'

Dove drew back her arm from Belle's shoulders. 'Run away? What do you mean?'

Belle shook her head despairingly. 'I can't tell you. Only … I must. I can't stay here and face — them. I don't know what to do. But — promise you'll do one thing for me, Dovekin.'

The protective arm came round her again. 'Of course. There's no need to ask.'

'Well, I *do* ask. If — if I get caught, will you tell them that whatever I say is true — that you knew about it all the time? They'll believe you if they don't believe me. You may get scolded a little but it will make things easier — oh, please promise!'

Her heart heavy with foreboding, Dove said, 'Very well. I promise.'

Mary's bedroom slippers were of the softest leather, trimmed with fur, and heel-less. Neither girl heard her approach their bedroom door, drawn by the sounds of weeping and anxious conversation. It was not like her to listen at doors, but now she did, for her children's sake, and that night she lay awake while Ephraim slept peacefully, until streaks of light showed between the curtains and life started up in the streets.

They were summoned to their mother's parlour next morning after breakfast. It was the room in which she audited the household accounts with Aggie, arranged the daily menus, interviewed any extra servants who might be needed, and dealt with important citizens calling on Ephraim. Over the years it had acquired a severe aspect. As the two girls stood awaiting their mother's remarks from the high-backed walnut chair, Dove felt her knees shaking.

'I may as well tell you girls,' Mary said, 'that I accidentally overheard some of your conversation last night.' Belle started to say something indignant, but her mother held up a prohibitive hand. 'I knew long before that something ailed you, Mary Ann.' Belle cringed at this use of her real, christened name. It could only mean bad news. 'Perhaps you'll now be kind enough to tell me what it is. I chose this morning to send for you because your father is at the Assizes all day and need not be troubled by it — unless I think it right to tell him later. Well?'

Belle held her head up and addressed the window-curtain behind her mother. When she spoke, her voice sounded very unreal to Dove, like an actress reciting a part. 'I didn't wish to worry you with it, Mother.'

'I'm already worried. What ails you?'

'I have ... fallen in love.'

Mary's faded blue eyes, behind their spectacles, were like sharp beams from a dark lantern. 'Is that all?'

'I wish to be married.'

Dove started, shooting a sideways glance at Belle.

'What do you mean, child?' Mary dared not put her worst fears into words.

Belle controlled the trembling of her jaw and her hands, holding on to a chair by her side. 'I mean what I said, Mother. I want to be married, and soon.'

In all their lives of youthful peccadilloes they had never seen their mother wear such a look. Dove thought it must be as bad as any aspect the circuit judges wore when they tried murderers. It aged the soft lines of her face and made her appear frighteningly stern. 'The man's name?' she asked.

'Joe.'

The room wavered round Dove, as her mother asked incredulously, 'Your *cousin* Joe?'

'Yes.' Belle was still staring in front of them.

'I'll thank you for proof of that, miss. Joe hardly visits these days. When have you seen him, pray?'

'We — met in the town sometimes. And exchanged notes. It — I'm quite resolved, Mother.'

'Aye, but is he?'

'You'd better ask him.'

Shocked and distressed, Mary scanned the girl's face, and the even paler face of Dove. Joe, their cousin, brought up as a brother to them — Joe the simple and honest, to behave so. She had had suspicions, when he first came home, but to find them true... She felt as though the roof had fallen, crushing her and all she held dear.

One hope remained, in Dove's face, which wore a look of equal shock. If this was some made-up tale, Dove would tell her.

'Is this so, Maria?'

Poor Dove, also shaken by the use of the formal name she had been given at the font, and bound by her rash promise, said almost inaudibly, 'Yes, Mother.'

Mary drew a deep breath, feeling the pulses in her neck beating thickly. She hoped she was not going to have the heart attack the doctor had kept threatening her with since her weight had increased so rapidly. Then she controlled herself.

'Some parents would order you to your room, both of you, on bread and water. I don't believe in such things. You may go about your ordinary business, but only in the house. Aggie will see to it that neither of you sends messages or receives any. And tonight I shall talk to your father.'

Out in the passage Dove turned on Belle, between rage and tears, uncaring that their mother might hear her. 'How dare you say that? It's not true, I know, even though you *said* you'd make him fall in love. And how dare you make me promise without knowing what you were going to say? Oh, Belle, tell me it's not true, or my heart will break!'

Weeping, she clung to her sister's arm, but Belle tore herself away and ran upstairs.

The misery that pervaded the house in St Leonard's Gate during that day was like a heavy fog, creeping into the minds of the puzzled servants and lying leaden on the spirits of the family. Ephraim, coming from court after hearing two death sentences pronounced on wretched housebreakers, found a domestic crisis waiting for him which surpassed court dramas.

At first he refused to believe Mary's story. Not his daughter, not little Belle. Even if the truth were not so bad as Mary feared, she would never have carried on an illicit courtship with their Joe.

'Where was the need? Why could they not ask our permission? We'd have considered it. A time imposed, perhaps, with both of them so young. But to go behind our backs … no, Mother, there's some mistake.'

'I tell you there's not. I thought I knew our children, but now I see I don't. I once felt there was something between them, but I never thought of this. And that's all there is to it. Joe must be sent for tomorrow.'

Ephraim shook his head, dazed. 'Why Belle? It doesn't matter, as things have turned out; either would be as bad. But why Belle, and not Dove?'

'Because she's like —' Mary would not speak the name — 'my wicked sister. I told you, when the girls were born, I was afraid one of them would turn out like her, light-minded. Well, if Belle breaks our hearts as — the other one — did my mother's, she's got a good example before her.' She laughed bitterly. 'I hope she does as well out of it.'

The next day was Saturday. Ephraim dispatched a note to Joe summoning him for Sunday, his free day; then, restless and unwilling to stay in the gloomy atmosphere of his home, he rode out on impulse to Ashton Hall. There, in a tiny cottage in the grounds, lived Roderick Mackenzie, now a crippled pensioner of the Duke of Hamilton, whose Lancashire seat this was. The old duke, his former master, had been dead three years, but his son willingly kept Roderick on for services formerly rendered as dispatch rider.

He was sitting outside the cottage, his face turned up to the August sun. Ephraim always thought of him as an old man, yet he was not really old, only broken by the wounds and privations of the Peninsular Wars, and lacking one arm, lost to a Frenchman's sabre. The long white scar across the left cheek was healed long since, now only a deep cleft; the white hair had grown to an unsoldierly length on the shoulders, and the long chin was bearded. He might have been an Old Testament prophet, thought Ephraim, not the husband of a still-young woman.

They greeted each other kindly. Ephraim brought out a kitchen chair and sat by Roderick's side. For a time they talked of common topics — the King's death; the general election that followed the opening of the new, sensational Manchester to Liverpool Railway that was to take place soon. Then Ephraim said, with an effort, 'Have you heard anything of Eleanor?'

Roderick turned mild eyes on him. 'What should I hear? I am a stranger to her now.'

'I wondered. We hear nothing, for Mary made it clear she wouldn't correspond. I think of her sometimes. Do you feel as unkindly towards her as Mary does?'

Roderick took off his spectacles, laying them down on the rustic table where his Bible rested. 'She reaps what she sows, I daresay. Is that no' aye the way of it? Her mother's death, and the breaking of the marriage tie. God is not mocked.'

Ephraim shifted uncomfortably. 'Every time I sit in court I hear harsh judgments on folk who don't seem to me to deserve them. I knew Eleanor well enough, and I felt she was silly and impressionable, if you like, but not wicked. I cannot think that

— that there's any real badness in our family — or hers. Don't you feel that the devil selects his children on their merits, not for their blood ties?'

The wrinkle-embedded eyes surveyed him keenly. 'Ye want to believe it, I can tell. But never take me for an authority on either God or the devil. I am a stranger in a strange land.'

To Ephraim's next remark he returned no answer, seeming either to muse or to have fallen into a trance. Sighing, Ephraim took the chair inside and went on his way, moodily wandering about the grand, familiar grounds, aware neither of the fine old trees and well-marshalled flower beds, now scarlet with geraniums, nor of the flag flying to announce that the duke was in residence, nor the bright eyes of one of the duchess's ladies peeping round a curtain at him. Nothing seemed real. That poor wreck of a man with the white beard could never have been the fiery soldier who had eloped with young Eleanor, and run Jesse Bradshaw through in an enforced duel for jealousy. The *cottage ornée* he was passing had been the very one where Eleanor had made a sort of dolls' house for herself during her lifeless marriage. Now a keeper's children were playing on the step, and washing hung on a line.

Yet nothing was more unreal than that one of his lovely daughters should be no better than a light woman, and the other one her accomplice.

Joe, standing in Mary's parlour (he had not been asked to take a chair) stared from his uncle to his aunt and back again, baffled. The note in his pocket had merely summoned him to the house — there was no mention of Sunday dinner. And they were not at church, an unheard-of thing. They said nothing to him, only fixed him with curious looks, and there had been no kiss and handshake for him when he arrived.

'Uncle?' he said at last.

Ephraim cleared his throat. 'Belle has told her mother that you have been trifling with her affections.'

Joe almost laughed with surprise and relief. 'Trifling with…? Are you joking, Uncle?'

'I wish I were. It's not my way to joke on such matters. You've been meeting secretly, I hear.'

'Sending notes,' put in Mary. 'And seeing her at all hours of the day and night. That day of the King's funeral service, when she pretended her sandal ribbon was broken … oh, we know all about that, my lad.'

Joe felt as though his face were turning all colours and his head spinning like a child's top. He managed to say, 'I don't understand you, Aunt. What sandal ribbon? I've never met Belle without your knowledge in my life — or sent her notes. Why should I?'

'To ruin her,' Mary snapped. 'An innocent girl brought up with you as a sister. My faith in human nature's gone for ever, I can tell you that. You, a boy I'd have trusted with my life —'

Joe broke in desperately. 'Aunt, I repeat I don't know what you're talking about. Of course Belle's been a sister to me, and so has Dove. I could think of them in no other way.'

'That's all very well, but facts are facts. She's made a full confession to me that you've compromised her, and she expects marriage. As we do.'

This was not quite truthful. Belle had not admitted to being ruined, and Mary had shied away from pressing the point. That dreadful fact, if true, need never be known if events could be hurried on fast enough. But there was no harm in letting Joe think all *was* known.

His stunned face confirmed to her that her guess was correct. But in Ephraim it raised doubts. He had seen many hundreds of prisoners in the dock, and he knew as nearly as any man could know the difference between innocence and guilt, and the various degrees of both. It was time that witnesses were called in this case. He pulled the bell and asked the maid to bring in his daughters.

Before the pale-faced, shaking girls, Mary repeated the charge. Ephraim watched carefully their reactions. Belle's chin had gone up defiantly. She was not looking at Joe, and her answers sounded rehearsed. When Mary asked Dove to confirm the story, there was a hesitation before the low-spoken 'Yes', and then a spreading blush which would have been more apt on her sister's face.

'Well? Are you going to admit it now you've heard them?' Mary asked Joe.

'No, Aunt. I can't, because it is not true. This is some very silly, cruel joke the girls are playing on me, and I don't know how I've deserved it. Won't you tell me why, one of you?'

He turned to them. Belle's poise was still defiant, but Dove's eyes brimmed with tears and her lips trembled. Suddenly, with a loud sob, she ran out of the room. He appealed to Belle.

'Why are you doing this, Belle?'

'I know best,' she answered sullenly.

Joe shrugged, then addressed Ephraim. 'If Belle wants me to marry her, sir, and you and Aunt wish it too, of course I will, though I swear to you there's no reason why I should. You both know I'm in no position to marry. I've my way to make in the world and only enough money to live on myself. I've no wish to get married — and, if Belle will forgive me — I've seen nobody I liked well enough to ask. Belle and I are both too young to tie ourselves up yet. There's everything against it. But, as I said, I'll do whatever you ask.'

Ephraim had listened and watched with keen attention. Now, without consulting Mary, he said, 'Belle, leave us.' She turned on her heel and went without a word. When the door was shut he brushed aside whatever Mary had been going to say. 'Not now, my dear. Sit down, Joe. We have much to discuss.'

Joe continued to stand. 'I've no more to say, sir.' The 'sir' was a stab to Ephraim. 'I think it best if I leave you to talk matters over yourselves.'

Mary spoke, and now her voice was again the gentle motherly voice he had heard all his childhood. 'It's a fine day, Joe. Won't you take a turn in the garden while your uncle and I talk? We must straighten all this out, you know.'

The flushed, distressed boy nodded and left them. They saw him from the window pacing up and down under the fruit trees. Both knew that there was no real need for discussion. Twenty-two years of marriage had established between them a personal telegraph system.

'What I was going to say,' said Mary, 'was that we've made a great mistake. Belle was lying, for some reason of her own. The lad's innocent of any knowledge of this wretched business.'

'I came to the same conclusion. Have you any idea why she should lie?'

Mary shrugged. 'Not the slightest — unless she's taken some fancy to a man who won't wed her, and she wants revenge, so picks on poor Joe as the scapegoat. There's been something going on — I got that much out of Aggie. To think a daughter of mine should be such a double-dealer... I'd never have credited it, though she was always the naughty one. What beats me is why Dove should say the same thing when she must know it's not true. Why, when she was a little thing she —' Mary stopped, realising what she was saying.

Ephraim went on for her. 'She could never tell the smallest fib to get herself out of trouble. That's what you mean, isn't it?'

'Yes, that's it. And I wonder now how many punishments she took because Belle wouldn't own up to being the guilty one. I can see it, Father. Belle's put her up to this tale, and she won't give her away.'

'Misplaced loyalty indeed, when Joe is asked to suffer for it...'

'Joe! She's no love for Joe, or for any of us, it strikes me. That I should bear such a child...'

Her anger gave place to tears. Ephraim patted and soothed her. 'She's still a child, Mother, and children will misbehave, even the best of them. Look on the good side of it — there's no harm done, after all, and we thought it was going to be such a commotion.' No harm done except to Joe's feelings, he thought, watching the lonely pacing figure in the garden. Perhaps only he, who had projected his longing for a son on to Joe, knew the boy's vulnerability. Leaving Mary to dry her eyes and straighten her cap he went out to join his nephew.

'Joe. Your aunt and I have talked it over. We know there's nothing in all this. Whatever the truth may be, it's nothing to do with you. I'm sorry — we both are — you've been dragged into it. Will you forgive us — and Belle, if you can?'

Joe did not answer; Ephraim saw that it was because emotion choked him. When Joe had been a little boy in trouble he had never hesitated to run to his uncle for a comfortable lap to sit on and a bright penny-piece for consolation. Now he was a grown man he must put aside childish things. Trying to smile, he managed to say, 'How could I do anything else, sir?'

'"Sir"?'

'Uncle. It's been a ... misunderstanding.'

'Yes, and a bad one. Let's try to forget it. Come along in to dinner. The girls won't be there, by the way. Your aunt has ordered their meal to be served in the old schoolroom.'

Joe shook his head. 'I'd rather not, Uncle, thank you. I'd like to go back now — if I can borrow one of your horses. Mine will be too tired after the journey up.'

'Of course. Ask Jack to pick you a good one. But come in, Joe, and take a glass of Madeira with me, just to show kindness.'

The wine was old and rich, but Joe could not enjoy it. A bitter taste was in his mouth: for the first time his beloved family had betrayed him. It might be all cleared up now, but they had believed the worst. The hurt would take a long time to heal. Ephraim, looking across the rim of his wine glass, saw in his nephew the man who had fathered him, young Francis, and prayed silently that a better fate might lie in store for Francis's son.

Going out to the stables, Joe almost collided with a flying figure. Dove had been waiting in the shadows of an ivy-covered arbour for him to emerge. She caught at his arm, clinging.

'Joe! Don't go without a word! I don't know what they've said in there, but please believe me — I didn't...'

He turned his face from her and shook her off. She watched him go, her hands at her throat, wishing she could choke out her own life, for all her loving hopes lay dead at her feet.

For two days the girls were kept away from the rest of the household, allowed no outings or shared meals. In the cheerless old schoolroom, half-converted into an extra bedroom, they whiled away the time somehow, reading or playing solitaire, each on her own. They had had a violent confrontation when Mary had sent them in disgrace up to the old schoolroom, Dove turning on her sister in the first passion of resentment she had ever shown.

'Why did you make me say that? They knew it wasn't true. *I* knew, as soon as I saw Joe. How could you do such a thing to him and me? I think you must have gone out of your head.'

Belle was silent and sulky, turning away her head. 'I thought it would do.'

'Do? Do what? Only make Mother and Father think we were both together in a story. Now I can't go and say I'm sorry because I don't know what for. Oh, Belle, you're very naughty. I think I hate you.' Whereon the tender-hearted creature burst into tears, and troubled, miserable Belle made no move to comfort her.

After that there was nothing much to say between them. From time to time meals were brought to them, but no word from their parents, and Aggie did not condescend to appear to the children she had almost brought up. They were thoroughly out of favour.

But on the third morning Belle leapt out of bed, bright-faced, and ran to Dove's bed, getting into it as she had always done when they were little girls. Dove's face was turned away from her. Gently she pulled the long gold hair until her sister was forced to look at her.

'Oh, come on, Dovekin! Let's not play sulks any longer. It's all over, and we've been punished, though you shouldn't have been by rights, and I'm sorry. Give me a smile and say I'm forgiven.'

Dove did not smile. 'All over?' she repeated. 'But I thought you...' She hesitated to put into words what she had thought.

'Thought I wanted to get married? Oh, I did have a silly fancy that way — I don't know what came over me — you know how giddy I can be. Well, I don't, and it *is* all over.'

It was: the growing fears of the last month that had tormented her girlish ignorance had been dispelled, and she need no longer give a minute's thought to the handsome young guard at the castle who had found the pretty Miss Belle entertaining, but had swiftly got himself transferred to a garrison two hundred miles away at her trembling suggestion that he might have to marry her as soon as possible.

The summer's sport was over, and it was Dove who had lost most.

CHAPTER FIVE

Saul Bradshaw sat at his office desk, sprawled in the armchair he had had brought from home, for he needed comfort these days. He was eighty and more; he didn't care to count how much more, for what did it matter to a man still with all his faculties about him, a fine mill running like clockwork, money pouring in as it had these fifty years? Certainly, he was not the one who turned the wheels. He had started the mechanism off then left it to be kept in motion by his son Shem.

Shem was the second son, the poor snuffy old maid with a brain like an adding machine, the one who had taken over when his elder brother Jesse ran away with a floyting miss, Eleanor Mackenzie, a married woman. *Aye, and still a married woman,* Saul chuckled to himself. That bond would never be broken while her broken old husband lived, and serve Jesse right. Members of Parliament stood squarely in the firing line when moral bricks were being flung. One day he, Saul, would see to it that an extra-large brick would be flung in Jesse's direction, to smash him and his doxy, lording it down there among London riff-raff, adulterers playing at being lady and gentleman.

The day when he had found Jesse's room empty and heard the story of how that loose young woman had stolen him away, had burned like a brand on Saul's memory, for she had been sister-in-law to his old enemy Ephraim Atkinson. Sometimes, now that he was so old, Saul found it hard to recall exactly what it was that Atkinson had done to him. There had been a law case; factory workers who had attacked his mill had been successfully defended by Atkinson. And other things, surely. Yes, not long ago, among the many riots against harsh conditions in the mills, Ephraim Atkinson had snatched half a dozen or so law-breakers of Preston away from the gallows. It was nothing to do with Saul, but he kept a score against his old enemy. There was nothing much to do, nowadays, except hate.

The door opened.

'Father?' said Shem. At first he was not sure whether the old man were asleep or awake: the grey head nodded forward, the big shapeless hands were flat on the ledger in front of him. Then came a stirring of the huddled form, and his father's eyes were unclosing, like the lidded eyes of a toad. Shem surveyed him calmly. He knew only too well how people hated Saul Bradshaw: his operatives, neighbours at Bradhope, men of Lancaster who were turning towards the new dawn of reform and away from the dirty image of the factory profiteer. So old, they said, so gross, so bloated with rich living — surely he must soon have the stroke that heaven had in store for him?

But Saul held on, 'pickled in spirits', as he called himself in his lighter moments. Port, sherry, brandy, Madeira and claret had gone to swell the fat of his body and colour the red veins of his cheeks and nose; pork, beef, and venison had enriched his blood; cigar smoke filled his lungs with fragrant fumes. Some died of such fare early; Saul boasted that he thrived on it. And Shem was in a strange way proud of the survival of his half-mad, choleric old father. There was a semi-contemptuous affection between the small, asthmatic middle-aged man peering through steel spectacles at column after column of figures and names, and the bloated old relic of the eighteenth century who relied on his son to run his mill, yet would not put his name to the least change.

The bleared eyes rolled open. 'Well?' Saul grunted, pulling himself upright. 'What's to do, then?'

'Nothing special, Dad. Only these for you to sign.' He knew they would not be read, but it would never have occurred to him to slip in anything of which his father would not approve. Scratch, scratch went the pen, as document after document was signed and put aside. Then the big red face was turned up to him, the mind distracted from accounts.

'This lad of Atkinson's that's come to Whittingham's.'

'Yes, Dad?'

'Well?' A fist thumped on the desk. 'What about him? What've you heard?'

'Nothing. Only that he's there. A partner, it seems. Though in nought special, by the sound of it. My guess is that Whittingham got him in for the money.'

'Oh, *money*, is there? Atkinson's doing well, then? Gratified clients — shekels rollin' in?' Saul made as if to spit, but at Shem's pained look thought better of it. 'So, out of the brass he's made from defending Walter Whittingham against me he's putting his pup relations in the seats of power. That's grand, that is. Next thing we'll be having this lad followin' in Uncle's footsteps, getting up on his hind legs preachin' about workers' rights and how a man can smash t'factory that feeds him and get off scot-free.'

'I believe,' said Shem with faint mischief, 'he's read law at Oxford.' With amusement he watched his father's cheeks turn from turkey-cock red to the dark plush of church kneelers, and heard the half-coherent splutterings that followed. He always knew when to check them before they grew dangerous.

'Jesse,' the old man was mumbling. 'If Jesse hadn't gone... He was o' my way o' thinkin' once. I coulda trained him up i' the way he should go. I'd'a had grandchilder round mi knee now, a dozen, mebbe, 'stead of a barren hearth. That the flower o' the flock should wander and nobbut the puny lamb be left ... aye, me, aye, me.'

'Come now, Dad,' Shem interrupted with thin good humour, 'you've not done badly out of the puny lamb. Cheer up, and get done with the signings, then we can be off home.'

Scratch, scratch, the pen covered page after page of blank spaces for signature. Shem knew better than to pursue the matter of Jesse. His father's mind was set obdurately against the handsome son who had deserted him for a woman and a butterfly life in London. Shem and his brother corresponded occasionally, guardedly. Shem was kindly disposed towards Jesse. He would have been glad to see him home, but their father's enmity was so often and bitterly expressed that he felt it his duty to warn the elder brother that danger lay in wait for him in the north. Old and maundering Saul might be, but a snake need not be newly hatched to strike.

'Tell me what young Atkinson does,' Saul was saying. 'Tell me every move he makes. If you dunna, I'll find out, never fear.'

Joe sat at his window in Whittingham's house. It was on the top floor, and had been a servant's bedroom when the household had boasted more servants than just a cook-housekeeper and a woman who came in to do the rough cleaning. It commanded a view of the dull village street, empty now but for a man bringing logs home in a cart. Factory folk went to their beds when the mill turned out — or to what passed for beds. After work hours, Bradhope was dead, or as good as.

Joe's spirits were low. He had a book or two by him from the lending library in Lancaster, but reading meant candles and candles cost money. Down the street a faint light came from the public house, the Red Cow. He could well imagine what poor cheer he would find there. A wry thought recalled to him the place he might have been in now, if he had not followed his fancy: Oxford in Easter term, a fellow-student's rooms, jolly company, eager talk and food and drink, green college gardens and sweet river air, bells chiming from the towers. Young, foolish, lonely, undeserving, he felt himself no better than the mouse which peeped at him from its hole in the skirting board by the fireplace then flitted across the floor to cower by the far wall. There were crumbs on a plate beside him, left from his supper: he flicked them lightly across in the mouse's direction. It fixed him with questioning bright eyes, then in a moment it and the crumbs were gone. Joe was sorry. It would have been company.

He was startled by a knock, soft, timid: too quiet to be the housekeeper's.

'Come in!' he called. Any visitor would be better than solitude.

A dark shape filled the doorway. As the light touched it Joe leapt up with a cry of welcome. 'Uncle Will!'

Will Raven's large hand clasped his warmly before they stood back to survey each other. The man who had been friend and partner to Joe's father was now in his late forties, his big frame slightly stooped, the head of once-dark curls greying fast. Life had marked his face with sorrow; Joe thought he had the look of a patient beast that had been driven too hard. Next to Ephraim and Mary, Will had been the person closest to the boy since Joe had come to live in Lancaster. Not only affection bound Will to him, but a set, immovable conviction that he owed the nephew to whom he was not even blood kin a great debt. Had it not been for Will's mad marriage long ago to Jane

Atkinson, things might have fallen out very differently. It was impossible to rearrange the past; but if only ... if only he had stayed at home on the night of the Waterloo rejoicings instead of going down to the furniture workshop, as much to get away from his wife Jane as to see that the place was safe from rioters.

If he had not gone rushing up to Kirkland and taken Francis away from his fireside to the ravaged workshop, then Francis would not have been killed by that falling weight of mahogany. And so Ann would not have died of grieving for her husband's loss, and little Joe would not have been left orphaned.

If only Will had let the child go to his nearest relations, Ephraim and Mary, instead of constituting himself guardian to him and putting him through those months of hell under Jane's tyranny. If only...

'Well, lad? How's tricks?'

'Not bad, Uncle.' He did not miss Will's slow appraisal of the dingy room. 'Plenty of work to do. I'm glad of a bit of time off in the evenings.'

'Aye. You never thought to tell me you'd come down to Whittingham's.'

'Didn't I write? No, I don't believe I did. I'm sorry. Then how did you find me? Oh — I suppose you called in at Lancaster?'

Will noticed the slight stiffness in Joe's voice. Some trouble there — that was a pity. He said, 'They told me where I'd find you. I thought it were time I looked you up, seeing it's been t'best part of a year.'

'Yes, just before Lent term started. It doesn't seem so long, but then so much has happened.'

They talked of Joe's new life, of the state of the industry, of everything but the cause of the disappointment and melancholy he could see in Joe's face, and of the family at Lancaster. Big, hulking Will had in such matters the tact of a woman. He was prepared for the question he knew he would be asked.

'How are — things at Kendal?'

A pause. 'There's been changes, Joe. Your Aunt Jane's been going downhill fast of late. Not in health, that's to say, but in her mind. Times she's as quiet as can be; other times she's like a wild thing. Last week she — well, she went for me. With a kitchen knife.'

'Uncle! You mean she stabbed you?'

'Nay, nobbut a scratch.' He glanced down at his forearm where the long wound still throbbed under a bandage. 'It's a good thing I'm strong. I got t'knife off her and held her down until t'fit passed. When doctor came he said she must go away. That is — be put away.'

Joe looked horrified. 'The asylum?'

Will nodded. It was not his way to describe the capture of his crazed wife by the two sturdy warders they had sent: her furious struggles, the falling down of her grey hair, the red marks her long talons made on the men's faces, her obscene curses of them and himself. The neighbours had come out to watch her being loaded into a cart like a beast, and he had been bitterly ashamed, heartsick. All this would only bother Joe.

'So you're all alone now,' Joe said.

'Oh, it's nought to me. I've t'shop to keep me busy, plenty to do and folks in and out all day.' Will lived these days by selling second-hand furniture and oddments in Finkle Street, not far from the fateful workshop of Atkinson and Raven, now the premises of a wine merchant, its tragic past forgotten.

'It's funny,' he mused, 'what a sale there is for knick-knackery. You'd not believe the stuff they'll buy. Last week I got shut of a stuffed bear with the mange and an owd-fashioned bed I'd not ha' given twopence for — black oak all over, fancy bits, naked babbies and roses and the like. Mind you, Frank — your dad — liked such things. He once restored a houseful of it for Howard at Levens Hall, that he did, and so you couldn't tell any difference. Then there's pictures. I've stacks of 'em leaning up against t'wall, oils so dark you can't see whether it's a man or a woman on t'canvas. *That* doesn't stop customers, bless you. It's seldom anyone comes in but they get down in t'dust rooting through all them simpering wenches and fat squires, looking for a Romney.'

Joe laughed. 'Do they ever find one?'

'Not they. Owd George may have died in these parts, but he didn't give much away beforehand. Better come up and have a look — might make thee a fortune.'

'Very welcome.' Joe shivered. The clock said almost eight. 'Come out and take a drink, Uncle. The Red Cow's not splendid, but it's better than this.'

'Well.' Will smiled shyly, 'ale's my weakness, everyone knows. Happen I'll take it moderate, though, with thee.'

The Red Cow was indeed far from splendid, a rough alehouse with backless benches and imperfectly scrubbed tables, thickly scented with coarse tobacco. Among its patrons were overseers from Whittingham's and Bradshaw's. Some glanced up and nodded at Joe, others stared blankly. One or two wretched shawled women were getting some custom; a heap of children lay asleep in a corner like puppies. Will took note, and regretted the place in which he found the boy. As they talked over the poor brew he realised more and more that somewhere Joe's life had gone wrong. In the face opposite him he could see Francis's likeness come and go, a very young and sensitive Francis, without the excited confidence and assurance of success. Fond though Will was of his glass — too often his only company and cheer — he could not get drunk tonight with all his thoughts intent on his companion.

Joe was talking on, about the poor conditions in the mills and his longing to improve them, his designs for machines. He took out an old letter and began to sketch on it an intricate thing of wheels and cylinders balanced on long thin legs. It looked to Will something like the new cottage piano, or its skeleton.

'It's for spinning bobbin-net,' Joe explained, 'only better than any there's been yet. It could be cheaper, too, for you see it's capable of being run by steam or water, and it's quicker, no doubt of that.' Will listened to his explanations without taking them in, only registering that Joe had some high-flown scheme for designing machines that would allow the workers more leisure time and bring the manufacturers in more profit.

'When can you try this thing out?' he asked.

Joe shrugged. 'When I'm given the opportunity. I know just how it works — I take notebooks everywhere I go, and I've learned more about cotton than I ever did about law, believe me.' He talked of West India Cotton, Surinam and Berbice, of Bowed Georgia, Pernambuco, Bengal and Surat, while Will's mind went on a tour of foreign parts where men wore turbans and robes, and women had jewels set in their brows and noses, and all had brown faces and rode upon elephants. He tried to pull himself back to reality and the encouragement of Joe, but it seemed that in the dull atmosphere of the inn encouragement did not flourish. Joe said less and less; neither was drinking with any enjoyment.

Suddenly Joe pushed away his tankard and told Will the story of Belle's accusation and his trial by the Atkinson family. 'It wasn't that I'm too soft to take such things,' he said fiercely. 'I hope I'm man enough for that. But that *they* should think ill of me — believe it — without even taking me aside and asking… It's not like them. Uncle Ephraim and his love of weighing the evidence — when did he ever damn a prisoner unheard?'

'Happen the girls' tale rang true.'

'The girls!' Joe's tone was bitter. 'Belle I've always known for a bit of a minx and a flirt, but to say I owed her marriage — I, that never gave her a thought but as a little sister. And Dove — I'd have said she liked me better than Belle did. Why should *she* lie? I'll never trust a woman again, I tell you that. It's like having a limb off, to lose faith in those two — in all of them, come to that.' He stared moodily into the remnants of his ale while Will surveyed him with deep pity and a dim understanding of what had happened.

'Belle was up to something, Joe. At her age they always are. She's deep and sharp, and like her Auntie Eleanor, but I don't think she meant you harm.'

'No harm — to make me marry her out of hand? Oh, come, Uncle.'

'She didn't think. Lasses don't. They can't see an inch beyond their noses. As for Dove, she's your mother all over again, all softness and love. She'd never hurt you, meaning it. You take my word, she was driven to it somehow. Nay, don't ask me, I wasn't there and I know nought. But this I do know.' He leaned forward earnestly. 'You remember what's just happened to you — keep it stored up. Don't say yes to a lass just because she says yes to you, or because she's got blue eyes or black eyes or a bedpost waist, or her mother thinks you'd look grand in t'family pew. Just talk to her, and look at her. Figure what she'll be like i' thirty years, what sort of a temper she'll have, whether she'll mother your bairns well. And Joe, I'll tell you this, for you're no angel any more nor me: if you feel fire i' the blood flare up between you, reckon nought of that either, for you can feel it as hot in a poor Saturday night drab.' He was thinking of his own brief, disastrous first marriage: the unborn child killed by its frightened young mother, the barren years of separation, and of his second marriage to a sex-starved bitter woman hungry for the life he could give her through their mutual passion, a passion that had turned to hate. He turned his head sharply to shut the visions out, and met Joe's worried gaze.

'Give it time, eh, lad? The offers'll come your way, never fear, with that bonny face on you and a good turn of speech. I'll never have the choice again, but you will. And Joe — if there's ever ought I can do to help, you've only to send me word. Never mind what it is, great or little, send me word. Think on, now.'

Joe smiled. 'I'll think on, Uncle.'

The beautiful, elaborate drawing of the bobbin-net frame made no more impression on Walter Whittingham the second time Joe showed it to him than it had the first, or, if it did, he concealed his enthusiasm well.

'I've laid out enough on new machines. I've no brass for more.'

'But this could produce so much more material, don't you see? — almost double what we turn out now.'

'Who wants to produce double? Stuff's too cheap to bother wi' doubling. Fourpence a yard, sixpence at most — there's a glut of it.' Whittingham turned away impatiently.

Joe left him, rolling up the precious drawing carelessly for once. He was getting tired of hawking it about with no success. He began to wonder whether he knew as much about machinery as he thought he did.

Unknown to him, he had aroused at least one party's interest. On the night when he had talked with Will Raven at the Red Cow, there had been among a group of men at the next table Thomas Swainson, one of Saul Bradshaw's overseers. Swainson was a personal crony of his employer's, a gambling and drinking companion who was sometimes asked up to Bradshaw Hall, for Saul had no friends among the local gentry. High on the list of an overseer's qualifications came sharp eyes and keen ears, both of which Swainson possessed. During a lull in conversation he had caught something of what Joe was saying to Will as he described his invention in an excited voice louder than his normal tones. Craning his neck, Swainson could see the drawing, though not in detail. Unlike Will, he knew what Joe was talking about, and it interested him enough for him to pass on the information to Saul.

Saul listened impassively. Then he said, 'Sounds no better than t'owd stocking frame.'

'Oh, it's more than that, Mr Saul, if what I heard was right. It's as delicate as a handloom, yet it'd take steam or power, the lad said.'

Saul looked up under bushy white brows. 'Dost believe it?'

'May be all a tale, for owt I know. But it sounded sense. I wished I could a' taken a look at it. If it's what he says, then it could turn out stuff that's produced by handlooms — stuff like super-fine muslins and India dimities — only at twice the rate.'

'I'll believe it when I see it,' Saul brooded. Swainson knew well what was in his mind before he spoke again. 'And I *will* see it.'

Discouraged by his failure as an inventor, Joe thought back to his uncle Ephraim's advice about his possible influence on conditions in the mill: *Find out good women ... persuade some pious young lady to start a school, or a crèche, or both ... get Whittingham to install a rest place where his people can sleep and eat during the working day.*

It had sounded very idealistic and far-away at the time, and it sounded so now in his mind. But, half-heartedly, he set about trying it.

CHAPTER SIX

On the outskirts of Bradhope, in the hamlet of Knott Green, Joe's social activities had come under the brown eyes of one of the village's great ladies. Miss Porteous was not gentry in the sense that the Duke of Hamilton was, or any of the old landed families. She had lived in Knott Green only a few years by their reckoning, and kept only a modest carriage and a few servants, nor was she seen at hunt balls. A lady of quiet life, yet without question distinguished. Her manners were of London, her speech elegant, yet so clear and unaffected that it might have been their own, and was approved by those who mocked southern accents. She lived in a tall stone house of the previous century, neither a villa nor a cottage, but a good sturdy Lancastrian dwelling with a prim well-kept garden at the back. Her household was made up of Londoners and highly respectable locals. A household which neither chattered over walls nor blabbed in pubs about its mistress's business, a household which was worthy but unimportant, for she had no business that could possibly have interested scandal-mongers.

Secure from the summer sun behind closed shutters, Miss Porteous sat surveying a document in her drawing room. It had been given to her by her friend, Mrs Leeming, wife of the vicar of St George's. As she read it — not for the first time — through dainty lorgnettes, expressions of amusement, interest, and something else chased across her long, slightly horsy face, which was neither handsome nor ugly, but, like the rest of her, distinguished. Her dark hair was dressed in the fashionable topknot backed by a Spanish tortoiseshell comb, partly veiled by a high-crowned cap, her long neck decorated by a simple, beautiful necklet of opals set in silver. Her brown dress of watered silk was cut in the popular mode of low neckline, balloon sleeves and exaggeratedly tiny waist, yet looked not at all ugly on her tall, slim form. She was perhaps forty, or less; one's guess depended on whether she smiled or looked grave.

The table at which she sat was of finest mahogany, its sheen concealed by a cloth of Indian manufacture, crimson and peacock colours interwoven with tinsel threads. Round the walls were books, shelf upon shelf of them: calf-bound, handsome, yet not so immaculately serried as to seem unread. Here and there a volume had been taken out and replaced hurriedly, or laid on top of others because it did not fit into its old space. They were loved, used books. The furniture, too, was used. A wing chair of the kind favoured by gentlemen was by the fireside; visitors had been known to eye it askance as being far too comfortable for a lady to slouch in. Yet Miss Porteous did not slouch, but carried herself uprightly with a natural grace.

She was sitting up very straight now, reading the document before her, with its large boyish signature: *J. ATKINSON*.

Schools, day and evening. Voluntary teachers. A doctor, or person instructed in nursing, to be within call. A place of rest and refreshment to be within the factory. A petition to Parliament to demand the restriction of child labour. Persons in the habit of making charitable gifts to be informed of the poverty among operatives. Ladies to undertake religious instruction…

'Well, well!' She rose and pulled the bell-rope. To the servant who appeared she said, 'Send the young man in, Ellen.'

Joe, coming from Whittingham's, sniffed with appreciation the scents of lavender and wax polish that met him in the hall and accompanied him up the wide oak staircase. He noticed the scent of flowers, too, on a *torchère* carved from marble, and in a copper bowl on the landing windowsill. There were no family portraits on the walls, only landscapes and some Bartolozzi prints of nymphs and cherubs. He recognised the room into which he was shown as being furnished with a taste equal to Uncle Ephraim's, expensive and — yes, slightly gentlemanly; nothing of the boudoir about this. Smarting from recent events, he had not been eager to be received by a lady alone. It seemed possible to be compromised without having had the faintest thought of improper behaviour.

But the sight of this lady reassured him: the plain face, the pleasant smile, the rich dress and the low-pitched musical voice which reminded him of the ladies he had known in Oxford, yet it was even more mellifluous, and with a different ring to it.

He bowed and took the chair she indicated, sitting in a shaft of sunlight that pierced the cracks between the shutters, making his hair a fiery nimbus and showing up the cotton specks and dust on his clothing. Suddenly shy, feeling very young and presumptuous, he lowered his gaze and studied the pattern of the carpet.

She was surveying him strangely, closely, almost eagerly. When he raised his eyes again the look had gone.

'Well, Mr Atkinson? It seems you have some very ambitious ideas for the betterment of your partner's mill. How came you by them?'

'I … they appear to me only sense, ma'am. If you had seen the condition of the workers — not so much at Mr Whittingham's, but at other mills — I think you would feel … I mean, I am sure you would agree…' he floundered.

She took him up neatly. 'I have heard of them. Tales of exhaustion, of foul atmosphere, little children crippled or killed by excess labour — filth, vice and ignorance among the parents. These tales are true, then?'

Joe, blushing slightly at such female frankness, replied, 'They are, ma'am. I've travelled widely in Lancashire and Derbyshire, and seen it for myself. I can't describe how bad it is.'

Her smile had a touch of mischief in it. 'I really knew nothing of these things until I read your paper, Mr Atkinson. It moved me to make enquiries. Having now seen you, I am sure all I have been told is true. Your zeal in bringing such matters to light is very commendable. Christian charity would do very little good if everybody kept silent.'

So she was a religious lady, he thought, murmuring aloud that he had only done what he felt proper. She was not in the least like Mrs Leeming, or any Lancaster charitable person, but he supposed there were variations. She was asking him about what he had seen, the reasons for the suffering and deprivation of the workers, the average wages. As he answered, she meticulously wrote on a sheet of paper already ruled out into columns.

'Spinners may earn as much as one pound fourteen shillings a week. Dressers, one pound ten and six. Weavers, twelve shillings. Carders, fifteen shillings, reelers twelve. Doublers, eight and six. Children between ten and fourteen, tenpence a day — fivepence if under ten years old. Correct? These seem to me fair enough wages, as they go — certainly compared with those of agricultural workers.'

'But not when you think of the hours they have to work, ma'am! Even with food prices down from what they were, how can they restore their health? The best meat and other foods could do nothing for them. And they've so many mouths to feed, they couldn't live at all without the children's labour. Yet the children fade away and die. Is it surprising? Quite apart from the long hours, their lungs are full of cotton waste — fly, we call it — stuff that builds up in the bad air of the factories and kills in the end. The scavengers, who collect the waste from the floors, get kicked and beaten as well...' He paused for breath.

'You're quite a Radical, Mr Atkinson. I think you should turn your attention to politics when you have done all you can for the cotton industry.'

'How strange you should say that, Miss Porteous. It was precisely what my uncle Ephraim advised me to do, but I have at present no thought of it.'

He either felt or imagined a stillness in the air, as though she had momentarily stopped breathing, but her face was quite composed. He noticed her hands, clasped together tightly on the table: long-fingered, rather bony hands that managed to be beautiful because of their smooth whiteness and polished pearly nails. There was more tenseness than repose in them. He wondered if he had said something to offend her. But she said, very calmly, in a tone of mild enquiry, 'Your uncle Ephraim?'

'Mr Ephraim Atkinson of Lancaster. It was he who brought me up after the deaths of my parents.'

She nodded, as if dismissing the subject, then rang for the servant and ordered sherry and biscuits. 'A habit of mine — it cheers the long morning, don't you agree?'

Over the refreshments he admired the shelves of fine books. 'They remind me of my uncle's study — but his deal mostly with law.'

'Mine range widely — over the years and the arts.' She rose and pointed to a section of newish bindings beside the mantelshelf. 'Those are from my own hand. It may be immodest to draw attention to them, but I take an almost parental pride in seeing them as real, true books, when I remember them as sheets of manuscript, trying my already much-tried eyes.'

Politely, Joe went to examine them, fully expecting them to be volumes of piety and grave moralising. He was startled to see the titles on their spines — *The Fatal Friendship, a Drama; Yseult of Lyonesse, a Tragedy; The Passionate Shepherdess, and other Poems; Florio and Ethelinda, a Romance.* This was in three stout volumes; he saw that many of its companions were also three-volume novels.

Miss Porteous read the astonishment on his face. 'Yes, I am that maligned thing, a female author. I hope you will not now fly abruptly from my presence, Mr Atkinson, for I can see you are a serious-minded young man.'

He tried to say that of course he would not fly, that he was surprised — honoured — that he had not actually read any of her work, but her name was of course familiar ... and in the course of trying to say all these things fell over his words and stuttered, blushing. He thought angrily that this cool lady would conclude he was always blushing. But her eyes and her voice were kind as she motioned him back to the table.

'Never mind. You're too young to have read so much weighty stuff, and I daresay romances are not at all your style. To be frank, they are not mine either these days; I should prefer to study the great figures of the past and write of them, as my friend Miss Agnes Strickland is doing at this moment. But I find that the public has an insatiable appetite for novels, and so I continue to write them. One must, after all, eat.'

Joe saw that in fact she was not eating the small delicate biscuits, but had already drunk one more glass of sherry than he had done. There was a faint colour now in her cheeks, and her voice had lost its slightly mocking note as she said, 'Enough of me. Tell me about yourself.'

More at ease now, Joe sketched out his life, leaving out its early tragedy and telling her only about his youth in Lancaster, his two years at university, and his decision to devote himself to the improvement of conditions in cotton. Her face, as she listened, was so expressionless that it was almost as though she were not listening, but thinking of something else.

When he had finished she put up her lorgnettes and scanned his face closely. 'What you did not tell me,' she said, 'was that your father was Francis Atkinson, and your mother Ann Bateman of Wray.'

'Yes ... but...' He was stammering again. 'How did you know, ma'am?'

'At first I was not sure, with my short sight, until I studied you. Later, when I heard you talk, I was sure. You are so like your parents, yet so unlike in many ways. I had heard of your bringing-up at St Leonard's Gate, but not of your coming to Bradhope — I was certain it must be you. You see, Joseph, I am your aunt Margaret.'

The room reeled round Joe, then steadied. He was conscious of someone outside in the garden, singing, and of the ticking of the clock. Thoughts whirled through his mind: the stories heard from Mary of her wild stage-struck young sister, who had run away with a company of players and had never been heard of since. Margaret the bookworm, the romantic young lady, the black lamb of the family, neither pretty like her sisters Eleanor and Ann nor staid like her sister Mary. Margaret, whom they had long ago decided must be dead.

She was re-filling his glass, pushing it towards him; when he had drained it her long hands reached across the table and enfolded his, and her eyes were bright with emotion. 'I'm sorry to tell you so suddenly. I felt I must, my dear boy. You are the first of my family I've spoken to since I was nineteen.'

'But — why — Aunt? They all think you died long ago.'

'I was so ashamed,' she said simply. 'I defied them and disgraced them. How could I expect to be received again? Better they should think me dead.'

'But you don't know!' he burst out. 'It was not like that at all, Aunt. I believe Aunt Mary was very much shocked at the time, and Uncle too, but they tried very hard to find you, and so did my father — he went to London and enquired everywhere. Then Aunt Eleanor ran away, and I don't think Aunt Mary has ever forgiven *her* — but they always spoke of you as "poor Margaret".'

She was silent. 'And my own parents? They died...?'

'When I was quite small, though I remember them very well. Grandpapa Bateman used to be a very jolly, robust man, but he grew thin and sad. And Grandmama Bateman died of a heart failure. Aunt Mary said it was from the shock of losing...'

'Both her daughters. Yes.' Margaret put her face in her hands. 'Oh, Joseph, how callous and thoughtless I have been. I was so sure they would not want to hear of me. And yet Mary and Ephraim were always so kind, and Francis and Ann. It was my father I was afraid of — he had a violent temper always. And I was ashamed that Mary should see what I had become.'

Her face looked older, and drawn, and pale; Joe felt through his bewilderment deeply sorry for her. He pressed the cold hands, noticing that they were ringless except for a heavy mannish signet ring on one finger.

'Won't you tell me about it, Aunt? I should like to know. Believe me, I won't judge you — only I'm so sorry for your mistaken idea that they would be angry. Please tell me.'

'Can you stay? Should you not be somewhere else? At work?'

'No, not this morning. Mr Whittingham is holding an audit and told me to make myself scarce. I have plenty of time, and … I don't want to leave you.'

She rose. 'Let us sit more comfortably. The chaise-longue is quite the most … yes, I think we'll sit there.' She drew him to the couch beside the window, and settled in one corner, while he took the other. As she began her story he sensed that she had dropped the pose with which she had met him, and become once more the young Margaret, but wiser and sadder, no longer the eccentric literary lady showing a mocking face to the world.

What could she tell him? Margaret wondered. She could not bring herself to speak to the innocent-faced boy (there was no mistaking the quality of true innocence) of the degradation and shame of her life on the roads with Harlow's touring company. Incapable of acting — how could she have had such dreams of glory? — incapable even of crossing the stage without tripping over something because of her mole's eyes, she had become the company drudge, dresser, stage-sweeper, anything that came handy. 'Maggie will do it, leave it alone. Maggie! Damn the girl, where is she?'

Tall, lanky, plain — dirty, even, as she was — nobody approached her to lead a life of wicked pleasure as a kept woman. There had been Pommeroy, the elderly actor who had promised to befriend her, and instead had pestered her and taken advantage of her poverty and wretchedness to make her sell herself to him for scraps of food. Even now, a strong shudder went through her and her skin crawled at the memory of his slug-like hands and wet lips. He had tired of her once the novelty had worn off, and had soon after left the company. She was glad to see the back of him, humbly grateful that there were no consequences of the horrible relationship; and very, very hungry. It was the end for her of any desire for sexual love, of the silly ideas of romance she had entertained, burst like bright bubbles to become ugly soap-suds. Ironic that she should later have made a handsome living out of weaving romances for others. All this she summarised for Joe's ears in a brief, selective account, so that he wondered what she was ashamed of about it.

She took up the story. 'One day our manager's wife, Mrs Reilly, sent me with a letter to a lady who had written some dramas we had put on — Mrs Mortison. (Though I think, Joseph, she was in fact a Miss.) She lived in a street off Piccadilly, to which I had to make my way on foot, and a poor business I made of it. My spectacles had long ago been broken, and I could see hardly a foot in front of my face. It was a long way from the street off Drury Lane where we were playing. I fell down things, and over things, lost the note I had of the address and went flat on my face once, and another time almost under a horse's hooves. When I got there at last it was more by Providence's efforts than my own, and near late afternoon. I was half in a stupor with terror and the fear of losing my place. At the door the maid was haughty to me and said she would deliver the letter herself. But Mrs Mortison was passing through the hall…'

Margaret would never forget the sight of that upright figure — grey-clad, grey-haired, with the severe cap over the hawk face — or the sudden kindly smile at the sight of her distressed self, the dismissal of the maid, the invitation to come up to the drawing room and deliver her errand.

'She looked so harsh, yet she was so kind. It seemed she was a distinguished writer who championed the cause of oppressed women on the principles of the late Mrs Godwin, and in me she saw an example. She talked to me as nobody had ever done before, gave me tea, asked me what skills I had — too few, alas! — but she seemed to think them enough. I talked, and I suppose I wept; I was almost at the end of my tether. I was in despair when she asked me to go back to Kitty Reilly — but in a coach, and with a letter asking whether I could be spared from the company to enter her service. Well, Mrs Reilly was a good enough woman — I don't blame her for thinking little of me — and when she read the letter I could see that she wondered if she had been quite fair to me, seeing that I came to her from a gentleman's family. But she wrote a letter back to Mrs Mortison and sent me with it the following day in a hackney, as I could evidently not be trusted to go through the streets by myself.

'And there, Joseph, it began. She took the dirty, sad, sluttish girl that I was, threw away my ragged clothes and gave me some of her own, some bought new, had me bathed in front of her kitchen fire and my awful hair cut and washed by her own maid. As for my poor eyes, she went with me to Dollond's for new spectacles with elegant gold rims, which made *me* feel elegant and gave me a new outlook on the world. I've never minded wearing them since, though I used to hate them so.' She toyed affectionately with the lorgnettes.

'I was not truly in service with Mrs Mortison. I did some errands for her, but mostly I worked with her in her library, looking up references, checking proofs, writing letters to authors and publishers. I was quite good at that, though it was not what I had imagined for my career. It was she who encouraged me to write, and told me what was wrong with what I'd written already. I blush to think of it: how crude, how naive I had been. I think now that her taste was a little puritanical, but it did me so much good, and there was enough of myself left to balance her. I had a play published and performed — not by Reilly's company — and then another, and some poems. I began to attend the salons to which literary ladies were admitted, but which real ones shunned. At some, Joseph, I saw your Aunt Eleanor...'

Joe started forward. 'Oh! What was she like? Did she know you?'

A head-shake. 'No. How could she, transformed as I was? Quite elegant, by that time, with none of the rawness showing. But she was beautiful, just as I remembered her, only with a London polish on. I avoided her, for there was nothing to be said. I thought — she would have felt as the others did.'

'But they did not, Aunt! Nor would she have done.'

'I know that now, from you. I thought quite otherwise, then, and Mrs Mortison agreed with me, when I told her my history. She said it was better to suppress the past and make a new life with a new name. She even gave me one. Margaretta Porteous — how grand! My first heroine was called Margaretta.'

Joe was remembering. 'Aunt — when you met Aunt Eleanor — was she married?'

Margaret gave him a long look. 'What did they tell you?'

'Very little. Only, somehow ... no, I must be plain. Uncle Ephraim said Jesse Bradshaw had seduced her and they were living as man and wife.'

'So they were, Joseph, when I saw them, and a very successful thing they made of it. Nobody there knew but I, and I'm sure nobody suspected. She is very pretty still... I think she...' Margaret suppressed what she had thought. There had been a young foreign-looking man with languishing eyes and shiny ringlets at Eleanor's elbow, who was known in Margaret's own circles as a very promising novelist of considerable dash. Once more she had seen her sister stepping aside from the path of virtue. It had even given her the basis of a plot for a story.

She saw the occasion still, the white-and-gold room with its throng of fashionable chatterers, and across it, only two or three groups away, her elder sister's fair curls with a diamanté aigrette in them, laughing and flirting her fan at the Eastern-faced youth, while a stoutish florid man who must be Jesse Bradshaw stood complacently by. Margaret had had a wild impulse to rush across and embrace her sister, the girl whose bedroom she had shared at Highriggs, in which they had read the poetry of Scott and romanticised together. Surely Eleanor would understand and forgive... But the crowd shifted, and the group was gone, downstairs to supper.

She came back to the present. 'So you see, Joseph, through Mrs Mortison's influence I came to be a writer like herself, and she was not in the least envious, only pleased she had rescued me from — what I had been. She died five years ago, quite elderly, leaving me many of her things. It was then I felt I had seen enough of London and Society. I longed to come home — so here I am at Bradhope, as near as I can get to it. I suppose Highriggs has gone.'

'Yes — it was sold off in lots.'

Margaret sighed. 'At least I have found you, nephew.'

Joe moved across the sofa and grasped her hand firmly. 'Aunt, you must believe me, they would be overjoyed to see you in Lancaster. It would be the best thing to have happened for years. *Do* believe me — I know them so well. My cousins, the twins...' He hesitated for a second. 'They have grown up into beautiful girls — they would be charmed with you, and you with them. Imagine, to have a famous author for an aunt! And, Aunt Margaret —' his keen sensitivity made him aware that she had not told him all her story — 'if there is anything from the past that saddens you, and would make them sad, there's no need to tell them.'

She pressed the hand that held hers, then gave it a firm shake. 'Joseph, you're a gentleman indeed. I think we shall understand each other very well. And I promise I shall think of what you have said. And now,' briskly, 'as to what you want me to do about these mill-hands of yours. If money is in question...'

The red head and the dark bent over papers, figures, lists of names. Of a scattered and decimated family, two had found each other.

CHAPTER SEVEN

Eleanor gazed appreciatively round the boudoir-library of the Countess of Blessington, London's newest and most talked-of fashionable hostess. It was worth looking at, this jewel of a room in what had been rapturously described as a jewel of a house. Long and narrow, its tall windows facing the trees of Hyde Park, it was newly painted in white and gold, its walls lined with bookcases (Lady Blessington's guests included many authors, and she herself had a turn for writing). Brilliant colour was everywhere: the blue of Sèvres vases, the delicate tints of porcelain fruits and flowers, the countess's armchair blazing in yellow satin. Everywhere on small dainty tables were displayed priceless relics of the famous — the Pompadour's watch bearing her portrait, the star-shaped jewel on the forehead flashing on and off as if by magic — snuff boxes covered with gems, tiny treasures of gold and enamel; and, on the table by the armchair, a sculpture in marble of one of Lady Blessington's lovely hands.

It was Eleanor's habit nowadays to assess swiftly the danger to herself of any new acquaintance's beauty, but that of her hostess disarmed her. There was something about Marguerite Blessington which won hearts on sight. Now in her early forties, she still kept the dazzling Irish complexion of her youth, the blackbird's wing shine of her dark hair, the white roundness of her superb shoulders and arms, displayed tonight in a simple gown of sumptuous crimson velvet. But more than all these was the beaming intelligence that shone from her eyes, and her air of calm sweetness. Just so, thought Eleanor, should angels look. Artists always made them simpering ninnies. She did not mind Jesse's undisguised admiration for his hostess.

What daunted her was the fact that all the guests were male, except for herself and a young lady in a fussy dress of pale pink who seemed to know everybody. She drew Jesse into a corner where they were sheltered by a Grecian statue and whispered to him urgently.

'Are you sure I should be here? My name *was* on the invitation?'

'You answered it yourself, my love.'

'Yes, but … could there have been a mistake? It seems so strange. I feel quite conspicuous. Who is *that* young woman?' She indicated the other female guest.

'That? Letty Landon. She writes — poetry, novels, that sort of thing. A great friend of Lady B.'

'Oh,' Eleanor thought for a moment. 'But *I* don't write — I'm not clever at all. Why should the countess invite me, when there are no other wives present? It seems very odd.'

Jesse did not answer for a moment. He knew well enough that Lady Blessington was regarded by certain members of London society as a woman of doubtful reputation. Her origins were humble. Her marriage to Lord Blessington, dead a few years since, had been the subject of much chatter because of the presence in it of Count Alfred D'Orsay, that stunningly handsome dandy who, it was whispered, had been the lover of both husband and wife, and had been married off to Blessington's shockingly young daughter to conceal the scandal. Both D'Orsay and his child bride were no longer living under Lady Blessington's roof, but the talk went on. Respectable women shunned her. Others, not absolutely disreputable but labelled as eccentrics, such as Letitia Landon, came to her salons eagerly, in the company of brilliant men of all sorts: politicians, poets, novelists, professional wits. Jesse saw them now flocking round her.

He knew that she considered him worth cultivating, a youngish Member with interesting ideas. When the invitation including both him and Eleanor had come, he had been puzzled. Either she mistakenly thought Eleanor to be a bluestocking, or had some uncanny inkling that they were not in fact married. Or she was merely trying, somewhat pathetically, to enrol some respectable ladies into her set.

He never knew which, for before he could answer Eleanor, Lady Blessington had swum up to them in a cloud of enchanting perfume and was bearing her off, chatting as they went.

And what chat! The women Eleanor knew, politicians' wives in the main, were dull. They had children, households, dinner parties, servants, and they talked of nothing else. Eleanor would never quite be able to recall what Lady Blessington talked of, except that it was scintillating, and yet that she herself seemed to be drawn into doing a lot of talking in return, even launching into an account of how she had in a way abducted Jesse from under his father's nose. She had never mentioned the escapade since they left the north, and could not imagine how she came to be telling it now. But Lady Blessington's beautiful eyes beamed with benevolent amusement, her musical voice with its fashionable hint of Irish brogue rattled on in witty comment, and Eleanor was altogether enraptured.

They had moved into the drawing room, an apartment even more dazzling than the other, with ruby red and gold for its colour scheme, glinting mirrors lit by shaded candelabra fixed between silk brocade panels. Nobody, least of all the dazzled Eleanor, could have believed that the countess existed on a miserly two thousand pounds a year left by her husband, and the exercise of her wits in writing and editing. In the middle of a thrilling account of Marie Antoinette's clock, which ticked away on the mantelpiece as it had done in the Petit Trianon, a liveried footman appeared like a piece of mechanism.

'Mr Benjamin Disraeli.'

Eleanor's heart seemed to stop and re-start. There he was, slim as ever but sunburnt to a biscuit colour, glittering with fobs, chains and rings, bowing over Lady Blessington's hand.

'My dearest lady! Your servant grovels — half an hour late. Forgive him, or else —!' He mimed self-murder with a dagger, and the countess laughed.

'Ridiculous boy. We don't dine for another —' she consulted the Trianon clock — 'yes, twenty minutes. Pray mingle with the company. But, of course, you know Mrs Jesse Bradshaw?'

Their eyes met, and Eleanor knew she had lost him. There was no dimming of his sparkling black glance, no difference in his lingering kissing of her hand, no harshness in his soft murmuring of her name.

'Mrs Bradshaw, my divinity.'

Yet something was gone that had been there: a complicity between them. A wall had sprung up instead. Eleanor knew, and with the perception of misery saw that Lady Blessington knew also: that the sad wisdom of those angel eyes recognised a pleasant little liaison, the sole reason for Eleanor's being invited at all, shattered. Her ladyship's mind, rich in quotations, was murmuring to itself:

When the lute is broken,
Sweet tones are remembered not;
When the lips have spoken,
Loved accents are soon forgot.

Eleanor had barely heard of the late Radical poet, Percy Bysshe Shelley, but she shared the sentiments. Throughout the exquisite meal in the mirror-lined dining room she sat, tasting nothing, caring nothing for the perfect wines served by footmen dressed like glorified lizards in green and gold. She only knew that her young lover was lost to her. To whom? Some Eastern houri, or a charmer of Italy, or Paris, or Spain?

He was sitting a few places removed from her. She talked little, in order to listen to what he was saying. Very sombre, he was telling his neighbour that the Grand Tour had turned into a tragedy with the sudden death of his companion William Meredith, his sister Sarah's fiancé. Could it have been this that had turned his mind from light loves, Eleanor wondered? But she knew that it was not. The way his eyes flicked away from hers when they met, his sedulous attention to the brittle, nervous chatter of Letty Landon, told her that she had been abandoned.

The summer months brought her confirmation. She encountered him in the park, where she had first seen him driving with a Dr Bolton. But now he was accompanied by a short plump lady with a high colour and a twirling parasol, who proved to be Mrs Bolton, his new flame. Eleanor disliked her on sight, but thought her an unlikely rival. It was not long before she was informed by the gossips' grapevine that Mrs Bolton had been quite ousted by the beautiful Lady Henrietta Sykes: dark, glittering, passionate, older than Disraeli — which he liked — and undoubtedly his mistress.

Quite extraordinarily, it was Lady Blessington in whom she confided her grief. As she drove down Park Lane one afternoon, lost in wretchedness, something drew her gaze to the front door of the house in Seamore Place, and impelled her to stop the carriage and send in her card.

Some fashionable hostesses would have been asleep, or entertaining a lover, or otherwise quite unprepared to entertain a female acquaintance. Marguerite Blessington was not one of them. Writing in her library-boudoir, she accepted Mrs Bradshaw's card with equanimity, requested the footman to send Mrs Bradshaw in, and ordered tea to be served.

Eleanor was glad of the tea, glad of the warm, sympathetic company. At first she talked platitudes. Then the truth began to come out, with no names named, for that would have been vulgar, but Eleanor knew herself completely understood.

Marguerite raised the daintiest of teacups, eggshell thin, patterned with fairy flowers, to her lips, and put it down, the tea untasted. 'My dear, we women are all sisters in these matters. We make temples of our hearts, and worship idols in them — until we find out that the idols were false gods. And then not only the idol is shattered, but the poor shrine.'

Eleanor said impulsively, 'You are so wise. It's quite true. But you — you are so calm, so cheerful; surely —' She stopped, with memories of the rumours. Had that particular shrine been shattered by the late Lord Blessington, or by D'Orsay, the girl-face whiskered exquisite who still graced his stepmother-in-law's salons? Surely no one so mature and beautiful could have seriously loved such a puppy. Eleanor remembered, with distaste, that he was one of Ben Disraeli's best friends. Perhaps they were all alike, all shallow deceivers. Her half-asked question went unanswered, and suddenly she was tired to death of everything: of herself, of Ben, even of the gracious lady at whose table she sat.

That night she quarrelled with Jesse over nothing, and ran up to bed weeping. Jesse shook his head and went back to his parliamentary papers. There was an important motion coming up in the House next day on which he must concentrate.

Something was the matter with Nell, poor girl, and it was not in his power to help. She had always been a spoilt child crying for the moon, and he had had nothing to give her except himself. Apparently that was no longer enough.

Next morning Eleanor did not come down for breakfast. Pink-eyed and snuffly, she was taking chocolate and rolls in bed when Jesse entered.

'Morning, my dear. Hope you slept well. Thought you'd like to see this.' He laid an opened letter on her tray. It bore the heading of a firm of solicitors.

Eleanor read it, her puffy-lidded eyes widening with interest. *'Re Mrs Lucetta Bradshaw, of Eagle Hall, Downham, Lancashire, deceased...'* She read, went back to the beginning and read again, then raised a bright face to Jesse.

'But how wonderful! The dear old creature, to leave us the house! That lovely house, I shall never forget it. That is I couldn't now, if I tried, for it's ours. Oh, Jesse, when can we go there? Poor dear, it's not that I don't grieve for her, but she must have been an enormous age. Fancy her thinking of us after all this time, when she'd only seen us the once. Remember that day, and that night? And when she gave us the money? When can we go? Tomorrow? Next week?'

'Steady on, steady on.' Jesse perched on the bed. 'It's not as easy as that. I can't leave London at the moment. Now, don't be downcast, we'll go when we can. But there's much to be done beforehand, letters to be written.'

She hardly listened to his explanation of the formalities that preceded taking possession of a house — even supposing possession were desirable. In her mind she was already living in the rambling, romantic, ancient building, mullioned and gabled, creeper-clad and banked with lavender, where her elopement with Jesse had been blessed by an old, old lady, and their pockets filled with gold earned in the days of the second George.

She continued to live in it in her imagination during the weeks that followed. While her body carried out its social duties, ordering menus, entertaining visitors to tea, yawning in the gallery of the House in order to be able to discuss a debate later with Jesse, however little she understood of it: all the time her mind was moving about Eagle Hall, remembering the shapes of windows, the turn of stairs, wandering from room to room. A house only once seen for a day and a night, yet so well remembered.

Sometimes, driving in town, she passed Disraeli and Lady Henrietta, a startlingly picturesque pair. Ben's bow and smile were no less courtly than they had been before, yet it hurt her to see him and the voluptuous beauty by his side. She became clever at drawing a mental curtain across them and their barouche, and finding herself once again in the old panelled room, standing in front of the great fireplace with its grotesque carvings, or playing with the ancient dolls' house and its tiny inhabitants who took their tea from fragile rose-patterned cups without handles, as had once been the fashion.

It was satisfying to choose new furniture and hangings for the house. The carpets and linen would be long since perished, eaten up by time and moths. She would begin at the front door, in the stone porch. Yes, the hallway needed lightening up, though not with the endless white and gold of London. The panelling must be kept, but perhaps one or two large colourful tapestries could be hung on the walls. Then there was the wide stone staircase; a rich red or blue carpet for that, and flowers in the halfway window (which would need a lot of cleaning to bring up the colours in the coats-of-arms). As for the room where they had first seen Jesse's grandmother, that should be kept in its original quaintness, with rosebud-sprinkled chintz curtains to match the dainty tea set... Then something would break her reverie, and she would come back to everyday life, blinking and smiling like a girl wakened from a dream of love.

One morning, when she was feeling particularly hopeful and cheerful, Jesse came to her from the study where he read his daily post, with a letter in his hand. She saw from the franking that it came from Lancaster, and her heart jumped.

'You'd better read this for yourself, Nell,' he said.

The writing was clear and businesslike — the hand of Shem, Jesse's brother.

My dear brother,

I thank you for yours of the 2nd, and pray you'll excuse delay in replying. I have obeyed your instructions in the matter of Eagle Hall, with the following findings.

The property, which has stood for some four centuries, is reported by the surveyor to be in very poor case. No repairs appear to have been made for many years, with the result that the roofing is in many parts deficient, a number of attic rooms being completely open to the weather. Extensive rot was found in the joists, floorboards and other woodwork, in some cases to a dangerous extent. The kitchen premises contain mould and some standing water, and no modernisations have been carried out, water being obtained from a well in the grounds and a single open fireplace and sunken ovens providing the only cooking facilities. Elsewhere rats, mice and birds have taken possession, with what destructive results you may imagine.

In short, the dilapidation is such that some thousands of pounds would be required to make it habitable, without taking into account the expense of redecoration, etc. My surveyor advises you strongly against undertaking what would be a major and vastly expensive work of restoration. The property and estate have potential value as building land; the firm of Jabez

Brown and John Hinkson have already shown interest in the purchase, and named a substantial sum.

Needless to say, his advice is also mine.

Re your enquiry as to our father's possible view of your being again domiciled in the neighbourhood, I must inform you that though now advanced in years, his faculties are unimpaired. He retains a lively memory of past events, and has, I fear, no more kindness for you and Mrs Mackenzie than he formerly entertained. It has displeased him greatly that his mother bequeathed her property to you rather than to him or myself, and has at times uttered threats that he would have the house burnt before you should occupy it.

While not regarding this latter threat too gravely, I would merely remind you of our father's disposition. I believe that he could make things more than a little unpleasant for you were you or Mrs M to return.

On another subject, I have had a meeting with Mr Ephraim Atkinson, who tells me that his lady wife has by no means forgiven her sister's escapade, and is unlikely to change her attitude. In all these circumstances I think it would be extremely unwise to proceed further in the matter of Eagle Hall, other than to set its sale in motion. Accordingly I append the address of Messrs Brown and Hinkson, and a note of the surveyor's fee. Perhaps you will be good enough to settle it direct.

I am, Yr affte Brother,
Shem Bradshaw.

Eleanor looked up from the letter to Jesse. He wore an expression of relief.

'There,' he said, 'so that's that. It was good of poor old Grandma to leave us her house, but you see it would only be a brick round our necks, and a very large brick at that. So, if you agree, I'll write to these builders as soon as possible.'

'If — I — agree?'

He was surprised at her tone. 'Why, I imagine there's no question of that, my dear. Shem makes it very clear that there would be no advantage...'

Eleanor jumped to her feet, knocking over the cup on the table and sending a stream of coffee over the cloth and her own lap. It was not like her to be clumsy. She was trembling all over and had turned very pale. Jesse moved towards her but she backed away from him.

'No advantage? No advantage? No, I suppose not, to someone who thinks about nothing except politics, politics, politics, all day and all night, a lot of stupid men airing their stupid views to each other like parrots, and never thinking of how women feel at home, nothing to do, nothing to care for...' She paused for breath and rushed into another tirade. 'At least some have children — I wasn't allowed them, was I? I suppose you think I "agreed" to that, but I never, never did. I always wanted ... and being alone here all day staring out at that hateful dull street, always the same...'

'But, my dear — you've always said you loved London life.'

'I don't now. I hate it, and I hate you!' She broke into the rhythmical sobs of mounting hysteria, beating her fists on the table.

Jesse caught her wrists and held them in a firm grip, ignoring her struggles. 'Eleanor, listen to me. Be quiet. Do you want the servants to hear you?'

'I don't care!' She was shaking her head from side to side, great tears spilling down her cheeks.

'Yes, you do. Hush!' He held her arms painfully tight, until the sobs lessened, then pushed her back into her chair. His face was set in lines very different from his usual placid expression.

'That's better. Now. I have no idea what this tantrum is about. I don't for one moment believe that you hate me, but if you think you do, we must find out why and see what can be done to remedy it. That's reasonable, wouldn't you say? Well, then, I accept that I'm away from home a great deal. I accept that you are unfortunately childless, for reasons we both understand very well. I accept that politics are uninteresting to women. But all these conditions have existed for years, and you've never complained. What has set you off now?'

Without looking at him, she half-whispered, 'The house.'

He was puzzled. 'Parliament?'

'No. Eagle Hall.'

'What about it?'

'I want it.' Now she looked up, and he was taken aback by the intensity of longing in her eyes.

Quietly he said, 'It matters to you so much, and I dismissed it lightly. Is that what set you off?'

She nodded.

'I see. Then I apologise, my dear. I thought it was something you would hardly care about. Very well, since you feel so strongly, I shall not do as Shem suggests. You and I will go up to Downham together and look at the state of affairs, and then we can discuss the whole matter and what's best to be done.'

Her arms came round his neck, her wet cheek was pressed against his.

'Oh, my dear, thank you, thank you! What a fool I was to make such a scene, when all I had to do was to ask ... but it matters to me so much, and I can't explain ... only that it was a sort of magic house, the place where we were so happy, the — the first time.'

He thought, as she was thinking, of the great old-fashioned bed, with its cupid guardians, and the night they had spent in it.

Their life together had begun there. Since then things had changed, and not for the better, he acknowledged to himself. He half guessed at Eleanor's cruel disappointment with Ben Disraeli; he had seen her face as they encountered each other one day. Poor Nell, and her empty life.

He stroked her hair. 'Don't trouble yourself any more, my dear. What I can do, I will.'

Shem was not over-pleased to hear that he might expect a visit from his brother. If their father came to hear about it his fury over Eagle Hall might swell to epic proportions, and there was no knowing what he might do. The old man was in a curious state nowadays, Shem thought: his manner was a blend of gleeful excitement and quite unprovoked bursts of anger, as though he nourished a secret, and was in turn delighted and irritated by it.

It would have surprised Shem very much to know what that secret was.

Old Saul chuckled to himself. It had been so easy. Tom Swainson had been sent to Whittingham's on a spurious errand, to enquire if Whittingham had any objection to buildings being put up on a piece of waste land between their two factories. Whittingham had been mildly surprised at his rival's consideration in bothering to ask, and raised no objections. Swainson, on his way out, wandered into the small office where Joe worked. He was out, as Saul had contrived to discover that he would be. It was only a guess that there would be copies of his machine design somewhere about. A hurried search with the door shut, and Swainson found it, in a labelled box: four or five copies, drawn with various degrees of detail. He chose the most useful-looking, pocketed it, and left unnoticed.

Now it was in Manchester, at a textile machinery works, being turned into reality. Saul's friend the manager viewed it with scepticism, but agreed to make it up — 'whatever good that'll do'. Soon it would be ready, an instrument of pleasurable revenge and, if Saul's guess was right, of considerable profit.

CHAPTER EIGHT

Few visitors could have looked more out of place in a drawing room than Walter Whittingham appeared in Margaret's, as he sat uneasily on the edge of a small chair, twisting his dusty hat nervously between his fingers. A drab figure in baggy clothes, he contrasted sharply with the elegant upright lady opposite him, and with the natural youthful grace of Joe.

Walter was not quite sure how he came to be there. Young Joe had nagged at him to come and see this lady, who was a sort of relation, and discuss with her the possibilities of improving the working conditions of his operatives. Walter could not see that they particularly needed improvement. He was not a hard master, though he said it himself. There were those among his workers who were bad cases, too weak or too feckless to look after themselves or stick up for their rights. But what was he to do about that? And where was he to find the money? Not from the precious hoard that was accumulating in the bank. That was for his old age, which wasn't far off. It was daft, giving in to Joe about this visit.

Yet here he was, and Miss Porteous was being charming to him, plying him with tea and delicate cakes and lending an attentive ear. There was enough of the actress in Margaret to adjust to all manner of people.

'Our young friend here has made me a complete enthusiast,' she was saying. 'With your help, we can make Whittingham's mill famous throughout the length and breadth of England for its humane conditions. Would not you like your name to go down to posterity in this way, Mr Whittingham?'

He shifted uncomfortably. 'I'd not thought about it.'

'Well, think now. To be surrounded by happy, healthy people who would turn out better work for you — what could be more excellent? I can see without knowing you well that you are a sincere and benevolent man, sir. Now is your opportunity to fulfil the deepest needs of your nature.' *And may I be forgiven,* Margaret thought, *for uttering such false sentiments, but at least the end is good.*

Walter sighed. 'Just what do you suggest, ma'am?'

Joe broke in eagerly. 'We could put a ventilator in, sir — in the machining room. That's where it's needed most, with the cleaning process releasing clouds of cotton flakes. Some of the people are nearly choked, and there's more time taken off for sickness there than anywhere else in the mill. If the room could be ventilated...'

'How? You'd knock out the windows, happen?' Walter's tone was sarcastic.

'No — simply put in the machine Brooks's have in Manchester. It revolves twelve hundred times a minute, and the air it produces takes the cotton waste out through a wooden funnel and a chimney outlet. The difference in the air is quite astonishing, I do assure you.'

'How much would a thing like that cost?'

Joe's answer was prompt. 'A hundred pounds. I had that from Mr Brooks himself.'

'It's a lot of money.'

'Not for the benefits it would give.'

'Well, I don't know, I don't know. I'll have to think.'

'There is something else,' Margaret put in. 'The special problems of the women and children. They need more rest, recreation — and above all education. Now, Joseph tells me there is a building on the ground floor of the mill which is at present disused, because the machinery in it is obsolete. Would it not be possible to clear it, install simple pallets where mothers and children could rest, and some sort of cooking arrangements, so that their food during the working day could be more nourishing?' She went on to elaborate on the extreme simplicity and cheapness of this enterprise. 'And then, coming to education, I hear from Mrs Leeming that the old Primitive Methodist chapel in High Street has been closed because of the decline in its congregation. Now, would not that make an excellent school, where the mill children could be taught reading, writing, arithmetic, and be instructed in the Scriptures?'

Walter looked alarmed. 'What, in my time? I pay 'em to work, not learn lessons.'

'It need only be on one day a week, or perhaps two, if a large number of children were concerned. The same premises could be used in the evenings for the education of older children or their parents.'

'And who's to pay the teachers, ma'am? For I tell you I can't.'

Margaret was ahead of him. 'They will not require paying. Mrs Leeming and I have spoken with a number of young ladies in the parish who already do church work, and would be happy to occupy themselves in teaching, The poor women who spin and weave for many hours a day are overworked — possibly,' she added delicately, seeing his expression — 'but believe me, Mr Whittingham, many ladies in better circumstances would be only too glad of agreeable Christian employment.'

'Don't know about agreeable — teaching a set of young numbskulls.'

'They would not be numbskulls long,' Margaret said. 'And I would be glad to provide school books, and other books which might form a small library for the workers. Now, does this sound a very costly project?'

'No,' he admitted reluctantly, 'not as you put it, ma'am.'

Margaret sat back, relaxing. She knew that she had won. Joe threw her a look in which the warm affection he already felt for her was joined by an equally warm admiration. She smiled back.

'Another cup of tea, Mr Whittingham? Or perhaps, as I see it is already eleven o'clock, a glass of sherry?'

In a matter of three months the ambitious scheme had become a reality. Whittingham grumblingly paid for the ventilation machine, swiftly installed by engineers from Manchester, and instant in its beneficial effect on the pale, snuffling, coughing creatures whose work of opening and cleaning the cotton had been so unhealthy and miserable. Now a large proportion of the 'fly' lived up to its name and flew along its funnel and into the outside air. Joe was so delighted with the improvement that he haunted the machining room merely to watch the happier, healthier people in it, and to listen to the gratifying hum of the ventilator.

Margaret was equally charmed by the speed with which she and her helpers had brought about the other changes. In an all-enveloping pinafore, with her hair scraped up under a plain cap, she and the plump, panting Mrs Leeming had personally worked on the rest room. Now it was clean, airy, provided with a row of cheap new mattresses and fresh linen; bowls for washing were supplied with water from the river, and soup and other food could be heated on a device like a large spirit-kettle, which Margaret had found, after a long search, at an ironmonger's in Preston.

The little school flourished equally. There, too, the ladies had worked tirelessly. The old pews, which would serve as benches and desks, were scrubbed and polished, the windows cleaned by Joe and some of the men, perched on perilously tall ladders, a long-disused fireplace restored to warm the cold little building. In the vestry Margaret's little library had begun to build up. Naturally, it would be expected to contain mainly religious books, but she slipped in two volumes of Shakespeare, the poetical works of her old favourite Walter Scott, and some of his novels. Minds were important as well as souls. She had never been happier: at last she felt she was some use in the world.

Joe, too, was happy. Some of the things he had set his heart on had been done. If only his machine could be brought to life! But Whittingham stubbornly resisted his pleas to have at least one built. The hundred pounds spent on the ventilator had drained his pockets, he said.

Joe was working in his room one evening on further improvements to the design —though surely he had already made a more detailed drawing? — when Whittingham's elderly, deaf housekeeper announced a visitor. Her tone was sharp.

'A person to see you, Mr Atkinson.'

He turned, smiling, expecting to see Will Raven, though Mrs Darwen did not usually describe him as a 'person'. But it was a woman who came out of the shadows.

'Evenin' to you, Mr Atkinson. You don't know me, I can see. I'm Rosie Giles.'

She spoke broadly, with the accent of the district, although she was polite enough not to address him as 'thee'. Later her refinement would slip sharply, but by then he would be beyond noticing or caring.

Time seemed to stop as he stared at her. He had never seen anyone more beautiful. She was not tall — few mill-hands were — but of a comely plumpness rare among those under-fed women. Her face seemed like a lamp in the room, bright blue eyes alight with laughter and allure, a wide, generous, sensual mouth always on the verge of smiling, dark hair clustering round pink cheeks and white neck. Her shawl had slipped back, so that he could see how lustrous that hair was, rich and shining.

She set her arms akimbo, the shawl spread open, revealing her splendid shape, full breasts straining at the cheap fabric of her bodice, small sturdy waist and wide hips. Consciously flirting with him, she assumed a dancing pose, one foot pointed in front of the other.

'Well? Aren't you goin' to ask me to sit down?' she enquired pertly.

Joe recovered himself and pulled forward a chair. 'Pray excuse me. I was — not expecting to have a visitor. Please sit down...' He glanced at her unringed left hand. 'Miss Giles.'

She sat with abandoned ease, one ankle casually thrown over the other, an attitude that would have shocked the vicar's wife or any other respectable lady. An artist's model might have sat so, or a courtesan: not that Joe had ever met any. Her smile widened at his embarrassment.

'Happen you don't get many young women to see you? Yon owd witch as showed me in seemed fair tekken aback.'

'Yes,' said Joe, gulping. 'I mean yes, she would be, and no, I...' He found himself floundering in a speech about it being an unexpected pleasure and his regret not to be better prepared for it. Then, to his horror and annoyance, he felt himself blushing, the scarlet flush of the red-haired, from throat to brow. She laughed outright, and he saw that she had a deep dimple to the left of her mouth which riveted his gaze and sent his mind leaping among the poems of his schoolday reading, where dimples had been described as cupids' nests and other fancy similes. If the ghost of his father hovered in that room, it would have shaken its head mournfully, remembering just such a meeting with just such a woman and the instant blazing-up of infatuation. The road to ruin.

She was talking to him, earnest now, forgetting to coquet. 'I come because of our Billy. You don't know me, 'cause I work at Bradshaw's, but you might know him. A little pale chap, walks wi' a bit of a limp. Him and me, we're all our mam's got left out o' ten, the first and the last you might say. Well, our dad went wi' the lung-rot two year sin', and Mam, she'd to work all the hours God sent, and see us work too. Now I'm as strong as a mare, you can see that, young master — oh, I saw you tak' note of mi rosy cheeks and the fat on me. Comes of sowin' seed and eatin' what comes up — cabbages, carrots, 'tatoes, owt. I've a little patch behind the house, where I grow 'em. Better nor old meat, I reckon.

'But our Billy, he were clemmed from t'start. Mam's milk give out and there were nobody else to nurse the little lad. I reckon I saved him, with a bit of this, on the side.' She mimed picking a pocket, and gave Joe a long slow wink. 'He's never been strong, though, an' we thought Bradshaw's 'ud see him in his coffin — if we could afford one. So Mam, she takes him away when she hears of what your lot were doin' here. Six month now he's been piecin' at t'mules for Whittingham, and such a change you never saw. A bit o' colour in his face and a smile now and then. Mam's left Bradshaw's and come to Whittingham's now. Owd Saul didn't like it, but there was nowt he could do. So here I am, to thank you, you and your lady friends for savin' our Billy.'

She gave him a smile like sunshine. He said something, some nonsense, feeling all blush and great hands, as if he were fifteen again. She was looking round the room curiously, noting what was finery to her, grand living, then at the drawings on the table. The smile faded to a lovely seriousness. 'I come about that, too. Yon machine.'

He looked down at the drawings, then at her, puzzled. 'I fear I don't understand, ma'am.'

She threw back her head, laughing. '"Ma'am." O Jerusalem! Fancy me livin to be called that. Joe Atkinson, I like you, but you're a born fool. Them pictures you've got there, and I can tell upside down what they're of, owd Bradshaw had one of em stolen. Sent a creepin' thing of an overseer to filch it while you was out. Oh, never look so frit, Saul's as fause as a weasel — cut his grandma's throat soon as look at her.'

Joe was almost speechless. Then he got out, 'I don't quite take your drift, Miss Giles. Mr Bradshaw had one of my drawings stolen?'

'Reet first time. *And* copied. *And* made up, by a firm he was in with. Lad, you've gone white as a ghost.' He heard the softening of her voice, saw her go over to the washstand and pour some water from a jug into a cup. Then the cup was at his lips, her strong brown hand on his shoulder, and her scent, which was the strangely heady emanation of her young body blended with something like heather and new-cut grass. He leaned his head against the warm fulness of her breast, listening to her talk, caring less and less every minute for the story she was telling.

'Aye, he had it made up, three models, a' a bit different from each other. And it didn't work — leastways, not as it were meant to. Well, Saul were as mad as a piper, fit to be tied, and it were noan at hisself for bein' fool enough to go to the trouble, but at you. So I'd watch out, lad. He loves you as Owd Nick loves holy watter. And never think noan o' this is true, for I got it from a feller I walk out with now an' then.'

Joe was in a daze of mixed emotions. He knew she spoke the truth; everything fell into place now, the missing drawing, the looks of fearful animosity Saul Bradshaw had given him when occasionally their paths had crossed. He had thought it the ill temper of old age. Now he knew. His invention was stolen — and he had never even taken out a patent for it. What was worse, he had been wrong: it was not as perfect as he had thought. He was an incompetent bungler who should have stayed at university and kept on with his law studies — for what good he would have been at them, he reflected bitterly. In his abject disappointment with himself he turned his face into the warm breast, and felt it heaving quickly, as though its owner were excited.

Suddenly, in a flash, his depression was gone, and he was gloriously, for the first time, conscious of himself as a man, and a lover.

Rosie knew the right moment to move away from him, and towards the door. 'This'll never do,' she said. 'I'll lose me good name if I'm from home longer. Think on, I only came to warn you, Mr Atkinson — and to thank you for our Billy.'

The door shut. He was alone; a different Joe from the one who had sat there before her entrance, drawing. He collected up the sheets of paper, crumpled them slowly and deliberately, and hurled them into the grate. Let Mrs Darwen find them in the morning and throw them in with the rest of the rubbish. It was nothing to him now.

All through the long, hot summer with its sudden volcanic storms that killed cattle and wrecked shipping, Joe's passion for Rosie Giles grew. No longer did he care to travel for Whittingham's; he would undertake such journeys half-heartedly and returning as soon as he could.

From his office window he could see the path that led to Bradshaw's mill, round the bend of the river. Rosie would walk that way sometimes, an unmistakable figure with her swinging gait, the shawl that was always slipping off her head to let the sunlight catch her hair, and her quick glance up at his window. She would never stay to let him look at her. Once, in the evening, he had gone round to the shack of a cottage where she lived with her mother and Billy. The child was asleep, a small quiet figure under a blanket in the corner. Mrs Giles was spectre-thin, grey and scant of hair, and almost toothless; it was almost impossible to believe that she was Rosie's, or anybody's mother. Her welcome was not warm when Rosie asked Joe in for a cup of the black, many-times-stewed tea that was their only drink.

'This is Mr Atkinson, Mam, as did so much for Whittingham's.'

'Oh, aye.'

Joe made her his best bow, but got nothing in the way of conversation out of her. If she felt any gratitude for the good that had been done to Billy she did not show it. To Mrs Giles, gentry hanging round a girl meant trouble: a misbegotten bairn, a body in the river or swinging on the castle gallows tree for killing the child at birth. After a difficult few minutes Joe gave up the effort and left. Outside, he said to Rosie, 'Where can I see you? Your mother doesn't like me, that's clear.'

'Oh, her. She likes nobody. Think nowt of it.'

He persisted. 'But I must see you sometimes. Oh, Rosie! I can't ask you back to my lodging — Mrs Darwen's spoken to Mr Whittingham about the last time. You work all day and half the evening, and so do I. So — when?'

His look was so comically pleading that she burst out laughing. 'Who's lost a guinea and found sixpence, then? Eeh, what a face, enough to scare t'crows.'

'Don't make fun of me, Rosie. I'm quite miserable, truly.'

She relented. 'Well, then. There's Sunday — the better the day the better the deed, eh?'

Joe was taken aback. Sunday was not, in his experience, a day for anything but church-going and seemly pastimes; certainly not for jaunts, though he remembered that Sunday evening was the traditional time for 'walking out' among both mill workers and country folk. He resolved not to be bothered by recollections of the way Ephraim and Mary lived; it had nothing to do with him any more. Thinking rapidly, he proposed that the next Sunday they should go up to Kendal, which Rosie had never visited, travelling in a hired trap with a hamper of food and starting early in the morning (when, his conscience reminded him, very few respectable parties would be up to see him. He had no great fancy for encountering Aunt Margaret on her way to church, or the Reverend Leeming hurrying back to breakfast after early service. Yes, they would start very early indeed.)

Rosie watched him down the street, hands on hips, half amused, half pitying. He was such an innocent. Any other man in his position, master to her servant, would have had her in the long grass where the fells began to rise from the river, weeks and months ago. She had given him plenty of opportunities, for sure. Yet he seemed not to understand or notice them, though she knew he was mad for her. She was very experienced in men, had been since her fourteenth year, and was sharp enough to have learnt tricks that had stopped her getting caught with a bairn. The men were sometimes generous, giving her a sixpence or a new ribbon, sometimes mean. Still, a penny bought a bit of food. There was no other way of adding to the thirteen shillings that was her weekly wage. And she didn't mind paying the price; often she enjoyed it, especially with the big rough lads who laughed and joked with her. Joe Atkinson was nothing like that, not really her kind, a bit soft, never taking the least advantage, even to force a kiss on her. Might it be (though it seemed impossible) that his intentions towards her were serious? Surely not; he was just the kind to have a regular young lady waiting for him in Lancaster, and it was only a hot fancy he had for her, Rosie, that he was too bashful to express.

And yet … he was out of sight, the street empty but for some children rolling on the cobbles, a few hens and a dog straggling about for scraps. Very thoughtfully, Rosie went in and shut the door.

'What's yon lad up to, then?' her mother asked.

'Come to see we've not died o' t'cholera.'

Her mother threw her a suspicious glance, and put the kettle on to boil for another brew of the strong, nasty tea. She had never known what to make of her daughter, and as time went on she knew even less.

Sunday dawned fine and cloudless. They were off soon after six in the morning, for they had almost thirty miles to travel. Rosie wore her best bonnet, which happened to be her only one, and a grey patched dress which she had brightened up with red ribbons and a cheap shawl from a stall at the fair. Joe would not have noticed if she had been clothed entirely in cobwebs. He only saw her vivid face and felt her exciting warmth next to him on the driving seat. She giggled and squeaked at the rocking of the trap, pretending to be frightened and clutching him — which he liked. Everything was new to her — being driven out for pleasure, riding behind a horse, feeling like Somebody, leaving the mill behind. Her gaiety was infectious. Joe, at first burdened by guilt at travelling on the Sabbath, soon cast it off and several years with it. Rosie was like a child out for a treat, and he slipped into her mood. Some of her jokes and expressions were not such as he had ever heard before on the lips of a woman, but he took them in good part, remembering the people she mixed with. One day, he promised himself, he would help her to forget them. Meanwhile, he laughed.

They reached Lancaster by mid-morning. The horse was tired and they were hot and hungry, so Joe steered them towards Giant Axe Field, where the nag could be let loose to browse under the trees, and they could eat their packed food on the grass.

'Come and see the castle,' he said. 'It's a grand old place.' He led her through the sloping churchyard, showed her the White Lady whose sad marble statue had always affected him as a child. Up by the church were family graves, his grandparents and great-uncle. Rosie was not used to reacting to serious matters, and was not quite sure what to say.

'Eeh,' she said, when in doubt. 'Just fancy.' And, occasionally, 'That beats cock-fightin'.' Joe thought her simplicity charming.

It was too early for churchgoers to be arriving — Joe had made sure of that. He had no intention of calling at St Leonard's Gate. He had not been there for some time, and knew in his heart that this was not the moment to drop in: better not to be seen by them as they went to church.

But one of that household saw him. Dove's school friend, Ellen Ashworth, lay ill at her parents' house in St Mary's Parade, which ran in a graceful half-circle round the south side of the castle, and Dove had got up that morning to pick plums and apples from the orchard to take with other comforts for an invalid. It would hardly do to take them into church, so she set off ahead of the family to deliver them early.

Enjoying the pleasant morning, her full basket on her arm, she turned the corner from steep little Castle Park Hill into the Parade, and saw them. The glint of bright auburn hair under an elegant grey hat, and Joe's smiling face, turned towards the girl on his arm. Rosie was on his other side and Dove could not see her very clearly, but got an impression of laughter and closeness. The bright, hot morning turned cold to her. No longer was she pleased to be going to see Ellen and cheer her up. Everything had turned dusty and hopeless. She felt the cobbles hurt her feet, her pelisse was uncomfortable, and there were tears starting from her eyes. She scrubbed them away, felt them start again, and hastily turned as if to examine a house number.

Through the long weeks she had kept the hope of Joe's return warm in her heart. The stupid business of Belle was over, and Belle was fully occupied in conquering other young men. Surely he would come back now. At least, if he did not comprehend her love for him, things would be as they had been, and she could see him, breathe the same air, hope and pray that he would one day turn to her.

Now it was over. He had another girl on his arm, had brought her to Lancaster. Perhaps, later, they would come to her father's house. Dove stood still, breathed deeply, and fought back the tears until they ceased. Then she walked on to Ellen's home, pulled the bell, and presented a calmly smiling face to the maid who answered.

Will Raven sat relaxed in the summerhouse behind his shop. He lived there now, having thankfully given up the rooms he had shared with Jane. In the two storeys over the shop he had a sitting room, a bedroom, and a lumber room where he kept things destined for sale which needed cleaning or restoration. With his experience in furniture, he was good at both. It was pleasant and satisfying to turn a neglected, decayed piece of craftsmanship into the comely thing it had once been, and it occupied the hours that might have been long and sad. Fifty, he was; an old man, he told himself, though he knew that his body was as healthy as it had ever been, and his mind clearer because of the trials he had passed through. He understood himself better now, and also poor Jane, whose reason had left her. He knew, too, that he was lonely, but what couldn't be cured must be endured. The birds in the trees of the little garden came down to him, and the swift red squirrels, too. Dogs loved him, even the fiercest, and the stray cats of Kendal's alleys knew that he carried scraps for them. Perhaps they sensed that he had few friends among his own kind, silent and selfless as he was. Sometimes, walking at night, a woman's shape and voice beckoned him from the shadows of walls, and his blood leaped towards them; then good sense told him that nothing would come of such encounters. He had earned loneliness; he must bear it.

His drowsy thoughts were scattered by the sound of the shop door knocker. A caller, and on a Sunday? It couldn't be a would-be purchaser, for trading on the Sabbath was forbidden. He went through into the shop and unlocked the door.

'Joe! It's never thee, lad!'

'It is, Uncle, none other. And look what I've brought you.'

Will looked. Instantly he divined what Rosie was, where she came from, and why Joe had brought her; his heart sank to his boots. But he greeted her kindly and invited them in.

'Being Sunday, I didn't expect callers. Come all the way from Bradhope, have you? Your nag'll be spent, won't he?'

'We changed horses at Carnforth,' Joe said. 'But that one would be glad of a bit of rest and shade.' He indicated the brown horse with its head sunk between the shafts, and Will went out to lead it down a nearby yard into stables where there was shade, food and water. In the shop Rosie was jumping about with delight.

'Eeh, what a grand place! I niver was in a shop before but to buy, and that not often. What's that? Can I see? Why in't it lighter?'

Will, coming in, heard her, and obligingly went out again and drew one set of shutters. 'Better leave the others, or we'll have church wardens round. That better, is it?'

It was. Rosie was running about like a child, picking up trashy jewellery and second-hand clothes, holding them against herself to a dark old mirror, laughing at a classic bust with its nose broken, playing with a doll.

'Whatever sort o' shop is it? I niver saw such a place before!'

'I call it a knick-knackery,' Will said. 'All kinds o' stuff for all kinds o' folk. I go out, when things are quiet, and buy up from houses where there's been a death, or old places being sold off. Some of it's good, some of it's nought. Some I like that much I keep it. It's nice to handle, better nor selling meat or groceries. Which minds me — you must be hungry after that drive.'

They were indeed, their young appetites unsatisfied by the frugal meal Mrs Darwen had put up for Joe. Will found in his larder a piece of ham, bread and cheese, a pottle of rum butter made for him by a fellow shopkeeper's wife. They fell on it avidly, and on the drinks Will provided, milk and ale. Rosie chose the ale and Will noticed that she drank it off like a man. Between sups and mouthfuls she chattered.

'We stopped i' Lancaster — oh, it's a fine town, I'd niver seen it afore. And Mr Atkinson took me to t'church and showed me all t'mon ... mominents, his family's and other folks, all carved and wi' letters on. He had to tell me what they said, 'cause I can't read,' she admitted frankly. 'An' there was the castle where folk get hanged — I'd be fain to see that, so I would.'

Will stole a glance at Joe, and was glad to see that he looked slightly shocked. But as Rosie babbled on his look changed back to adoration. Will made up his mind that he must speak to Joe. It was not possible while Rosie was there; he racked his brains for an excuse to get rid of her.

'There's a bonnet shop up the road,' he said, 'where the lady's had her shutters blown down and not had time to put 'em back. You'd like to look in there, Miss Giles, I'll wager.'

She clapped her hands. 'Oh, I would that!'

'Well,' he opened the shop door, 'you turn left and keep going. It's next to Wilson's the printers, you can't miss it. Knock when you get back.'

She was off, bounding up the street like a young animal. Will drew Joe back into the parlour behind the shop.

'Joe, what's all this? Where did you find that lass?'

Joe stiffened visibly. 'She came to see me, about her brother.' He described the circumstances briefly. 'Then we became friendly.'

'Friendly? Friendly? What sort of friend is that for you, a rantipolling young madam wi' a roving eye — it lit on *me* once, though I dare say you'll not believe it — and no better than a factory hand?'

'I told you she was a factory hand,' Joe said coolly, 'a weaver. What's wrong with that? She's a young woman of great spirit and intelligence, judging by what I know of her. There's many a lady of good circumstances couldn't hold a candle to her.' He thought of the church helpers, respectable beyond reproach but dull in the extreme. 'And such a beauty — Uncle, you can't deny that! Did you ever see such a face? I never did in all my life. She's too good to leave on the dustheap.'

'So what are you bound to do?' Will asked. 'Pick her up?'

Joe looked surprised. 'Yes, of course. Improve her. Marry her, if she'll have me.'

Will groaned. 'If she'll have you! She'll jump at the chance. And you, Joe, you'll be done for. Who's going to want you, with a wife like that? What chance will you have in management? And what are your family going to say? You'll be taking chalk to cheese, that's what you'll be doing. Forget her, lad, while there's still time.'

Joe shrugged. 'Too late for that. And I didn't expect to hear you talk so, Uncle. It's not polite, to say the least. However, we won't strain your hospitality. As soon as Rosie — Miss Giles — comes back, we'll leave.'

'Joe, Joe, don't speak like that to me! You know I only want the best for you.' He thrashed round in his mind for arguments. 'Couldn't you, what's it called, seduce her and have done with it? I'm sure it's all she expects. You must have had plenty o' girls while you were at Oxford — and don't put on that prim face with me, I know lads and their ways. Now, lad, don't tell me you never...'

But the blush Joe hated had crept over his face, betraying him. He turned away from the light of the window to hide it, saying, 'I don't know what you mean.'

Will was silent. He knew Joe so well; the meaning of the blush was not lost on him. The lad had somehow contrived to come through university and attain his twenty-second year without losing his virginity. That such an innocent could survive in this wicked world: he shook his head. Aloud he said, 'We've not much time. Can I tell you a story?'

The story he told was of Joe's father, another young man with an honest soul and an eye for beauty, who had gone to London and met a charmer he would never have introduced to the wife he loved dearly. He had become infatuated with her and might well have ruined his life had not fate stepped in and taken that life first. Will told the story well, looking all the time for the boy's reaction. But before it came there was a lively rapping at the door; Rosie was back.

When they drove away no more had been said, and the parting was cool on Joe's side. After their departure something made Will look round his stock. From a box of second-hand finery a little necklace of green and coral stones was missing.

CHAPTER NINE

It was not until three months after he had made his promise to Eleanor that Jesse Bradshaw was able to inspect Eagle Hall, during the parliamentary recess. He arranged to meet Shem in Blackburn, to avoid any possibility of running into his father, and their meeting took place at the hotel where he was to stay for two or three nights.

As they shook hands the brothers sized each other up. After nineteen years changes had come to both of them; Jesse had become florid and plump, almost stout, though it suited him, and Shem, always sickly, had grown bent with years and office work. He looked almost an old man.

'Nineteen years — it doesn't seem possible,' Jesse said. 'I'm glad to see you, brother. If it hadn't been for Father's stubbornness ... well, things might have been very different. How is he?'

'Stubborn as ever. Worse. I'd say he was turning senile if his head for business weren't as sharp as it is. He always had the devil's own temper, and the way it is now he might well burst a blood vessel one of these days.'

'Does he ever mention me — or Eleanor?'

'Only when he's had a drop too much and starts raving on about the folk who've crossed him in his time — and there's been a tidy few of them. You're not forgiven, that's as sure as anything can be. I keep off the subject, myself. No use starting hares.'

Jesse shook his head. 'A pity. Come and have some supper, and we'll exchange news.'

'You mean you'll tell me *your* news,' Shem said drily. 'I've none, unless you'd like a statement of accounts for Bradshaw and Son.'

Over the meal it was indeed Jesse who talked, and Shem who listened.

'You've done well for yourself. You were right to break away when you did.'

'Was I?' Jesse sipped his wine. 'Sometimes I wonder whether I ought to have stood up to Father like a man instead of running away, or whether I ought to have let Eleanor compromise herself with me. It's been hard on her in some ways, our life. She's lonely, she misses her family, and she wants to come home. That's why I'm here. How soon can we visit Eagle Hall?'

'Tomorrow morning. I've arranged to pick up the keys from the old chap who looks after the place. But I warn you, Jesse, you're in for a shock.'

Even after so much preparation, Jesse was appalled by the state of the house he remembered as only mildly neglected. The description in Shem's letter rather understated the extent to which time and the lack of upkeep had reduced it. Windows were broken, doors hung off their hinges, gaping holes in ceilings showed the lath-and-plaster of their construction. The fine broad old floorboards creaked arthritically as the two men moved from room to room, and some had collapsed through dry rot, the sweetish sickly smell of which filled the musty air. A rat ran scuttering in front of them and disappeared into a hole. In the room where Jesse and Eleanor had been introduced to Madam Bradshaw there were skeletons of birds and mummified bats which had flown in and been unable to get out again. Two attic rooms were obviously in too dangerous a condition to enter.

Jesse's spirits sank lower and lower. He was glad when they emerged into the sunshine, and Shem had turned the key and pocketed it.

'Well?' Shem asked. 'I didn't exaggerate, did I?'

'No. I suppose I hoped you had. What a damned waste of a grand old house! I wish to God I could put it in order, but you were right when you said it would cost thousands, and I haven't got them. We live well enough, but it takes money.' He looked back sadly. 'I'd like to restore the place for its own sake, as well as Nell's, for it holds happy memories...'

'It's a rotting corpse,' Shem said. 'You can't restore 'em when they get to that state.'

'No. I suppose not. Well, what'll happen to it?'

Shem appeared surprised. 'I told you about Brown and Hinkson's offer, didn't I? Surely, now you've seen for yourself, you'll take them up on it. Might even get the price up a bit more, if you leave it to me. They've got plans for an estate of Gothic villas, the sort of fashionable houses folk like now — I reckon they're eager to purchase.'

After a moment, Jesse said, 'No.'

'No?'

'I'll wait. I can't spoil Nell's dream yet. At least I'll let her think something can be done. I'll spin some tale. I'm used to talking. Thank God she didn't come with me, that's all.'

Shem shrugged. 'As you like. I think you're daft, but it's your property. I'll do what I can, though it isn't much — a tarpaulin over the roof would keep out some of the weather in winter, and the ratcatcher could do a bit of good. Mind you, it's wasted effort.'

Jesse turned to him. 'Thank you. I wouldn't have thought of such things, but you were always the practical one. And send me the bills.'

As they walked back to the waiting phaeton, Jesse asked, 'Any news from Lancaster that I can take back to Eleanor? She's always wondering how they are, and her friend there's a poor correspondent.'

'Well, I'm the last one to ask, with the name Atkinson a black word at Bradshaw's.'

'He still keeps it up, then, after all this time?'

'Keeps it up? He feeds it like a babby, takes it out and nurses it every day. It's not so much Mr Ephraim that rankles with him now, but the nephew, young Joe, Whittingham's partner — and you'll recall how Father always hated Whittingham. It seems this lad, a bit of a dreamer with a college education, got hold of some notion that he could design a loom that would do what no loom ever did before. Well, Father got to hear of this, and what must he do but get one of his toadies to steal it, then have it made up. And lo, it didn't work, after Father had gone to all that expense. Well, you can imagine what a red rag to a bull *that* was. He goes on about how he'll destroy the lad as he'd like to have destroyed the uncle, not to mention your Eleanor, and I wouldn't be surprised if he managed it somehow. He's full of resources, our dad.'

Jesse stopped. 'But that's criminal! To steal an invention, and then ... I didn't think even he was capable of that.'

'Believe me, he is. Oh, never fear, I'll watch him. Joe Atkinson's a harmless lad, and enough wrong's been done already. I happen to know he's walking out with one of our hands, a brazen young piece if ever I saw one, but I'm keeping that from Father in case it gives him some sort of handle to damage Joe.'

'Shem — why do you stay with him?'

His brother shrugged bowed shoulders. 'Not much else I can do. And it's my duty, I suppose. Don't be sorry for me, Jesse.

Life's half over before we know what use it's been — mine may be some use yet, who knows?'

As they passed the church, Jesse said, 'Is Grandma buried here?'

'Aye, in the new plot at the back.'

'I'd like to see the grave, just to tell Eleanor.'

Behind the old church, among several others in an area where the grass was newly sown and closely cut, they stopped by a mound of earth that bore no tributary flowers. But at its head was a white marble stone, lettered in gold, to the memory of Lucetta, wife of Jedediah Bradshaw, aged 98 years.

Yet shall thy grave with rising flow'rs be dressed,
And the green turf lie lightly on thy breast.

Jesse read it twice. 'Father never put that up?'

'No,' Shem answered quietly. 'I did.'

'But…' Jesse stared at the grave, the strange hopeful inscription. 'It was good of you,' he said. It came to him that he hardly knew his brother at all.

It took Will Raven several days and plenty of courage to make up his mind to go to Lancaster. He felt that Ephraim must be warned about Joe's unsuitable sweetheart, but the thought of interference in a family matter, and the fear of disloyalty to Joe daunted him. He was afraid to take action in the boy's life, remembering how he had twice almost ruined it.

What decided him was his weekly visit to his wife. Every week, by duty bound, he went to the lunatic asylum. It was useless, for Jane either did not know him or poured out a torrent of abuse. But he felt he must do it, for there was nobody else.

She was sitting hunched at the table in the tiny room where they had put her because she was too violent to be housed with the other inmates.

'She's quiet now,' said the woman keeper who admitted him. 'But she's been right rough lately. I'll stay, just to be on the safe side.'

Any beauty Jane had owned was gone, for it had lain in her air of elegance. Her thin features were obscured in fat, the result of lack of exercise and a starchy diet. Sharp eyes peered up at him from a pale, puffy face, but she did not speak.

'Jane? It's me, Will. How are you today?'

He found talking to her agonisingly difficult. But he forced himself to go on. 'It's been very fine, this week. They've got the crops in already. I — I was up by Ullswater last Thursday. The lake was right blue, like they say the Italian ones are...' He rambled on in commonplaces, seeing her glance flicker to his face, then back to the ground, but getting no other response.

'It's no good,' the attendant said. 'She's gone into one of her sulky fits.'

Just then she moved, got up, and began to walk towards him. He smiled and held out his arms, though his flesh crept with revulsion.

'That's right. That's a good girl. Come on.'

In a lightning movement she had pulled something from her gown and was striking at him with it, uttering animal shrieks. He fell back as the attendant pulled her off him and forced her back into the chair, grasping her arms. A small pair of scissors fell from her loosened hand to the floor.

'There, you see, she's not safe. Get out while you can, Mr Raven. I'll tie her up again.'

He went, shuddering and sickened.

So it was that he plucked up courage to visit Ephraim and Mary. If ever there had been a mistaken marriage it was his; he could but try to stop Joe making one.

He had not been expected, for writing letters was not his forte. To his embarrassment, when he was shown into the Atkinsons' drawing room they were not alone. It was early evening — he had chosen that time because Ephraim's work would be over for the day — and he saw that they had finished dining and were taking the tea which followed the meal. It appeared to be something of an occasion: Mary, Dove and Belle were in their best dresses and Ephraim wore an imposing and expensive cravat. Will recognised two of the guests as Jack and Arabella Dilworth. Jack was a member of the rich sail-making family, lifetime friends of Ephraim, and Arabella had stood godmother to the twins. They were a comely, prosperous-looking pair, Jack plump and cheerful, Arabella keeping her prettiness remarkably unscathed.

The other guest was unknown to Will. Young, not much more than twenty, he wore the uniform of the Merchant Navy and had the typical brown, clean-cut, somewhat hard face. The twins sat one on each side of him, and Will noticed that the young man turned often to Dove, while Belle sat fanning herself and drinking tea in quick sips.

Ephraim greeted him, warmly, seeming relaxed and happy. 'My dear Will, how unexpected and delightful to see you. Is this a fortuitous visit, or were you informed?'

'Informed? No, I didn't know there was ought special…'

'Oh, but very special!' Mary broke in. 'I don't believe you've met George Dilworth, Dove's betrothed. The engagement was settled this very day. Now, what a pleasant surprise that you should have arrived, Mr Raven.'

Will murmured that it was indeed, and quite by chance, and congratulated the young couple, while he looked from one to the other, to the young man's confident bearing and obvious contentment, to Dove's shyness, her head bent, her look not quite meeting her betrothed's or anyone else's. Will saw now a distinct difference between Dove and her sister. Was it one of expression, bearing, or actual features? Hard to tell, yet he would have known one from the other anywhere. Belle, in a fashionable and striking lilac gown, with artificial lilacs in her hair, moved and smiled and talked a great deal, while Dove was still, self-effacing; Dove's face was more delicate, more spiritual. Yet Belle was very beautiful, and Will sensed that she was not happy.

'George has been promoted First Mate,' Ephraim was saying, 'at an unusually early age. As he must shortly sail for the West Indies, they thought it the right moment to announce their betrothal. Isn't that so, my love?'

Dove smiled up at her father, then the smile faded quickly. Will saw George Dilworth's brown hand close over hers, remain there, then be displaced as hers moved to her lap.

Belle gave a tinkling laugh. 'My nose is quite put out, you see, Uncle Will! I shall be an old maid yet, shan't I, unless the gentlemen hurry. Wanted, eligible young man, for pining young lady, aged nineteen. Requirements, a handsome income, broad acres, the looks of Count D'Orsay and the form of Gentleman Jim, together with town house and country seat and a stable of fine hunters. What offers do I hear?'

'Belle.' Mary's voice was quiet but firm, though Arabella was giggling and her husband's face wore a broad grin. 'That will do. Your time will come.'

The conversation became general. Will found himself beside Belle, eating sweetmeats from the dish she offered him, noticing how downcast her face was in repose. A moment ago he had thought Dove the sad one, but now she was smiling and talking animatedly. He wondered whether the tribulations he had passed through had made him in some way sensitive to the feelings of others. It was almost painful to share their feelings, read their faces, suffer or be in suspense with them. He knew that, whatever Ephraim might say, these two lovely girls were not happy, and there was something very wrong about this celebration.

'Keep cheerful,' he said to Belle in an undertone, 'it may never happen.'

She laughed spontaneously. 'Isn't that just what I said? Here's me with the oncoming disposition and Dove the shy one, yet she's the first to get the ring.' She held out her own left hand, white and dimpled, with nails like pink polished shells. 'It would look well with a diamond on it, don't you think, Uncle?'

'Very well.' He wished she would not call him Uncle; he felt old enough as it was, with so much weighing on his mind. 'Just bide your time, Belle. The lads won't be backward in coming forward, that I'm sure.'

'Ah, but they *have* come forward, and either they don't like me enough or I don't like them. I can't tell which. What do *you* think will happen to me — a nice young man like George? Not that I'd have him with a pound of tea.'

Will hesitated. 'I'm not a fortune-teller, Belle. I think you'll get what you need and deserve — and that's a lot in your case.'

'Is it?'

Their eyes met, hers dark hazel, sad and questing, for all the merriment of her mouth, his soft and brown, and vulnerable as an animal's. The talk in the room had quietened for Arabella Dilworth's rendering at the piano of a romantic solo full of lark-trills and gentle reflective passages. And in a moment, scarcely as long as it took Arabella to strike a chord, something had changed between Will and Belle, an electric meeting which turned them from adoptive uncle and child-niece to something else, though neither could have told what. He knew a strange sympathy for her, and for the little sister at her side, whose ringed hand lay so passive against the silk of her dress. Then he pulled his thoughts away from them, and went to Ephraim.

'I came to see you in particular, Mr Atkinson, but I see it's not a good moment. I'll come back another time.'

'No, no. Mary can entertain the company. Come up to my study.'

In that brown, quiet room, sitting opposite to Ephraim in a deep upholstered chair, he told him of Joe's visit, and the girl who had been with him, and his own fears. Ephraim was writing sporadically on the paper in front of him, as he did when in court or listening to a client. When Will had finished his story, Ephraim looked up over his spectacles.

'I see. Would you say this was a passing infatuation ... a young man's fancy?'

Will shook his head. 'That's not Joe's way. He was as serious as the grave. He's too sound a lad to play tricks, and too honest not to say, if he was. He means matrimony with Miss Rosie, and God help him if it comes to that. I know her sort, ten a penny in China Lane, out for a good time and what's to be made out of it.'

'There might be roses among the thorns, Will.'

'Not i' this case. If there was good in her I'd ha' seen it, but I didn't, not a speck. And what's more, she's a thief.' He described the disappearance of the necklace. 'Is that the wife we want for Joe, or the wife he'd want himself, if he could see clear?'

Ephraim continued to make notes. 'We knew there was something wrong, or altered. For months we have hardly seen him, even on his birthday. We thought it was ... a misunderstanding that took place.'

'I know about that,' Will said. 'And I think it did rankle. His feelings get hurt easily. He was innocent in that business, I know as well as you, and he's innocent now — aye, that's the trouble, as innocent as a babe newborn. I don't like to interfere, Ephraim, but I felt bound to in this case. Now there's no more I can do, for he won't listen to me. It's up to you.'

'I dislike interference, too, Will. At times I felt like interfering in young George's courtship of Dove, when she seemed not to realise the boy's worth and promise — a First Mate at twenty, think of that, and without any particular influence. But I stayed my hand, left it to her, and suddenly she seemed to have a change of heart, and now we're all very happy for them. However, in Joe's case I think I must make an exception.' Will could see that he was a good deal more troubled than he appeared. 'I shall go to him rather than ask him to come here; it's hardly a matter for family discussion.' He looked up, smiling. 'Leave it to me, Will.'

The light from the study window shone down on to the darkening garden, where Dove walked with George under the trees.

'We may be stationed out there nine or ten months,' he was saying. 'But you'll have plenty to occupy you, I don't doubt. They say it can take a young lady a whole year preparing for her wedding. What in heaven's name do they do?'

'I don't know. I haven't given it any thought.'

'Not given our wedding any thought?' George's tone was pained.

'Oh, of course,' she said hastily. 'I mean that I had not thought what I shall do in your absence. Much the same as usual, I expect.'

'You sound deucedly matter-of-fact. Come, give me a kiss, Dove.' He pulled her round to him and planted a sound kiss on her cool mouth, annoyed at her lack of response. She looked so beautiful in the fading light, a glimmering angel in her white dress with a sparkling shawl over her hair. George could hardly believe that he had won her at last.

And Dove, strolling with him through the night-shadowed, sweet-smelling garden, wished with all her heart that George were already in the West Indies, and that it was Joe who walked there with her, close and tender, sometimes talking quietly. She would have lifted her mouth for his kiss, clung to him, lingered with him until they were called in, and treasured every moment of it. If only she had not seen him with that girl! It had driven her to accept George, whom she mildly liked, but could never love. And yet she had been right, she told herself. Joe *had* appeared enraptured with the girl. And instinct told her that Will Raven's coming tonight had something to do with it.

She looked up at the stars. No use to think and torture herself.

CHAPTER TEN

Bradhope was quietening down when Ephraim arrived. He had meant to be earlier, but a meeting with the executors of a complicated will had gone on far longer than expected. It was evening, the mills out, a few men lounging in doorways or around the alehouse. The place had the depressing air of a deserted village. Ephraim wished profoundly that he had not felt bound to visit Joe.

At Whittingham's house Mrs Darwen told him that Mr Atkinson was not back yet. No, she didn't know where he was. Something censorious in her eye suggested that she had a fair idea.

'Try t'school,' she suggested. 'He's sometimes there of an evening. Though not so much, these days,' she added, possibly hoping to draw Ephraim into a discussion of his nephew's habits. He avoided the bait, merely asking where the school was. Her reply was disappointed and brief; she had hoped for a bit of a gossip.

No school in Bradhope sprang to Ephraim's mind. He wandered down the High Street, hating its shabbiness and dirt. There was nobody about to ask. He reached the church, a newish building already tarnished with the atmosphere, its cemetery fuller than it should have been after only twenty years or so. A small, plump, plainly dressed woman, with *vicar's wife* written all over her, was shutting the gate. He raised his hat.

'Would you be so kind as to direct me to the local school, madam?' he asked.

Pleased to see a manifest gentleman in those parts, Mrs Leeming beamed upon him. 'Yes, indeed. We hold it in the disused Methodist chapel, only a few steps from here. You have heard of it, then, sir? I'm told it is quite famous already among philanthropists.' Ephraim was treated to an enthusiastic account of its creation.

He caught the name Atkinson, and asked, 'Would that be Joseph Atkinson, ma'am?'

She beamed even more broadly. 'The same. An excellent young man, a real acquisition to us. He and Miss Porteous together have done *so* much. If only...' She stopped. 'Here we are. I'm sure you'll find Mr Atkinson inside, sir — the evening school begins in half an hour, and he usually helps to lay out the books. If you will forgive me I must leave you. A large family and a busy husband — so little time...'

He thanked her and went into the chapel, noticing the neat conversion of pews to desks, the cleanness of it, the only relic of its original use still emblazoned on the end wall: GOD IS LOVE. Joe was not there. A young woman and an older one were going round placing books and papers on each desk. To his enquiry, the younger one, a brisk young lady whom Ephraim guessed to be a prosperous farmer's daughter gave him a pretty smile and the information that Joseph had not been in that evening. 'He's often got other things to employ him now we're so well established.'

The other woman said nothing. Pale and shaken, she was staring at the brother-in-law she had not seen for twenty years. There was no doubt it was he, for all the greying hair and the spectacles, even if she had not heard him ask for Joe. She felt her knees trembling and looked round desperately for the nearest door. She could not, would not meet him like this, at a disadvantage, taken by surprise. The teacher stopped her imminent flight.

'Miss Porteous, have we got another copy of *Russell's Modern Europe,* Part Twenty? I can only find seven and there ought to be eight. It *was* sixpence a part, so perhaps we didn't buy any more, but I thought we did.'

Forced to answer, Margaret kept her voice down in case its quivering was noticeable. 'There should be another; try the desk in the vestry, Jenny.'

Ephraim glanced towards her, struck by the soft, clear voice that had a trained quality so rare to his ears. And by something else — a dim sense of familiarity, though nothing in her appearance suggested that he might have met her, and he seldom forgot a face. Well dressed in a quiet way, long-visaged and plain yet pleasant; just another philanthropic lady devoted to churchgoing and good works; he remembered no Miss Porteous.

'Perhaps, ma'am, you could tell me where I could find Mr Atkinson,' he said to the young teacher. 'In fact, he is my nephew, and I have urgent family reasons for visiting him.'

Miss Jenny looked faintly uncomfortable. 'Oh, as to that ... he might be at Mr Whittingham's house where he lodges, or — or anywhere. He won't be at the Red Cow, that's for certain. He's not that kind of young man, is he, Miss Porteous?'

Margaret murmured that he was not. To conceal her agitation she picked up a book and pretended to look through it, first through her lorgnettes, then pulling them off to peer closely at the pages with an expression so intent that it gave her a look of bad temper.

She had always done just that, ever since she could read.

Ephraim must have given some exclamation, for she looked up and their eyes met. Young Jenny, sensing the strained atmosphere, slipped away mouse-like into the vestry at the back of the hall, closing the door behind her.

Ephraim could not be sure. It seemed so unlikely, and yet ... he remembered the action so vividly, and a girl who was always reading, long ago.

'Margaret,' he said, almost under his breath. Perhaps she would look puzzled, and snub him for using a first name to her, without even an introduction. But her face changed, softened, then was contorted as if with agony, and he saw in it the long-vanished girl. Without a word they moved towards each other and she threw herself into his arms, sobbing and babbling incoherent words, while he stroked her hair and patted her shoulder, as overcome as she.

'I can't believe it — I can't believe it,' he said, over and over. 'My dear, we were sure you were dead.'

'No, no, but I knew you thought so, and I wanted ... I wanted ... oh, Ephraim! Don't let me go, don't...'

He put her a little away from him, to calm them both. 'But why did you never communicate with us? You caused a lot of suffering, my dear. Poor Mary has shed many a tear over you, and your parents both spoke of you on their deathbeds.'

She shook her head violently, as if to shake pictures from her brain. 'I thought everyone would be angry ... ashamed.'

'Why, what had you done, child?' It seemed natural to call her that, impossible to think of her as a woman. For the first time she managed a smile.

'Nothing very dreadful, now I look back. I'll tell you soon. But — sit down, let me look at you before the others come. You haven't changed at all.'

'Flattery, my dear. I'm an old man — or almost.'

'And I'm — what you see. A very grave lady. Not wild Margaret any more.'

He had been thinking. 'Why Porteous? Did she say *Mrs* Porteous?'

'No, it's my *nom de plume*. It's a very long story and I can't tell you all now. The class is due to assemble and Jenny will think we are keeping a rendezvous. Come home with me — I live only a few minutes away. We will have supper and everything shall be explained.'

'How I wish I could, Margaret. But I have an errand I must carry out first.'

'Of course. You came to see Joe.'

'And you are Joe's co-worker! Your vicar's lady very kindly led me here and told me about your charities. Then — Joe knows who you are?'

'I told him — and made him promise not to tell you or Mary.'

Ephraim looked grim. 'Little chance of that, since he hardly comes near us these days.'

She glanced quickly at him, but went on, 'He told me what you have done, that I'd be welcome back, but I feared it might be his young warm-heartedness speaking, not true perception. Yet he made me think I could perhaps approach you, after all. And I would have done, I'm sure of that. But since things have fallen out as they have, I shall not have to screw up my courage after all.'

She kissed him. She was almost as tall as he now, for he was a little stooped with years and she had not finished growing when she ran away from home.

The vestry door opened discreetly, and Jenny peered round it. Margaret beckoned her.

'Jenny, the most extraordinary and agreeable thing has happened — this gentleman and I find that we knew each other years ago — we are, in fact, related. Neither he nor I expected to meet here: now isn't that remarkable?'

'Well, now! I *am* pleased for you, Miss Porteous.' Jenny evidently scented romance, and Margaret hurriedly went on, 'Did you find the Russell?'

'No, it doesn't seem to be anywhere.'

'We must do without it this evening, then. That is — I shall not be staying, but Mr Patton and Miss Hinde will be here soon. Indeed, someone is arriving now.' The door opened, to admit a little group of people, men and women from the mill, neat and washed, talking cheerfully. Margaret took Ephraim's arm.

'If anyone asks for me, Jenny, tell them I have gone with Mr Atkinson and can be found at home later?'

Jenny's eyes were round as she watched them leave. Mr Atkinson? And he had come asking for Joe Atkinson. So, if he and Miss Porteous were related, then... She gave it up and welcomed the arrivals.

Outside Margaret said, 'There's something I must tell you. Not about myself, but Joe. Something I am not very happy about.'

'You are the third person this evening to make me wonder why people are not very happy about Joe.'

'Oh dear! I wish I had not to tell you.' They walked arm-in-arm the way Ephraim had come. 'You see, Joe is so idealistic a fellow, so full of good intentions, that I suppose he does not see things and persons as they are. I believe he embarked on this with the best of motives, but ... he is still very young, younger at heart than most men of his age, I think ... and very easily taken in.'

Ephraim glanced at her curiously. Whatever it was she had to say, she was finding it difficult. They were passing the church, and had reached the gate of an ugly house next to it, whose architect had attempted the Gothic style and failed singularly. The door was shutting behind two people who were approaching down the path. Margaret and Ephraim stopped simultaneously, and Joe, too, halted.

'Uncle!'

'Good evening, Joe. I was looking for you. Your aunt and I met by chance, and now we are all met, very fortunate.'

Joe looked swiftly from uncle to aunt, and opened his mouth to say something, but turned it to, 'Yes, Uncle. A very good moment. May I present Miss Rose Giles?'

Ephraim took in from shawled head to ancient boots the figure of Joe's companion, and the pert, boldly pretty face. He felt Margaret rigid at his side. She was not going to help.

'Miss Giles,' Ephraim repeated with the sketch of a bow. He could not say he was delighted to meet her. But she gave him a wide coquettish smile.

'Well, I *am* pleased!' she said. 'How d'you do. That's right, isn't it, Joe? He keeps me up to scratch wi' t'manners, you know,' she added to them. 'I'll be talkin' proper before you can say Jack Robinson.'

Ephraim gave a wince of a smile. Round her plump neck he caught a glimpse of a necklace, green and coral, and his heart plummeted lower. It was as Will said. Margaret spoke, cold and clipped.

'I think we should be going, Ephraim.'

Joe led Rosie through the gate and stood in front of them, his arm round her. 'Before you go, Rosie and I have something to tell you. We have just called upon Mr Leeming and asked him to put up our banns.'

In Margaret's parlour a stormy scene was taking place. They had prevailed on Joe to accompany them to the house, against his will and very much against Rosie's. She knew quite well that these two stuck-up people were determined to separate her from Joe, and she was equally determined that they should not. She had got him to the point of asking her to marry him, even to the triumphant moment of calling on the vicar, and now his precious relations were trying to interfere. It took all Ephraim's skill at exercising his authority before she sulkily relinquished Joe's arm, disappointed of the 'courtin' saunter', and her raised voice brought the Leemings to their window. The vicar's wife shook her head.

'Not even a church-goer.'

'It won't do, Joe. You must know that yourself. Otherwise you would have presented Miss Giles to your family before you took this serious step.' Ephraim was pacing the hearthrug in Margaret's parlour, too agitated to keep still. They had been reasoning with Joe for what seemed like an hour, yet he remained unmoved, sitting with folded arms and the look of one who has made up his mind.

'I knew you would think the match unfitting, Uncle, so I waited until a chance came to tell you of it naturally. Well, it has come, and you and Aunt have taken it as I guessed you would.'

Ephraim struck the mantelpiece with his fist. 'Confound it, the match *is* unfitting! How can you, an Atkinson and a gentleman, even consider marrying this — this mill-hand?'

'I thought you more democratic, sir. A mill-hand may be made into a lady, with proper training and instruction. You heard Rosie herself say that she was improving already.'

'No one,' Margaret put in, 'can become a lady who is not already one in essence, and the accident of birth has nothing to do with it. I suspect that if Miss Giles had been an earl's daughter she would still have been unsuitable to be your wife.'

'Perhaps I know her a little better than you, Aunt. You've only met her once before this evening, when you were very cold and curt with her after she had spoken civilly enough to you.'

'Because I could see what she was,' Margaret snapped, 'and your state of infatuation with her.'

'Call it infatuation if you must.' Joe's voice was tender. 'I love Rosie very, very deeply, as I never knew one could love. She's beautiful, innocent and good, everything a young woman should be, except for lacking of refinement … and believe me, compared with many others of her station she's refinement itself.'

Ephraim snorted. 'Beautiful? A pair of red cheeks and a head of black hair that will be as grey as mine before she's forty. As to innocent and good — do you know she's a thief, Joe?'

For the first time Joe's confidence was shaken. 'I don't believe that, Uncle.'

'Then listen. When you and she visited Will Raven she stole a trinket from his shop. He described it to me. I saw her wearing it tonight.'

Joe hesitated. 'There must be a mistake. She told me her necklace came from the shop in the village — they sell all sorts of second-hand gear. She saved up for it — tonight was the first time I'd seen her with it on. You see, you're mistaken.'

'I wouldn't call your uncle a liar if I were you,' Margaret said. 'I've known him since my childhood, and a man less likely to tell a lie never existed. He would hardly begin now.'

Joe shrugged. 'Very well. If Rosie did chance to pick up the thing, I'm sure she meant to put it back. And when she found it — in her pocket, perhaps — she couldn't bring herself to return it.' He smiled fondly. 'She's very poor, and — girls like pretty things.'

Ephraim and Margaret exchanged a long, despairing look that said, *Our last trump card.* But Ephraim pressed on in a last effort to breach Joe's defences.

'Many have been hanged because they couldn't bring themselves to return stolen objects,' he said. 'The law has now been amended. Stealing from a dwelling-house to the value of five pounds is punishable by seven years' transportation. Lesser amounts earn lesser sentences. Miss Giles may think herself lucky that Will chooses not to prosecute; though he might well change his mind.'

Fear flared into Joe's eyes. 'Uncle Will? He'd never do that — and to the girl I love. Surely he isn't thinking of it? I'll go and see him if you feel there's the slightest danger...'

'I have no idea what may be in his mind. I merely put the facts before you.'

Joe looked relieved, but said, 'Thank you. It makes no difference.'

Margaret bent forward, close to him. 'Joe. Do you know Miss Giles's family?'

'I've visited their house. Well, cottage. Yes, I know them.'

'Will you try to imagine, my dear, how they would appear at a gathering — a wedding reception, say — of your own people? Your uncle and aunt, their friends...'

'Do you think Belle and Dove would find them agreeable?' Ephraim enquired. 'Chat with them easily, exchange confidences? And do you think they would be altogether at home at St Leonard's Gate?'

A dull red crept into Joe's cheeks. He saw in his mind Mrs Giles, sluttish and toothless, without what Rosie would have called a word to throw at the cat, and Billy, puny, always with a running nose, his speech so thick that it was not easy to understand what he said. By no stretch of imagination could Joe see them at home in Ephraim's house. But he was not going to give in.

'Perhaps they are not altogether … like ourselves at the moment. But Rosie will improve them, as she learns herself, when we're married. She has a very strong character, Uncle. She would not wish to leave her mother and brother in a state of ignorance.'

Ephraim drew a long, deep breath. 'Unless you have anything to add, Margaret, I think we've said all that can be said. I'm sorry you are not more amenable to reason, Joe. I thought you a young man of good sense. I see I was wrong. Very well, by all means take your own course and ruin your life. Your aunt Mary will be sorry to hear of this, I believe. Margaret, my dear, I must ask you for a bed for the night; it's far too late to return.'

Joe rose and bade them goodnight. He was disconcerted and unhappy. In all his life he had never had an undeserved cross word from the man he looked on as a father; they had never even had an argument until he wanted to become Whittingham's partner. And Margaret, whom he had known such a little time, had already become a friend as well as a relative. He was fond of her, fonder still of his uncle.

But he loved Rosie with a passion unawakened until now.

Mary's reaction to Ephraim's report of the evening was violent. He had told her about the girl's existence, though not in the strong terms Will had used, and she had said flatly that she was sure it was all a nonsense, just a boy taking a girl out for the day. 'Joe's only human — every lad likes a bit of fun sometimes.' Let Ephraim go and investigate, by all means, but he would find there was nothing in it.

She heard him out to the last detail, her colour rising and her lips tightening. Then she spoke.

'If anyone else but you had told me, I wouldn't have believed it. Well, I *do* believe it, every word, and I'm shocked, Ephraim, shocked. Our Joe and that common, low doxy. Yes, doxy! And there's worse words for a girl like that, only I hope I'm too much of a lady to use them. To think of the love we gave that boy! Brought up as our own, cherished like our daughters. I'd such hopes for him. Many a time I've planned his wedding, and what I should w-wear, and how grand he'd look...' She began to weep, noisy uncontrollable sobs.

Ephraim drew her to him. 'Don't upset yourself, love, don't. You know it isn't good for you. Here, take my handkerchief. Where are your smelling salts? There now, be calm. You know what we've always said — worse things happen at sea.'

When she could speak, she said, 'There couldn't be much worse than this, unless it was one of our girls running off...' She mopped at her eyes. 'I'll go myself, that's what I'll do. I'll see Joe. He'll take it from me when he wouldn't from you. It needs a woman, Ephraim, to explain these things...'

'Mother', he said in the gentle tone he always used when he was going to say something important. 'Mother, I've something else to tell you. Now don't be alarmed, you remember what the doctor said. It's nothing bad, indeed it's wonderful news, but you must keep very calm. Promise me?'

She nodded. He could feel her heart beating very fast. Quietly, making as light of it as possible, he told her about his finding of Margaret. Told her too of Margaret's story, which he had heard the night before after Joe had gone; they had sat by the fire, trying to put the distress of the evening behind them. He dilated on Margaret's cleverness, her elegance, the books she had written, her well-appointed house, the good work she did in the parish. Gradually, he felt Mary's tense body relax, her heartbeats become less dangerously rapid. 'So you see, Mother, some good has come of all this. Now aren't you a little happier? And you'll forgive Margaret, and welcome her, when she comes to see us?'

'The silly lass,' Mary said almost conversationally. 'Keeping away from us all this time. Yes, I'll be glad to see her, of course I will.' She burst into tears again, overcome by the double shock. Ephraim led her upstairs and called Dove to put her to bed and sit with her.

Four weeks later a letter came from Joe, telling them that he and Rosie were to be married the following Saturday. Ephraim read it aloud to Mary, who listened expressionlessly, then took it from him, tore it across, and flung it into the fireplace.

CHAPTER ELEVEN

Joe stood by Rosie's side at the altar. The service had seemed long because she had needed so much prompting. She had not been able to rehearse it, being unable to read, and her unusual state of nervousness made her deaf to Mr Leeming's gentle reminders of the responses. It seemed strange and sad to Joe that none of his own family were there, only Rosie's mother, with Billy, some of her workmates, and Mrs Leeming, disapproving but showing a Christian forbearance. Joe, after all, was one of her husband's flock.

Joe was acutely conscious of Rosie's presence at his side: the warmth of her thigh, her quick breathing, her hand clutching his whenever it could. He knew without looking at her that her colour was even higher than usual, and that she was proud of the new dress, bonnet and shawl he had bought her. The dress was a very bright blue, the bonnet white, the shawl a mixture of all colours. She thought they were beautiful, but Joe knew nothing about such things, only seeing her in them, young and vital. He wished she had had one of her own family to give her away. As it was, an elderly overseer from Bradshaw's had performed that duty.

He heard the vicar speaking the last words of the service. 'Husbands, love your wives, even as Christ also loved the Church, and gave Himself for it, that He might sanctify and cleanse it with the washing of water, by the Word; that He might present it to Himself a glorious Church, not having spot, or wrinkle, or any such thing; but that it should be holy, and without blemish...'

So, he promised himself, would he love Rosie, helping her, educating her, gently separating her from the imperfections of her birth and rearing, bringing her into the charmed circle of the women he himself had grown up amongst. Under his loving care she would learn to speak well, hold herself gracefully, read books and join the band of ladies who did good among the poor of Bradhope. Soon nobody would be ashamed of Rosie; he was not, never had been in their short acquaintance, never would be in their long life together. He saw little children in Rosie's arms, at her lap, red-headed boys like himself, dark laughing girls like her, and, strangely, a fairy-faced creature with silver-gilt hair and dusky eyes.

He shook off the vision. Mr Leeming was coming to the end of his reading from the Scriptures.

'...*whose daughters ye are as long as ye do well, and are not afraid with any amazement...*'

Joe became conscious of giggling in the back pews where the mill girls sat, and of Billy loudly demanding to be taken out. What were they all waiting for?

'The register,' Mr Leeming murmured. 'The bride's mother should attend the signing.' He smiled and beckoned to Mrs Giles, who stared back at him and stayed where she was. After a moment, the clergyman moved off towards the vestry, Joe following him with Rosie. The registers were open in the stuffy little room, the clerk in attendance. Joe wrote his name and status, then handed the pen to Rosie, who looked at it blankly.

'What's this, then?'

'You must sign your name, love. First your maiden name, then "Rose Atkinson".' The words were hardly out before he remembered what he had, in his dreaming, forgotten. He threw an embarrassed glance towards Mr Leeming.

'My wife —' how proudly he said the words — 'my wife doesn't write clearly.'

Mr Leeming understood only too well. 'If you'll make your mark here, Mrs Atkinson … and here.'

'Oh, aye.' She scrawled a cross twice. 'Owt else, or can we go?'

Mr Leeming sighed. 'That is all. God bless you both.' They left the church, Rosie clinging to Joe's arm and smiling to right and left, preening herself before the stray observers who hung round the church gate, and laughing with the friends who threw wildflower at the couple. There had been no music at the service, and only a preliminary clanging of the little church's single bell, with its dull funereal toll. Still, thought Joe, it was a cheerful enough occasion; at least he hoped it was so for Rosie. He was preoccupied with his own passionate devotion and dream-building, for which a whole nuptial mass such as the Roman Catholics held would not have been too solemn or protracted.

Mrs Giles was beside them. 'Where's breakfast, then?'

He started. 'What, ma'am?' He still had not found the right form of address for her.

'T'weddin' breakfast, Mam means,' Rosie explained. 'There's to be a fiddler, i'nt there, an' a grand feast an' dancin' an' singin'. Where's it to be, Joe?' She was on tiptoe with excitement.

Joe stared at her, utterly baffled. 'I … I don't know anything about it. Has someone arranged it?'

'Someone? Someone? Who but thee, lad? Come on now, tell us.'

'Aye,' grumbled Mrs Giles, 'they're all waitin'.'

'Upon my word,' stammered the embarrassed Joe, 'I've made no such arrangements. I didn't know it was usual … that is, in, er, cases of simple weddings. I thought…'

'You thowt what?' snarled the bride's mother. 'Thowt my daughter weren't good enow for a proper bridin', is that it? Whoever 'eard of a groom as didn't bid neighbours to a feast? Come on, I'm listenin'.'

Joe, scarlet as ever at a crisis, was appalled and speechless, looking round for help. Mrs Leeming was just leaving the church porch. Relinquishing Rosie's arm, he hurried over to her and stuttered out his predicament. She looked at him with kindly pity.

'Dear me. Yes, it is the custom. They think a lot of it, though of course it's a pagan affair. Well, you were not to know, Mr Atkinson.' She thought, and brightened. 'If you and your bride and … any friends you think fit will return with me to the vicarage, I shall be very pleased to give you some tea and cold refreshments. I think we have a ham…' She reviewed mentally the resources of her larder. They were not great, with six children to feed, and a husband, and numerous parish droppers-in. 'Yes, I'm sure we can spare something.'

Mrs Giles was behind her, a spitting fury. 'Tay? Tay be hanged. We want none o' your tay. Cakes an' ale's what we want, and what we'll have, or my name's not what it is, an' this young whippersnapper's goin' to pay for it.'

The vicar's wife stiffened, drawing herself up to her full height, short though it was. 'We keep no strong drink. The vicar would not countenance it for one moment. If you want it you must go elsewhere, though I'd advise you to go home and remain sober.'

Mrs Giles replied in words Joe hoped he would be able to forget, and Mrs Leeming turned her back and walked rapidly away. Rosie was crying loudly, the other girls crowding sympathetically round her. Joe tried not to see what Billy was doing after his long confinement in the church.

'Well, who's for t'Red Cow?' asked Mrs Giles, receiving a chorus of approval. She set off at the head of a procession down the street. Joe stood there, feeling the most ridiculous, miserable figure of a bridegroom that had ever existed. How could he have been so inept as not to find out the local custom? Why had Rosie not told him? And if he had known, what could he have done? At that moment a fish out of water would have been more comfortable and relaxed than Joe.

Rosie came back from the gate where she had been waiting. She had dried her tears at the assurance of a proper celebration and was really quite sorry for Joe. He knew no better, she could see, but in time he'd learn. The ring was on her finger now, she was Mrs Atkinson, the manager's wife, and she was going to enjoy herself and brighten up Joe's life a bit, for he was a bit of a long-face, no doubt about it.

'Come on, Joe. Nowt wrong as can't be mended.'

Two hours later, in the tap-room of the Red Cow, Joe wished profoundly that his aching head could be mended. He wished they would all go away, these chattering, shrieking people, with their voices pitched to overtop the noise of machinery, their coarse jokes that made him blush, their unquenchable thirst for ale, every drop of which must be paid for out of his pocket. Mrs Giles appeared to have gone out of her mind and was lying on a bench uttering monotonous witchlike cackles. Somebody standing on a table was singing 'Grimshaw's Factory Fire', while another with an even more strident voice had started up the ballad of 'The Bonny Gray':

'Come all you cock-merchants far and near,
Did you hear of a cock-fight happenin' here?
Those Liverpool lads, I've heard 'em say,
'Tween the Charcoal Black an' the Bonny Gray.'

A big man, with a girl hanging on to him, slapped Joe with painful heartiness between the shoulders, making him cough.

'Hey, sing up, Joe! Tha's bahn t' tek an interest i' cocks on thi' weddin' day — eh, Betty? Show me t'lad as doesn't, then!'

Joe pushed him away furiously. He felt sick. Across the room he saw Rosie with a man's arm familiarly encircling her. Resolutely he pushed his way through the crowd (where had they all come from? Only a handful had been in the church) and took her arm.

'Come. We're going home.'

She stared, surprised, laughing. 'Home? You may be — I'm not. What, leave a bridin' with folks so merry? Here, tak' a sup.' She pushed a mug towards him full of dark brown ale.

Suddenly, desperately, he lifted it to his lips and drank it down, then called for more. It made the whole nightmare scene a little more bearable. He hoped he was not a milksop to find it all ugly and wrong, but if this was rustic merriment he disliked it very much.

Home, when they got there at last, early in the evening, was a cottage on the outskirts of Bradhope. It was small, detached, built of grey stone: a mansion compared with the hovel the Giles family lived in, and the best Joe could afford to rent, together with its few but adequate pieces of furniture. Its situation was picturesque, backing on to open land, Hawthornthwaite Fell looming up to the east, its stark outlines softened in sunset cloud. There were two small rooms and a lean-to kitchen downstairs, two bedrooms upstairs, and a good dry shed in the yard. Not a bad start for married life.

Inside, Joe shut the door and leaned against it, his eyes closed.

'Feelin' bad?' Rosie enquired.

He nodded. He had never felt worse, even after his first mild debauch in Oxford, or after the famous rowing match. He had been drunk before, he had heard bawdy talk before, but not on an occasion which he felt should have been private and sacred. It had been wrong, wrong. And he had so much missed those who would have made it all that it should have been: his uncle, Aunt Mary, Aunt Margaret, the twins, the kindly, respectable Lancaster faces that had been about him since his childhood. How could they have deserted him? And yet, if they had come … Ephraim's words were in his head. *Do you think they would be altogether at home at St Leonard's Gate?* He remembered Mrs Giles and Billy at the Red Cow, and shuddered. No, they would not.

Rosie was taking off her shawl, untying her bonnet, admiring herself dimly seen in the window-pane reflection, since there was no mirror. She moved about quickly, banging things down. He realised that she was angry. He moved to her and put his arms round her from behind, feeling as he did so a surge of the desire that had consumed him for so long. She turned to him, smiling.

'Well, that's better!' She leaned against him, warm, smelling of the lavender water someone had given her as a wedding present. He did not notice that she also smelt of ale, having drunk it himself, or that she was only pleasantly affected by the quantity she had taken, for she was used to it.

'Shall us, then?' She jerked her head in the direction of the ceiling.

Joe was certainly surprised, if not shocked. He had not imagined the suggestion would come from the bride. But then it was like Rosie to be utterly frank, with no pretence or hypocrisy. Closely entwined, they went up the narrow stairs together.

She was more beautiful than he had dreamed: a plump nymph, a Bacchante, gloriously naked with her black hair loose about her, lying sprawled on the bed. He had never seen a naked woman before; it was a shock of delight to him, undreamed of in all his imaginings. The awful blush, which had been with him all that day, crept over his face again, and Rosie laughed.

'Nay, there's nowt to be shy about, lad. Will I do, then?'

He gulped. 'So beautiful ... I...'

'Well, get on wi' it.' As he undressed, his back to her, he wondered in his confused mind why his desire was tempered with another feeling — could it be disappointment that she had not veiled herself from him, revealed her charm modestly, behaved as he had expected a virgin bride to behave? Then he was angry with himself for ungratefulness. She was his, his own at last.

He was hot, and limp, and exhausted. Sweat damped his hair and ran on to his pillow. He had been so inept, and she had tried to make it so easy for him. How did she know...? He was a man now, yet he felt less than a man. And she — how long had Rosie been a woman? For he had read that brides suffered and resisted. Perhaps it was not true, or perhaps she was different. Now she lay curled up beside him, fast asleep, breathing heavily, and he wished, perversely, that he might get up and go to a bed of cool linen where he could sleep alone.

In another bedroom, in another house, Belle lay awake in the darkness listening to a very soft, muffled regular noise from the four-poster where her sister lay. Dove was crying, had been crying since the candles had been snuffed. Belle's heart ached for her. Yet there was nothing she could do but pretend to be asleep.

The Indiaman *Chloe*, bound for Barbados, rode at anchor off St George's Quay, waiting for the tide. A handsome ship of 230 tons' burden, spanking bright in new paint; her figurehead, a gorgeous full-bosomed woman, was resplendently ebonied, her jewels picked out in gilt, her mouth poppy-scarlet.

Among the bustling crowds on the quay stood two women, a young man and an older one. George Dilworth was being seen off by his parents, his betrothed, and her mother.

He looked up at the creamy clouds scudding across a bright blue September sky. 'A fair wind — we shouldn't be long now.' Not all the conventional sorrow at parting with his dear ones could keep the excitement out of his voice.

'I don't believe you're in the least sorry to be leaving us,' his mother said. 'You'd as soon be back among the monkeys and the palm trees as in your own good home.'

'And why shouldn't he?' asked her husband. 'I know which I'd have preferred, at his age. Plenty of time to settle down when youth's done.'

Arabella dug him in the ribs and threw him an admonitory look. 'Have some thought for poor Dove's spirits, to be parting with her sweetheart when the ring's scarcely on. Cheer up, Dove dear — George'll be back far sooner than he thinks, I'll be bound.'

George, who could not keep his eyes from the ship, replied absently, 'To be sure,' while Dove showed no sign of distress.

Mary noted with approval that she was looking at George intently, as though learning his features. It was time the child showed some real interest in George; but then her coolness was commendable enough after Belle's flirtatious ways. Of late Dove had been coming down to breakfast with puffy eyelids, and that too was a good sign, meaning that she had been weeping for George's coming departure. Perhaps it was as well that he was going away. Absence notably made the heart grow fonder. By the time he returned she would be more than ready for marriage.

Dove was indeed memorising George's face. Though they had been boy and girl together, she found it unaccountably difficult to remember what he looked like when he was away from her. Yes, it was a good, comely face, open and cheerful, the fair hair beneath the hat a bright butter-gold, the complexion ruddily healthy. In foreign climes it would turn deep brown. No girl in her right senses could have called George unattractive.

He was strong and sensible, too, with fine prospects; he could offer her security, a home of her own, children. A future of spinsterhood could be nothing but dreary. So she must be able to recall George when he was away, conjure up his image often — though there was always Aunt Arabella's portrait of him painted by a local artist two years ago, with a very pink face and a very blue uniform.

George caught her look. 'What a moping face!' he said. 'I'm not going for ever, or to the other end of the world, you know.'

'Oh, it's not that. I was just remembering how you used to chase me when we were little, and frightened me very much because you said you had a wasp in your hand — though I suppose I knew you hadn't, or it would have stung you.'

George laughed. 'The deuce I did! You've a better memory than mine. What a young Turk I must have been. I won't do it when we're married, I promise you. Ah — there's the signal.' He embraced his mother. 'Goodbye, Mama. Don't fret, your boy will behave himself and come back to you all of a piece.'

Clinging to him, Arabella wept a little. 'Do take care, my darling boy. And bring me an India shawl back, won't you?'

'As if I'd forget — a parrot too, if you like. Goodbye, Father.' A hearty handshake and a clap on the shoulders from Jack. He turned to Dove, tilting her chin up to kiss her. 'Dove. Don't forget me. I'll write to you when I can, though you know I'm not much hand with a pen, and you must write and tell me all the news. Goodbye, sweetheart.'

'Goodbye, George.'

Waving and smiling, Arabella applying a handkerchief to her eyes, they watched him run to the jolly-boat. A sailor lent him a hand to enter it, then the oars were flashing through the waves, bearing him towards the *Chloe*. They saw it reach the side, and George swarm nimbly up the boarding ladder to the deck.

'Well,' Jack said, 'he's aboard. It'll be some time before she sails yet. You ladies want to stay?'

'Oh, yes!' Arabella cried.

'Oh, no,' said Dove. She shivered. 'It's very cold. I don't think George would want us to catch chills.'

'Quite right.' Jack patted her arm. 'Seeing folk off's a melancholy business at the best. Let's get back home and warm ourselves up.'

As they left the quay, Dove turned to look back at the beautiful ship, rocking on the tide, her sails swelling and straining to be gone. Suddenly she wished she were already married to George, sailing away with him to islands of golden sun and bright seas, away from the cold grey town and the prim old house which seemed to hold for her now nothing but sad memories. It might be her salvation to put the world between herself and Joe.

Belle had been left at home with the startings of a cold and an upset digestion which Mary diagnosed as a chill on the stomach. She sat by the fire, wrapped in shawls and blankets, layer upon layer of them added by Aggie, who hovered over her like a fussy hen.

'Oh, do leave me be, Aggie. I'll be well enough. It's only the shivers. Just mend the fire and let me stay quiet.'

Aggie continued to hover. 'I hope it's not the Spanish 'Fluence.'

Belle tried to laugh, though she did not feel like it. 'Of course it isn't. Where could I have caught such a thing? They say it passes from one person to another.'

'That it does, I well remember. The poor lads come back from the Peninsula wi' tales of their comrades dyin' like flies. I shouldn't wonder, now, if you hadn't catched it from them paupers you and your ma's allus visitin'.'

'Oh, nonsense, Aggie. Be sensible. Just because Mama and I take food to them, it's not to say they're lepers. What an idea! I'll be perfectly well if I can just get warm.'

Aggie peered at her. 'You're a funny colour. I've got some chicken broth heating in the kitchen, I'll just fetch you a bowl.'

Belle opened her mouth to protest, but Aggie had bustled out. She sighed, and settled herself into her cocoon. If only she could get comfortable. The broth must have taken some time to heat, for she fell into a light, uneasy doze from which she was awakened by the entrance of Dove with a steaming, fragrant bowl of it.

'Aggie told me to bring this to you. Gracious, Belle! You look quite dreadful. What a blessing you didn't come with us — it was perishing cold on the quay. Here, drink some.'

Belle shook her head irritably. 'I couldn't touch a mouthful. Aggie knows I couldn't, yet she will keep bringing things in. You have it. You look cold enough.'

'I am.' Dove helped herself to the broth. 'Oh, this is good — you ought to try some.'

Belle's tone was unwontedly sharp. 'I told you. I don't want it. Never mind me. How did George's departure go?'

'Very well, I suppose. The *Chloe* looked magnificent, and George seemed very elated to be leaving for the Indies.'

'Well he might be, leaving this terrible cold place. Why did we have to be born in the north, Dovekin? I'd much sooner have been brought up in the south, among the flowers, where it's always warm and one can wear delightful muslins all the year round. Oh, to be in London like Aunt Eleanor, even if she *does* live in sin! Do you suppose she's very, very happy? How I wish we could visit her... But Mama wouldn't allow it. Poor Mama, if she only knew.'

'Knew what?'

'How wicked one can be. She thinks ... she thinks...' Belle's voice slurred. Dove tucked the blankets round her shoulders.

'You ought to be in bed,' she said. 'I'm sure you've caught a very nasty cold. And you're not at all wicked, so don't think such bad thoughts and make yourself unhappy. If you're wicked, then so must I be, for you and I are the same, are we not?'

Belle fixed her with a swimmy look. 'Ought to be. But you're in love. How delightful, to be in love. I wish I were.'

'Don't mock me! You know how things are with me.'

'I know.' Belle nodded sagely. 'Though nobody else does. You wouldn't care a pin if George never came back from Barbados, would you?'

Dove flushed, putting her hands to her cheeks. 'Of course I would care! Poor George. How can you say such a thing? As for … the other, I don't want to talk about it. Please leave it, Belle. Mama must never know.'

'I shan't tell.' Suddenly Belle began to shiver, long convulsive shudders that made one of the shawls covering her fall to the ground. Her teeth were chattering violently. Dove hurried to her and touched the icy hands and the hot brow. Belle looked up imploringly. 'I feel as if … cold water … trickling down my back. Ache all over…'

Dove pulled the service bell sharply, twice. In a moment Aggie entered and took in the situation at a glance.

'Upstairs with you, milady.' Her arm supporting Belle, she turned to Dove and snapped, 'Isaac's in t'kitchen — tell him to get a kettle on and bricks made hot. Then let your mother know, and say doctor's to be sent for.'

The doctor, arriving half an hour after Belle had been put to bed under a mound of blankets, looked horrified.

'I'm sorry to tell you, Mrs Atkinson — Miss Belle has the cholera morbus.'

CHAPTER TWELVE

It was the beginning of a nightmare. Mary, when told, declared that it was impossible Belle should have caught cholera. She had been nowhere near the asylum or the workhouse, where the infection was known to be raging. It was Aggie who reminded her of a visit Belle had made to the Stubbs family, the wife and children of a labourer who had been killed in a building accident. Bet Marsden, the young servant who maided Belle and Dove, had heard of their plight from her own people, neighbours of theirs. Food was put aside weekly in the Atkinsons' larder for the deserving poor, which they distributed themselves, as did many other ladies in St John's parish. Mary recalled with horror that Belle had gone to the Stubbs' the previous week.

'But they were not ill!' she cried. 'Only distressed and hungry. Belle went to see Mrs Fearnside about them because she thought they were in need of more help than we could give. There was no illness in the house.'

'There may be now,' said Dr McAndrew. 'The disease has spread to the town, particularly among folk living in crowded conditions. More than likely one or more of the Stubbs children was sickening for it. However that may be, Miss Belle certainly has it.'

'How dangerous is her case?' Ephraim asked.

The doctor's silence was sufficient answer.

Ephraim took Mary's hand and held it. 'Then what must we do?'

McAndrew shook his head. 'Very little's known about the thing. It's thought to have come from the East in the first place, then spread to Europe — last year was its first appearance in England. It's a terrible complaint, Mr Atkinson. The patient suffers continuous high fever, rheumatic pain, violent sickness and intestinal cramps. There's nothing I can do myself, for no treatment is known at present. I think you should let me find you a nurse from the fever hospital — or have Miss Belle taken there.'

'No!' Dove broke in. 'I'll nurse her myself.'

'That you won't!' snapped Mary. 'Isn't it enough, having one of you stricken down, without risking the other? I won't hear of it, Dove.'

'No, no,' McAndrew agreed. 'It would never do. These women at the hospital are used to infection and scarcely ever catch diseases themselves. I can find you a clean respectable woman, I'm sure, without difficulty.'

But Dove was adamant, standing up calmly to her father's opposition and her mother's rising hysteria. 'What use is my life to me, if my twin dies? Nobody shall look after her but me. I'm quite strong, you know — and quite determined, Mama. Don't cry, for you won't stop me.'

Another volunteer nurse joined her in the large attic they had set aside for a sickroom. Little Bet Marsden, bitterly distressed that she had been the one to bring the news of the Stubbs' disaster and cause Belle's visit to the infected house, insisted on helping. 'I've had all the ills there is, smallpox an' scarlatina an' all, so I'll not catch this 'un, will I? It's too much for poor Miss Dove, that it is.'

When the implications of the calamity came fully home to Mary, she collapsed. Her mother's heart weakness had descended to her; without complete rest, the doctor said, he would not answer for her. Aggie undertook to care for her. Downstairs, Ephraim tried to eat, but the empty chairs round the table laid for one were too much for him. He went up to his study, but work was beyond him; the letters swam before his eyes and he soon laid them down. His family had been so lucky, so blessed in their good health. It was as though the sky had fallen on him.

Within a day or two Aggie reported that Mary was recovering, but not surprisingly was still very low in her spirits. 'If I was you, Mr Atkinson, I'd send for Miss Margaret. From what you say she's a lady of leisure, not tied at all, and it'd do Mrs Atkinson a world of good to see her.'

Ephraim managed to smile. 'Aggie, you're a fount of wisdom. I'll write today, and Isaac shall ride to Bradhope with it.'

Within twelve hours Margaret was with them, and it was clear from the beginning that Aggie had been right. Deeply disturbed though she was by the news of Belle, she was strong enough to assume a convincing cheerfulness which she was far from feeling, and her natural calmness and good humour were the perfect tonic for Mary. Deliberately she refrained from giving in to emotion when she first stood by her sister's bed.

'Well, Mary, I must say that for an invalid you look blooming. If I didn't know your age I would never believe it. What a beautifier marriage must be.'

She sat down, and glided into a stream of cheerful trivia that diverted Mary's mind from the gloomy channel it ran in. Her life had been so diversified, so full of amusing incidents and people (or she made them seem amusing if they were not) that Mary actually laughed, and began to recover from that moment. Calm, capable, and strong, she took the wretched household in hand, saw that Ephraim ate properly, talked to

Dove and Bet through the sickroom door and herself brought up food and drink for the girls. It was strange to her to know the grown-up Dove only as a peaked little face peering through the scarcely-open door: the child who had been one year old when Margaret ran away. In only a few days they came to like each other, Margaret admiring Dove's bravery and devotion, Dove recognising Margaret's kindly strength.

'Don't fear for me, my dear,' Margaret said when her niece begged her not to come so near the infection. 'We've had some cases in Bradhope, and I expect the plague has taken a look at me and flown away. Look after yourselves, keep the window open whatever the doctor may say, and take nourishment when you can.'

At Margaret's suggestion, a saucer was placed outside the sickroom containing powdered nitre into which oil of vitriol had been slowly dripped. It was, she said, an infallible weapon against the spreading of infection to other parts of the house; and, whether by virtue of its powers or by good luck, nobody else in the household sickened.

Belle had been ill for almost a week when Dove reported tearfully, 'She has no strength left, Aunt. She can keep nothing down and her skin is quite cold. Her thirst is terrible, but when I try to get her to drink, the water runs out of her mouth. Oh, what shall I do?'

'Keep calm. Wash her face and arms to moisten her skin. It is very dry, is it not?'

'Yes. Like tinder, and blueish.'

Margaret said no more, but hurried downstairs and called for the trap to be brought round. Ephraim would have been horrified if he had seen her destination: the lunatic asylum outside the town, a place unpopular with strollers and seldom visited. When she came back she entered the parlour briskly.

'I learned something this afternoon. Out of two hundred and more cholera cases at the asylum only ninety-four have died.'

Ephraim and Mary stared at her, horrified. 'You've never been up there, among the infection?' Mary cried.

'Only to the gatehouse. They sent someone out to talk to me. It seems that they were advised to give the patients the juice of oranges and lemons. Water is useless to assuage the thirst, it only disappears like all other liquids in the body. Ephraim, can you get some fruit very quickly? Belle has reached that stage in the illness when it might help her. I asked at all the shops in town, but there was none.' Even Margaret was becoming agitated. 'We must get some, if we have to go to Preston for it, and by then…'

He was out of the room, and out of the house before Mary spoke. 'And without the fruit … there's no hope?'

'How can we tell? It's in God's hands. I've done what I can, Mary. She has youth and those two brave girls nursing her. How they've carried on with such patience, day after day, washing the linen in the next room, throwing it down to be dried, sitting by her hour after hour…'

Dove was sitting by her sister's bed at that moment; and, an hour later, had not moved, the dry lifeless hand in hers. The girl in the bed was not recognisable as Belle. On a pallet on the floor Bet was asleep, taking her turn to rest. Belle's head moved weakly on the pillow, then turned towards Dove, her lips moving. Dove bent down.

'What is it, dearest?'

It was hard to hear what the cracked, husky voice was murmuring. Then Dove recognised the familiar words, the rhyme that belonged to a game they had played as children.

There had been a tune to it then, but now it was only a harsh whisper.

'Water, water, wild-flower, growing up so high,
We are all young maidens, and we have got to die.
Excepting Mary Watkins, she is the fairest flower...
Fie, fie, for shame...'

The whisper faded. Dove bent closer. *'Turn your back and tell your beau's name.* Isn't that what you were saying?'

There was a faint movement from the pale lips of the girl in the bed. 'Got to die,' she breathed. 'Die.'

'No, Belle. No. Hold on to me. I won't let you die.'

She was still holding Belle, talking to her softly and getting a little response, when the door flew open. Margaret stood there with a china pitcher balanced on her hip.

'Aunt!' cried Dove. 'You should not be in here.'

'Nonsense.' Margaret brushed past her and set the pitcher down. 'Too late to think of such things now. I learned today that the juice of oranges and lemons is sometimes of great help in these cases. There were none to be had in the shops, but your father went down to the quays and tracked down a consignment waiting for unloading. Some were unripe and some were going rotten, but he bought them all, and Aggie and I have extracted the juice with the cider press. Here is a sponge — easier than a cup. Now, you hold Belle's head and I will trickle the juice into her mouth.'

It was a slow process, needing much patience. At last Margaret said, 'Enough. Leave her. Now, light another candle, Dove.' The candle lit, she peered at the face on the pillow. 'A little difference, I think. Not much, but time will tell. Go and rest, child. No, don't disturb Bet, she needs her sleep as much as you do. The doctor said the risk of infection was less now than before — for what he knows about it, which I suspect is as much as cuckoos know of cows.'

There was another day of suspense, close watching, then growing relief as the dreadful blue colour began to fade from Belle's skin and moisture crept back into it. Margaret sent the exhausted Dove and Bet off to their own beds, making them take a precautionary bath beforehand, and then she herself took charge, sitting by the bedside, taking occasional naps, refreshing the patient with sips of juice and doing whatever else was needed. She was quite unruffled, but sat there with her pince-nez to her eyes and Scott's *Tales of a Grandfather* on her knee.

The following morning she went downstairs and returned with Ephraim and Mary, who climbed slowly and leaned heavily on his arm. 'You may look at her now, my dears.'

The face on the pillow did not look at all like Belle's. Her hair had not been cut off during the high fever, for Margaret, when consulted, said it was a ridiculous practice which led to severe depression in the patient when she was enough recovered to be able to look in the glass. But the beautiful hair was lank, matted, straggling over the pillow, and the peach-like face a sunken mask with dried, cracked lips and grey cheeks. Her parents approached the bed, treading softly, but Margaret said, 'You won't disturb her. She is in a natural sleep.'

'Thank God,' Ephraim said, and again, 'Thank God, for saving our girl.'

'God and His agents,' said the practical Margaret. 'He arranged your sending for me, Dove's wonderful devotion to her sister, and Bet's bravery. And furthermore He arranged for us all to remain level-headed and sensible in the face of danger and adversity.' She closed *Tales of a Grandfather,* polished her pince-nez, and beamed benevolently upon them.

'Margaret,' said Mary, 'I always knew you were a remarkable girl, and we all thought you would grow up to be something extraordinary, but none of us could have guessed you would be what you are.' She went to her sister and kissed her cheek.

A few nights after Belle's first step on the road to recovery one of the most awful storms ever known in Lancashire began to rage. For five hours a hurricane blew, the gentle Lune swelled until it burst its banks, flooded Lancaster's cellars and lower-lying streets, tore off the roofs of houses, blew down chimneys and sent the stained-glass windows of St John's Chapel shattering to the floor within. Ephraim's office building had a door torn off its hinges; the street outside was like a beck coursing down a Lakeland hillside. The vessel *Mary Ann,* moored at St George's Quay, drifted into mid-river, her cable broken. At Poulton-le-Sands many fishermen lost boats, nets and stakes, and would have found themselves penniless had not a public subscription been raised to help them. Sodden, shaken, damaged, Lancaster prepared to pay the bill.

But the cholera morbus had gone; washed away, people said.

The weeks of Belle's illness, brief as they were, brought changes to all the family. Ephraim's hair thinned and grew greyer, lines of anxiety and sleeplessness carved themselves on his face. Mary, over-plump before, had become haggard, the flesh of her cheeks and throat sagging; she seemed years older. But the greatest changes were seen in the sisters. Dove was no less beautiful, but her face had sharpened a little and a new maturity had come to her look and manner, as though she had passed through some vale of experience. And Belle, herself again but very weak, was almost unrecognisable. The soft, round contours of girlhood were gone, the bloom that had been upon her skin had faded. At the base of her long neck deep hollows had formed. Her eyes no longer bright, were sunken, and the hair spread on the pillows had lost its moonlight lustre.

When she asked for a mirror, and Dove reluctantly gave her one, she handed it back after one glance. 'I look like a corpse. Don't let me see myself again, Dove.'

'You'll mend! You won't always look so, I promise! Aunt Margaret says that good nourishment will bring back all your colour. You're to have the best of everything — Mama and Aggie are preparing all sorts of delicate things for you downstairs.' But Dove's eyes were full of tears, and Belle reached for her hand.

'Don't cry, Dovekin — you, of all people! I'm not at all mopey, only thankful, thankful to be alive, and it's because of you and Bet that I am. Why should I care about my silly looks?'

'It was as much Aunt Margaret and Papa,' Dove murmured, drying her eyes, for Belle must not be upset. She was grieving partly for herself, she knew. It seemed to her now, though she had never thought of it before, that part of her lived in Belle, and that with the destruction of her sister's beauty her own suffered a kind of eclipse. Vanity, vanity, to feel so. But she prized her own face just because Joe was still in the world, though lost to her, and for him she was proud to be beautiful.

To put such thoughts out of her head she pretended to be very busy tidying up their bedroom (for Belle had come back to her own pretty bed and the pleasant view of the garden). Then she went briskly downstairs, where, in the kitchen, the most tempting delicacies were being prepared for the invalid. Chicken and duck broth, beef tea, strengthening jellies made from wine, eggs beaten up with cream and brandy: even a person protesting that she had no appetite must succumb to their charms, yet as often as not Belle sent away her tray hardly touched. Mary viewed the returned dishes with despair.

'What are we to do, if she won't eat?' she asked Margaret. 'She can't be forced. But the doctor says she must take nourishment.'

'How gratifying to know he has *some* opinions on the case,' said Margaret dryly. 'He was little enough use when Belle lay at death's door. I have an idea, however, which is this. When you were very low after the shock, I often sat reading to you as well as talking, and it seemed to divert your mind. Now, if I were to send for some amusing books, and read to Belle at mealtimes, might it not calm her nerves (for I'm sure she mopes, whatever she may tell Dove) and stimulate the appetite? They practise this in monasteries, though of course from religious works, and it's said to have a most salutary effect.'

'Trust you to know what goes on in monasteries!' Mary retorted. 'But at least we can try it, and you're so often right.'

Margaret was right again. Her lively readings from the most comical parts of *Tom Jones, Joseph Andrews, Roderick Random,* and other novels which would certainly not have been read aloud in monasteries, made Belle laugh in spite of herself. Margaret's acting ability may not have been remarkable in her youth, but her stage experience paid off now. Dove and Mary took to sharing the sessions, cunningly eating their own meals from trays, so that from sheer social habit Belle began to eat hers. Gradually, by slow degrees, she began to look less skeletal and to recover her spirits.

Visitors came: girl friends, neighbours, the vicar and his family, all with flowers, or presents. And one day Will Raven called, presenting himself bashfully enough in that extremely feminine bedroom where he felt like a bull in a china shop.

His first sight of Belle shocked him out of the light pleasantry he had carefully worked out on the way upstairs. He had known her as an enchantingly pretty little girl, as a lovely young woman — and now this.

'Eh, dear,' he said before he could stop himself, and Dove, sitting with her embroidery in the role of chaperone, shot him a glance of reproach. But Belle smiled and held out a fragile hand, all bones.

'Never mind, Uncle Will. Eh, dear, indeed. But I'm not as bad as I look, I promise you.'

'You'd better not be, lass. How are you feeling, in yourself, though?'

'Oh, so much better I can't believe it. They've all been so good to me and even made me eat when I thought I couldn't. I'm getting fat already — look at this.' She showed her thin forearm, half-veiled in the lace of her bed-robe. 'You should have seen me before.' Then, suddenly, she said, 'It's so good of you to visit me — and so good to have you here. I've had a lot of callers, haven't I, Dove? but I don't know any I was more glad to see than you.'

He was still holding the small hand, studying her face. When he had first come into the room he had felt uncomfortably large, clumsy, and out of place, and his first gaffe — showing Belle how shocked he was by her appearance — had put him out even further. But now, perched on an elegant chair far too small for him, he was more at ease, even happy, glad he had nerved himself to call.

The three of them chatted, Belle becoming more and more animated, until Dove began to wonder if visitors were altogether advisable. Will talked about the shop, about affairs in Kendal and his recent buying trips, finding a loquacity usually foreign to him. He realised that he was doing Belle good and was glad of it. Sometimes it felt to him as though he had done nothing but unintentional mischief to people all his life, and here was someone he could at least help a little, even if it was only by rambling on in his own way. It seemed to please her, though she must have heard better talk.

Dove had been longing to ask him something, yet afraid, in case she gave herself away. At last she got it out, looking down at her sewing. 'Have you seen Joe lately?'

'Aye. Two or three weeks since.'

'Was he … how did he … did you visit him?'

'I did,' Will said heavily, 'and I'm sorry to say I didn't like what I saw. I'll not trouble you two wi' it, but it sent me away saddened, I can tell you. I knew how things would be, when he took yon wench to wife.'

'And how are they?' Dove negotiated the re-threading of her needle, turning her face away towards the light from the window, for she felt the colour burning in her cheeks.

'Bad. She's given up work — too fancy for that now. It's all fine frocks and feathers in her bonnet, and spending Joe's brass on all manner o' rubbish. He's not that much to spare, I know for a fact, but a lot she cares for that, if she even knows it, for I doubt she's a whole brain in her daft head. A lad like Joe needs a proper woman, a lass to feed and care for him like he should be fed and cared for. I told him how it would be, but he'd not listen…' Will realised that he was saying too much; in a minute he'd be letting out the tale of the theft. And this was no kind of talk for a sickroom. To Dove's disappointment, he changed the conversation.

Mary came in and greeted him warmly. 'Won't you stay till Ephraim comes home, Will? It would do him a world of good to see you and hear some man's talk after living with a gaggle of women — and he'll be home early, I know.'

Will looked wistful; he wanted to stay. 'I'll be tiring Belle if I bide much longer.'

'You come downstairs with me and I'll see you get a good tea while she rests. Draw the curtains, Dove — it's time she had a little sleep.'

Ephraim was more than glad to find Will at home. They talked over a pipe and a decanter of wine, and Will, warned by his rashness upstairs, said nothing of Joe. His friend had had enough troubles lately without loading him with more.

Before he left he visited Belle again, seeing with pleasure how her eyes brightened at his entrance. Shyly and nervously, he took something from his pocket, a small package clumsily wrapped.

'For you. I thought as something pretty might do you good…'

'What *can* it be?' She was busy unwrapping it. From the coil of paper emerged a dainty, delicate ring, small enough for a fairy's finger, he had thought when he first saw it. Tiny diamonds, pearls and garnets twinkled in a simple chased setting.

Belle gave a cry of delight. '*Pretty?* It's quite beautiful. I never saw such a charming ring.' She slipped it on. It fitted her finger only a little loosely. 'When I'm plumper it will be the exact fit. How did you guess?'

Will did not know how he had guessed. He smiled sheepishly. 'I know you well enough,' he said.

Impulsively she reached up to kiss him. As her lips touched his cheek both suddenly shared the feeling that had come to them on his last visit, months before; a sort of belonging, a recognition of each other that was as though each had discovered a person familiar, yet quite new, and very important.

She sank back on the pillow, and their eyes met in a long look. Neither spoke, until Will said, 'Goodbye. It's been grand seeing you better.'

When he had gone she looked at the ring on her finger again and again, and put it to her lips.

Will was not, in fact, her uncle. He was no blood relation to her. As the thought sank into her mind, her heart lifted.

CHAPTER THIRTEEN

Christmas dawned wet and wild that year. At Bradshaw Hall trees lashed with bare branches the windows of the room where Saul Bradshaw sat slumped by the smoky fire, a decanter of port at his elbow. Now and then the wind brought fitful snatches of church bells calling to service, but he took no heed of them, or of the entrance of Shem.

'You don't want to be taking that stuff at this time of day,' said his son, nodding towards the decanter. 'You'd enough last night to sink a ship.'

'I'll drink what I like when I like. Sit down. I've summat to say to you.'

Shem obediently sat. 'Well?'

'I'm buying Whittingham out.'

'You're *what*?'

'You heard. I'm taking his mill over, lock, stock and barrel.'

Shem stared. 'What the heck do you want it for? Isn't ours enough for you?'

'I've a fancy for it. I've a mind to be the biggest fish in t'pond. And don't you go telling me I'm past taking on new responsibilities, for I'm not. My mother lived to be ninety-eight and I'll do t'same, mark my words.'

Shem was thinking. 'That's not all, is it. You want more than that mill. You want to get hold of young Atkinson. Come on, admit it; that's your real intentions.'

The old man looked cunning. 'It may be, or it may not be. Never you mind. You tend to your own business, which is figures, and I'll want some out of you tomorrow, when you've talked to Whittingham's accountants.'

'Tomorrow's Boxing Day.'

'Damn it, I'd forgotten. Blasted holidays! Too many of 'em, if you ask me. Well then, day after that.'

'How do you know Whittingham's going to agree?'

'I know owd Walter. He'll agree, if there's money in it, and there's plenty.'

Shem sighed. He knew that his workload was going to be doubled, and he foresaw all kinds of complications ahead. But when his father made up his mind there was no shifting him.

It was the strangest Christmas Joe had ever spent. Always he had been with his family, even on the last three Christmases, when an unease still lingered between them and him. Now there was only himself and Rosie.

The familiar savoury scents of Christmas dinner cooking were absent, for roasting was not possible on the small kitchen hob, and Rosie had taken the beef down to the bakery. She had not made a pudding; it was too bothersome, she said, they could make do with bread and jam.

Joe had mildly suggested that now she no longer worked in the mill she might devote some time to learning the art of cookery. He was getting very tired of the hash of cheap meat and potatoes which was Rosie's standard dish; he even missed old Mrs Darwen's cooking, and she had kept his room cleaner than Rosie kept the cottage. But he refused to blame her, brought up in poverty as she had been. For the same reason he tried not to complain about her extravagance. Since they had been married she had spent money right and left, buying herself clothes and finery, though Joe's shirts went unmended and his linen became so grey with bad washing that he had asked her to take it to the washerwoman.

A fine lady, a manager's wife: that was how Rosie saw herself. The airs she put on had already offended their neighbours, with the result that when she felt inclined for a good gossip it was not to be had from those downright, sharp-tongued women. She missed the badinage and horseplay of her companions at the mill; she was lonely. Joe knew it and was sorry for her. That was another excuse for her preoccupation with dress. If only she had tried to improve her mind and her speech as well as her appearance, but her promises to learn had never come to anything. When he gently corrected her speech or manners, she snapped at him that she'd been good enough to marry, hadn't she, and she'd talk as she pleased.

And yet he was still in love with her, hopelessly enslaved by her physical allurement. She had opened a new door to him, leading to a world of wonder and excitement. A look or a touch from her set his pulses racing; careless, vain, a bad housewife, sometimes coarse in her ways, she yet charmed his senses.

Restless and tired of his thoughts, Joe wandered to the window and looked out at the ceaseless rain. There was no sign of life; everybody was indoors, keeping Christmas at home. He wished it were dinner time.

Two figures turned the corner of the street, coming towards him: a woman with a shawl over her head and a boy who limped. Joe's heart sank. He knew them all too well.

Swearing under his breath, a thing unusual for him, he called upstairs. 'Rosie!'

'What?' She appeared at the stair-head, half dressed, sluttish and beguiling. But Joe was not, for once, in the mood to be beguiled.

'Your mother and Billy are coming up the street. Are you expecting them?'

'I asked 'em, didn't I? 'Course I'm expectin' 'em.'

'I think I might have been told. It *is* our first Christmas together, after all. I'd have preferred us to spend it alone.'

She tossed her head. 'Well, I wouldn't. I can do wi' a bit o' company, the life I lead i' this place. Besides, I couldn't leave our Mam and Billy on their own, could I now? An' I didn't let on to you 'cause I knew you'd pull a face.'

Already they were knocking at the door. Joe could not bring himself to smile as he opened it to them. He knew it was his duty to love Rosie's relations, but, try as he did, he could not even like them. Indeed, he disliked them very much. Their presence was as detestable to him as Rosie's was enchanting. In spite of the money and presents Rosie heaped on them, they remained dirty and malodorous, and their habits were revolting to the fastidious Joe. It outraged him to see his mother-in-law spit on the floor, or Billy blow his nose on his sleeve. To speak about such things only turned mother and daughter against him, though Rosie herself, to do her justice, would sometimes object.

'Come in,' Joe said. He would much rather have said, *Go away.*

'Turned up again like a bad penny,' Mrs Giles observed, cordially for her. Removing her sodden shawl and draping it over a chair by the fire, where it steamed rankly, she looked sharply round the room and especially at the unlaid table. 'Well? Aren't us to get a drop o' drink for Christmas?'

Joe was aware that she had had a drop already. Since Rosie's promotion in life Mrs Giles had taken to visiting the gin shop. 'I'm sorry,' he said politely. 'There is none in the house, except for some wine we were intending to drink at dinner. Rosie and I,' he added pointedly.

Mrs Giles cackled. 'Wine? What sort o' fancy stuff's that? Well, if there's nowt better it'll ha' to do.'

In silence Joe went to the corner cupboard and brought out the small bottle. He was careful not to keep any quantity of drink in the house, fearing that Rosie, alone all day, might get a taste for it; he had not forgotten her behaviour at the wedding. He poured a glass for Mrs Giles, who pushed Billy forward. 'Little lad'll tak' a sup, too.'

Billy choked and spluttered at the taste, and promptly spat out the mouthful he had taken. Mrs Giles drank her glassful almost in one draught, and placed the glass suggestively near the bottle. Rosie came down, gorgeous in red, embraced her relatives and exclaimed joyfully at the sight of the wine. Joe poured some for her. They were going to have none left to celebrate their first Christmas. He was thankful when it was time to go to the bakery for their dinner, relieved to be out of the house. A vista opened up before him of years filled with visits from the Giles family; worse, of Rosie insisting that they move in under the same roof.

Walking through the rain, wishing he might stay out in it, he thought of Ephraim's kind letter, inviting him to spend Christmas with them as usual and to bring his wife *if you feel it would give her pleasure, though I must warn you, my dear boy, that your aunt has not yet become wholly reconciled to your marriage, for reasons you will no doubt understand. Time will unquestionably modify her attitude.* In other words, he was being gently warned off. Ephraim went on to add that Belle was not entirely strong yet, though very cheerful in her spirits. Joe took the diplomatic hint to write refusing the invitation, because of his cousin's delicacy. He longed to have been able to accept it, to have been at St

Leonard's Gate with a Rosie magically transformed into a being with her own looks and allure but with ladylike manners and language. He longed, most of all, not to be going back into his mother-in-law's company.

It was a relief to return to the mill after Christmas and take up his work. At the end of the day a message came requesting his presence in Whittingham's office.

'Joe. Come in, lad. I wanted a few words...'

Joe sat down and waited. Circumlocution was a speciality with his partner, but for once he came straight to the point.

'I'm selling out, Joe. To Saul Bradshaw. Aye, you may look surprised, but I'm getting an old man and I want a bit of peace in my last years. Saul's made me a handsome offer and I've closed with it, but for the paper-signing. I've a sister at Barrow I could go and live with. No sense in keeping on when you can get out easy, is there?' Relieved to have broken the news, he sat back.

Joe sat in stunned silence. Whittingham's words had not only been a shock in themselves; they brought with them a premonition of trouble, as though a black, suffocating cloud had suddenly filled the office. At last he managed to speak.

'What will become of me?'

'Oh, you'll stay on, o' course. You're bound to, by the agreement. It's more than a year to run yet.'

'I'd rather not work for Mr Bradshaw,' Joe said. 'By my uncle's account he's got a grudge against all our family. I'd not be happy with him, nor he with me.'

Whittingham raised his eyebrows. 'Well, that's rum! He asked particularly how you were fixed, and said I was to keep you on at all costs. I didn't know you knew each other.'

'I've barely exchanged a word with him, and I doubt if he knows me by sight. There seems no rhyme nor reason in his asking that I should stay on — unless he's had some kind of change of heart, being an old man.'

'Aye, it's possible. You're content to stay, then?'

'No!' Joe's eyes met the rheumy eyes of Whittingham squarely. 'I prefer to work for employers I know to be friendly toward me. And as far as concluding our agreement goes, that should be easy enough, my agreement being with you, not with him.'

Whittingham's gaze shifted. 'Well, it's not as simple as that, Joe. Seeing he's so set on keeping you, I'd not like to disoblige him.'

'Meaning...?'

'When your uncle and you and me drew up that contract, it was laid down that you couldn't break it prematurely before the five-year period was ended. Now nobody can stop you breaking it — only, if you do, you'll forfeit two hundred pounds. You remember, your thousand was calculated to cover the five years, and eight hundred's been written off by now. So, if you choose to leave, the balance of the money stays in the firm.'

Joe pondered, staring out of the window at the lines of shabby slate-roofed houses beyond the river. He knew instinctively that there was something twisted and sinister about this arrangement. He was, in effect, being blackmailed for some purpose he could not guess. If he were to go by instinct and leave, would he be taken on readily by another mill owner? He knew himself better now than when he had signed on with Whittingham. In temperament he was too soft for the life of the factory. The failure of his stolen invention had shown him that he was technically inept, however grand his conceptions. The only real satisfaction that had come to him from his years with Whittingham was the achievement of the room for rest and refreshment, and the establishment of the school; and the practical details of those had come from Aunt Margaret.

He realised that he would be glad to be quit of the cotton industry. It had not so much failed him as he had failed it, and himself. Yet there was nowhere else to turn. His capital was gone, all but the two hundred pounds. He had no training for anything beyond two years' study of the law; how could he ask his uncle to pay for his return to university?

And there was Rosie. The extravagance of her tastes had once or twice brought him to the edge of debt. How could they exist if he were workless and penniless? Wryly he thought that it would at least keep Mrs Giles and Billy from his door, but that would be the only consolation in a barren prospect. And Rosie would be angry.

For a moment he thought of appealing to Ephraim for help. None of his own studies had covered anything like this situation, but Ephraim would know all about it and perhaps be able to extract him from this pit of his own digging. No; it would be too lowering to his pride to turn to the man who had warned him. There was nothing for it but to accept Whittingham's shady terms and to work his way through a year of Bradshaw's rule, little as he liked the thought. A man who could do the iniquitous thing Saul Bradshaw had done in stealing his machine would do anything. A cold premonition weighed on Joe's heart as he said to Whittingham: 'I've not much choice, sir. I'll stay.'

'Good lad!' Whittingham was immensely relieved. It had been a gamble, even with this unworldly boy, and he had not been looking forward to reporting failure to Saul Bradshaw.

It was spring in Lancaster. The wet weary winter was forgotten, young green leaves jewelled the trees round the castle, lambs played in the meadows by the Lune. At St Leonard's Gate a great spring-cleaning was in progress, making Ephraim thankful that he had an office to escape to from a house with curtains taken down, carpets being beaten on a line in the garden, an aggressive smell of washing in the air, and his study almost useless to him. He was, on the whole, reasonably happy, because his family seemed so. Belle had lost the dreadful thinness left by her illness. She had put on weight, the lustre was back in her hair; only the soft bloom of girlhood had gone, and the contours of her face were changed, refined into something that seemed maturity, but was not. For the first time in their lives she and Dove were completely distinguishable from each other, Dove seeming much the younger.

Ephraim was glad that they were seeing so much more of Will Raven these days. It did the poor fellow good to get away from his musty shop and the knowledge that his mad wife lived out her existence only a mile away. His conversation interested Ephraim, broadened as it now was by Will's interest in acquiring objects for what he still referred to facetiously as his knick-knackery, but which Ephraim guessed to have become something of a life-saver to him.

If not that, something else had. Even to the unobservant eye of another man, Will had altered in the last months. Ephraim could not have said exactly what it was, but it certainly improved him. He asked Mary, who always knew about such things.

'Well, there's no doubt of it. He's lost pounds in weight, and that shamble he used to have, like a great bear. And then he dresses better, and shaves cleaner … I declare, Father, it's taken ten years off him, looking after himself properly. He was a handsome enough lad in the days when Jane set her cap at him; I thought he'd let himself go too far.'

'You've a sharp eye, Mother. And to what do you attribute this transformation? It must surely be the interest of conducting his own business.'

Mary laughed. 'What funny creatures you men are, to be sure! As if any business ever invented could change him so. No, you take my word for it, there's a woman in the case, as you'd say in your jargon.'

'I doubt it,' Ephraim replied primly. 'That is, I doubt that I would put it in exactly that fashion. As to your premise, it is probably quite correct. However, poor Will's diversion can be only temporary, tied as he is to that unfortunate woman.'

'That wretched serpent!' Mary burst out. 'I wish nobody had ever seen her in our family. First poor John, now Will, married to a fiend. Why can't the law do something about such cases, Father? It's wrong and unnatural that a man should be tied for life to a madwoman — or the other way round, if it comes to that. Why can't he be set free before she dies — which may be donkey's years?'

'Divorce *a vinculo matrimonii* is not possible in such cases. One day I hope it will be. Changes are coming that we custom-shackled lawyers will never see.' He thought of the old King William, ruling over a kingdom without a male heir; the crown hovering above the head of a young girl. Princess Alexandrina Victoria, scarcely out of her nursery at Kensington Palace. 'Meanwhile, the lady who has cheered our Will up so much must accept that under the law illicit love must be their portion.

Mary looked downcast. 'I don't like to think of Will in that way. He's one who needs a domestic hearth and a wife to come home to, not a fancy piece.'

'My love, we have no evidence that Will's lady — if she exists — is a fancy piece. He has made two matrimonial mistakes, certainly — but a third?' He shook his head. 'A man of his age must surely have more sense. Without wishing to condone licence, we must be glad that he has found some consolation in his loneliness.'

It did not occur to either of them to wonder why, in that case, Will was spending so much more time at their home.

Only Belle, with her new, secret smile and faraway look, knew the truth. It had begun even before the day when Will had visited her and given her the little ring. The time came when she was up and about again, able to sit well wrapped in shawls in the new conservatory of which Ephraim was so proud, and there Will found her.

There was no need of words. A few moments' verbal fencing, and they were in each other's arms.

'I never knew it was you,' she said. 'That is, I think I knew all the time, but I hadn't the sense to realise.'

He stroked her hair. 'I thought of you as a little lass, till one day I looked at you properly. Since then I've had you in my mind night and day.'

'I wanted someone to love, so much,' she admitted. 'I used to flirt dreadfully. Once I even went further, though I've been ashamed to tell anyone about it, and I got myself into such trouble, and Dove and Joe as well.' She told him frankly of the young officer, Gilbert, their clandestine meetings and her fears. 'It was all nonsense. I knew nothing about men or the world. But it frightened me so much I've hardly dared even to flirt, since. Until now.'

He looked down at her small white hand, in his large brown one, the ring he had given her glinting on the second finger.

'But it won't do, love. We must face up to it. I'm middle-aged and you're — what is it? Twenty?'

'Twenty-one — twenty-two this year,' she said quickly.

'Well, then. That's a lot of years between us.'

'It doesn't seem so. No difference at all.'

'Nor to me. Nor to me. But it's not just that, Belle. There's Jane between us as well.'

She turned her head away. 'I know. How could I forget? I try not to wish … bad things. I *don't* wish them. Only … it seems so sad and wrong, your being tied to her.'

Will let go her hand, sighing. 'There's so much sad and wrong, my lass. Even if I were free, how do you think your dad and mam would feel about us getting wed, when I've always been called Uncle to you and Dove and Joe? And I'm not free. Jane could outlast me: aye, and you, with bad luck. She's older nor me, and mad, but she's no bodily illness, and plenty o' food and a quiet life … so far as her life can be quiet. I wouldn't count on anything there, if I were you.'

'Then what are we to do?'

'Oh, Belle, little Belle. What can we do but forget all about it?'

'*I* don't intend to forget all about it,' Belle said mutinously. 'I love you, Will, and this time it's not a silly hoydenish flirting behind a fan with a spotty boy. I'll never love anybody else but you, I'm sure of that.'

He took both her hands now and held them firmly, searching her eyes. 'Don't spoil your youth for me. Belle. A lass as bonny as you has a lifetime before her, but half my lifetime's gone. Let's be content to have found what we have, and let it be at that.'

'Very well,' said the minx who looked as ethereal and calm as the lilies growing in a pot beside her. 'But as nobody seems to be coming to bother us, you might like to kiss me — that is, if you've nothing better to do.'

Dove knew. But because her twin chose to say nothing, she kept quiet, only wondering how it would all end. The disgraceful affair of Gilbert was old history now. Would Belle be rash enough to repeat it, and with a man old enough to be her father? Well, this time there would be no Joe to blame. Ephraim had told them of the selling-up of Whittingham's mill, and of Joe's new employment by Saul Bradshaw, but only to Mary had he mentioned his grave fears about the arrangement. Out of touch with Bradshaw, knowing nothing of his theft from Joe, he yet had no faith in this particular leopard having changed its spots. Joe seldom wrote, and very briefly when he did; since that unlucky marriage they had not seen him in Lancaster. Sometimes, overcome by her weary longing to see him, Dove thought of wild excuses for visiting Bradhope, or getting her mother to summon him to them. At least she would be able to see him and hear his voice. But she never plucked up the courage, and it was better so.

What a pair we are, she thought. *Both in love with married men, and mine doesn't even care for me. At least Belle is loved again, judging by her looks. But for me what hope is there, what future?*

George: people were always talking about him, asking about him. He had been away six months. Very occasionally she would get a dashed-off, dog-eared letter that had been through many hands, containing a highly selective account of life and scenery at his ports of call: the bright-coloured birds, the women in their flounced skirts and elaborate turbans; all the things he thought a young lady would like to hear about, if he had only had the skill to describe them vividly. Always these letters would end *Your affte. and obed., George Dilworth.* They were far from lover-like, but it was agreeable that George wrote them at all, and they deserved the stilted little letters she wrote in return, on such fascinating subjects as a series of local robberies, the flower show at which her mother had won a prize, and the report of increased tonnage at Glasson Dock.

When an invitation came from Margaret for the girls to accompany her on a visit to London in order to visit publishers and the great libraries, Belle refused on the plea of not being strong enough yet to face the excitement. But Dove accepted eagerly, as a princess imprisoned in a high tower would have welcomed the chance of escape, even though the prince would not be there.

CHAPTER FOURTEEN

London!

Before she saw it, Dove had thought Lancaster a fine town. Now it seemed a grim, grey, drab place compared with this wonderful city of fine modern houses, of elegant terraces and vistas created by the great Nash, of new pink bricks and painted stucco, its wide streets filled with 'fashionables' in silks, feathers and jewels, riding in highly polished carriages emblazoned with coats-of-arms and drawn by equally polished horses, sometimes attended by gold-laced footmen. Nobody in Lancaster ever looked or rode like that. The grandest sight Dove had ever seen in Lancaster was the procession of judges from their historic lodgings to the castle for the Assizes, in their robes and wigs. Their memory faded and vanished altogether behind this splendour.

Margaret viewed her niece's excitement with kindly amusement. At any rate, the child now looked cheerful. Even the coach journey up, long and tedious to Margaret, who felt she could hardly wait for the day when the new railways joined north and south with their speedy if dirty carriages, was like the unwinding of a fairy tale to Dove. Each halt took her further and further away from familiar scenes, showed her a new sort of country and people, drew from her rapt silence or excited squeaks, to the entertainment of the other passengers in the stuffy, rocking coach. Arrived in the capital itself, she was dumb with awe at its size and population.

Their lodgings were in Manchester Square, just north of the Oxford Road, close to Hertford House: very stately and respectable surroundings indeed. Margaret always lodged there when in London, with the convenience of a resident housekeeper and servants. Her own maid, Jane Bryan, had travelled with her. Dove would like to have bought Bet, as a reward for the great service her nursing had done for Belle, but Mary thought the girl was not yet ready for such an experience. And so Dove sat before the dressing table in her elegant bedroom, having her hair dressed into fashionable loops and whorls by Bryan, while her aunt surveyed her from an upright chair. Dove thought her aunt looked much more easy and at home here than she had done in Lancaster.

Margaret, watching the country mouse being groomed for a town appearance, reflected what a pity it was that Mary had always been such a stay-at-home, not taking her daughters about. Perhaps it made for contentment, and perhaps not: but certainly it failed to develop the mind. What a pity, too, that Dove and Belle, unlike so many provincial young ladies, had no suitable relation in London to play chaperon to them in the Season, smooth the edges off them and introduce them to Society. When one had suffered from being gauche oneself it was sad to see others having it imposed on them. She thought she had found a solution; it remained to see whether she had.

Dove turned on her a glowing face and shining braided hair. 'Look at me, Aunt! Hasn't Miss Bryan changed me, and isn't she clever?'

'Very clever. Thank you, Bryan. We will take our tea up here, if you'll kindly advise Lucas.' The tall, quiet maid sketched a curtsey and left.

'We are going to a small assembly tonight,' Margaret said, 'where you will be presented to a few people I have known for some time. There will be a few young ones among them, I hope, so you won't lack for amusing company. Shall you like that?'

Dove hesitated. 'I think so ... it's been very dull at home. But I'm so afraid I shall seem awkward and not know what to say or do.'

'Nonsense! A well-reared young woman like you should be at no disadvantage even if Queen Adelaide were to invite you — which is unlikely, so pray don't look so startled. Walk into the room with your head up and a smile on your face, as though you were the guest they were all eagerly awaiting. Smile before you speak. Remember that everyone there is in his or her way as anxious to make an impression as you. Keep your eyes wide and your ears open, and listen before talking.'

Dove, though trembling a little, did her best to carry out these instructions, with the result that the soirée in Portland Place was a painless, even pleasant, introduction to London life.

'What a charming, modest gel,' said another lady of letters to Margaret, surveying the pink-faced Dove eating a lemon ice, while a dazed-looking young man bent over her. 'She don't look in the least like you, though. How on earth did they breed her in those wilds you inhabit?'

'Even the wilds produce occasional flowers,' Margaret replied, and drifted across the room to listen inconspicuously in case the conversation needed terminating. But it was a perfectly innocent affair of stammered beginnings on the youth's part and limpid looks from Dove, who was enjoying the ice and rather wished he would fetch her another instead of going on about a horse his mother owned. Margaret smiled and drifted away again.

She let another day or two pass before writing her letter. Then she wrote it, with extreme care, and sent it off by messenger.

The reply came within a few hours, in a handwriting that showed excitement and emotion, slanting across the paper and blotted in places.

My Dearest Sister,

I hasten to answer yours. How could you think I might be displeased to have it? Tho' I admit it came as a great shock to me and at first I trembled very much. If I scold you at all my dear, it must be for your unkindly long silence. You and I were always close in the family. I could never have felt towards you as I know Mary feels to me, I have no unforgiving thoughts at all even towards her. What you say is very right, that Pride has been the enemy of all of our generation, keeping us apart when a frank word and admission that we have perhaps been Wrong would have saved all these years spent so foolishly apart.

I cannot write much more at present for the strength of my feelings, but I do implore you to visit me with our Niece as soon as possible. I have told Jesse the news and he is all impatience to see you. Pray do hasten.

Your loving Sister, Eleanor.

Their meeting was tearful on Eleanor's part, controlled though happy on Margaret's, for she had no intention of giving way to her feelings this time, after her untypical display of emotion at her reunion with Ephraim. Eleanor's colour was high, she chattered and laughed and alternately skipped away to look at her sister and skipped back to embrace her.

'My stars, how you've changed! You were always such a little dowd — that is to say such a tall one — and now you're so *elegante,* so *soignée,* yet the same, somehow … it's your eyes, I think. Now tell me, have I changed?'

'Only to grow more mature,' Margaret said tactfully. 'Besides, I have seen you not too long ago, though you did not see me.'

'What? Where? Oh, how cruel, not to make yourself known!'

'You were in company. I thought it not quite the moment.'

'As if I should have minded. What company?'

'A gentleman, I think — yes, a dark, foreign-looking young man.'

Eleanor's lips tightened, but she gave a brittle laugh. 'Oh, Ben Disraeli. Yes, he escorted me once, when Jesse was too much engaged at the House. At least, I think it would be he — one meets so many gentlemen. But never mind that. Where is our little niece all this time?'

'Walking in the park with my maid. I told them to keep close to the road so that one of your people could find them easily.'

Eleanor dispatched a page-boy to do the errand, and the two sisters subsided on the seat by the window where Eleanor had spent so many lonely hours. As they talked, barely stopping for breath, Margaret felt herself slipping back into her girlhood, losing the weight of years and the new personality she had built for herself. There was so much to say, so many tales to recount. They had barely begun when Dove was shown in.

Eleanor ran to her, arms outstretched. 'My dear!'

Dove had been prepared for the meeting, but she was taken aback by the elegance and beauty of this new relative. Somehow she had expected a lady whose looks were a cross between her mother's and Aunt Margaret's. Instead she found a Londoner of Londoners; Dove felt a little shy, remembering stories of the scapegrace girl who had left her husband and run away.

But Eleanor was so happy to see her, so astonished at the baby she remembered transformed into this lovely young creature and chattered away so naturally, that Dove soon lost her shyness. Then Jesse came in, and Dove liked him at sight, as he did her. At supper she looked from one to another, full of happiness in her new family.

Eleanor noticed her ring. 'And you're to be married! Who is the fortunate bridegroom?'

Dove looked less embarrassed than disconcerted. She had not expected to have to talk about George. 'Oh, he's First Mate on a merchantman, in the West Indies just now.'

'How exceedingly romantic. Do I know him? I mean his family, that is?'

'Probably, Aunt — he's a Dilworth.'

'Dilworth! Of course. Your godmother was a Dilworth, and Ephraim's friend Thomas … there were hordes of them.' She plied Dove with questions, getting only perfunctory answers, and at last gave up, deciding that the child was too shy to chatter about her betrothed. 'Well, well. We must see how we can entertain you to pass the time in George's absence.'

Dove would never forget those three months of London days and nights. There were breakfast parties in charming villas by the river, excursions to Richmond, Kew, and Windsor, where Dove saw the King and Queen bowing from their carriage, and thought how red-faced and pop-eyed the old King looked, and how sad and sweet the Queen. Firework displays irradiated the evenings; scientific lectures sobered them. At musical parties Dove sat entranced by the playing of professional musicians. She had hardly heard any music beyond her own performance with Belle of 'The Battle of Prague' on the pianoforte; at the Haymarket Theatre she heard and saw opera for the first time, Verdi's *Otello,* with Mademoiselle Grisi in the role of Desdemona, classically beautiful of face and astonishingly piercing of voice. On another evening Grisi sang in a new opera by the popular young composer Rossini, and afterwards came another wonder, the ballet. Dove could hardly believe that Mademoiselle Taglioni was not in truth the fairy creature she represented in *La Sylphide,* flitting several feet up in the air (it seemed) around the sleeping Scotsman James. Then came other celestial beings, Fanny Elssler and her sister, and Monsieur Theodore, dancing the *Pas de Trois,* the ladies seraphic in muslin tutus hardly whiter than their powdered arms and swan necks, their neat shining hair crowned with roses.

One thing distracted Dove's attention from the stage. In the royal box sat the King's niece, Princess Alexandria Victoria. Eleanor whispered that the people with her were her mother, a somewhat swarthy, heavily made lady, her brother-in-law Charles, Prince of Leiningen, and two gentlemen attendants.

'She will be queen one day,' Eleanor added. 'Take a good look at your future monarch.'

Dove found it hard to believe that such a tiny creature could grow into a queen. No taller than a ten-year-old child, though she was fifteen, the Princess was like a charming doll, except that her animation was anything but doll-like. She stared raptly at the performers, clapped spontaneously, flashed her bright toothy smile from one to another of her companions, and called *'Brava!'* at the end, in a high clear voice. Self-possession radiated from her, and an air of being 'someone'. Curiously, Dove found that it was the Princess's image which remained in her mind when the floating forms of the dancers had flown out of it.

The time was coming for her to go home. They had been in London almost three months, Margaret's business with the publishers and libraries was done. Eleanor conferred with her.

'I never saw anyone enjoy themselves more than that child has done. It made me feel even more…' But she could not talk to Margaret about the children she would never bear now. 'Yet so unspoilt and fresh, even with the men making such a furore over her. Young Dartington offered for her hand — did Jesse tell you? And Clara Montford's boy said he wished her fiancé no harm, only that his ship would founder with all hands. Yet she took it all very coolly, far more than we would have done at her age. Is she *so* devoted to her George? I can hardly get a word out of her on the subject.'

'I doubt,' said Margaret carefully, for it did not do to put ideas into Eleanor's busy head, 'that she is deeply devoted to him at all. The match seems to me to have been largely an arranged one, which is quite right and proper, of course, if the young people can like each other enough. But Dove has a warm heart and talks a great deal about those she loves. I fear George is not among them.'

Eleanor sighed. 'What a pity. She was made for happiness … Margaret, do you think Mary will scold her — and you — when you get back, for being so much in my company and Jesse's? I do hope not.'

'I told Mary all about it in my first letter after we arrived. I said that Dove needed to see something of a wider world than Lancaster before she settles down, and I added that it was quite stupid of Mary to keep up this enmity to you, when you could be of such help to her daughters. Though I put it more tactfully, of course.'

'And no answer?'

'No answer at all, nor any mention in her letters to Dove.'

Eleanor sighed deeply. 'Oh, well. I suppose what I did takes a lot of forgiving. But it was so long ago I can hardly remember how it was myself. I only pray Dove will be luckier in marriage than I was.'

Jesse and Eleanor accompanied them to the inn from which the coach was to leave: Bryan, who was London-born, was to remain behind for a week's holiday with relations.

As they said farewell in the coach-yard Eleanor said wistfully, 'I wish I could come with you.' As the coach moved through the archway that led to the road Dove looked back to wave. Her aunt was standing at Jesse's side, a forlorn figure, clinging to his arm as though it were all she had in the world to lean upon.

'How strange. Aunt leads such a wonderful life. Why should she want to leave it?'

'A long story, my dear.' Margaret told her of the legacy of Eagle Hall, its woeful state, and Eleanor's longing to take possession of it. 'Your uncle Jesse is not in fact very rich. It would be quite beyond him to restore the place to a decent condition, and in any case his father keeps some sort of stranglehold upon him. It seems very unfair, but then life is unfair.'

'Do you know Mr Bradshaw? He sounds a terrible man.'

'I have never met him. I don't particularly wish to.'

Dove looked out of the window, intently contemplating a haycart which was trying to pass them and failing. 'You know,' she said, her face still turned away, 'that Joe works for him now?'

'Yes, your father told me.' Margaret knew that something important was about to be told her.

'He hardly ever writes,' Dove said in a rush. 'Father says he must be too busy, but *I* know it's something else. Mother told me all about Mr Bradshaw's behaviour to Uncle Jesse, and that he hates all of us. I can't believe Joe is happy working for him… Why do you suppose he stayed at the mill? There seems to me to be some mystery about it.'

'I truly have no idea, Dove. I have hardly seen Joe since he joined Bradshaw — indeed, since his marriage. Without being too unkind, his wife is hardly an inducement to his relatives to visit him.'

There was a pause before Dove asked, 'What is she like, Aunt? Father said very little about her to us.'

'Your father is an extremely charitable man. I would describe Joe's wife as coarse, in a word.'

Dove was silent. At the next stage three more inside passengers got in, filling the coach with their persons and conversation. The miles rolled past, Margaret making notes or dozing, for the jolting of the vehicle made writing difficult; Dove looked out of the window, glad to be quiet with her thoughts. She was sad to leave London, Eleanor and Jesse; the heaviness of anticlimax was upon her and the realisation that she was physically tired after so many hectic days and nights. Yet amidst the dullness there was an excitement in travelling northwards. For Joe was there; they would pass close by the mill. She would give all the brilliant memories of the past three months for just one sight of him.

At one of the musical parties a song had caught her fancy — simple enough, among so many elaborate operatic arias and sentimental outpourings:

If I had but two little wings
And were a little feathery bird,
To you I'd fly, my dear.
But thoughts like these are idle things,
And I stay here.
But in my sleep to you I fly;

I'm always with you in my sleep —
The world is all one's own.
But then one wakes, and where am I?
All, all alone.

Whether she woke or slept throughout the long journey, the lines haunted her, and so did Joe's face. Night came soon after they left London. The Midlands went past them in darkness; when dawn came they were beyond Leicester. Derby, Ashbourne, the beautiful Derbyshire dales, and the valley of the River Dove, her namesake. She was tired and stiff, glad when they stopped at Macclesfield, with its silk mills and castle-like church high on a hill, to take a hasty inn meal of cold meats and coffee. There was almost three-quarters of an hour to spare, and her young appetite was quick to be satisfied. Margaret steered her back to their places in the coach, and, sitting comfortably back, asked, 'And now, what have you to tell me?'

Dove was startled. 'Tell...? How did you know?'

'My stock-in-trade for years has been the study of romantic young ladies. Out with it, now.'

'I wondered ... if we might ... if I might...'

'Well?'

'Stay with you at Bradhope tonight.'

Margaret's eyes were twinkling bright behind the lorgnettes she raised, the better to outface poor Dove.

'And tomorrow?'

The reply was almost inaudible. 'See Joe.'

Margaret gazed interestedly towards Macclesfield's church tower, and recited in her soft, pleasant voice:

'Wenn ich ein Vöglein wär',
Und auch zwei Flüglein hätt',
Flög' ich zur dir!
Weil's aber nicht kann sein,
Bleib' ich allhier.'

Dove's eyes were round. 'What does that mean?'

'It's German, child. How neglected your education has been. And it means, roughly, *Would that I were a little bird, with two little wings, I would fly to you; but since I cannot, here I stay.'*

Dove went scarlet, then laughed. 'Aunt Margaret, I do believe you're a witch.'

'If only I were — the white variety, that is — I should indeed make my presence felt. If it comes to that, a short wielding of the black art might be uncommonly useful and satisfactory.'

'But that was the song! The one that has been going through my head. How did you know?'

Margaret polished her lorgnettes. 'I may be short-sighted, but not so much as not to see a church by daylight, as they say, or a young woman half-swooning at a song. There's no magic in it, my child. The song is charmingly translated by Samuel Coleridge, I was there when it was sung, and it fits your case very well. Isn't that so? Don't look so afraid. I have known for some time, but kept it to myself. I think we must stand up to this together, don't you? So, as the coach does not reach Lancaster until almost ten o'clock, we will leave it at Garstang and I shall send a message to your parents that you are overtired and staying with me for a night or two. How does that please you?'

Dove laid her brow against her aunt's shoulder. 'Very well. And … I do thank you so much. I never knew anyone like you.'

Margaret patted her shoulder. 'And never will, I dare say. Well, who knows what will come of it? Trouble, perhaps. But I am so tired of all this waiting and doing nothing in our family. For nineteen years the chessboard stayed untouched, the pieces stationary, glaring at one another. I was as much to blame as any of the other pawns; so, as I seem to be the only one to be able to do anything about it, I propose to take action. No, don't say anything, we can talk tonight.'

By the welcome fire, in the comfortable house in Knott Green, Dove poured out the story of her love for Joe, her grief and frustration. Margaret nodded slowly, then reached suddenly for the bell-rope. 'Time for a hot nightcap, and bed. You won't dream tonight, child.'

Dusk was touching the sky on the following evening when Margaret's own neat gig drew up in the street that ended in Joe's cottage. Briskly alighting, she looped the reins round a post, and lent Dove a hand to descend.

'Nothing to tremble for, except the cold.' She threw a blanket over the horse's back and, her hand on Dove's elbow, approached the door. A light burned in one downstairs window. Margaret's hearty bang on the knocker produced only silence. She repeated it. The door creaked open, to show a young woman in a colourful ruffled bedgown standing there, a rolling pin in her hand.

'Who is it?' asked Rosie. 'What d'you want?'

'It is Joseph's aunt, Mrs Atkinson,' Margaret replied pleasantly. 'His cousin and I felt it was time we paid you a social visit. May we come in?'

There was nothing Rosie could do but make room for them to pass her, though she looked sullen enough about it.

One candle lit the room, and the faint redness from a low fire. On a chair beside it a figure slumped, turning its head languidly towards them. Dove realised with a shock that it was Joe, and that she would scarcely have known him.

CHAPTER FIFTEEN

Even in the poor light it was obvious that he had lost much weight. The bones of his face stood out like an old man's, the deep-set eyes were sunk far back in their sockets. His clothes sagged on his body, as if they had been made for a bigger man. With a sinking heart Dove thought of Belle's wasted form at the worst of her illness.

His face brightened at their entrance, though. 'Aunt Margaret — and Dove,' he said. Dove was gladdened that he did not take her for Belle. He tried to rise, but broke into a prolonged fit of coughing and subsided into his chair.

'I'm afraid you're not well, Joe,' Margaret said. 'How long has he been like this, Mrs Atkinson?'

Rosie shrugged. 'Month or two — maybe a bit more. It's nowt, only t'mill cough. A lot of 'em gets it.'

Joe was able to speak. 'Rosie, find chairs, please. I'm very ... glad to see you both.' His voice was low and husky, and he seemed breathless. Dove saw a faint growth of stubble on his chin, once so fastidiously shaved, and a sort of greyness overlying his skin. There was a faint miasma in the room, formed of untouched dust, the smoke blown down the chimney in gusts, and the very strong perfume Rosie used. Dove began to feel nauseated, and Margaret wrinkled her nose distastefully.

'I'm ... not very well,' Joe gasped out, 'but the doctor says ... it's common. If I ... keep away from the mill ... a few days, it...' He was coughing again.

'You ought to be in bed,' Margaret said. 'Why is he downstairs, Mrs Atkinson?'

'It's warmer, that's why. There's no fireplace upstairs, an' doctor says he needs keepin' warm.' She read accusation of herself in their shocked faces, and was ready to do battle if these stuck-up females wanted it.

My God, my God, thought Margaret. She was not often frightened of anything, but a prickle of dread ran down her spine when she looked at Joe. She had seen the illness before — 'spinners' phthisis', as it was called — and she knew how it often ended. The lungs of workers exposed to cotton 'fly' over a long period became congested and inflamed, a cough set in, becoming worse and worse, the body wasted away.

'But how could you have contracted this, Joe?' she asked. 'Surely you don't spend enough time in the mill to be affected?'

He tried to answer, but she said, 'No, don't speak. You tell me, Mrs Atkinson.'

'Well, since Bradshaw bought out Whittingham Joe's been took off buyin' trips, Manchester an Liverpool an all that. Owd Saul said he'd to spend his time in t'mill, "supervisin'", he called it. One week in t'cardin' an' preparin' room, next in t'spinnin' rooms, next wi' t'dressers, next wi' t'machiners, then back to t'start again. That's how he got like this, not bein' used to it.'

'But,' Margaret said, 'surely Mr Whittingham installed a machine to extract the cotton flakes in the room where they were most likely to cause harm?'

'Took it out,' Joe whispered.

'Aye,' said Rosie, 'it cost him money to get it took out, but he did it, owd devil that he is, and now things is bad as ever. Two childer died last week, and there'll be others yet.'

'But *why*?' Margaret asked. 'Joe made it quite clear to Mr Whittingham, in my presence, that the machine was essential to the health of his workers. Surely that was explained to Mr Bradshaw? In any case he must know it for himself, as an experienced employer.'

'Didn't want to know,' shrugged Rosie. 'Said 'twere new-fangled an' he'd have none of it in his mill. He shut up t'rest room, too, because it were time-wastin' an' makin' the folk as used it soft. That's what he's like.'

Margaret was very angry, angrier than she had ever been in her life. The room for rest and refreshment had been her own idea and creation; she had been so proud of the good it had done. Now it was destroyed, the benefit reversed, and there was nothing she could do.

'I towd Joe, time and time again, he should stand up to owd Saul,' Rosie said, 'but you know what he's like, no fight in him. That's true, Joe, you know it is. He tried once, I'll give him that, but it got him nowhere.'

Joe shook his head weakly. He remembered all too well how he had gone to the old man's office in the hope of reasoning him out of the senseless removal of the extractor. The language Saul had used to him was such as Joe had never heard even among the roughest operatives. There was no way of answering or stopping the tide of invective; he stood like a schoolboy under the lash, he who had known nothing worse than the gentle, reasonable reproofs of Ephraim and the mild sarcasm of tutors at Oxford.

Except once. His mind went back to himself at eight years old, a room in Kendal, a half-mad woman who out of hatred for him had tried to murder his dog. It was pure, personal hatred that had attacked him now, pouring out of the scarlet-faced old man.

When Saul took a breath Joe managed to speak. 'I don't know what you have against me, sir. We have hardly met before to my knowledge. But whatever wrong you imagine I've done you, I beg you not to take it out of your workers.'

'Workers? Damn the workers, idle swine. Let 'em die if they choose, I can get more where they were spawned. Aye, and *you* die if you choose, young Atkinson! There'll be no tears shed for you i' my house, I can tell you.'

Joe said quietly, 'I cannot continue to work for you. Please accept my resignation.'

'Resign, that's it, resign!' Saul mocked. 'If you do, I'll sue you, and your precious uncle won't be able to get you out of it.'

Joe turned and left the office. He was still shaking when he got back to his own, so that his clerk looked up questioningly. For a time he sat with his head in his hands, thinking, trying to recover. Then, telling himself that his best plan was to try to cool down the situation, he wrote a painstaking memorandum to Saul, in which he said that as a result of their conversation he felt compelled to terminate his service with Bradshaw's, but in fairness he proposed to work out the month.

The weeks that followed were weeks of tedium, petty humiliation and mental misery. Saul sent the overseer Swainson over from the other mill with particular orders to see that Joe spent every minute of his time in one or other of the departments, in the same conditions as the hands who looked on him with pity but dared not speak up. Either Joe was in poor health already, or the death sentence Saul had invoked for him began to work, but whatever the cause he began to sicken of the workers' disease, the increasingly bad cough, weakness and wastage of the tissues.

Rosie called him a fool. 'Face up to the owd bastard and get what's left o' your brass! There's little or nowt he can do. A

222

nice mess you've made of things, that I must say.' She feared the loss of his money and position more than the decline of his health, he knew, and was sick at heart because of it, yet so ill that emotions mattered little. His mother-in-law and Billy came no more to the cottage, Mrs Giles having a dim superstitious idea that spinner's cough was catching.

Every day he intended to go to Lancaster and throw himself on Ephraim's mercy. But he was never well enough. In the end he stayed away from the mill, and sat where Margaret and Dove had found him, mostly without Rosie, who was irritated and depressed by his condition.

He came out of his thoughts, conscious of his cousin and his aunt gazing at him in consternation. He was genuinely glad to see them, angels from a bright world he had left, as he felt he would soon leave the dark world of his existence. Dove would make a most fitting angel. He had fancied, long ago, that she was one...

She saw the troubled, wandering look in his eyes and moved her chair to sit close beside him and take his thin hand in hers. The skin of it was hot and dry, but sweat stood out on his brow. More and more she was reminded of Belle's illness. Was she fated to see those she loved best at the gates of death?

Margaret went into action. 'That fire needs more coal on. Where's the scuttle? It's half empty — go and get some more, girl. What medicine is he taking?' She studied the bottle of dark-brown stuff, uncorked and sniffed it. 'Liquorice, mainly. It may soothe his throat, but that's all. Who is his doctor?'

'Parrish, in t'village. He looks after all Bradshaw's hands.'

'*Does* he?' remarked Margaret grimly. 'Is he in partnership with the coffin-maker, by any chance?' Rosie stared, uncomprehending. 'Never mind. Joe must be got out of here and nursed properly, Mrs Atkinson. I hope you agree with that.'

Rosie looked uncomfortable, but undeniably relieved. 'Well, miss, there's nowt much I can do, you see. It's a draughty owd place, this, and I never was much of a hand wi' sick folk. If you want to tak' him away…'

'I do, at the soonest possible moment. Oh, not now — my gig will only take two people, and he should not go out in the night air.' She rose. 'Keep him as warm as you can tonight. Bring down some blankets and make a bed up in front of the fire, with plenty of fuel on it, and give him warm drinks. Tomorrow I will come back with suitable transport.' She fixed Rosie with a stern eye, her lorgnettes raised. 'Your husband is very ill. Care for him while you can.'

Rosie began to whimper. She had not really thought of Joe dying on her hands, and she was very anxious for her own comforts, which began to look as if they would vanish down the wind.

'Go and get the bedding, child,' Margaret snapped. 'Dove, we must say goodnight to Joe and be off. We have many arrangements to make.'

Joe looked up with the ghost of a smile. 'I heard,' he whispered. 'Not too … bad to take things in. Thank you … Aunt. And Dove.'

'I've done nothing for you!' Dove cried despairingly. 'But I will, Joe. I nursed Belle and I'll nurse you.' She kissed his cheek; he took her hand and put it to his dry, cracked lips.

She was weeping as they climbed back into the gig. But Margaret was dry-eyed and grim. She drove at a sharp pace back to Knott Green, barely replying to Dove's distracted questions. At home, she rang for the elderly maid who had stayed up for them.

'Tell Frederick he is to ride to Lancaster first thing in the morning with a message. He must hire a coach there and come back in it, change horses and return to Lancaster with a sick person.'

Dove looked a question. 'Joe?'

'Of course. Mary is the one to nurse him, in his own home. And don't remind me that your mother has a weak heart, for such things take second place at a time like this. Besides, it will take her mind off your introduction to your aunt Eleanor.'

Joe lay in his own bed, in the room he had slept in all his boyhood and youth. It looked like a chamber of Paradise after the gloom of the Bradhope cottage. Miniatures of his father and mother hung above the pier glass, and a childish drawing one of the twins had made of the dog Adam. Mary had set the servants to scouring, sweeping, dusting and polishing. The sheets smelt of lavender and rosemary, and were warm from the shelf above one of the ovens where clean laundry was kept. When his sweating made him uncomfortable, they were changed.

The window was open, autumn air coming in with a freedom no doctor would have approved, but Mary believed firmly in fresh air. At her father's farm it was always said that the rich smell of pigsties, shippons and hay would cure a cough. The air brought with it a distant waft of wood smoke and cut grass, for Sam the gardener was scything the lawns. The old apple tree that grew just outside the window was full of red ripe fruit, glistening in the morning sun. The poultice of linseed and mustard on Joe's chest was not comfortable, but he sighed with sheer contentment.

The nightmare of Bradhope was over. It had been wrong to go there, wrong to stay, wrong to marry Rosie. He had muttered something of the kind to Ephraim, the day they had first brought him to St Leonard's Gate, and Ephraim had said, 'True, true, but nothing to fret for now. Put it out of your mind and leave all to us.'

At first Joe had felt very ill, choked by his persistent cough, chilled and undernourished. There had been a day or two when he was not clearly aware of anything; then he began to recognise the faces bending over him. Mary, Belle, Dove — particularly Dove, who always seemed to be the one to bring him the drinks he liked best.

Because he had been ordered not to talk, she talked to him. She told him stories of London, pleasant things that would not excite him too much or distress him at all: the magnificent dancing horses at Astley's Circus, the grandeur of the opera, the wonders of the great castle of Windsor, the Diorama in Regent's Park, in which before the eyes of amazed spectators a picture appeared to come to life by a trick of lighting; the little Princess Alexandrina Victoria framed in the gilt and plush of the royal box, her chignon twisted with real pearls.

Joe listened dreamily, happy to be so pleasantly reminded of things he had seen himself, though he would not have let Dove know it for the world. She told her little stories so well. He thought her much improved by her London visit — more sure of herself, more amusing, more womanly, and even prettier than she had been. And so very different from Rosie.

But he was not able to think for any length of time about Rosie, or Dove, or anything else. He was being dosed with a medicine containing a strong sedative, prescribed by the doctor Mary had called in to replace the unsatisfactory McAndrew. Dr Calvert had come to Lancaster from a practice in Manchester, where mill conditions were at their worst, and had worked with the celebrated Dr Kay, whose report on *The Moral and Physical*

Condition of the Working Classes Employed in the Cotton Manufacture of Manchester had become a textbook for reformers. He treated Joe with a calm knowledgeability that reassured her and spared her the worry that had made her ill herself when Belle was stricken down.

He agreed with an indulgent smile that Joe should also have a supply of Mary's favourite cough mixture, the recipe handed down by her mother: honey, lemon juice and paregoric elixir.

'It will do no harm and may well soothe the patient in the night, but be sure that he receives the opiate as well.'

Night after night Mary lay awake, in the small room next to Joe's into which she had removed herself, listening to the coughing that seemed to tear her chest as it did his, and when it was particularly bad, going in to tend to him; all day she was in constant attendance on him, as she had been when he was a delicate child.

'You'll be next,' prophesied Aggie darkly, catching her mistress making yet another trip upstairs to the invalid's room.

'You leave me be,' Mary returned. 'I can manage very well.'

And indeed, she was surprised to find that she was happier than she had been for a long time. Joe's partial alienation from the family, drastically worsened by his marriage, had struck her deeper than anyone knew. To have him back at home, under her care, looking at her once more as though she were the mother she had once been to him, brought her what she had almost forgotten: contentment.

Left alone in the cottage, Rosie was at a loose end. She had resented Margaret taking Joe away, yet had been relieved by it. She sensed that his time at Bradshaw's was over in any case, and knew that she had been quite mistaken in thinking marriage to him the passport to improvement in life. It had brought her nothing but hard-faced looks from other women, loneliness, an inexperienced husband nothing like the lads she had known, for all that he was so soft about her.

She had some fine clothes, that was true. She laid them out on the bed, admiring the red dress with the flounces, the green bonnet trimmed with poppies, the brightly patterned shawl, the smart kid boots. There were some bits of jewellery, too. She held up the long earrings of pinchbeck, imitation gold, letting them swing agreeably against her neck. The mirror reflected a highly satisfactory image. Rosie had made up her mind.

The next morning she surprised her mother with an early knock. Mrs Giles opened the door, yawning and blear-eyed with last night's gin.

'What the heck do you want?'

'I'm going back to t'mill. Thought you'd like to know, Mam.'

Her mother surveyed her from head to foot, red dress, bonnet and shawl.

'Like *that*? Bradshaw's don't employ peacocks.'

Rosie tossed her head. 'They can like it or lump it. I've got to earn, haven't I, now Joe's gone off wi' them fine folk of his? I happen to know they're short of spinners.'

Mrs Giles snorted. 'Got up the way you are, you look like earnin' on your back. Well, get on wi' you. An' Rosie — I could do wi' a shillin' or two.'

'You'll have to wait, Mam. I've nowt left. Wish me luck!'

Work had begun long ago when Rosie reached Bradshaw's. The familiar din of the long spinning room roared in her ears as she walked in. The workers at the looms nearest to her caught sight of her and stared, but it was more than their job was worth to stop. A bright jaunty figure among those drab overalls, she sauntered along the aisle between the great machines until the overseer came into view; he was examining a faulty wheel.

Tom Swainson was not pleased to see her. He remembered her all too well: her loud laugh, the distractions her charms provided for his men, the noisy friendships or noisier enmities with the other girls. Certainly, he needed two or three experienced hands, but he would prefer none of them to be Rosie Atkinson. He feared, besides, the repercussions on himself if Saul Bradshaw heard that anyone connected with Joe had been taken on.

He said doubtfully, 'I can't say yes, Rosie, not wi'out Mr Bradshaw's agreement. And you know...'

'I know he'd a grudge against Joe, but I'm not Joe, am I? Well, go on, ask him!'

Swainson took a lot of persuading. Only the sight of the three unattended looms made up his mind to go and face the employer who purported to be his friend but might at any moment turn and rend him. As he went to the door leading to the management offices Rosie caught up with him.

'I'll come, too. Let Saul see what he's getting, eh? He's never set eyes on me, as I know of.'

'Well, if you must. But you keep a civil tongue in your head — none of your "Saul". It's "Mr Bradshaw" or "sir" when you talk to him, and the less you say the better.'

'Yes, *sir*,' replied Rosie demurely, following him up the stairs.

Saul liked to be in his office on time, on the days when he came in, and he liked plenty going on: letters to answer, requests, complaints, visits, anything to make him feel important and powerful. He knew perfectly well that Shem would have much preferred his absence, so that he might get on with things in his own quiet fashion, but that was not Saul's way. He looked up at Swainson's knock.

'Well? I'm very busy.'

'Sorry to bother you, Mr Bradshaw. But this young woman wants to be taken on as a spinner. She's worked for us before, and we need hands. I thought as you'd like to see her before…'

He had no need to push Rosie forward, for she was already advancing, all confidence and smiles.

'You don't know me, Mr Bradshaw, do you? Rosie Atkinson.'

The old man stared, his cheeks beginning to turn the purplish hue that betokened a burst of temper. Swainson prepared for the worst, wishing he had never agreed to Rosie's daft idea of making a personal appearance. But Saul only said, tonelessly, 'Nay, I don't know you.'

'I'm Joe Atkinson's wife — sir. He's been took bad wi' spinner's cough an' gone home to his own folk, so I've got to earn me livin' again. I thought you might be good enough to take me back. An' seein' as Joe got into a bit o' trouble, it's only fair to tell you who I am, rather than sneak back.'

To Swainson's astonishment, Saul nodded slowly. 'Aye. Quite right. Very honest and proper.'

Hearing the name he hated had given him a momentary shock, and a starting-up of one of his rages. But the girl herself was so unlike anything he connected with the name of Atkinson. Here was none of that holier-than-thou, stuck-up, do-gooding attitude, or the long-nosed good looks and superior voice. She was an ordinary working lass — dressed to kill, for sure, but not in Atkinson taste. If she had worked for Bradshaw's before he must have seen her, yet he would have remembered; that startling, flaring beauty must have stood out in any crowd. Yet under the quenching cap the women wore he would not have noticed her luxuriant hair, and the long overall would have hidden the swelling curves of her figure. He stared at her until even she, in her cheerful arrogance, began to wonder whether she had done right, and Swainson, behind her, twitched with apprehension.

Then Saul said, 'All right, Tom. That'll do. I want a word with the lass.'

Thankfully the overseer retreated. Rosie remained standing, one hand on her hip, her head quizzically on one side. She was not in the least afraid of him, old devil though she knew him to be, and she recognised the look dawning on his face. She had last seen it, oddly enough, on Joe's, the first time she had called on him.

Saul nodded towards a chair. Rosie sat down, unobtrusively loosened her bonnet strings and let the ringlets cascade round her shoulders. In that grey morning light she seemed like a rainbow that had alighted in the dull office. She knew instinctively how things were going to go, but waited for him to speak first.

'He's gone, then,' he said flatly.

'Aye. I doubt I'll see much more of him. We didn't suit, you know.'

'No. No. I can believe that... You *were* wed, were you?'

She flashed the gold wedding band at him, at the same time displaying her plump dimpled hand. 'Wed proper.'

'Well, we'll forget that. You'll work under your maiden name if you work here.'

'Glad to. It's Giles, Rosie Giles.' She was saying as little as possible, cleverly giving him time to take in her beauty and allurement. She could read him like a book, or better: a greedy, power-mad, gross old man who found his excitements nowadays in bullying. She guessed that he had let women go out of his life as the years crept on, though there were nasty tales that had come down in legend from the days when Saul had been younger, tales, only whispered, about his debauching of female workers: a woman who had gone on the streets in Preston after he had finished with her, a mother and daughter summoned to his office together, and the door locked; a young girl who had killed her baby, and been hanged for it, without Saul lifting a finger to save her.

Oh, he had been a womaniser in his day, Rosie knew. And now the lecherous look was creeping over him again, after years of abstinence, and she, Rosie, was going to benefit from his reawakening. It would be a lot better fun than living with Joe.

She crossed her feet, showing her ankles, and moved a little nearer, so that her powerful scent crossed the desk to his nostrils.

'Well, Rosie,' he said genially, 'I hope we're going to know each other better.'

'Oh, I'll be bound we are,' she said. 'Sir.'

CHAPTER SIXTEEN

Within two weeks — no less, for it did not do to seem easy to get — Rosie was Saul's mistress.

The news travelled swiftly to Lancaster, as scandalous news will. A client of Ephraim's was the first to tell him, with a wealth of embellishment. The girl had not worked in the mill for more than a few days. Now she was living at Bradshaw Hall in the highest style, with the old man slavering over her, and Mr Shem removed to the far end of the Hall in his own quarters, not associating with them, and running the mill single-handed, for his father no longer went to it. She was seen driving out in the carriage, four horses drawing it. She had rejected finery that had belonged to Saul's dead wife, kept in attic trunks, and had gone to Preston for new dresses and all sorts of gear. She ruled him with a rod of iron, some whispered with a whip from the stables, for she was extremely adaptable in her ways.

The old man was cock-a-hoop, bemused, infatuated, whatever you liked to call it. Rosie's mother and brother had been put into a cottage on the estate and were living on game and all sorts of fine fare. It was the talk of the district.

'I knew it,' Mary declared. 'I knew she was a bad woman from the first moment I heard about her. You kept it from me, Father, you know you did.'

'Nothing of the kind,' protested Ephraim mildly. 'I told you exactly what she was like, and you formed your own conclusions. As it happened, mine were the same. Well, now we know the worst, what's to be done? Is Joe to be told?'

'No, indeed!' Mary was outraged. 'Mending so nicely, and to hear something that might set him back weeks? Never. It might kill the boy.'

Dove spoke up unexpectedly. 'Tell him.'

'What?' Her mother's voice was sharp. 'What do you know about it, miss?'

'I saw her,' Dove said. 'I know *exactly* what she's like, and it has nothing to do with Mr Bradshaw. She was bad for Joe, always, and he would have separated from her in time, even if this had not happened. Oh, she was very handsome, and that was what won him. But the illness has put an end to his feeling about her, I think.'

'*Do* you?' Mary had never heard Dove say so much in one speech. She was faintly jealous that the girl should know more about Joe than she did herself. 'Well, if you're so wise about it all — and I can't think what experience you've had in such matters — pray tell him yourself, but be careful about it.'

Dove did tell him. He was indeed much better, propped up on the high pillows that made it easier for him to breathe. There was a tinge of colour in his face and brightness had come back to his eyes. Dr Calvert was very pleased with him, very gratified that his treatment of the spinners' disease in its early stages had had such good results. He was writing a monograph on the subject in his spare time.

Joe listened to Dove's story expressionlessly, looking out of the window at the tossing boughs of the apple tree. When she had finished he said, 'Poor Rosie. I'm glad.'

'Poor? Glad?'

'Yes. She was poor, you know, she and her family, very poor. They had nothing at all. Eight of the children died, and her father. Rosie looked after her mother and Billy very capably, and never grumbled about it. She deserves some reward for that, don't you think?'

Dove did not answer.

'I couldn't give her enough. Oh, I believe she thought I could at first. I think she even liked me,' he added wistfully. 'But she was so beautiful, and she must have known how far she could go, given the chance.'

'She *has* gone far,' Dove said as spitefully as she could. 'As far as anyone could, by the sound of it!'

Joe shook his head. 'It's not a matter for shame. What else can a poor girl do, outside marriage, and the mill, and domestic slavery? I don't blame her at all; why should I? I ought never to have married her, but I was under a sort of spell, Dove. Rosie is the last survivor of the Lancashire Witches, and good luck to her for escaping the fires.'

Dove sprang up and faced him, anger sparking from her eyes. 'Joe Atkinson, I suppose you'll only be happy when you're a saint in heaven, and it's only thanks to Mother and the rest of us that you aren't one now! How *can* you be so ... so horribly reasonable about that dreadful woman? You ought never to have married her indeed, and you ought to be thoroughly shocked now, instead of sitting there smiling!'

'I was smiling at you, Dove; you look so very like an angry kitten. I suppose I must begin coughing again, to win your sympathy back?'

She came close to him, the shine of tears in her eyes, though she tried to laugh. 'Don't you dare. I ought to shake you, and I would if you were well enough.'

'Try,' he said, holding his arms out. He looked particularly elegant in a ruff-necked lawn nightshirt, bands of lace falling about his slender hands, his auburn hair long and flowing, like a poet's. Dove flew into his embrace, laughing and crying at the same time, while he patted and hushed her.

It was a moment of enlightenment for him, of utter abandon for her, her hidden feelings out at last. He knew now, in the wisdom of tribulation past, what his little cousin had felt for him all these years, and what he could feel for her, as soft and desirable in his arms as Rosie had been, but sweet and gentle as well: his other half.

He kissed her wet eyelids, and pushed her away from him; it was safer so. 'Softly, Dovekin.' He had never called her that before, it had always been Belle's name for her. 'If Aunt hears you we shall both be shockingly scolded. Sit down and be quiet. Good girl.'

When she was calm he asked her, 'Shall we forget this?'

She met his eyes frankly. 'No — my love.'

He lifted her hand and laid it against his cheek wordlessly.

Autumn passed into winter, winter into spring. A few changes came to the house in St Leonard's Gate. Ephraim, declaring that it would be most undesirable for Joe to return to Bradhope in any capacity, took him into his own office as a kind of superior clerk, paid a nominal salary to assist with the work and learn at the same time. Booth, Ephraim's partner, was about to retire, and Ephraim needed all the help he could get.

Joe was happy, or happier than he had been for a long time. He enjoyed the work, enjoyed exercising his brain on its complexities and his body in the walks and rides on which Ephraim sent him to deal with clients who were unable to come in for consultation. The life of the mill seemed as though it had happened in another century, and he might never have been married to Rosie at all, so dreamlike were his impressions of her.

He said to Belle, 'When you came through the cholera, did you feel that you were in a sense a different person?'

'Why, yes, exactly! It was as though my mind had been away, and came back to me knowing something it had not known before.' She smiled, remembering Will's visit, and the ring she must not wear. 'Such illnesses are terrible at the time, but if one is lucky enough not to die of them one is in a way reborn.'

It was a ponderous thought, coming from the once-frivolous Belle. She had indeed changed, thought Joe. Back in the family, closer to the twins than he had ever been, it seemed to him that they, the three young people, were all leading a secret life unknown to their elders. Ephraim, deep in a complicated and contentious dispute about an inheritance, was only concerned with food, rest and sleep when he came home in the evening. Mary had seen Belle and Joe through their crises; now she devoted herself to rebuilding her own health. A stay with Margaret, a further one with family friends in the fresh air of Wray, a series of absorbing appointments with her dressmaker, now that she had lost flesh and attained a slimmer waistline, all took her attention from the air of strangeness about the three young ones.

They were each acutely aware of their own dilemmas, and of the problems of the others, but they said nothing of it aloud, for what was the use? Joe knew very well now that Dove loved him deeply. He knew too, that, thanks to Rosie, he could see her at last as a lovely and desirable woman, not as the little cousin-sister she had once seemed. But he fought back his longing to tell her of his changed feelings; let her guess if she would, to bring them out into the open could only cause harm, since he was legally tied to Rosie and she contracted to George Dilworth.

He watched when a letter came in George's bold hand from one or other of the West India stations. Dove always gave it to her mother to read, and its contents were certainly anything but private. He expected to be away some months more, he had had one of the nasty fevers so common out there, the mosquitoes were driving them all mad; it would be jolly to be back in England.

To Dove the prospect did not seem at all jolly. But what was the use of breaking off her engagement when a future with Joe was impossible?

High on a grassy slope that overlooked the shining rippled sands of Morecambe Bay Belle lay closely embraced with Will. Larks sang above them, poppies blazed scarlet among the grass, the air was balmy, tinged with the healthy tang of seaweed. Suddenly Will disengaged himself from her arms and sat up.

'It won't do, love. Call the little lass back.' Bet Marsden had driven out with them, since it would not have been proper in Mary's eyes for Belle to be alone with a man, even an old family friend.

Belle pouted. 'She won't have had time to pick many flowers yet, and she isn't far away.'

'Far enough,' Will said grimly. 'It's not fair on either you nor me, being like this. No, let go, I'll not be tempted.'

'Just because I was foolish once…'

'I'm not talking about that. I'm talking about being foolish now. You know very well the road to trouble's an easy one, and we're not taking it, Belle. Tease how you like, you'll get nowhere wi' me. I'm old enough to be your dad, so you'd best take orders from me, not the other way round. And don't think you can force my hand.'

'I was not thinking so much of your hand...' she said demurely.

'Now, none of your naughtiness, Miss Belle, don't try me too far. It's enough of a struggle, as things are. You said you'd be content to be friends — now you don't want to stick to the bargain.'

'No, I don't!' she burst out. 'It's so silly. What's the use of Parliament passing their stupid Reform Bill if they can't reform the way ordinary people live? It's all votes and the workers and such stuff; not a word about the way a man can be tied to a woman as mad as a piper, who doesn't even know him for her husband! I wish *I* were in Parliament. I'd soon change things.' She clenched her fists and looked fierce.

Will was half-laughing, half-angry. He was weary of his shackled state, frustrated, ashamed of the deceit he was practising on Ephraim and Mary, and he had no intention of doing them further wrong. He pulled Belle to her feet and propelled her towards the gate in the hedge. Up in the higher meadow a small form could be seen, its arms full of wild flowers. Will shouted, Bet raised her head and waved, she began to run towards them. The idyllic interlude and the near-quarrel was over, and nothing was solved.

Candlelight from a hanging chandelier shone down on the massive table with its load of good but old-fashioned porcelain, glass and silver. The tablecloth was yellowed with age, but of fine Brussels lace, deserving better treatment than the wine splashes it was receiving from the trembling hand of the old man at the head of the table, and the careless pouring of the young woman at the other. Saul Bradshaw wore his best clothes, which were as out-of-date as the table: the breeches and silk stockings which had gone out of fashion years before, the swallow-tail coat and high cravat which caused his thick neck to bulge over it. His face was scarlet with wine and excitement, as was Rosie's. There were jewels round her neck, her shoulders were bare, her new gown of puce velvet, her hair ornamented with feathers on the top, but dressed with ringlets flowing on the shoulders, as Saul liked to see it.

'What d'you want to sit that far off for?' he asked. The table's five-foot length separated them.

''Cause it makes me feel grand, that's why. Like a lady.'

'I'll make you a lady,' he growled. 'You'll be as grand as any in the County Palatine before I've done wi' you. Nay, but I'll never be done wi' you. You and me's one, Rosie. Any as looks down on you now must reckon wi' me, and I dare 'em to do it.'

Rosie tossed her head, making her earrings swing alluringly. 'They'll look down on me so long as they know I'm nobbut your wench. I'd lief be Mrs Bradshaw, Saul.' She mimed kisses, throwing them across the table.

'Then what did you want to wed yon snicket of an Atkinson for? But for that...'

He took a long draught of wine, brooding. Rosie was the sort of woman he had always needed: needed more than ever at this time in his life. With her at his side he let the affairs of the mill alone, content to stay at home, gloating on her, playing with her, driving out with her in the light phaeton, perched up beside him in her finery and feathers to be shown off. He particularly enjoyed driving in Lancaster, seeing with satisfaction the stares of admiration, or at least astonishment, hoping to be seen by the humiliated Atkinsons. Mrs Joseph Atkinson, whore to the most powerful man in the district, and far better than them now: Mrs Joseph Atkinson, a fine spanking woman and a raving beauty, his property and his pride.

He wished he were a younger man, virile as he had been once. Useless to pretend that he could satisfy her as he would have liked (though she put up a commendable show of ecstasy) or that she could give him the pleasure he had once enjoyed with women. It must be enough to share her bed, take her lavish favours, do what he could with her, even experience an illusion of youth returned. In all his life he had not known love, only lust; now he thought he knew something like it — enough, at least, to want to make an honest woman of her for her own sake, because she wanted it.

But the obstacle was there, not dead of spinners' phthisis, but maddeningly alive. It made Saul choke with anger to think of the irony of it: he might so easily have been rid of the fellow by now.

He refilled his glass and raised it. 'Here's to you. Sup up and get to bed.'

The servants, clearing away, furtively watched them go out entwined, walking slowly because Saul could go no faster. Old Black, footman promoted to butler, and his wife Alice, now the housekeeper, dared not have sniggered even if they had wanted to. With set, expressionless faces they piled up plates and scraped the left-over food into a dish. The young girl who had recently been taken on as maid was kept downstairs; it was not suitable for her to witness such scenes.

At the opposite end of the big house Shem's candles burned late. He always remained at the office as long as possible, until the mill shut down after its twelve-hour day, and brought work home with him. All his food was brought up to his sitting room, and he used his own staircase to the grounds. He was not an emotional man, but his whole being rose up in protest against Rosie. Determined to conquer, she had once waylaid him and coquetted.

'Come on, Shem, give us a smile. Not shy, are you?'

'Not in the least,' Shem said coldly. 'If I appear unsmiling it's because I don't like you, ma'am.'

She stared after him, open-mouthed and disappointed.

Joe entered Ephraim's office with a letter in his hands.

'This makes curious reading, Uncle.' He passed it over. Ephraim put on his glasses. It was written on thick paper in an unclerkly hand.

Dear Mr Atkinson,

It may surprise you to hear from me, having as I take it broken your connection with Bradshaw's, but I have something to tell you that cannot well be put on paper. Believe me I mean you nothing but well. If you will meet me at the Elephant in Skerton about eight of the clock on Wednesday present I will tell it to you then.

Yours obediently,

THOMAS SWAINSON.

Ephraim handed it back. 'Well? Do you know the gentleman?'

Joe had long since told him of the theft of his design.

'It was Swainson who stole my drawing, Rosie said. He had a bad name at Bradshaw's for being in with Saul Bradshaw, though I never knew any worse of him. He's one of those men whose face you can't remember until you've seen it quite a hundred times. I can't imagine what he might want with me.'

'So. Will you go? It seems an eccentric rendezvous.' He mused. 'Is it not on the river side of Skerton? I fancy I've passed a small house of that name. Why should Mr Swainson make the longish journey from Bradhope to meet you north of the town?'

'I've no idea. Perhaps it's kept by some connections of his. But why should he want to see me? He must know that I know about the theft, and that I'm hardly likely to want to associate with any friend of Bradshaw's. There's no unfinished business about the partnership, is there?'

'No,' Ephraim said shortly. He had held a long, tedious, acrimonious wrangle with the firm of Bradshaw over the matter of Joe's partnership, how much was owing to him in balance and compensation for the illness he had contracted, and how much, if anything, Bradshaw's were entitled to retain. Some cool letters had been exchanged between Ephraim and Shem's solicitor, and the outcome was not entirely satisfactory to either party. Ephraim rather hoped he would never hear the name of Bradshaw again, thought it seemed unlikely.

'What else can it be, then?' Joe was still scanning the letter.

Ephraim ostentatiously set up a pile of papers on the desk in front of him and dipped his pen in the inkwell. 'To know that, you had better go and find out. Now I have matters to attend to, and you are due in Castle Park — dear me, about five minutes ago.'

Joe sensed that he had been dismissed. All day his mind returned again and again to the curious summons. Could it be to do with Rosie? In which case, what good could news of her possibly do him? Swainson's note seemed to hint that the meeting would be to Joe's benefit. He gave up the puzzle.

It was dusk when he left St Leonard's Gate. Ephraim was shut up in his study. Mary and the girls were at the theatre with Will, who had called in during the afternoon and offered to escort them to a performance of *The Stranger,* an old melodrama which Mary had seen in her youth and declared she longed to see again. They had set off in a bustle, delayed because the kitchen chimney had got on fire after dinner, and in the resultant chaos Mary's best cap had been ruined by soot and the front of her dress blackened; it took all three of them to set her to rights again. Will and Joe exchanged wry glances.

'Why don't you come with us, Joe?' It was not far from Will's mind that Joe might prove a pleasing distraction for Dove, giving him more of Belle's attention. Then, reluctantly remembering his new-found resolution, he decided that he would place himself next to Mary, and Belle beyond her, to prevent temptation.

'No thanks, Uncle Will, I have to go out.'

Will was trying to compose a sentence. Finally, with difficulty, he got it out. 'Don't you think you might leave off the "Uncle" now, Joe? It makes me feel — well, right elderly.'

Joe looked surprised. 'I'd never thought of it. I suppose it *is* rather comical, but it's a lifelong habit. Certainly I'll drop it ... Will.'

Will reached out his hand and shook Joe's, saying no more.

Left alone after the theatre party had left, Joe reflected on the general oddness of things. First the puzzle of Swainson's letter, then Will's sudden request. In China, he remembered, certain years bore the names of religiously significant creatures: the Snake, the Lion ... was 1835 by any chance the year of the Sphinx? But no, for the Sphinx was only half a lion, the rest being woman. He shook off such pointless speculations, and set off to Skerton on foot. He had been told by Doctor Calvert that he should walk when he could, ride when he would, and travel in a closed carriage only when he must.

He crossed Skerton Bridge and paused to look back at the town, the crouching might of the castle, its battlements etched against a twilight sky, the proud outline of the Priory Church tower; below them the huddled grey roofs blending into shapelessness as dusk came down, and the curving river bearing boats large and small, a merchant ship at anchor, the dark sails of fishing vessels, a bobbing light here and there. When would the *Chloe* sail back to St George's Quay, with Dove's bridegroom aboard?

Across the bridge Skerton showed pinpoints of light from the windows of cottages and tenements crowded together close to the river bank. This northern outcrop of Lancaster was old, ramshackle and not over-respectable. Joe remembered a recent legal dispute between the tenant of a good substantial house and his next-door neighbour about rats and mice. He imagined the rat population of Skerton to be large; they always abounded by rivers and Smith's shipyard was their delight. A stale, decayed smell hung about the place, dominating the smell of the river.

He found the Elephant Inn by asking a man lounging outside a doorway. It was in a narrow street behind the shipyard, and seemed to be popular, judging by the noise proceeding from it and the crowd gathered round its doors. Some event was going on to the accompaniment of cheers, shouts and screams and the light of flares. With some effort Joe pushed through the outskirts of the crowd, through people who were either too small or too weak to press forward. Unable to see over the heads of the front ranks he asked a small man, craning on tiptoe, what was going on.

'Fight,' was the answer. 'Two prime 'uns.'

Joe was not particularly anxious to witness a boxing bout; he only wanted to reach the inn and get over the business with Swainson, whatever it might be. He had no desire to linger in the unsavoury district. But only by pushing through the spectators to the front could he enter the inn. Cursed and jabbed by sharp elbows, stepping on feet, he came at last to the roughly cordoned 'ring' which covered the width of the street, and was lit by four flares, tied to posts at each corner. A canvas had been spread over the cobbles. On it two figures sprawled and writhed, cheered on with shrieked obscenities and wild shouts. Joe saw that the sport was wrestling, an even more brutal pastime than bare-knuckled boxing. He paused to glance at the wrestlers, one of whom half rose before being dragged down, and saw that it was a woman.

Both were women, both naked to the waist and tied-skirted below, filthy and blood-streaked, for they not only wrestled but scratched and bit each other. One, middle-aged, grossly stout, was now grappling the neck of the younger, a scrawny creature muscled like a man and scarcely breasted, in grotesque contrast to her opponent's enormous swinging bosoms. The big one was evidently the crowd's favourite.

'Go on, Sally, kill 'er! Give 'er the backheel!' they were shouting, as the antagonists swayed on their feet. Sally obliged, hooking her great bare foot behind the other one's heel, so that she was forced backwards and only recovered by a visible effort, gasping and grunting; then she screamed as Sally seized her long straggling hair and yanked it viciously.

Joe watched in horrified fascination. This was not Cumberland wrestling as he knew it from boyhood, though he recognised certain holds, the hank which brought both wrestlers to the ground together, the inside click that locked a leg after the other wrestler had been jerked violently forward, the cross-buttock, one hip turned under the opponent's body, with a backward strike, lift and throw; all these were familiar, but not the fist blows, bites and cruel wrenches the two practised on each other.

A man reached over the rope and handed Sally a pot of porter, which she drank down at one draught. 'E's 'er man,' someone said. In that pause she momentarily lost concentration. The younger woman crouched, straightened, landed a straight punch on Sally's mouth, and followed it up by clawing one of the huge breasts with her nails. The crowd yelled as Sally clutched at her face, her chin streaming with blood. Two of her front teeth had been bashed in by that small but iron-strong hand. The man with the pot leapt over the rope and hit the girl, but was dragged out by his mates, while Sally spat out the teeth and retaliated on her own account with a kick at her opponent's leg that was violent enough to break the bone. The girl fell heavily, and lay moaning on the ground, as cries of 'Foul!' broke out on every side.

If that was a foul, Joe thought, what were the other variations of the rules? Sickened, angry with himself for pausing to watch the degrading sight, he pushed through to the door of the inn.

The bar parlour was almost empty. A potman was washing mugs in a bowl; a group of men who looked like seamen or shipyard workers were playing cards in a corner. A single ceiling lantern lit the room; Joe wondered how they could see to play. At another table sat Swainson, a pot of ale before him untouched. At Joe's entrance he got up and pushed back another chair.

'Joe, lad. I thought you'd been kept. Sit down.' There was a distinct air of relief about him. Joe greeted him coolly and accepted the drink he was offered, though it tasted poorly enough in the atmosphere thick with the smoke of cheap tobacco.

'That's a rough piece of work outside,' he said. 'Do they go in for such exhibitions round here?'

Swainson nodded. 'It gets custom. Every man out there's got a measure of ale or porter in his hand, and they'll be back for more. It's different, see. Two chaps having a mill's one thing, two wenches is another.'

'Hardly an improvement. It's beyond me how women can let themselves fall so low. What are they, those two? Not wives and mothers, surely?'

Swainson glanced up under his eyebrows, and Joe knew that he was being written down a stiff-necked prig.

'They're 'ores,' the overseer said. 'That, and t'other way's how they get their living. They're used to it, bless you. A couple of teeth tonight, a lump of hair out tomorrow, it's all the same to them. As to being wives and mothers, I've not seen their lines, but they've two or three babbies apiece, that I do know. You don't want to be so soft about wenches. Which brings me to the point. Have you heard from Rosie, Joe?'

Joe had to concentrate hard to be able to answer the question. The thick miasma of shag smoke seemed to have got into his head, and the din outside was ringing in his ears, so that Swainson's voice seemed far away. For a second he could hardly remember who Rosie was. Then he shook his head to clear it.

'No. Not a word. I did hear ... about...'

'About her and Saul. Aye.'

Swainson was looking hard at him, as if trying to read something in his face. Was he supposed to express great emotion at the mention of Rosie's name? It seemed ridiculous, for he felt nothing at all, only a faint choking sensation and a haziness in the head. He dimly remembered that he had been told to avoid smoky, unventilated places, and automatically he began to cough.

'You're not well,' Swainson said, leaning closer to him. 'You're not well, not well, not well.' The words kept echoing through his head, while his eyes registered the strange look on Swainson's face, something between triumph and anxiety, and he was aware of the face growing larger and larger and more distorted, until it seemed like a balloon hovering in the air, about to burst.

Out of the corner of his eye he saw figures moving towards him. The seamen had left their card game and were coming towards him, though he only saw them as moving shapes, almost shadows. He wished his head were not so muzzy, and a qualmish feeling had come over him. Bad ale.

He fell forward, his hair spilling like a sheaf of autumn leaves on the grimy table, his glass overturned, pouring what remained of its contents on to the ground.

CHAPTER SEVENTEEN

He never saw the four men closing in on him like a pack of intent wolves, or Swainson's hurried retreat from the table. He was only conscious of someone grasping him and pushing him face downwards over two chairs, half under the table, out of the way of the conflict that was raging between his assailants and Will Raven.

Will was furiously angry, his blood was up, and he was more than a match for the four men who had been drinking to keep up their courage. In his youth he had been a notable fighter. Now that skill came back to him, sending a punch to a jaw here, a low-hitting jab in another direction, putting an arm lock on the small foreign-featured man who had sneaked up on him from the side. He had them by surprise, at a disadvantage, and now men from outside the inn were coming in, drawn by the struggle, seeing one man fighting four. Regardless of who was against whom, they joined in, intoxicated by the stimulus of the wrestling match, ready for violence of any kind. In the resulting mêlée the attackers silently melted away, leaving Will standing alone over the table beside the slumped body of Joe, while Swainson cowered against the wall alongside, unable to retreat.

'All right, lads,' Will said to his uninvited helpers. 'They've gone back to their holes. They were out for trouble and they got it, thanks to you. Tell him there to draw you a pint apiece.' He nodded to the barman, tossing across a guinea.

Murmuring gratitude, though disappointed of a sharper battle, the stragglers went to receive their reward. Outside the wrestling had stopped. There was some talk, and laughter, and a woman's voice cursing and crying. Will knew that the winner would soon be led in to be congratulated with drink. He turned his back on the door and pulled Joe upright, slapping his cheeks with sharp alternate blows until his eyes opened and he looked about him, dazed. All the time Swainson had stood by the wall like a hypnotised rabbit, unable to move. Will turned to him. 'Well, what was the game, then?'

Swainson stared back at him, speechless.

'You were to get him here and have him taken — was that it?'

Swainson nodded.

'Then what? They're no pressmen, that gang. So — disposed of, knocked on the head?' He could see by the man's terrified expression that he was somewhere near the truth. 'Well, well. And the river so nice and handy. A drugged man doesn't fight, does he.' The whole picture was forming in Will's mind. 'And so Saul Bradshaw'd have his revenge, or whatever he calls it, and his new missis. He did put you up to this, didn't he?'

Swainson nodded. The barman was now serving new customers: the thin girl wrestler with a shawl draped round her upper half, a man touching her avidly, excited by the recent violence, five or six hangers-on all clamouring to be served. Nobody took any notice of the three at the table. Will went on in a quiet voice that carried all too clearly to Swainson.

'What a pretty business, and it might have all gone through, but for me. Sorry, are you? Or happen you don't care one way or t'other?'

The overseer licked his lips. 'I've got to do what I'm told. It's as much as my life's worth.'

'Is it?' Will looked and sounded very dangerous. 'Let's see what your life's worth. Joe, stay there. Here, you'll need this.'

He picked up a canister of water from the bar and dashed a liberal amount of it over Joe's head, then, leaving him gasping and coughing, he led the unresisting Swainson out of the inn across the now dismantled site of the wrestling match into the next street and through a narrow stinking alley to the path that ran by the river. The man began to put up a struggle, but Will had him in a bulldog grip. He looked up and down, ascertained that there were plenty of boats moored alongside the bank, then put Swainson in front of him and gave him a mighty push in the middle of the back. With a scream, Swainson catapulted into the water. There was a wild splashing and floundering, and muffled cries to which Will listened with satisfaction. With luck the would-be murderer would rescue himself by clinging on to one of the boats tossing on the water. The light from a flickering lamp would show him the way back to the bank. Otherwise, the rats might be pleased to find another body in the river. Dusting his hands, Will walked away.

They were back at St Leonard's Gate, talking in the garden house, for neither was anxious that the family should know what had happened that evening. Will had made Joe walk all the way back, to clear his head, though the rain had begun while they were still in Skerton, and was soon coming down thick and fast. They had not talked much on that walk. Now Joe tried to work things out, but slowly, for he was still confused by the drug Swainson had slipped into his glass.

'I don't know how you came to be there just at that moment. It seems like a miracle. Was it?'

'Who's to say what's a miracle? It so happened that when we got back from the theatre your uncle happened to mention where you'd gone. He'd been thinking, and wasn't satisfied he ought to have let you go — at least without Isaac or one of the other men. I was capped, I can tell you. I know the place and I know the man, and he's as false as a weasel. I said I'd go and meet you there, just to see what was up, and by God's mercy I was in time. Call that a miracle if you like.'

'It would have been the end of me otherwise. Why the devil can't I conduct my own affairs without getting into such scrapes — to say the least of it? First Aunt Margaret has to rescue me, now you. But, Will ... what was it for? I never did Tom Swainson any harm, that he should want to have me kidnapped, or whatever the plan was.'

Will did not tell him what the real plan had been. 'Swainson lives in Saul Bradshaw's pocket. It's my guess that he wants rid of you, because of Rosie; happen he's a mind to wed her, though it's not like him to make honest women of his fancy bits. With Swainson as the lure and four hired bullies, he could ha' had you nicely out of the way, easy as winking.'

'Out of the way where?'

Will was still evasive. 'Aboard a ship, hidden in the hold till they were at sea ... how should I know? Well, it came to nought, and our best plan is to say as little as we can to them in the house.'

Joe nodded. 'No need to alarm them, since there's no harm done.'

It was not so easy to pass the evening's happenings over as casually as they hoped, for once they appeared in the full light of the parlour candles it was obvious that Will had a gashed knuckle and a bruised cheek, while Joe's pale face and dazed expression aroused awkward enquiries. The women fussed over them, but accepted that Joe had contracted a bad headache and that Will had fallen over in the dark. Only Ephraim looked unconvinced. After the others had retired Will told him the truth.

'I thought I had ceased to be subject to shock,' Ephraim said, 'but I see I was wrong. What a dastardly business!' He clenched his fist. 'If I could get proof I'd have Bradshaw up at the next Assizes for attempted murder. There's no chance of getting proof, I suppose? The men are obviously untraceable, but Swainson might be made to speak if we can lay hands on him. Where did you leave him?'

'In the river,' confessed Will sheepishly. 'Seemed the best place to dump him, wi' the other rats. Oh, never fear, he'll have got out all right — he wasn't two yards from a boat. A wetting's the worst he's had, more's the pity.'

Ephraim sighed. 'Will, Will! Watch your temper, or you'll be up for attempted murder yourself one day. You could have drowned him, and that would have done Joe no good, or any of us, for that matter. So: there's no proof, and Joe is still in danger from Bradshaw if your guess is right.'

'And what do we do about that?'

'What can we do? The lad can't be kept in cotton wool, and wouldn't wish to be. No, he must go about as usual. As for Bradshaw, I'll think hard, and look up some parallel cases. And I'll start now, if you don't mind.' He went to his bookshelves and selected three or four volumes.

Will lay in the dark of the guest bedroom he always occupied. It was disturbingly near the room shared by the twins; he had schooled himself not to think of Belle, but to go to sleep instantly. Tonight he lay awake and pondered, not unhappily. He had nearly killed a man — perhaps *had* killed him, if for some reason Swainson had not been able to reach the moored boat. But he had saved Joe's life, and thereby made up to him for the loss of his father. A great debt was paid.

He turned over, and only then fell into a deep sleep.

Fate, with its infallible gift for knocking its victims down at the moment of triumph, dealt Will a blow the next morning. At breakfast Mary was quieter than usual, and Belle was not there. Perhaps, thought Will, Joe or Ephraim had after all told them the truth about what had happened at the Elephant.

When the meal was over and the table cleared Mary said, 'Will, I have something to say to you. And you should hear it, Ephraim.' (So, he was not 'Father' this morning.)

Ephraim glanced at his watch. 'If I must — but I would like to be in court on time, so make it hasty, my dear.'

She moved to a chair by the window, and looked out for a moment, gathering her thoughts, before she spoke.

'It's very painful for me to say this, Will, but I must ask you not to come here again — for the time being, at least.'

Both men stared at her, startled. Then Will said, 'May I know why?'

Her eyes met his frankly. 'Yes, you may. Belle is the reason. I see you know what I mean.'

'*I* don't,' Ephraim said. 'What nonsense is this?'

'No nonsense at all. Only that Belle imagines she has fallen in love with Will. And Will, you've encouraged the silly girl, you know you have. I must say, I never thought you capable of such behaviour, and you can't deny it, can you?'

Will flushed darkly. 'No.'

'I can't believe this,' Ephraim said.

'You must, Ephraim. The thing has been there before our eyes for months, but I only came to realise it last night, when she made a ridiculous fuss about sitting next to Will, and I noticed how she looked at him, and her tone of voice. I had it out with her at bedtime, and she told me everything, including your drives together when Bet was sent away on errands.'

'There was nothing to tell!' Will cried. 'I never touched her, only in affection … love, if you like. I wouldn't harm her for the world. I did my best to stop it all, but…'

'I know exactly how it was. Belle's very stubborn and headstrong; she'd be a match for you any day, and I'm quite prepared to believe she did most of the courting. However that may be, it must all come to an end before we have a scandal on our hands. You're a very old and dear friend of ours, Will, but I'm sure Ephraim will agree with me that our daughter's good name mustn't be put at risk any longer. I shall start looking for a suitable husband for her at once, to take her mind off all this business.'

'It wasn't as you think,' Will said wearily. 'We love each other, Mary, however daft you may find it. If I were a free man I'd have asked you for her hand long since, and I'd wager a guinea to a farthing we'd have been a happy pair, for all I'm so much older. Belle needs someone like me to take her father's place, when she leaves home.'

'I'll thank you to let me be the judge of that,' Mary retorted. 'As it happens, it doesn't come into question, with your wife alive. So you'll oblige me by stopping away until she's married and gone.'

She rose briskly, as though everything were settled, but Ephraim stopped her as she went to pull the bell-rope. *Ringing for me to be shown out,* Will thought bitterly, *after so many years, as if I were a tradesman come to present a bill.*

'Mary,' Ephraim said sternly, 'I wish you'd spoken to me about this before. I value Will's friendship very dearly; I thought we all did, too much so to send him away like a servant caught stealing. There are things you don't know…'

Will caught his eye, shaking his head.

'I can't credit you with meaning any harm to Belle, Will,' he continued. 'All I'll say about that is that if you were a free agent I would happily consent to your marriage with her.' Mary began to speak, but he put up his hand. 'I think Mary may be right in asking you not to visit us so often, for your sake and Belle's. But our door will never be closed against you while I'm master in this house. Life has not been kind to you, and I won't be one to add to your troubles.' He took Will's hand and shook it heartily.

Will could hardly speak, but he managed to say, 'Thank you, old friend.'

Mary knew that her husband was very angry with her, and she had begun to realise that she had acted too swiftly, but she was too much woman to resist a parting gesture of dismissal. She took something from her pocket and gave it to Will. 'I made Belle give me this to return to you.' It was the little ring of diamonds, pearls and garnets.

Without a word Will put it in his pocket and strode out. In the hall they heard him asking Isaac for his coat and hat, then the shutting of the front door.

'What else could I have done?' Mary asked. And then, 'I'm sorry, Father.'

Ephraim made no reply, but brushed past her and left the house. She knew he would catch up with Will and try to comfort him. And though it was the brightest time of morning, her heart was heavy, and the room seemed full of ghosts from the past.

Ephraim's active nature was irked by his inability to help anybody in his unhappy family. He said no more to Mary, sensing that she knew herself in the wrong. There was nothing he could do for Belle, who was always in tears these days and barely able to speak to her mother. Dove went about with swollen eyelids and lines of tiredness on her face; George had written to say that the *Chloe's* return had been postponed for a further six months, but that they must be married as soon as he came home.

'No wonder the child frets,' Mary said.

Joe's nerve had been badly shaken by the attack on him, but he obstinately refused to take the least precaution in travelling about. Let Bradshaw try to ambush him again if he must, and perhaps succeed next time; he would face up to it like a man after his humiliating experience of falling into an old and elementary trap.

Ephraim worried greatly about him. He read up case after case, finding none that bore any relation to the circumstances, improbably lurid as they were. Having no proof of Bradshaw's intention to murder by proxy, or even that he was behind the attempt, there was no way of touching him. The man had committed no crime in the eyes of the law, except that of cohabiting with another man's wife...

Ephraim ran his pen through his hair, as was his habit when thinking deeply, then rang for his clerk. 'Send Mr Joseph in to me.'

When Joe arrived he was smartly motioned to the chair in which clients usually sat. Ephraim came straight to the point.

'I should like to know your feelings about the possibility of bringing an action for damages against Bradshaw, on the grounds of Criminal Conversation.'

'For —?'

Joe was familiar with the common law suit which enabled a husband to take his wife's paramour to court, and with luck to get damages based on the deprivation, loss of domestic comforts, public scandal and general affliction he was supposed to have suffered by the seduction of his wife. It had produced many a lively scene in court, and given Counsel for the Plaintiff unrivalled opportunities for dramatic, tear-drawing oratory. Only ten years or so before London had rung with the sensational details of Cox versus Kean, the suit brought by a City Alderman against Edmund Kean the tragedian. Joe remembered some of them, and scabrous caricatures passed round at his school.

He shook his head. 'What good would that do, Uncle? A lot of muck-raking with perhaps a few hundred pounds at the end of it, and bad feeling all round. Bradshaw could well afford the money, and the action wouldn't break him. I'm not sure what it would do to me, but nothing good, certainly.'

'True, true, O wise young judge. I merely toyed with the thought of attacking the man, perhaps persuading him to leave the district, object of scandal that he would be.'

Joe laughed shortly. 'Only an earthquake would do that. They don't have many of those round Bradhope. No, he's too old a fox to be caught, and he's used enough to scandal. You'd be surprised at the stories...'

'I probably know most of them. Very well. What would you say to embarking upon a suit for divorce?'

Joe sat up straight, startled. 'Divorce? But ... isn't it very rare? Has the firm handled many cases?'

'None. Not a single one on our files. The people of Lancaster appear to be either matrimonially fortunate or gifted with a high degree of resignation.' Ephraim permitted himself a smile at his verbal felicity. 'The suit is unpopular, naturally, being complicated, expensive, and uncertain in outcome. In some cases, that is. I fancy yours would be fairly straightforward.'

'How?'

'A mere admission of guilt is not sufficient to prove adultery. In other circumstances, your wife might declare at the Market Cross her association with Bradshaw, yet still remain legally married to you, for all the action the law might take.'

Joe shuddered. 'Rosie would probably enjoy that greatly. I can picture her in her best bonnet and shawl, standing on a barrow to entertain the crowds. You were saying, Uncle...?'

'That in this case it can be proved that opportunities exist, and have existed, for the parties to gratify their illicit passion, since your wife lives openly under the same roof as Bradshaw, and has been publicly seen in suggestive circumstances with him. On those grounds a *prima facie* case could be made out, and canon law satisfied.'

'I see.' Joe got up to pace the room. 'I'm quite ignorant of these things, Uncle. So what would be the procedure?'

'I must confess I don't know. I remember roughly what it used to be when I first read law, but that was long ago. Things are probably much changed. To find out, I think it would be advisable to me to visit London and consult those who would know. But, Joe, we mustn't be too hasty. It is only our assumption that Bradshaw wishes to marry your wife. I can think of no other reason why he should want to dispose of you, but the whole question is still in the air. Before taking action we must have more facts to go on.'

Joe was pondering, weighing an ivory paper knife in his hand as though it were his fate in the balance. At last he said, 'I shall call upon Shem Bradshaw.'

'Oho! Isn't that rather entering the lion's den — or putting your head into the cage?'

'Not at all. I hardly know the man, but he has a reputation for honesty and fair dealing; I wouldn't expect trouble from him, and in any case I am the innocent party in all this. Why should I be afraid of Shem?'

Ephraim nodded. 'You'd visit him at the mill, I take it, not at...'

'The Hall? That would be senseless, wouldn't it. I should probably get knocked on the head as I passed the lodge. No, I'll go to the mill. I know the best time to find him there.'

Shem's face gave nothing away as he listened to Joe. He drew neat geometrical patterns on a piece of headed paper, and embellished the result with a border of complex design. When he had finished he said, 'I see. You want to know my father's intentions towards your wife. Well, I can tell you in one word. Marriage.'

'We thought so.'

'Aye. For some reason that bitch, if you'll pardon the word, has taken his fancy. He wants to give her the earth — or as much of it as he's got to give.'

'You don't like her.'

A tinge of heat crept into Shem's pallid face. 'I loathe her. She's a noisy, flaunting trollop. I can see how an old dotard like Father might be hooked by her, but a sensible-seeming young man like you, Mr Atkinson ... well, it beats me.'

Joe said nothing.

'However, there's no accounting for tastes. Now, from my own point of view for Father to marry the woman would be a calamity, no less. If she turns into my stepmother, God help me, I'll leave the Hall; I might as well, for it'll be hers when he goes. Everything will be — my mother's jewels, the pictures...' He drew a square and filled it in with harsh strokes of his pen. 'So I might as well pack up sooner than later.'

'I'm very sorry for you,' Joe said, meaning it. 'All this trouble has come to you through me, I know.'

Shem looked up. 'Don't you fret about that. We can't order our lives to stop evil coming to others, can we? No, you go ahead and try for your divorce, and good luck to you. Never worry about me. Most likely I'll be disinherited anyway, who knows?' He rose and held out his hand.

A few days later, leaving sheets of instructions on running the office with Joe and his clerk, Ephraim departed for London.

CHAPTER EIGHTEEN

Ephraim stood at the window of his friend Blanchard's sitting room, on the third floor of the line of buildings called King's Bench Walk, in the Inner Temple. Many barristers kept their chambers only for their practice, living elsewhere, but Percy Blanchard, a bachelor fond of his comforts, had chosen to see clients in the darker, less attractive office behind this one, so that he might enjoy a front outlook in a room uncluttered by dusty books and deed boxes.

Ephraim thought he would have done the same in Blanchard's place. From the high window of the graceful old house he looked across a spacious courtyard to the Temple Gardens, dressed in the first green of spring, and beyond them the Thames, a grey river under grey skies, enlivened by many little boats round which fluttered and squawked hungry seagulls, waiting for scraps. In the Temple itself every building was gracious, stately, built by masters, breathing the leisured life of the law. Crown Office Row, Paper Buildings, Mitre Court, Middle Temple Hall where Queen Elizabeth had danced and Shakespeare had acted, the round church on whose floor lay ancient effigies of cross-ankled Crusaders, the oldest church in London: all had a calm delight for the eye and a blessed silence for the ear.

For many centuries this had been a place of quiet, though just beyond it Fleet Street clattered and rattled. Ephraim thought with a sigh of his own cramped premises in a little congested street, a wall opposite his only view, the constant noise of town traffic filtering through the windows. Here in the

Temple he felt more peaceful than he had done for a long time, free of home troubles. A waft of his youth came back to him.

How different might his life have been, had he chosen to practise here instead of in his native town? For, north country man that he was, he felt at home here. It was pleasant to feel a bachelor again, to enjoy a bachelor's life of tasty dinners brought in ready cooked, with no domestic problems attached, and to eat them waited on by a respectful manservant; pleasant to enjoy male company, when a few of Percy Blanchard's friends dropped in for a smoke and a few bottles of excellent Madeira; pleasant to stroll in the gardens where the wars of York and Lancaster had been declared by the plucking of red and white roses, to sit in Fountain Court, listening with half-shut eyes to the splashing of the water, or to meditate in Pump Court on the message of its sundial: *Shadows we are and like shadows depart.*

He enjoyed the smiles of the pretty girl who collected and brought back Blanchard's laundry. She was pleased to have an extra gentleman to admire her neat waist and coquettish gestures, and pay her compliments in what she thought of as quite a foreign voice. It was many years since Ephraim had flirted. He thought wistfully that he would have liked more opportunities.

St Leonard's Gate seemed very far away, an infinite distance. Released from its pressures, Ephraim realised with surprise how many of them he had carried over the years. There, the troubles of his young people had kept his brow in a continual furrow and weighed upon his heart, troubles which here felt almost light. Yet he must not forget them, for it was Joe's business that had brought him to London.

Blanchard, that sophisticated man of law with the cynical eye and the portly form, had been a happy choice for consultant. He specialised in matrimonial cases and knew all there was to be known about the diseases of marriage and the remedies, the law offered.

'Crim. Con. keeps me in port and sherry,' he told Ephraim. 'More and more of it all the time, now men are realising that with a little help from me they can screw a very pretty sum out of their wives' lovers. They were afraid of scandal once, but there's so much of it in the air these days they've ceased to care. It's become quite a skill, spying on the little woman, letting her beau have his fling, then making him pay for it. And why not, pray?' He lifted his wig off its stand and smoothed its wiry strands tenderly. 'There's no call to look so shocked, my dear Ephraim. Times have changed since old King George's day, thank God.'

'I have very little experience of such cases,' Ephraim said, sounding and feeling prim. 'But what of divorce, which affects the present instance?'

'Ah, what? I always hoped the late King would come down on the winning side of the Delicate Investigation. With morals like lusty Caroline's...' He drew a heavy breath. 'I could have handled it for him single-handed and sent him out of court a free man. Well, well, it was not to be. In view of His Majesty's own domestic arrangements there might have been a small matter of *compensatio criminis,* but I fancy we could have got over that fairly smoothly.'

'The King married foolishly, ill-advisedly, at the least. So did my nephew, who is quite as much in need of the law's services to free him, if not more, being a completely innocent party. What can be done for him?'

Blanchard blew some dust off his desk and trimmed a pen, preparing to enjoy himself in a burst of exposition. 'The law of divorce, based on the canon law of Rome, has remained almost unchanged since Henry VIII put away Queen Anne of Cleves. That is, the power to separate husband and wife lies with the Church, following more or less the *lex Julia de Adulteriis,* modified somewhat by the Emperor Justinian but repealed by his successor. The principle then remaining was that there could be no divorce *a vincula matrimonii,* from the bonds of marriage with freedom to take a second partner, but only *a mensa et thoro,* from bed and board — in other words, judicial separation. The same applies today. Via the ecclesiastical courts, divorce *a mensa* can be obtained … at a price.'

'But,' Ephraim said impatiently, 'what use is that, merely to put aside an erring partner? My nephew requires to be entirely free, in order that his present spouse may remarry — or that he may remarry himself,' he added, wondering why he did so, for there had never been any talk of Joe's wanting such a thing.

Blanchard untied the ribbon of the wig and lovingly retied it, smoothing out the creases. 'Ah, well. The Church has always reserved unto itself the right to grant absolute divorce, on sufficient grounds, such as cruelty. There was the classic case of Evans v. Evans in 1790…' His eyes searched the shelves for the appropriate work of reference.

'No cruelty is involved, only flagrant adultery.'

'Even so. It can be done, but the machinery is complex. The first approach must be to the appropriate diocesan court — in this case, the consistory court of York. An appeal must be made initially to special delegates appointed by the Crown *ad hoc.*' He noted Ephraim's air of bafflement, and added with a twinkle of his small bright eyes, 'But the case is altered, and only this year. The Privy Council has now been granted the powers which lay previously in the hands of the diocesan courts. So, you see, corners can be cut. In other words, Parliament may now wield the knife that severs the matrimonial cord. And here you stand, my dear friend, on the fringe of its petticoats.' He jerked his head in the general direction of Westminster.

'A private Act of Parliament, in fact.'

'Precisely. Rare in the old king's time, not too rare nowadays. But costly still. Has your client the means?'

Ephraim shook his head. 'All he has was sunk in Whittingham's mill. I could get nothing out of Bradshaw, not a penny. So the cost must be mine. How much would you reckon?'

'Seven hundred pounds, more or less.' Blanchard watched his friend's gloomy face. 'A great deal of money.' Then, the human being speaking for the lawyer, 'I would let you off my part of it, for old times' sake.'

Ephraim smiled. 'You're a good fellow, Percy. I know you would. Even so… Well, I have some stocks and shares. I bought some in the railway which have soared, the accountant tells me. My daughters' dowries will be poorer, but the sacrifice must be made for Joe's sake.' For the first time he told Blanchard the full story of Bradshaw's feud, the affaire of Rosie and the attempt on Joe's life. The barrister's bushy eyebrows rose and he whistled faintly.

'Strong stuff, eh? I thought such matters belonged on the stage of Drury Lane. Dear me, what a tame life we lead here in the Temple. I thought the case of Lord Tunnicliffe sensational enough, but it ended merely in a friendly duel.' He meditated. 'You're quite sure a comparatively simple separation wouldn't do?'

'Emphatically not. I know Bradshaw.'

'And your nephew — he has some thought of remarrying?'

'No,' Ephraim said, and was surprised by an odd feeling of doubt that accompanied his reply, for nothing had ever been said or suggested to him about Joe's having any attachment. What was the half-realised knowledge that haunted him? A look in someone's eyes, a tone of someone's voice? But he repeated, 'No.'

Blanchard had drawn forward a sheaf of paper and was beginning to make notes. 'Now. Names, dates, circumstances?'

Ephraim said, 'I'm very much obliged to you, Percy. Not only your time, but the cost...'

'Think no more of it, old friend. Crim. Con. is the port and sherry, divorce the champagne. If I bring this off, and from what you say there seems to be a sporting chance, the Law Society shall hear of it to a man, and I shall get every case that comes up and buy myself a new wig. But, mind you, the unravelling of this business will take time.'

Even before coming to London Ephraim had resolved to call upon Jesse and Eleanor. Mary had kept a grim silence about the visits of Margaret and Dove to that household, and the silence had been more condemnatory than if she had breathed fire and brimstone at them. It was time, he thought, for her own sake and everybody else's, to put a stop to the old enmity. He wrote to Jesse in those terms, and received an amiable reply. So it came about that he sat comfortably in Bryanston Street, regarding his sister-in-law and her lover, very much at home, very glad to have reached out a hand of reconciliation to them.

'First Margaret and Dove, then you,' said Eleanor happily. 'It seems as though the years were melting away and we are coming together again, we who were boys and girls together. If only Mary…'

'Ah, if only. But she's far from strong, Eleanor, and I can't force her to listen to me. Let's be thankful the rest of us are reconciled.'

Eleanor sighed. 'If only we could come back, just for the parliamentary recess! Even though Eagle Hall isn't fit to be lived in we could lodge somewhere and visit. I long to see Belle and Joe, and the old places. But Jesse is quite firm that his father would make trouble.'

Jesse said suddenly, 'About my father, Ephraim. You say he has upset all the improvements Margaret and Joe brought about in the mill. I wonder if he has complied with the stipulations of the Factory Act?'

Ephraim looked startled. 'The…? I read of it — a year or so ago, I think. But as to applying it to Bradshaw's — that would be Joe's affair, and I don't recall him mentioning it. Perhaps you'd remind me of its terms.'

'Three and Four William the Fourth, c. 103,' Jesse recited promptly. 'Compulsory education for two hours a day, and night work forbidden for all workers under eighteen years of age. Children between nine and thirteen to work only forty-eight hours per week and nine hours per day. Young persons between thirteen and eighteen to work not more than sixty-nine hours per week or twelve hours per day. No child allowed to work in a factory without a certificate from a surgeon that he or she is of the ordinary strength and appearance of a child of nine years or over. And so on.'

'It has not come my way, in the course of business. I should have thought Joe would have made some use of it against Bradshaw … but we're very much in the country, you know, away from the seats of judgment. And all this trouble at

Bradshaw's has arisen so recently. But surely some investigation would have taken place by now?'

'Ah,' Jesse said, 'so it should have done. But can you give me a guess how many factory inspectors have been appointed?'

Ephraim shook his head.

'Four. Four, to cover the whole kingdom, with factories springing up like mushrooms wherever rivers flow. Papers have been sent out to mill owners, I believe, but either torn up or left to gather dust, and I warrant you my father was among the tearers-up. Well, I'll look into it. A fine is the worst he'd incur, more's the pity, but it might do some good. Young Joe won't benefit by it now: is it too much to hope some of those poor children may? You knew, I suppose, that Malthus died a little over a year ago.'

'Malthus?'

'Thomas Malthus, the workers' best friend, the man who advocated the improvement of man by the limitation of population.'

'My dear,' Eleanor said gently, 'I'm sure Ephraim would rather hear about Malthus some other time. Just now we wish to talk of family matters.'

Jesse laughed. 'My old hobby-horse. Nay, but it's more than that. When I get back into the House I'll make them listen to me.'

'You've still not regained a constituency?' Ephraim asked.

'No, nor would it do me much good under Melbourne. He said not a word, you know, when the Tolpuddle Martyrs were sent overseas, only that "the law had been most properly applied". It was Grey who saw the Factory Act through, and now he's gone and that lounging lord's back in office, caring about nothing but the shine on his boots and Mrs Norton's ringlets.'

Eleanor shook her head warningly. 'Jesse. You'll make Ephraim think you a complete Radical, and a gossip besides.'

But Ephraim had listened attentively. 'Who is Mrs Norton?'

'Sheridan's granddaughter, a bluestocking with a fine pair of eyes and an even finer pair of ... very well, I'll be quiet, Nell. Enough to say that there's talk of Norton suing Melbourne for Crim. Con.'

Ephraim had not meant to say anything of his reason for visiting London. Professional discretion fought with family feeling, and lost, perhaps because of his unusually relaxed state and the pleasure of being reunited with Eleanor, combined with the delights of Jesse's excellent wine. He told them of the threat to Joe's life, and the solution he sought.

Jesse was appalled. 'The old devil! I always thought he had murder in him. But this ... I can scarcely believe it, even of him. My own father, in a plot to kill an innocent lad.'

'There's no proof,' Ephraim said quickly, wishing he had not spoken. 'Please forget I even hinted at it — I should not have been so indiscreet. But at least we know from your brother that marriage with Joe's wife is your father's aim, and if that can be brought about Joe may be free from persecution.'

'Divorce,' Eleanor almost whispered. 'Divorce. It's possible, then?'

'Possible, but extremely difficult,' Ephraim said hurriedly. 'In your case — if I may say so — I fear there would be no chance of it, unless your husband were prepared to bring an action, and had the means to pay for the proceedings.'

He saw the light die out of her face as she turned back to the embroidery which had fallen in her lap. It was many years since he had last met her, this younger and flightier sister of Mary's, yet he felt he knew her well. He saw from what strain his daughters got their silver-gilt hair and perfect skin, and recognised Belle's nature in the older woman. With bad luck in love, and mishandling, Belle might come to this. He thought of her unfortunate attachment to Will Raven; perhaps after all it was as well that Mary had taken the drastic action of parting them.

It was clear to him, already, that Eleanor longed deeply to be married, and that her relationship with Jesse had somehow led to disappointment and emptiness. He sensed that Jesse's ambitions were greater than his emotions. A decent, honest man, yet unable in himself to make a woman happy, unless she were able to create her own world. Watching Eleanor, as she sat by Jesse's side on a low stool, the firelight catching glints in her fading hair and moulding hollows in her cheeks, he felt deeply sorry for her and wished he had not raised her hopes even momentarily.

They talked of Lancaster affairs. 'How I should love to go home,' Eleanor said wistfully. 'Do you think it did the least good, Dove coming to see me? Margaret hoped it might.'

'So far as I know Mary has never said a word to Dove about it. I tried to broach the subject once, but Mary immediately talked of something else.'

'Women!' exploded Jesse. 'How many years has it been — twenty, twenty-one? I thought Mary a sensible creature, but it seems the sex are incapable of reason — begging your pardon, my dear, and always excepting you. Ephraim, I count on you to tell your wife of the grief she has caused her sister all these years, when a kind word would have made all the difference.'

Eleanor laid her hand on his. 'No, no. Better leave it. In any case, your father is a sufficient barrier to my returning to Lancaster. Let's talk of something else. What an enchanting child you have in Dove, Ephraim!'

'I rather think so,' replied the modest father. 'She's everything we could wish.'

'And such a beauty. The young men went down before her like ninepins; she could have made a good marriage had she been free. Yet Margaret told me she's unhappy with the match, and doesn't care for her George. What a sad pity!'

Ephraim started. 'Not happy?'

'Oh dear, perhaps I've let my tongue run away with me. You may well frown, Jesse, I know I'm always doing it. Margaret only said that she gathered the betrothal was an arranged one, and after all, they sometimes turn out the best, don't they, when the parents are wise enough to ... to...' She heard herself chattering on to a stricken-faced Ephraim.

'Mary and I certainly wished her to marry George,' he said. 'We thought him suitable in every way, and they had been friends since childhood. Yet you say... She seemed to accept the idea willingly enough, after a certain hesitation. She was very young, after all. Lately she has not seemed happy, but we took that to be caused by George's long absence.' He remembered Dove's listlessness, her swollen eyes at breakfast. Then there were George's letters, passed across the table as if they had been trade circulars, the air of mysterious sorrow about her that was surely more than pining for an absent lover. Now he had a clue to follow, and follow it he would, if it led to his daughter's happiness.

'I should never have spoken,' Eleanor said nervously.

'On the contrary, I'm glad you did. Parents are not always the first to see their children's troubles.' He pushed the problem to the back of his mind, and led the talk to general matters: King William's failing health and the betting odds on how soon his niece would succeed him, the construction begun on the Great Western Railway, the new waxwork show opened in London by a lady who had once modelled from heads cut off by the Paris guillotine. The evening passed pleasantly, and no more was said either of Ephraim's business in town or Eleanor's indiscreet remark.

Ephraim lay in bed that night thinking, thinking. Dove, Belle and Joe: Joe, Belle, and Dove, and around them floating faces like pantomime masks: Saul Bradshaw, Will Raven, George Dilworth, Eleanor and Jesse, Percy Blanchard's manservant, a hawker seen in the street. At last they merged into dream, as the Temple owls hooted in the trees and the moon sank over the pointed cap of the round church.

The divorce suit would be a long one, Blanchard warned. 'First must come a Crim. Con. action. Your nephew must sue Bradshaw for damages.'

Ephraim debated. 'How much?'

'Counsel will decide that. We shall have to engage Counsel, by the way; you may leave that to me. Evidence of the illicit association will be brought during these proceedings — you know the sort of thing, letters, witnesses to guilty scenes, all the grubby details the public loves.'

'I think it highly unlikely letters exist between Bradshaw and Joe's wife. She is illiterate, and he is not a man to pour out his soul on paper.'

Blanchard waved away the objection like a passing wasp. 'Then there must be witnesses, servants, that sort of thing. Mrs Atkinson seems not averse to public embracings, from what you tell me, and a guinea to a maid can produce whole orations on the private variety. Your nephew need not appear — I see you have apprehensions about that.'

'Well, I had. Joe is the sort of chivalrous young man who might well wreck his own case. I presume Bradshaw's presence isn't called for either?'

Blanchard shrugged. 'In my experience the co-respondent usually attends to safeguard his own interests and harangue his counsel between sessions. I can, if you like, arrange for the action to come on in London, at the Sheriff's Court. It is frequently done, if a divorce case is pending, since that can't be dealt with in the provinces.'

'Excellent. That will keep unpleasantness away from Lancaster. And you think the Crim. Con. suit will succeed?'

'In this instance I'd bet a pin to a case of pistols on it. So, with luck, your man will win a substantial sum, and believe me every penny will be needed to finance the Bill of Divorcement. That may go to the Lords once, twice, three times, how can one say? It depends on their lordships' temper and state of health, and the number of pious bishops who always rise up in their righteousness to forbid the parties to remarry.'

'But that,' said Ephraim, 'is the whole object in this case. If Bradshaw cannot marry … this young woman, then there's no point in proceeding, surely.'

'Ah, dear friend, I know that, and you know that, and their lordships will doubtless know it too; but devil a bit of difference will it make if the holier-than-thou faction are sitting, and the free-hearted lads are away shooting or doing a bit of whoring on their own account. No, no, we must take a chance on it. And, by the way, before the presentation of the bill the case must be heard in the appropriate consistory court, under the jurisdiction of the bishop of the diocese — which means, I fear, that Lancaster must come into it after all.'

Ephraim groaned. 'On the doorstep. As I feared. Percy, is all this rigmarole going to be worth the candle? I begin to wonder.'

'Your decision, dear boy. All up to you. For me it means a fee to handle the London end and anything else you like. Obviously to my advantage, then, but you know well enough that I'd waive it without a second thought if you so decided.'

In the branches of a plane tree outside the window a starling was perched, sending out its sweet shrilling call to attract its mate, sometimes plunging its beak into its glossy feathers. How lucky were birds, Ephraim thought, to have no legal ties, no harassing complications in their short lives. But he, alas, was trapped in the human condition. He turned to Blanchard.

'I'll proceed — with your help.'

CHAPTER NINETEEN

A coffee pot overturned, flooding the cloth on the breakfast table, as Saul Bradshaw sought among the plates and dishes and among the sheets of the *Gazette*.

'Damn it, where's my spectacles?' he roared. Rosie, yawning and dishevelled in a yellow bedgown with a double lace collar, pointed to the missing article lurking behind the butter dish. It always made Saul bad-tempered to lose his spectacles and therefore have to admit that he needed them. He perched them on his nose and scrutinised the letter addressed to him in beautiful copperplate, with a London frank on it, broke the seal and began to read. After a few words he threw it down.

'It's come to t'wrong shop. Some sort of law business.' He tossed it aside.

'Has it got your name on it?' Rosie enquired, through a mouthful of kedgeree.

'Aye. Inside as well as outside. But they don't know a B from a bull's foot, yon wiggy chaps. Likely it's meant for some other Bradshaw.'

'Funny it should come to your address, then, in't it?'

He had picked it up again and was painstakingly following the opening lines of the letter. '*Notice of... Sheriff's Court ... in the case of Atkinson v. Bradshaw...* here, what's this?' Without reading further, he banged violently on the handbell used for summoning servants. Black appeared promptly from the corridor: it didn't do to be too far away when the master wanted a second helping. But Saul bawled at him, 'Fetch my son, and quick!'

Shem, who deliberately took his time in appearing, found his father purple-faced and breathing heavily. Ignoring Rosie, he asked, 'What's the matter, Father? A bit early, isn't it?'

Saul tossed the letter across to him. 'Read that.'

Shem ran his eyes down the single page, his expression changing as he read from impassivity to something like suppressed amusement.

'Well?' Saul snapped.

Slowly, enjoying it, Shem said, 'It's notice of the hearing of an action for Criminal Conversation, served on Saul Bradshaw, Esquire, by Joseph Atkinson, Esquire. To be heard at the Sheriff's Court, Bedford Row, London, on Monday, March 16th.'

Saul stared. 'Criminal ... what the heck's that? I've done nowt criminal.'

'I think,' Shem suggested demurely, 'it's the term used for seducing another man's wife.'

Rosie, all eyes, startled out of her drowsiness, exclaimed, 'Me!'

'And what about it?' Saul demanded. 'They don't hang you for it, do they?'

'I don't believe so. It's a way of making a man pay for his fun. At least I think so, but then I lead a very quiet life.' He laid down the paper and slipped out of the room, followed by a torrent of roared blasphemies, the crash of crockery, and Rosie's screams.

Shem smiled broadly to himself all the way to the mill. What if the action did lead to his father's remarriage and his own disinheritance? It would be well worth it.

The word *divorce* was not breathed at St Leonard's Gate. Ephraim felt he had already gone far enough in mentioning it to Eleanor, and thereby unintentionally increasing her discontent. Its very sound would alarm Mary; divorce was a thing which happened only to royalty and the aristocracy in the most scandalous circumstances. It had been breathed in connection with the late uncrowned Queen Caroline, fifteen years before; details of her alleged indiscretions had made the papers quite unfit to be read aloud at the breakfast table. The idea of involving Joe in its horrid processes would be quite unthinkable to Mary. So Ephraim kept a guilty silence, knowing full well that she guessed he had a secret. Joe, too, kept quiet, gladly enough. He loathed the thought of a public exposure of his situation and a possible confrontation with Saul Bradshaw and Rosie. Better to be still and take the consequences of a marriage which had been his own choice. But Ephraim was implacable; the wheels had been set in motion and must run on. Reluctantly enough Joe accompanied him to London for the hearing of the Crim. Con. action.

Bedford Row had a solemn, legal air. Its tall, plain houses looked as if they would stand no nonsense or frivolity of any kind. Their windows were bare of curtains, canary-birds in cages, or potted geraniums, their paint was shabby and peeling, as though no housewives cared for them. A March wind swept the dusty pavements, sending grit into the eyes and a chill to the bones. Joe felt as if the chill had reached his heart and settled on it, as he sat by his uncle on a hard bench with an upright back. In front sat Mr Bethune, his counsel, and Mr Tripp, junior counsel. On opposite benches were ranged Bradshaw's two advocates, and Bradshaw himself behind them, Shem at his side.

Joe met Bradshaw's eyes, fairly and squarely, receiving such a glare of hatred from them that he looked away, observing the witness box, empty as yet; the jurymen, who on the whole appeared cold, sleepy and uninterested; the judge, Mr Justice Ryland, whose enormous shabby wig must at least keep his head warm, Joe reflected, if it did nothing for his dignity.

Mr Bethune rose to open the case for the plaintiff. A man of severe and scholarly aspect, his was the ideal manner for breaking down the confidence of the other side. In long, rolling phrases shot with barbs of biting sarcasm, he invited the court to consider the situation of a worthy young man, Mr Joseph Atkinson, scion of a highly respected north country family noted for acts of philanthropy which had cheered and alleviated the lives of many mill workers toiling in conditions unimaginable to those present in court.

'Conditions, gentlemen, unimproved by the stipulations of the recent Factory Act: an Act mercifully reducing the work hours of children and young persons, permitting them two full holidays a year and eight half-holidays, and demanding that they be provided with a Christian education.

'It is a remarkable circumstance, gentlemen, that the stipulations of this Act — nay, its very existence — would seem not to have reached the ears of the defendant. We live in days of communications by road and railway unknown and undreamed of by our forefathers. Speed is our watchword, the might of science smooths our way wherever we may tread. Is it not, then, strange that the defendant, a man of ripe years and sufficient intelligence to control the workings of a large factory, should be unaware that for some fourteen months he has been breaking the law by omission?

'True, the defendant is not alone in his inexplicable innocence or ignorance. Reports have come to our ears of mill children whose education was administered to them by the factory fireman in the coal-hole.'

He paused for laughter, and Ephraim murmured to Joe, 'He's done his homework, I must say.'

Mr Bethune went on to point out that this woeful state of affairs had been remedied by one man alone — his client; at which Joe blushed painfully and wished he were a hundred miles away. He heard his modest achievements at Bradhope built up into something to be envied by the well-known reformer Lord Ashley, that friend of the poor and oppressed. His character, he learned, was a cross between that of the late Saint Sebastian and Mrs Elizabeth Fry.

'My young client, gentlemen, not content with tireless efforts to improve the lot of the oppressed workers, went further: he took one of them to wife.'

Murmurs in court and many stares concentrated on the unhappy Joe.

'The young woman, Rose Giles,' Mr Bethune went on, 'was the sole remaining daughter of a widow, and like her, a factory hand in Whittingham's mill, of which my client was junior manager. Connected as he is, might it not be supposed that he would not lower his eyes to a female so far beneath him in worldly status, but rather seek a young lady of his own station in life? It might. But such was not the case. His fancy charmed by her appearance, many would have forgiven him had he but toyed with her affections. Such behaviour was beneath him.

'Of her virtue, gentlemen, I cannot speak.' (Cries of 'Shame!') 'I can produce no witness to testify to it. That my client believed her to be wholly chaste there is not the slightest doubt, or he would not have taken the great and precarious step of marrying her.

'Raised as she was to a condition in life far beyond her expectations, do we now see her wholly devoted to the husband who had taken her from, so to speak, the gutter, and placed her in a palace: that is, a modest comfortable home where she might develop and exercise those qualities of womanly meekness and self-improvement of which my client, no doubt, looked forward joyfully to seeing the blossom and fruit?

'Alas, it was not to be. I shall bring before you witnesses to testify that in her husband's grave illness, contracted in the vile atmosphere of the defendant's factory, she did not care for and tend him as a wife should; and, even more shameful, no sooner had he been removed by his friends to their own care than she returned to her former work, and within a week had succumbed to the seducing wiles of the defendant, whose paramour she soon became.'

The judge pushed his glasses down his nose and interrupted mildly, 'I think we must allow that to emerge in evidence, Mr Bethune.'

The counsel bowed and continued. 'I cannot condone it, gentlemen. Which of us can, indeed? Yet, *honi soit* … it is my firm belief that Mrs Atkinson would have remained, even in separation from him, true to her spouse, but for the vile allures practised upon her. You see the defendant, gentlemen: mark his white hairs, his well-fleshed form, his costly clothing, and ask yourselves why a man so affluent should stoop to a young woman far below him in birth, though elevated by marriage? Then ask yourselves further why one so near the dread moment when he must answer to his Maker should imperil that moment by dragging down such a woman, hitherto honest (to our belief) to a depth lower than hell itself? Are there no whorehouses for such a man's pleasure, that he should debauch the wife of an equal?'

Amid the mutters, gasps and titters, Joe saw Saul Bradshaw struggle and heave, held down by Shem, and utter words which fortunately could not be heard for the general noise. In the next minutes he was described variously as a viper in the bosom, a wrecker of pious hopes, a living corruption, and Antichrist. Ephraim was smiling broadly.

'We've got the right man on our side,' he whispered to the embarrassed Joe. 'He's pitching it rather strong, but they're eating it up.'

The oration at last over, witnesses were called. A neighbour from Bradhope testified to Rosie's swift return to work and disappearance from her cottage, and added a few tart remarks about her neglect of her husband. Saul's manservant, Black, and a maid, Deborah Smith, gave damning evidence of the relationship in which their master and Mrs Atkinson lived at Bradshaw Hall, their bedrooms adjoining and the possessions of one frequently being found in the apartment of the other. When they had finished no possible doubt was left in the minds of the hearers that the couple lived together in every sense. There were unfortunately no letters to be read out, a loss to the hopeful jury. But the woman neighbour, recalled on a point, let herself go with some of the legends of Saul's dealings with women still current in Bradhope, until Mr Justice Ryland stopped her on the grounds that hearsay and repute were not evidence. Still, they had made their mark.

After the dinner-time adjournment it was the turn of the defendant's counsel, Mr Carthew, to dilate on his client's long and prosperous reign at Bradhope, his record of honest dealing, his pathetic widowerhood, the disgraceful elopement of his younger son with a female relative of the plaintiff's, whose virtue, he implied, was nothing to boast about. As to Rosie, his only possible line was to imply that she had thrown herself at an aged, compassionate man, who had opened his house and purse for her protection, since when she had taken full advantage of his indulgences to obtain a vampire-like hold on him in order to secure his wealth for her own use. There could, he averred, be no valid claim for damages where the defendant had no clear motive for procuring the dishonour of a woman so far beneath him.

It was not a very strong defence, particularly in view of Saul's violent, choleric appearance, the very opposite of the snowy-haired patriarch drawn by Mr Carthew. He appeared, to the jury and the court, the picture of a vile seducer. The type was common, an overhang from the last century into this more moral one, the situation commoner still. Everyone could call to mind fat royal dukes and low-born mistresses, not to mention stories in the papers of discarded women found drowned or hanged from trees. They had not seen Rosie herself; she might well be a sweet girl, for all Mr Bethune's somewhat censorious picture of her, which could have weakened his case.

By five o'clock on that dark cold afternoon, anxious to get home, the jury retired briefly and returned to award the plaintiff the sum of three thousand pounds damages.

On the way back to the Temple Joe said, 'I wouldn't go through that again for all the tea in China. How can men make a living by talking such twaddle? I was even sorry for old Bradshaw. It might well kill him.'

'Nothing of the sort,' Ephraim said happily. 'At least I hope not, as it would also kill the action. No, he'll pay up and bask in the reputation of having conquered a young woman at his advanced age. And that's the first round in the game won, my dear Joe. The consistory court should take a rosy view of your case, after that. Come, you'll never make a living out of the law if you don't accept its little fictions. "Only pretty Fanny's way", you know.'

Joe pulled up the collar of his greatcoat against the wind. 'I begin to wonder what I *shall* make a living at,' he said bleakly. 'So far I've proved uncommonly poor at everything.'

Ephraim glanced sympathetically at him, knowing very well the humiliation he was feeling even though he had been on the winning side of the unsavoury game. He was pleased to remember that Percy Blanchard had promised to lay on a good supper, to be supplied by the inn across the way, either for celebration or consolation. Thank God it would be celebration.

George Dilworth was coming home. The letter arrived in the usual sea-battered state on a bright morning of early April. Dove read it, then laid down her knife and fork and pushed her plate aside before passing it across the table to her mother. Belle, next to her, read the foreign frankings on the back of it and wondered what was to come. The three women were alone at table, Ephraim and Joe still away on the mysterious business in London about which their family had been told nothing.

Reading, Mary smiled. 'Well, what splendid news. Early next month, George says. Let me see: June brides are said to be lucky, but July would be just as good. I must speak to the vicar quite soon, there's such a call on him for summer weddings, and I shall call in on Arabella this afternoon...'

'Mother.' Dove's tone was ominous. 'There will be no wedding.'

Mary's mouth dropped open. 'No wedding? But, my dear...'

'I can't marry George. Oh, I've dreaded telling you. I've put it off, again and again, but now I must speak. I don't love him, Mother. I never have, but I knew you wanted it, and I thought it would be … better than a single life. All the time George has been away he's seemed … not quite real, a memory of someone I used to know who might never come back. Sometimes I hoped he might not come back.'

'You wicked girl!'

Dove met the accusing glance squarely. 'I know I'm wicked. But I meant George no harm, only that if he met another girl, or went to … to America, perhaps, I should not have to make up my mind. Well, I have made it up, and I'm so very sorry, Mother, but I can't marry him.'

Mary was looking suddenly old, her face collapsed into sagging folds. 'My spirits of salts, Belle,' she said. 'In my reticule.'

Dove jumped up and ran to put her arms round her. 'Mother, please don't distress yourself, it's not the end of the world, and you must have known I didn't love George. Come now, confess! I've been honest with you, now you're to be honest with me.'

Mary sniffed the salts. 'You weren't sleeping,' she said. 'We — I thought you were pining for George.'

'Wouldn't I have said so? Did I ever speak of him — as a lover, or in any other way? Belle knew, didn't you?'

Belle nodded.

'I think you all did, in your hearts, but you said nothing,' Dove went on. 'Well, now it's out, and I'm glad. You must tell Aunt Arabella, and I shall write to George at once so that he will know before he sails from Antigua. In a little while it will all be forgotten, and you'll be thankful I didn't let it drag on and then run away at the altar, or some such dreadful thing.'

Mary shook her head helplessly. 'But I don't understand. George is such a pleasant creature. How could you not like him? Or is there another attachment? No, I can't think that.'

She began to weep quietly. 'We've been so unlucky in our family. Why should it have happened like this? One of my sisters living in sin, the other unmarried, one daughter...'

'We won't speak about it!' Belle flashed out.

Mary mopped her eyes. 'I've tried to be a good mother ... I don't know where I've failed. Oh, I wish your dear father were here, or Joe... I think I shall go back to bed.

'I'll take you,' Dove offered, but Mary pushed her away.

'No, not you. Ring for Aggie.'

The men, on their return, were not surprised, both knowing what they did, though Ephraim was ignorant of Joe's involvement. He comforted Mary as only he could, assured her that girls were changeable, Dove was still very young, there were plenty of other eligible young men and no wars to take them away; Mary must not think of this as anything but a little disappointment. She smiled up at him and dried her tears, but he knew that she was very unhappy.

Joe asked Dove, 'Why did you do it?'

'You know,' she answered levelly.

'Yes, God help me, I do, and how do you suppose it will help either me or you?'

They were in the old schoolroom, now made into an informal parlour where the three of them could entertain friends without trespassing on adult preserves. From the window they could look down to Adam's grave, and the big pear tree in which they had once had a swing. Dove knew that if you looked carefully you could still see the frayed ends of its ropes knotted round the branches. It was comforting to look at, making time seem all one and the pains of today less sharp. She picked up an old doll she had kept through the years, a battered, noseless creature in a faded lace dress, and, holding it to her, went to sit by Joe, on the low window seat.

'Look at Jemima,' she said. He glanced down at the doll cradled in her arm.

'Well? What about Jemima?'

Dove said softly, leaning against him, 'She was always my favourite baby, when we were children. I still have her, you see, and I don't care if I never have any real babies of my own.'

'You don't know what you're saying.'

'Yes, I do, very well. I don't want children if I can't have yours. I don't want to have to go away and live in a strange house with a strange man, and never see you except at family parties. I'd rather be dead, up in the churchyard beside the White Lady. Joe, do you know what Belle remembered when she was ill, talking nonsense? It was an old game we used to play — we, and Ann Ashbury and Penny Colthard, out in the garden there:

Water, water wildflower, growing up so high,
We are all young maidens and we have got to die…'

He pulled himself away from her. 'Don't, Dove. Don't say such things.'

'Well, we *have* got to die, haven't we? Only we shall be old maidens, not young ones, Belle and I, living here at home, and I shall pretend I'm your sister, just as when we were little, and none of us will ever think of how it might have been.'

She saw the emotion in his face and was sorry that to indulge her own wretchedness she had tortured him as well as herself. When he moved to the door she ran after him and caught his arm. 'Don't go.'

'I must. I'm going for a walk.'

'Where? Let me come with you.'

'No. And I don't know where. Caton, perhaps, or Bowland. Tell Aunt not to keep supper for me, I'll find some at an inn.'

He walked rapidly, purposefully, like a man escaping from relentless fate, along the road that led eastwards into wild hill country, streams and forest, grazing land and moor. It was in his mind to do anything desperate that would break the web they were caught in: walk to Bradshaw Hall and drag Rosie away by force, to live with him as his wife again, putting an end to Dove's foolish impractical plan to ruin her life for him, and to this endless tedious lawsuit, which any time now would come on in Lancaster and draw in every journalist in the county to note down its sordid details.

Or, more simply, to walk and walk until he came to High Wolfhole Crag, and climb its steeps, and never come down.

CHAPTER TWENTY

'Come in here,' Belle said in a furious undertone, and pulled Dove by the arm into the small sitting room that opened off Mary's parlour. Kicking the door shut, she turned on her sister.

'How could you be such a fool? I've kept my temper till now but I must speak out. I've lost all patience with you, I declare! I thought you were resigned to George even though you don't care for him. And now to throw away your chance, and all for what?'

'Let go — you're hurting my arm. What do you mean? Why are you so cross?'

'You know very well. You've upset Mother and Father, and even Joe won't thank you...'

'Joe knows already.'

'Oh, does he? And was he pleased?'

Dove looked away. 'No.'

'There, you see! You've made a martyr of yourself to no purpose at all. But then, I suppose you'll enjoy that, won't you, drooping about like one of those females on a mourning brooch, and going off in a consumption if you can manage it.'

Dove's cheeks flared into angry colour. 'What a cruel thing to say! I shan't enjoy anything about it. Do you realise I have to face Aunt Arabella and Uncle Jack, and all the other Dilworths, not to mention George when he comes home? I'll be called a heartless jilt at the best, I suppose, and a promise-breaker, and all sorts of things. I tell you, Belle, what I did this morning was hard to do — I got no pleasure out of it, and I shall get no pleasure out of anything that comes out of it.'

'And what do you suppose you *will* get out of it?'

'How can I tell? Peace of mind. The knowledge that I've wronged neither George nor myself by marrying him.'

'And afterwards? Have you thought about that, year after year of living at home, being Mother's spinster companion, fading away until you're a dried-up old lady in a shawl and steel spectacles, dying alone, without even a kiss to remember? What sort of future is that?'

Dove was by now as angry as Belle. 'It's the same future as yours will be!' she retorted. 'What about your situation, moping and pining for Will when you know he can't marry you? You could perfectly well make up your mind to settle down with somebody else, and Mother did put several young men in your way at the Assembly Rooms only last week, yet you wouldn't look at any of them. Don't you call *me* names, Belle Atkinson, when you're as stubborn as a mule yourself!' She paused, breathless.

'It's not the same,' Belle said sulkily.

'How? How? What will you do, except turn into a poor old maid?'

Belle hesitated. 'Something.'

'Yes?' Dove laughed suddenly, throwing her arms round her sister. 'Belle, you silly goose, we're quarrelling, you and I. Twins, quarrelling! And all about nothing, for we're in just the same situation. Don't you see, it's because we're really one person that we've got into such a pickle ... the *same* pickle. So shall we stop this silly fight and kiss and make up, as we always have?'

Belle hugged her tightly. 'Oh, Dove. I'm truly sorry. I was angry for *you,* you see, not for myself or anybody else.'

'I know. Pax?' They had picked the word up from Joe's schooldays.

'Pax. And no more to be said.'

Mary stayed in bed all that day, waited on by the girls and a silently reproachful Aggie, who would dearly have loved to give Dove a piece of her mind, but dared not. The twins went about their business, Dove visiting her friend Ellen Ashworth to take a party of relations round the antiquities of the castle and Priory Church, Belle staying at home, thinking, moving to and fro restlessly. She had been wrong to attack Dove, she knew, and everything Dove had said in her unaccustomed anger had been justified.

She spent a long time in their shared bedroom. That evening she sat working at a cross-stitch panel for a chairback, very intently, saying little, while Dove wrote her letter to George. The candles had not been lit above an hour when she began to yawn.

'Oh, dear. It must be the dull weather, I feel I could sleep till Christmas.'

Dove laughed. 'You? You should have walked as far as I have today, all round the castle, the court … all those coats-of-arms and portraits! Even the prison cells, though we hurried past those. There was a poor young woman there nursing her baby — imagine it, how cruel, and on show to anyone who cared to look! We must have read every gravestone in the churchyard, including our family's. I felt quite proud to have so many relations buried there.' She nursed her feet in turn. 'All very well for Ellen, living almost next door to the place.'

'Well,' said Belle, with another artistic yawn, 'I may not have walked as far as you, but I'm uncommonly tired. I'll look in on Mother on the way upstairs. Say goodnight to Father for me. Is Joe home yet? I haven't heard him.'

'No. One of those walks of his. Aggie will keep some supper hot for him.'

'Yes. Goodnight, Dovekin. Let poor George down lightly.' She dropped a kiss on her twin's hair and went upstairs.

Once there, she worked with feverish activity. Taking off her dress and hanging it up, she took a simple gown from the wardrobe, and a cloak with a hood. These she laid inconspicuously over the back of a chair. Then she put on her nightgown, voluminous, long sleeved and high-necked, ornately frilled, over her underclothes: petticoats, chemise, stays, drawers and stockings. Her nightcap on, she climbed into bed and settled herself among warm soft goose feathers, so comfortably that she was even dozing when Dove came to bed. Her resolution was made, cost what it might.

Peace of mind, Dove had said. Very well, a bold stroke might secure her own peace of mind.

She slept for two or three hours, fitfully. When she finally roused herself the room was in pitch darkness, not a glimmer penetrating the heavy curtains. Dove was breathing quietly; Belle imagined her lying half on her face, as she always did, one hand touching her cheek.

Softly, skilfully — for she had practised it earlier — she drew off the nightgown and laid it on the bed. From under the pillow she took a box of matches, the friction type which had only a few years earlier succeeded the old, clumsy tinder box. A scrape of one of its thin wooden splints on the strip of sandpaper, and a tiny flame had sprung up to show her the dress and cloak, the ankle boots hidden behind the valance of the bed, and the small bundle beside them. By the light of the match she tiptoed to the door, her arms filled, gently turned the knob, and was out on the dark landing.

Thanks to the number of bedrooms in the house, she was some distance away from her parents. She lit another match to locate the dress and cloak. When its flame had died and all was dark again, she slipped on the boots and tied their ribbons as best she could without seeing; they would have to wait to be fastened properly.

Downstairs — and how stairs creaked, when one didn't wish to be heard! — she made her way to the small parlour where, earlier that day, resolution had come to her. A half-glazed door separated it from the garden, only secured by bolts at top and bottom. Softly she drew them and stepped out into the dark coolness. By the faint light of the stars she made her way round the house to the stables. There was the lantern on its accustomed hook. She lit it, fastened her boots, and went to the fourth stall, where Joe's mare, Rinalda, was stabled. Rinalda was a chestnut, gentle and biddable, a filly whose dam had once won the coveted Town's Plate. Both girls rode her in Joe's absence.

Belle chirruped to her and heard a sleepy whicker in reply. She entered the stall, patted and caressed the mare and harnessed her, praying that nobody in the house was awake to see the light. A huge oak tree overhung and shadowed the stables; once she and Gilbert had hidden in its shade from Joe, unsuspecting Joe. She shivered at the memory.

'Rinny, come on, girl. Out. Softly, now.' Puzzled but obedient, the mare followed her into the yard, along the carriageway leading to the road. Once out of it, and beyond the house, on the corner of Church Street, where a mounting block was built into the railings. Belle climbed on to the mare's back. It was fortunate that a side saddle was kept in the stable; modern skirts were not suitable for riding astride, and no convenient male garments were available for this rash enterprise.

How rash it was she would not let herself think. Dove's reproaches had shown her what she knew in her heart: she must break prison and go to Will. There had been other flights in the family, with unlucky endings — Aunt Eleanor's elopement with Roderick Mackenzie, Aunt Margaret's vanishing with the company of players. This too might end badly, but she must take a chance on that. Will might not want her. No, he would, he must, and they would face her family together. Anything would be better than this half-life in a troubled house. She thought of her mother's weak heart, and the worried frown her father so often wore nowadays, but put the thoughts from her.

The night was moving towards dawn, the stars paling, the sky brightening. Even in the town streets the air was fresh, exhilarating. She could smell the river, and the sea, and gardens at the backs of houses. Her blood tingled even with the gentle trotting of Rinalda. She longed to urge the mare to speed, imagining herself a heroine of romance galloping with her hair streaming behind her. But it was still too dark to risk galloping, and she very much doubted whether Rinalda would take kindly to the idea, after a life of staid progresses with Joe in and around the town. And it would make dreadful havoc of Belle's neat ringlets to let them loose in the wind. She had her appearance to think of when she reached Kendal.

They were over the bridge, on the Kendal Road at last, sometimes passing scattered houses and farms, sometimes travelling between tracts of open country. Fortunately it was not highwayman territory, and in any case she had brought only a few shillings with her, and none of her simple jewellery.

Dawn came, a sunless, grey dawn, finding her past the village of Burton, almost half the distance she had to travel. The birds were awake, chirping and twittering in competition with the crowing of cockerels and the dolorous moos of cattle going to first milking. Glad that darkness was gone, Belle began to sing under her breath, and to dream of her arrival at Kendal, of Will's astonishment and delight. He would scold her at first, of course, but then she would make him see that she had done what was best for them both in coming to him. She visualised his face, gloomy as when she had last seen it, then brightening with joy at her presence. What would his shop be like? She hardly knew Kendal. Merely to know herself drawing nearer to him every minute was heady excitement.

Her dreams were broken by Rinalda stumbling on a patch of stony road, almost throwing Belle off her back. Shaken, she pulled the mare up.

'You clumsy thing, Rinny. Can't you look where you're going?' She shook the bridle reins and they moved off again, but Rinalda was limping. After a few paces Belle halted her again, dismounted, and picked up the forelegs one by one. In the right hoof a sharp stone was wedged between the shoe and the frog of the foot. Without a sharp instrument there was no means of dislodging it. Belle got to her feet and stroked the mare's neck.

'Yes, I know, you're hurt. Well, never mind about it, we'll walk.'

She walked, leading Rinalda at a gentle pace, for more than two tedious miles before they came to a farmstead, the first sign of human life. There was movement in the farmyard, cows winding their way from the shippon, somebody feeding hens with loud cries of 'Chucky, chucky, come then!' Belle tied her mount to a post and went to investigate. A woman in a gingham bonnet and all-concealing pinafore stopped, tin basin on hip, between the poultry pens and the back door of the farm, staring Belle up and down.

'My horse has gone lame and I must get to Kendal,' Belle explained. 'Would you be so kind as to put her up and find me some kind of conveyance? Perhaps you have a spare horse, or a gig?'

'And p'raps we've not,' the woman snapped. 'You want an inn, not a farm. Good day t'you.'

She turned on her heel, Belle calling after her, 'Won't you at least keep my mare? She's in pain, she can't go much further.'

The farmer's wife turned, irritably enough, but to her a horse in trouble was quite a different matter from a put-out, stuck-up young lady who was probably no better than she should be, riding alone at that hour. She shouted something unintelligible to Belle, then produced a young man in a smock who listened impassively to the story, scratching and yawning. Belle was relieved to see him make his way back to the road, untether Rinalda and lead her back to the farmyard, watched darkly by the farmer's wife. Doubtless, Belle thought, she imagined the creature to be stolen property.

'I'm very grateful to you,' she said to them both. 'If you would rest and feed her...' She fumbled in the purse at her waist. 'There's four shillings towards it, and I'll come or send for her within a day or so. If you *could* find me another mount...'

'We've none to spare,' said the woman. 'Up t'road they'll happen find summat for you.'

'How far is it?' enquired Belle, her heart sinking.

'Three mile, maybe four.' The woman turned her back and retreated. Rinalda and her keeper had already disappeared. There was nothing for it but to set out on foot, however unwillingly.

The distance to Endmoor village was more four miles than three. Belle reached it tired, footsore in her pathetically inadequate laced boots, hungry and cross. It was no consolation to find Endmoor's only inn, the Green Dragon, barely stirring, a sleepy servant scrubbing the steps, another inside clearing up the bar room. Belle's polite requests for breakfast in the first place and transport in the second were received with uninterested stares.

'There's a coach comes by at half past ten,' the domestic told her. 'We put breakfast on for that — there's nowt before.'

'But,' said poor Belle, 'there must be something you could give me? I don't mind what, anything.'

'Anything' proved to be a piece of fatty ham served with bread and butter which had obviously been cut the previous day, and a lukewarm cup of tea. If she had not been so avidly hungry she could not have touched it. She gulped it down somehow, and laid yet another of her shillings on the table. Her enquiries about transport to Kendal met with blank looks, until someone said, 'Owd Meg's bound for Kendal market.'

And with Owd Meg, an ancient, gipsyish crone smoking a blackened clay pipe, Belle eventually set out, perched uncertainly next to her companion on the driving seat of a farm waggon packed with vegetables, eggs, poultry and a loudly complaining pig. Mercifully, Owd Meg's conversation was limited to an occasional curt direction to the stout horse. They drove northwards out of Endmoor, Belle blissfully unconscious that they had passed the very cottage where Will had lived secretly with Jane Atkinson, now his lunatic wife.

It was late morning when they reached the southern end of Kirkland, where Kendal began. Belle elected to get down there and walk the rest of the way, thanking Owd Meg graciously and bestowing two shillings on her, which were received with a stare and a mutter which might have meant anything, but certainly included disapproval of flighty madams travelling on their own.

Stiff and sore, feeling her lack of sleep and the stresses of the journey, she walked northwards up the long high street that was all one thoroughfare calling itself by different names as it went along. Finkle Street, she was told, lay to her right, almost opposite the Fleece. It seemed a long, weary way, pushing through crowds on their way to the market, and she was only buoyed up by the thought of the welcome that awaited her.

At last she came to it, turning the corner by the new town hall. Its carillon of bells was playing the melody of *Highland Laddie*; three hours later it would oblige with *Rule Britannia,* and at six would sign itself off with a hymn tune.

Butcher, haberdasher, pawnbroker, grocer … with a jump of the heart she saw the name RAVEN painted up over a shop window containing a jumble of objects. She put a hand to her hair, pushed back the hood of her cloak, hoped her face was not dirty after the harassing journey, and opened the shop door.

A loud clangour sounded from its bell. The shop was empty. Curious shapes loomed up, a small piano or organ, a half-suit of armour. On the walls hung garments, old flags and pennants, shawls, antique bonnets; a counter was piled up with oddments. The atmosphere was stale, redolent of old neglected things, and of dust.

Belle waited for what seemed like minutes, then opened and shut the door again, renewing the shouting of the bell. Upstairs there was movement, footsteps, an opening door. The footsteps began to descend the stairs that went up from behind the counter, and round the bend of the staircase Will appeared.

He stopped abruptly, blinking; she thought he must have been asleep. Then he said, 'Belle?' as though he could not quite believe what he saw.

'Yes. I've come to you, Will.'

It sounded oddly stagey, she knew as she said it, but he seemed not to take it in. Slowly he descended the stairs and was face to face with her. If he had been asleep so late, it must have been in his clothes, which were crumpled, his cravat unpressed, creases in his jacket. He looked pale, heavy, unshaven, as she had never seen him look.

'Belle,' he repeated. Then, 'How did you get here?'

'How did I get here?' Her tone was tart. 'With a great deal of difficulty, I can tell you. First my horse went lame, then I had to walk for miles until my soles were nearly through, and I finished by sharing a cart with a crate of hens and a pig. And here,' sketching a curtsey, 'you see me. Well? Aren't you pleased?' She put her cheek up for a kiss, but he only looked down at her in the same drugged way.

'I'd not expected you,' he said. 'Happen you've heard?'

'Heard? I've not heard anything from you, my lad, for a very long time, and I thought something must be done to end all the nonsense, so here I am, and — Will, I'm starving! Please can I have something to eat?'

He seemed to rouse from his half-dream, saying, 'Aye. Of course. The kitchen's upstairs.'

She followed him up the uncarpeted stairs, sniffing distastefully at the general dustiness. Men, bachelors, they had no notion of keeping a place clean. The kitchen, a lean-to affair built out of the back of the first storey, was no more appetising, with its dresser scantily laden with crockery, its littered kitchen table, a loaf of cut-into bread left unwrapped, a fireless grate. He looked about him helplessly.

'There's an egg or two ... and a bit o' haslet. Can you eat that?'

'I expect so,' she returned a trifle impatiently. 'It couldn't be nastier than what they gave me at Endmoor.' Seeing him peering hesitantly into a cupboard with a wire mesh front she pushed him aside and looked into it. 'Yes, there are three eggs, and some haslet, and — what's this? cooked potato? You'd better let me do it, and have some with me.'

'No,' he muttered. 'I'm used to it.'

She watched him, puzzled, as he moved slowly about, kindling a spirit stove, putting lard in a pan, breaking the eggs and slicing the pig's fry clumsily. Where was the welcome she had hoped for? But she was too hungry and jaded to stop the preparations with talk. When the food was ready she drew up a chair to the table, pushing its clutter aside, and eagerly attacked the plate he handed her. He took nothing, only a cup from the black teapot.

'There,' she said, replete at last. 'Now I'm better. Well, aren't we going to talk to one another? You *are* glad to see me, Will, aren't you? I can see you're tired — or perhaps not very well?' She touched his hand gently, her fingers lingering on his, but he did not respond. 'I didn't mean to take you by surprise. But Dove and I had a talk yesterday — at least, more of a quarrel. She has actually broken off her engagement to George after all this time, and was talking a great deal of nonsense about living like a nun. Then, when I scolded her, she said that I was proposing to do the same — and suddenly I saw that she was right, and I must pluck up courage and come to live with you. Now Mother will know that I really mean what I said, and that you did. Why should we both waste our lives, Will?'

He said, 'Jane's dead, Belle.'

She withdrew her hand sharply. 'Dead?'

'Aye.'

'But when … how?'

'Two days since. She found a window as hadn't bars, and threw herself down. They picked her up with nigh every bone broken.'

Belle drew a deep breath. 'Well! That's a problem settled, then. Poor woman, she's best out of her misery, and you're free at last.' Her eyes glowed. 'Oh, how wonderful the workings of Fate are! But ... why didn't you come at once and tell us?'

'I've had the funeral to see to. It's on Monday. I saw no call to ask any of your folk, even though she was an Atkinson.'

'No ... but you could have told *me*. You must have known how delighted I'd be. I think you might have sent word even if you couldn't come yourself.'

He looked at her strangely. 'Is that what you feel? Delighted? Aye, I can see it is.'

Belle tossed her head. 'I didn't know her, did I? And from all I've heard she was a thorn in everybody's flesh, not least in yours. I suppose I could pretend to cry, but it would be extremely false behaviour. And I don't see why you're putting on all this show of grief, if that's what it is, and not even saying you're pleased to see me, after I've come all this way and...'

Will shook his head with a half-smile. 'Belle, Belle. There's decencies to be observed in these things. Apart from which, I've my own feelings about it. Jane was my wife. I took her with my eyes open, even though we were a sort of poison to each other. If she'd wed another kind of man she might ha' kept her senses, and not died a dreadful death. Can't you see that, lass?'

'No.' She swung round at the table, her back half to him, angry, disappointed, contemptuous of him, wondering why she had come so far and gone to such trouble for this reception. 'I didn't think you were so soft,' she said. 'I thought you were a man, a big strong sensible man, not a sentimental baby.'

'And I thought you were a woman,' he said sadly, 'but I see you're a bairn still. I told you it would never do, you and me.'

'You told me you loved me!' she flashed back. 'You told me *and* Mother and Father we could be happy if they'd only let us marry. And what did it all mean? Nothing. Nothing at all.' She was breathing fast, trying not to break into sobs, helped by her fury. Looking across the table at him, she saw not the lover of her dreams but a large, unkempt, bristle-chinned man looking a good ten years older than his age, and the magic that had happened in a moment was undone in a moment. Bright, angry dark eyes met melancholy brown eyes, their signal unmistakable.

'I'm sorry, Belle,' he said helplessly. 'Happen we'd best not see each other for a while … until I've got over it. These things, they weigh on me, you see.'

She did not understand. She would never understand about his past life and the burden of guilt, real or fancied, that he had carried on his shoulders. It had gradually lightened, but with the death of Jane the load had once more descended to crush him. He felt nothing for Belle, numbed as he was, but a remembered tenderness and longing that must not be revived now.

She jumped to her feet. '"Happen we'd best not see each other for a while!"' she mocked him. 'Never, if it lies with me. I shall go back now and you needn't even trouble to see me to the door, thank you. They'll be exceedingly cross with me and I daresay I shall be punished, which I'm sure will please you. I hope you have a very fine day for the funeral and manage to find another young lady to console yourself with.' Saying which, she snatched up her cloak and ran down the stairs and out of the shop.

Will heard the door crash shut behind her and the bell give a protesting tinkle. He tried to think how she would travel back, whether she had money with her, whether he should go after her. But, sleepless and half-crazed as he was, his brain refused to work. He sat down at the table again and laid his head on his arms.

CHAPTER TWENTY-ONE

It was Aggie who saw Belle come home, peering from a front window; a slow-walking, bedraggled figure trying to make itself inconspicuous. She darted round to a side door and beckoned fiercely. Belle scuttled in past her, to face the wrath to come.

'So you've come back, milady, have you? And I'd like to know where you've been, frittenin' us to death? Look at you! Straw all over your skirts an' a face full o' dust. What wickedness have you been up to? Come on, I will have it!'

Wearily Belle pulled back her hood, struggling with the strings of it. 'Oh, Aggie, please don't scold. If you knew how glad I am to be home. The straw was blowing all over the coach...' She picked at pieces of it. 'Are they all anxious for me?'

Aggie snorted. 'Anxious? It's a wonder your poor sister's hair's not gone white, and mine would if it weren't already. A good thing for you your father's not in yet, being up at court house wi' Joe.'

'And Mother — does she know?'

'Oh, you've given some thought to your poor mother, then, have you? A likely story, and her with a heart that could carry her off any minute. Well, you'll be glad to know me and Dove made her stay in bed again this morning, and Dove kept her mouth shut about that note you left. Aye, I saw it, you might well blush — a lot of play-actin' twaddle no decent person coulda written. A nice job we had, I can tell you, with your mother asking, "Where's Belle? Why doesn't she come and see me?" every few minutes. But for the lies we told, you might well have come back to a corpse, and that's the truth.'

'Please, Aggie,' Belle said desperately, 'I know I've been very wrong to run off without telling anybody but Dove, and I'm very, very sorry for it, but I *am* so tired and I don't think I can bear any more. Please let me go upstairs.'

Aggie surveyed her, tight-lipped. 'Go on, then. I'll fetch some hot water up. Get them things off, they look lousy.'

Dove had appeared, silently taking in the conversation. As Aggie bustled off to the kitchen the girls exchanged a look that said much on both sides. Together they went upstairs.

Dove said nothing until Belle was bathed, changed, and lying on her bed, a vinegar compress on her aching brow. Then, gently questioning, she heard the whole sorry story, bitterly told.

'You needn't call me a fool. I know I've been one all the time. Mother and Father were right, and I was wrong. Will was too old for me and too … I don't know what to call it … sombre, serious. I seemed to see a different man this morning from the one I thought I loved. Oh, Dove, why did he change? Did he love that wife of his, do you think?'

Dove shook her head. 'One needn't love a person to be bound to them. I think she made him suffer very much — perhaps made it impossible for him to be truly happy, with you or anybody. If you hadn't gone to him just now, just after her death, things might have been otherwise. Poor Will. But you — have you really stopped loving him? Was it not just an unfortunate quarrel this morning? You know your temper.'

'Yes, I do, and I said awful things. I shouldn't have said them. But I was so hurt, after I'd gone all that way, and lamed poor Rinalda.'

'And where *is* Rinalda? Joe won't be pleased to find her missing.'

'A boy from that farm's bringing her back. I don't know how I'll explain it — say I went for a gallop, perhaps.'

'Not quite the horse to choose for a gallop. But you must make up your own story. How did you get back, with no horse? Had you any money?'

'A few shillings. I spent some on the way. After I left Will I remembered that he once said something about knowing the vicar of the parish church. So I walked down to the vicarage and said who I was and that I'd lost my purse in the market, and he kindly put me on a private coach — there's a new service opened between here and Kendal, twice a week.'

Dove laughed in spite of herself. 'Oh, Belle. You took a very great risk.'

'With the vicar? He seemed an amiable man.'

'No, stupid thing. In going to Kendal at all. Now, listen carefully. Mother must know nothing at all of this, by accident or any other way. You must tell Joe if you have to, because of Rinalda being missing. But it would make Mother very ill and distressed, remembering Aunt Eleanor and Aunt Margaret. When your head is better you must go in and see her, and say you've been out in the country riding and sightseeing with ... oh, anyone you can think of. She may guess something, sometime — but not now. Yes?'

'Yes. Oh, my head.'

'I'll fetch you some of Aggie's lemon wine.' She dropped a light kiss on Belle's cheek and went downstairs. It was no time for reproaches or for anything but comfort and well-intentioned dissembling. Belle was suffering enough from the pain of disillusionment; it was their mother who must be thought of now. Dove had taken care to send to the doctor's for his medicine prescribed for heart spasms, a strongish compound containing ether and opium, spirits of lavender and camphor. Usually Dove was wary of mixing it at full strength, but throughout the day she had given her mother doses as for severe pain, though Mary was not suffering. The result was to keep her calm and sleepy, unlikely to enquire too closely about Belle's absence.

As, yet again, Dove measured out the liquid into a medicine glass, she saw herself doing that same thing, through the years, to her mother, perhaps her father or Aunt Margaret when they were failing, too; a patient, meek figure. What had Belle said? *A dried-up old lady in a shawl and steel spectacles.* She glanced into her mother's dressing-table mirror, from which there looked back at her a face still fair, still fresh and young. For how long would it remain so, before the lines and shadows came?

The proceedings of the consistory court hearing in the case of Atkinson v. Bradshaw were heard in Lancaster, though under the jurisdiction of the diocese of York, to enable those concerned to attend more easily. It was held in the Nisi Prius court, adjoining the Shire Hall of the castle where the Crown Court was housed. Like all such chambers it was cold, stuffy and hard-seated. The case, though simple enough compared with some, was dragged out over three days, which seemed to Ephraim interminable.

The first two were taken up with confused bumblings (it appeared to him) about the holy condition of marriage, its theoretical indissolubility, the evidence required by the Church before dissolution could even be considered. He gathered that most of the clerics present had never attended such a hearing before, and that the machinery of it was even more rusty than the law's.

He, too, had never attended such a court before. In place of his colleagues' wigs and gowns, he saw on every side the black suits and white neckcloths of the clergy. It seemed they were all present, enjoying a holiday from their usual functions on this secular, comparatively entertaining occasion. There was a representative of the Archbishop of York, another of the diocesan bishop, both their clerks, the High Sheriff's chaplain, the now ancient Mr Manby, vicar of the Priory Church, who had married Ephraim and Mary and whose extreme age caused apprehension whenever he stumbled on the pulpit steps. His newly appointed curate, Mr Armytage of Huddersfield, was beside him, and there were others whom Ephraim did not recognise. He was slightly cheered by the presence of Percy Blanchard, the barrister representing the civil court which had been held in London. From time to time they exchanged significant looks and folded notes, impatient on Ephraim's part, mainly facetious on his friend's.

'Damned dull, an't it?'

'Get on with the sermon, we want our dinner.'

'How long, O Lord, how long?'

On the third day Percy's crisp summary of the proceedings of the Crim. Con. action provided quite the liveliest moments. Knowing what was expected of him by the incident-starved clerics, he outlined the events of Joe's career, marriage and betrayal in moving terms, causing young Mr Armytage to blush very much. Then he turned to the history, character and behaviour of Saul Bradshaw, keeping well on the right side of slander but painting a picture of the mill owner that could not be anything but prejudicial to the minds of the hearers. His best efforts were expended on Rosie.

'A young woman on whom, gentlemen, Almighty God has bestowed His gracious gift of bodily comeliness, learned

Counsel, in conducting the civil case for the plaintiff, informed the court that her chastity before marriage was not in question. Be it so: we may neither know nor judge. Yet, in her conduct only months after her troth had been given at the altar to Joseph Atkinson, may we not at least deduce a degree of light-mindedness — of a nature so ready to fall from grace that her virtue may be gravely questioned?

'I think we may. Let us not impute to this young woman any natural wickedness. Her previous life had been one of toil, and toil not undertaken in God's open fields, sowing and harvesting the fruits of the earth, or tending the harmless lamb or the feathered creature. No: that life had been spent in the dark squalor of those mills which may have contributed to our national prosperity — which, indeed, have done so; but what of their effect upon the human souls employed in them? I ask you, what?

'There are others better qualified than I to testify to the vice prevalent in such places. Ministers of the church and many other godly persons have reeled in horror at the conditions of cotton workers employed in such mills as have not benefited from the rule of an enlightened employer; and we may take it, from evidence which will be presented to you, that Saul Bradshaw was not such an employer.

'*O Opportunity, thy guilt is great!* So observes the Bard of Avon; nor, may I say, could I have put it better myself.' Percy's beam round the assembly produced appreciative laughs for a much-needed touch of lightness among such grave matters. He went on. 'Man and woman, boy and girl, toiling side by side, too often half naked; it is a sad picture indeed. What could be the recreations of such people, without Christian education, but the alehouse and the gin shop? I do not tell you that Rose Giles frequented either, or was renowned for insobriety. I have not heard as much, and I must be honest. But you will hear in the testimony of the Reverend John Leeming of Bradhope, who is present in this court, that she had *not* received a Christian education, nor had she or any of her family ever attended his church or that of any other denomination.'

He paused for effect, and was rewarded by shocked expressions and some murmurs.

'The edifice over which Mr Leeming presides,' he continued, 'has been founded within recent memory. It is possible that some of Rose Giles's earlier-born sisters or brothers received Christian baptism elsewhere. She, alas, did not, and when her husband-to-be requested Mr Leeming to put up the banns he was reluctant to do so, on this count. That he consented was a triumph of Christian optimism and that ever-welcoming faith which the Church extends, not only to sinners, but, as it is so beautifully expressed in the General Confession, to those who have not done what they ought to have done.' He paused and drank some water. 'Not pitching it too strong, am I?' he enquired of Ephraim out of the side of his mouth.

'Carry on,' was the reply.

Percy spread his hands eloquently. 'As to this young woman's life before marriage, I cannot speak with authority.' In the pause that followed there was some expectant rustling; he knew how to throw suspense into his voice.

'However, I will bring one testimony to your ears. It came to mine — I will not tell you how — by a providential chance, let us say.' He might have added that a deliberate stop-off from the coach at Bradhope, a few questions asked at the right moment in the Red Cow, and the passing of some money, had led to the production of this useful evidence. It came from James Ollerenshaw, a burly man of twenty-five or so: *mill-hand* written all over him, with a gash of a mouth always on the grin

311

and an accent so thick that the archbishop's representative's ear trumpet proved quite useless against it, and required the services of a clerk to repeat Ollerenshaw's replies in stentorian tones and with translated dialect.

Yes, Ollerenshaw had worked alongside Rosie Giles at Bradshaw's. Yes, he had courted her — or whatever the gentleman liked to call it — when she was sixteen or so, he didn't know her age. Had he 'courted' her beneath her mother's roof, or in the house of some relative? No. Pressed to describe the spot, he said it was usually down by the river, beyond the mill, where there were plenty of bushes and not many folk.

Percy polished his spectacles, refreshed himself with more water, purring almost audibly. 'This courting you speak of. Was it of a physical nature?'

His witness looked blank.

'Did you woo the young woman with sweet words, gifts, that sort of thing: a tender assault of youth upon maid, as it were?'

The witness, struggling to remember what he had been told to say by the generous gentleman from London, replied, 'I 'ad her on t'grass and I gi'ed her a sixpence.'

Percy smiled, looking modestly down at his notes, as a wave of shock went round the courthouse.

'*What* did the man say?' enquired the archbishop's legate, inclining his trumpet to his interpreter, who, turning a fiery pink, tried to repeat the evidence at a pitch that would convey the message without reaching the general ear. He was quite unsuccessful. Reluctantly, the men of the cloth began to laugh: a laugh suddenly stilled by Percy, who with a solemn face brought them back to the serious business of the court.

'Did this — occurrence — take place once, twice, many times?'

'I dunno 'ow many. A good few.'

'And you gave her sixpence every time?'

'When I'd got it. Sometimes it were a penny.'

Ephraim produced his large, snowy handkerchief and buried his face in it, leaning forward as though convulsed by silent coughs. Through it, while his eyes were streaming with suppressed mirth, he heard his friend delicately demolishing Rosie Giles's reputation, even to a description of the Bacchic events at the wedding, at which he had been a guest. Another witness, the husband of a neighbour of the married couple, testified to Rosie's grumbles to an assembled group, including himself, of her dissatisfaction with her husband. Swiftly Percy brought his case to a close.

'I think I have made my point, sir. A Christian marriage cannot exist when the tenets, practices and conduct of one of the parties is not Christian.'

The bishop's representative rose, double-jowled and pompous. 'The marriage took place in a Christian church with proper ceremonies. How might it be described otherwise?'

'That is understood, sir. I speak of the spirit of it; of an innocent, godly, well-intentioned young man deceived by a woman little more than heathen.'

A conference followed, mutterings and note-passings between the clerics, while Percy stared at the ceiling and Ephraim tied his handkerchief into knots. At length the bishop's legate rose to ask, 'Would the vicar of Bradhope inform us whether Mrs Atkinson ever partook of Holy Communion at his church?'

Mr Leeming replied that she had not partaken, and that after the first weeks of the marriage her husband had attended morning service alone.

At a signal from the bench the jury, if so it could be called, shuffled out and remained away for what seemed hours to the yawning, uncomfortable men remaining in court, but at least they had some spicy details to discuss in whispers. When they returned and settled, the bishop's representative, now seated beside the proxy for his archbishop, conferred with him in writing, as a private conversation would have been impossible with one so deaf. At the end of the conference he rose and addressed the assembly, at enormous length, sprinkling his speech with quotations from the Scriptures and works in Greek and Latin. But to Ephraim the tedium of it was worth the conclusion: the consistory court had decided, in its wisdom, that the marriage of Joseph and Rose Atkinson was suitable to be dissolved *a mensa et thoro* from the marriage tie of bed and board.

But for the solemnity of the occasion Ephraim would have clapped Percy on the back in his delight. As it was, they shook hands gravely. 'You're a clever old fox,' he said.

'I know it,' replied Percy. 'I've caught a few chickens in my time. I fancy today has added to my bag.'

'Bribery and corruption, Percy!' Ephraim shook his head in mock reproof.

'Well, hardly prayer and meditation, old boy. It don't work in our line.'

It was then that Ephraim noticed two men who had been sitting behind them busy scribbling in notebooks. With horror he realised what he had known, but had forgotten: at this, the most newsworthy day of the hearing, the press would be present. And there they were: Clark of the *Lancaster Gazette* and his opposite number from the rival paper. As they rose, putting away their notebooks and pencils, he hesitated, wondering whether he should go up to them and plead, for his family's sake, that they should suppress the worst details of the case.

Percy saw his frown and interpreted it. 'No go,' he said. 'They'll print, whatever you say. Nothing more the public likes than a good fat scandal. Call me a fox if you like — they're wolves, the scribblers. At least the *Gazette*'s a respectable paper — they won't turn the business into a pedlar's broadsheet.'

Ephraim, disconsolately watching the reporters leave, said, 'Then I shall have to tell them at home tonight.'

'You haven't said anything yet? Astounding reticence.'

'I didn't want to alarm them. My wife's delicate, and has gone through a great deal. But now I suppose I must face it.'

'I tell you what. Will you let me come with you? I fancy I might lighten the occasion a little — and the King's Arms is a damned dull hotel. Besides, you know, things have gone our way. If the old crows had thrown out our plea it would have been all up with us; as it is, the case can go on to the Lords. So we might turn the evening into a little celebration. I told you, didn't I, that Crim. Con. keeps my cupboard supplied with port and sherry? Well, then, divorce means champagne, and that I propose to purchase from my landlord, who will certainly sell it to me at an exorbitant price. But what of that, when it comes out of the damages?'

'My family are quite unused to it,' Ephraim said primly, but on their way out collared an usher who lived in his direction, with instructions to tell Mrs Atkinson that he would be bringing a colleague home for supper. There was always plenty to eat in the larder; champagne might well be the very thing to wash it down.

The presence of Percy Blanchard acted upon the spirits of Ephraim's household as cheeringly as the unaccustomed sparkling wine. He and it were the perfect combination of elements to lighten the gloom that had hung over the house for so long. Sophisticated, quick to size up character, with a lifetime's experience of women from female felons to duchesses, he charmed the three ladies as effortlessly as he landed fish — another accomplishment of his. It was a long time since a man had complimented Mary on her blue eyes and clear complexion.. She smiled, bridled, and felt twenty years younger for his gallantries, while the twins, more used to compliments, were flattered at being treated like society ladies. Joe laughed spontaneously for the first time in months. As for the champagne, the mere worldly wickedness of drinking such costly stuff increased its potency.

Ephraim waited until after supper, when they were all relaxed, before telling them the news of the court hearing and its result. Joe went white and looked about to faint.

'But,' Mary gasped, 'why did you not tell us this was going on?'

'Merely in order not to alarm you, my dear. Joe knew, but I persuaded him not to attend.'

'These things are like straws in the wind, ma'am,' Percy said. 'A puff of clerical breath in the wrong direction, and they're gone. We were lucky today that Boreas blew the other way.'

'But I don't understand,' Dove said. 'There have been two trials, you said, sir. What was the first?'

At a nod from Ephraim, Percy outlined smoothly and succinctly what had happened at the Crim. Con. hearing, softening the details and making it all sound very workaday. 'So, Mr Joseph, you became a rich man at very little trouble. It only remains for us to persuade the defendant to pay up, which he shows some reluctance to do, I hear.'

'The money is nothing,' Joe said. 'At least, it is, in that the costs won't fall upon Uncle, as we feared they might. What matters is the result of today's hearing. I can hardly believe it, even now.'

'It was a very clear case,' Ephraim said. 'The, er, evidence…' He glanced at Percy, who took the hint.

'The press attended, of course. I'm afraid you may find some unsavoury details reported in this week's newspapers, and I'd advise you not to give yourselves the trouble of reading them.' (But he knew they would.) 'Such matters are quite commonplace in our trade, I assure you. The outcome is the all-important thing, and we should be highly satisfied. But I do beg you not to let your hopes soar too high; we're not at the end of the road yet.'

'Hopes?' Dove was watching Joe, still pale, a nerve twitching in his cheek. 'Is there more to this than a separation for Joe?' She turned to Ephraim. 'Father?'

'It's possible, my love. The case must now go to the judiciary committee of the Privy Council for final consideration.'

'And then?' They were all hanging on his words, but Dove sat forward in her chair, her hands clasped tensely, her eyes fixed on her father's face as though a sentence of death might come from his lips.

'If the committee decides favourably, my dear, Joe's marriage will be dissolved.'

'And I shall be free to marry again?' Joe too, looked at him as a prisoner at the bar looks toward the hanging judge. Ephraim found himself unable to speak, but Percy stepped in.

'That is, of course, what we all hope for. The tendency in these days is to permit remarriage for both parties. Until the passing of this year's amendment to the laws of divorce, a stubborn element among the peers concerned was all too likely to forbid it, on the grounds that marriage is a religious rather than a civil contract.'

'How wicked!' Belle burst out. 'What has it to do with peers, silly old men? Most of them no better than they should be, I expect.'

'I've no doubt you're right. Miss Belle. But the laws governing marriage go back to Roman times and Roman mores, and further back, to the beginnings of Christianity,' Percy said gravely. 'They are still taken very seriously, too seriously in cases like Mr Joe's. But the wheels are turning faster, and the humbug grows weaker as the years go by. We shall see changes…'

He was aware of extraordinary emotion in the room that stopped him in mid-sentence. Dove had moved to Joe's side, his arm was round her shoulders, their hands were clasped. Mary's face was a perfect study of startled enlightenment, and Ephraim's of realisation. All his questions were answered now, his instincts vindicated. Now he knew his most beloved daughter's secret, and Joe's, hidden so long and so painfully. He noted Belle's face, blazing with joy and excitement; she had known, of course.

'Well!' Mary exclaimed. 'Joe … Dove … what's this?'

Percy made a great display of taking out his watch and comparing it with the mantelpiece clock. 'Dear me! I've trespassed on your time much too long, and I must be on the coach more or less at dawn tomorrow.' His thanks, hand-kissings and farewells covered the moment of revelation. At the door Ephraim shook his hand strongly.

'Thank you, Percy. I couldn't have managed it half so well.'

'Neat, wasn't it? I thought so myself. See you in town for the next round in the game, old boy.'

With many delays and protractions, letters passing to and fro, witnesses summoned but failing to appear and having to be sought out, the case of Atkinson v Bradshaw wound its way through the corridors of Westminster. At a point when its result seemed seriously at peril, an appeal by Ephraim to Jesse Bradshaw brought backstairs influence into play, smoothing out the difficulty.

In rather less than three months, Joe was a free man, and Rosie a free woman. Their Lordships had found no reason to forbid the remarriage of either.

CHAPTER TWENTY-TWO

Dove and Joe walked by the canal, southwards, along the narrow towpath fringed by lush weeds. There was utter silence around them, but for the small sounds of nature, on that still day of late autumn, as though they were receiving a special gift of peace after the trials of the last years. A coot pursued its jerky progress across the water, like a little black steamboat; a water rat swam gracefully from its hole in the bank, just visible below the dimpled, quiet surface of the canal.

'Look, the gnats are swarming,' Dove said. 'Father always said it meant a fine day tomorrow.'

'Every day is a fine day now,' Joe said lazily. 'No more bad ones.'

'Ssh, don't tempt Fate.'

'Fate knows perfectly well what I mean. While I have you, God send, for always.' He loosened the ribbons of her bonnet, so that it fell back and lay on her shoulders, letting the green-gold sunlight filtering through the trees touch her beautiful hair. He laid his cheek against its softness, holding her closer to him, and lifted her ungloved hand, so small, still childishly dimpled, the light blue veins at the wrist inviting kisses. A packet boat bound for Preston came in sight behind them and sailed by while the passengers' eyes raked them, weighing them up, passing on, leaving them in their own private Eden.

Dove turned her head. 'Aldcliffe Hall's over there. Do you remember, when we were children we said we'd live in it one day?'

'Yes, very well. Do you care where we live, now?'

'No. Well ... somewhere pleasant. But not too near home. They've been so kind and good, love, and so pleased for us, after we've deceived them all this time. But...'

'I know. We must be ourselves now, our own family.'

Dove was dreaming aloud. 'Our children will come here. A little boy and girl, perhaps twins like me and Belle, and we'll show them where the water rats nest, and the woodpecker's tree, and Cromwell's Tower.' They looked across the water to the small castellated building where, tradition said, Cromwell had stood to view some parliamentary skirmish, though nobody remembered what.

'I should like to shut you up in that,' Joe said, 'and keep you to myself, all winter through.'

'Wouldn't it be cold?'

'Not at all. We'd have a fire, and blankets, and a quilt, and a store of ... apples and nuts and cake and buttermilk; and stay in bed till it was spring again.'

Dove laughed softly, and began to sing, in her sweet high voice.

'By the banks of Allan Water,
When the sweet spring-tide was o'er,
There I saw the miller's daughter,
But she smiled no more.
For the summer grief had brought her,
And the soldier, false was he;
By the banks of Allan Water
None so sad as she.'

Joe gave her a little shake. 'Why sing such a sad song?'

'I don't know — only that it makes being happy somehow even better. I wish the grass wasn't so wet — we could sit down.'

'Mercifully it's completely sodden, otherwise I wouldn't answer for the consequences. When shall we be married?'

'Very soon. After George comes home.'

'What the deuce has George to do with it?'

'Only that I've treated him badly enough already. It would be too much to greet him as someone else's wife. Not that I think he'll care too dreadfully... In any case, we must give Mother time enough to enjoy all the preparations and make sure that everybody wears the smartest clothes that were ever seen at any wedding, anywhere.'

Joe looked down at her quizzically. 'And what does the bride want?'

After a moment she answered, 'Nothing, but to be married to you. And that it should be quite different from — anything you remember.'

He kissed her hair. By the farm gate they were passing grew a clump of red campion, rough-leaved and bright-flowered; he picked a bunch of it and put it in her hand. She laid the cool pink blossoms against her cheek.

'I wish this were my bridal bouquet,' she said.

Shem sighed, and told his father for what seemed the hundredth time, 'You'll have to pay up. The case was decided against you, no amount of argument's going to change that. Three thousand, and costs. You know you can afford it — what's the use of sticking out like this?'

Saul banged the desk with his fist. 'I'm not seeing my good brass go into Atkinson pockets, whatever their damned courts say. Let them whistle for it.'

'They'll do more than whistle. They'll send an officer for you and haul you up to the castle. D'you fancy seeing out your days on the Male Debtors' side? And don't growl at me. I didn't make the rules, I'm only trying to save you trouble. Come now; you've got Rosie's freedom through this. Why can't you pay the price and look pleasant?'

The old man was momentarily distracted from his wrath. 'Aye, Rosie. All mine now. We'll be wed before the month's out.'

'Why,' Shem asked with genuine curiosity, 'do you want to marry her?'

'Oh, I know you hate the mortal sight of her, more fool you. Don't know a fine woman when you see one.'

'It's not that, though there's no love lost, true enough. I mean why d'you want to wed her, when you can have her for nowt?' He saw an unusual expression on his father's face, a sort of blankness, and knew it for a sign of senile forgetfulness. *So,* Shem said to himself, *he doesn't even know what all this pother has been about, and the Atkinsons might have saved their trouble.*

'I want Rosie to be Mrs Bradshaw, for 'em all to see,' Saul said at last.

'But you said you wanted to make a scandal for the Atkinsons by keeping her as your ... by keeping her. Now you want to make her respectable; I'm only asking why.'

'I know what you're after,' the old man said with a great air of cunning. 'It's the inheritance, isn't it? My brass, and Bradshaw Hall, and the rest of it. No, don't bother answering back, I know what I know. Well, Shem, you've been a good lad to me, and I won't cut you out entirely. You shall have what I think fit, what's due to you for all the years you've put in at t'mill. There! That's fair enough, isn't it?'

'Thanks,' Shem said without enthusiasm.

'I'm sending for yon lawyer chap tomorrow — what's his name — Knapp. I'll stay at home and he can come up to t'Hall and draw up a new will. That way it'll be all settled by the time we're wed.'

'Who will you get to marry you to Rosie, by the way? You'll have a job to find a parson, after the way you've flaunted her about.'

Saul laughed contemptuously. 'Parsons? They're like any other folk. They'll do owt for a handful of guineas.'

'I doubt it, Father. Things aren't what they were in your day, when the daftest lad of the family went into the Church as a matter of course, and then spent more time hunting than preaching. There's a new spirit in the air these days. Folk are sick of old kings and loose ways and churchmen that might as well be butchers or farriers. I read the other day about some move to stop bishops putting their relatives into good livings. I tell you, it's easier said than done, getting wed in a situation like yours.'

'We'll see about that. I'll happen take her to Manchester — there's nobody knows me there, if I keep out o' sight of 'Change. I'll get a licence, that's what I'll do, and save all the fussation over banns. I've got it all plotted out, you see!' He laid his finger knowingly alongside his nose, grinning.

'Clearly.' Shem was suddenly sick of the futile conversation. He picked up his papers and left his father alone in the office.

That night the dining table at Bradshaw Hall was laden with enough food, as Rosie commented, to feed a regiment. She watched Saul eat his way through pea soup, game, mutton, a dish of cod in a rich sauce, and a pudding, all washed down with ale. He looked up from time to time, seeing her only picking at each dish, the plates sent away almost untouched, and said at last, annoyed, 'What's t'matter with you? Isn't the food to your liking?'

'Oh, it's grand. Only I've never been used to eat like this, and ever sin' I came here you've loaded me up like a baconer. I feel right choked wi' it tonight. I'm getting too fat, besides.' She patted her stomach, and sketched the curves of her bosom, which threatened to spring out of her green satin bodice.

Saul paused, his fork halfway to his mouth, struck by a sudden notion almost unthinkable, yet possible, possible…

'You're never breeding, lass, are you?'

Under his eager bolt-eyed stare, hearing the excitement in his voice, Rosie debated with herself, but only for a moment. She was quite sure that she was not with child — that it was out of the question, with Saul as old and enfeebled as he was. But in her way she was mildly fond of him and wanted to please him; besides, it would do her no harm and make him all the more eager for a swift marriage.

She fluttered her lashes, looked down and then up, and said coyly, 'I can't be sure.'

The fork dropped with a clatter on to his plate. He struggled out of his chair and round the table to seize her.

'Rosie, Rosie, say it's true! Eh, this'll be the grandest day of my life, if it is. You don't know, lass…' He was babbling, slopping kisses on her cheeks and neck, while she laughed, pushing him away.

'Now then, ease up — you'll have t'table over. There's nowt to get so hot about. It's early days yet. Let go, do.'

He went back to his place, refilled his glass, and held it towards her, his eyes brimming with tears. 'To us. Us … three!'

Rosie raised her own glass, feeling touched and ashamed.

He came to her that night like a bridegroom, wearing his tent-like old-fashioned cambric nightshirt and a nightcap that hid his baldness. Because of the guilt she felt she particularly wanted to give him all the pleasure she could, and so had left off her own nightgown and lay sprawled in deliberate abandon on the bed's dark velvet coverlet, like a painted Venus. Breathing heavily, he watched the play of the candlelight on her shining skin, the rich heavy curves of breast and belly, the white round arms raised to spread out her hair for his delight.

'Rosie,' he said hoarsely. 'Rosie.'

Smiling, she reached out her hand to draw him down. As he stooped, he suddenly wrenched his hand from hers and clutched at his chest with a great cry. As she sat up in alarm she caught at the coverlet to steady himself, missed it, and fell heavily to the floor, groaning.

Rosie leaped off the bed, not even bothering to cover herself, ran to the door and shouted for help. But, even as she pulled on a night-robe and went to kneel at his side, she knew that it was already too late.

They buried him in Bradhope churchyard, among the graves of men, women and children who had worked for him. Mr Leeming read the service as solemnly as though he were reading it over a man of upright life and good works. Round the graveside were gathered only a few mourners: Shem, Jesse — sent for from London — Black and the other male servants from the Hall, Saul's clerk from the mill, three overseers. Women did not attend funerals; Rosie had remained at the Hall, and Eleanor, who had come north with Jesse, at their hotel.

Shem ordered a handsome, ornate tombstone of the best marble. It was the last thing he could do for his father. He was surprised at the depth of his own feelings; impossible to share one's daily life with someone, even Saul, for almost fifty years, and not experience a blank when they were gone.

The reading of Saul's will was not so much a reading as a brief statement. Mr Knapp, the attorney of Scotforth, took perhaps five minutes to tell Shem, Jesse and Rosie, assembled in the morning room at the Hall, that all money, land and property were bequeathed solely to Mr Shem Elias Bradshaw, but for a legacy of fifty pounds to the manservant Black. The will had been made twenty years earlier, after Jesse's leaving home.

Rosie, who had been crying almost unceasingly since Saul's death, burst out again as she heard the end of her hopes pronounced. Mr Knapp surveyed her disapprovingly over his glasses. He could not imagine why Shem had not bundled her out at once, neck and crop.

Shem struggled with his conscience, which won. 'I know that my father's intention was to leave Mrs Atkinson the bulk of his property,' he said, 'in anticipation of their forthcoming marriage.'

'Intention has no meaning in law, I fear,' replied the attorney.

'Couldn't I sue?' she gasped through her tears.

'Not unless you can produce a later will, madam.'

She looked helplessly towards Shem, who shrugged. There seemed no point in further discussion, at least in Mr Knapp's presence. As soon as the lawyer had left, disgruntled that the will would bring him no further work than to put it through probate, Shem politely asked Rosie to return to her own room and ring for some tea.

Alone with Jesse, he said, 'I'm sorry about this,'

'No need for you to be sorry, brother. I expected nothing else, with the hatred he had towards me.' He was cheerful, not at all bitter. 'We'll be no worse off than we were before, and

Nell certainly won't be disappointed. Anyway, she's so up in the air with being back north she wouldn't look round if you told her she'd been left the Crown Jewels.'

'Aye, I expect so.' Shem's tone was abstracted. 'You're staying for a bit, I take it?'

'As long as we can. I've a by-election coming up to fight, but not yet. I want to get her back together with her family, if it's at all possible.'

'I'd ask you to stay here, but…' Shem spread his hands. 'It wouldn't be decent, with Rosie still about.'

'I wouldn't think of it. No, we'll stick to the Bear; they've made us very comfortable.'

As things turned out, Mr Knapp's services were again called upon, and another fee went into his pocket. His mouth dropped open when Shem requested him to draw up a deed bestowing half of the total sum of Saul's property upon Jesse.

'But … but…' stammered Knapp, 'I don't know of any precedent for this. Such an act is outside my experience as a lawyer, in forty years of practice.'

'Well, it's in it now,' said Shem. 'I want it signed and sealed before my brother returns south.' To the astounded Jesse he said, 'It's nothing to shout about, only fair play. But for Father's pig-headedness you'd be equal heir with me. Now, I've been called some things in my time, but pig-headed's not one of 'em. You and Eleanor are going to take your rightful share. I shall go on living here and running Bradshaw's, which will do me very nicely. What do I want with a lot more brass? I'm not a well man, Jesse, I've always been sickly, you know that. I'll not make old bones. I'm content to live the way I always have done, in my own home, with my own things round me — oh, and if there's anything you'd like from the Hall, just take it.'

'I don't know what to say.' Jesse was overcome.

'When in doubt, say nowt. Just you go and tell Eleanor, and see if she's not as pleased as Punch.' *Or as I am,* he added to himself, with one of his rare smiles. At last, in a humdrum life dominated by another personality, he had done someone a major service and cancelled out twenty years of family warfare.

When the estate of the late Saul Bradshaw was proved and its worth totalled, the result surprised even Shem, from whom the old man had kept secret many investments and holdings, including shares in the Liverpool and Manchester Railway and the projected extension of the line to Kendal. Between them, with the sale of some land and dwellings neither wanted, the brothers possessed a small fortune.

Eleanor laughed and cried, embraced them both and executed a wild waltz with Jesse. 'Eagle Hall!' she said. 'We can have Eagle Hall! I can't believe it. Oh, how wonderful! Dear Shem, I don't know why we kept away so long, however much of an ogre your father may have been, when we had a brother like you.'

'Well.' Shem was embarrassed. 'Seems you picked the right time, after all, sister Nell.'

To Rosie he said, 'I want you out. You, and that mother and brother of yours.'

'That's right!' she flared. 'Turn us out into t'dirt and watch us starve. Me, that should have been stepmother to you and had all this. And my poor mam and that little child — where are *they* to go, I'd like to know?'

'Back to where they came from, I suppose,' replied Shem calmly. 'It's done your mam no good to drink herself silly on my father's brass, and your brother needs to be with his own kind — there's nowt for him here. I want no arguments nor tantrums, now. It's all decided, so sit still and listen to me. I've settled a bit of a pension on you, for my father's sake, not yours.'

She mopped her eyes, and he saw the acquisitive gleam in them. 'How much?'

'A hundred a year — that's till you marry again, and then it stops. If you don't marry, but get taken into keeping by a rich man, it stops likewise. And if you leave the district and go away with some chap, as I can see you're thinking you might do and so get married without our knowing, we'll find out where you are from the registers. Did you know all marriages must be registered, from this year on?'

She shook her head, sulking.

'Well, then,' Shem got up in dismissal, 'you might as well go and pack.'

'I can keep my clothes?' she asked sharply.

'Keep what you like that my father gave you, all except my mother's jewels, if he parted with any of 'em into your keeping. And to make sure you only take what's yours, Alice shall go up and watch you pack.'

She flung out of the room. Hovering in the hall, he heard at the top of the broad staircase the bangs and crashes of Rosie's impending departure, and Alice's loud demand that such language should not be used in her hearing.

When they came down Rosie was shawled and bonneted and carrying a large shabby carpet-bag which Shem recognised as being from one of the attics.

'It's all right, Mr Shem,' said Alice, following his glance. 'I thought she needed a bag for her things. She's just taking what you said.'

'Goodbye, Rosie.' He did not offer his hand, nor she hers. She looked for the last time round the hall, up at the staircase gallery, towards the doors of the fine rooms in which she had been queen, and he was a little sorry for her.

Tossing her plumed bonnet, she hurried out through the door Black was holding open. A chaise had been hired, in which Mrs Giles and Billy were already glumly sitting. The driver cracked his whip and they were away, down the drive, out of Shem's life.

'Thank God,' he said. 'Shut the door, and let's get the place straight.'

It was with the greatest trepidation that Jesse took Eleanor to see Eagle Hall, or what remained of it. She had been alternating between high spirits and tears since their return to the north, wearing out Jesse's nerves. He hoped the sight of the ruined house would not send her into the depths of depression, and as their phaeton wound its way along the steep lanes, and came within sight of the gates, his heart seemed to have slipped down to the region of his boots. Eleanor sat beside him, tense and silent.

They turned the corner of the overgrown drive, long branches scratching the sides of the vehicle, and came face to face with Eagle Hall. Eleanor gasped, and Jesse's heart began an upward progress. The place looked far better than he had feared. Sheets of tarpaulin fastened to scaffolding covered its roofs; yes, Shem had promised to arrange that. Jesse remembered shattered windows, but could not see one broken pane. A door which he recalled had been hanging loose on its hinges was now firmly fastened. It came to him that that secretive angel, his brother, had once again been performing good deeds by stealth.

'Oh, my dear old house,' Eleanor breathed. 'Poor thing, how it has suffered.'

Jesse helped her down, and, still anxious, unlocked the front door. The key turned easily; the lock had been oiled and kept in use.

Nobody could have called the condition of the hall perfect, or even presentable, but Jesse remembered the broken floorboards and the rats. There was no sign of either. As they walked through the house, Eleanor rapt in her own joy, he noted where repairs had been done to stop deterioration growing worse. It was clear to him that a firm of builders — perhaps that very Brown and Hinkson who had offered for the Hall — had been instructed to patch the place up, temporarily at least, and to clean up the worst of the mess. For Eleanor's sake, he was heartily thankful.

They stood in the upstairs room where old Madam Bradshaw, that lady from another age, had made their life together possible. There she had sat, there had stood the dolls' house, there the court cupboard that had held her treasure.

'I can smell her perfume — can't you?' Eleanor said. 'It was made from roses. I know how to prepare it; I shall sprinkle it in this room, when we live here.' She was transformed, since they had crossed the threshold, a ship becalmed after many storms. She looked up brightly at Jesse, and took his hand. 'For we *shall* live here, shan't we?'

'Of course, my dear.' Never mind about the complications, the London base he needed, the parliamentary seat he hoped to win, many miles south of Downham. They were rich now: he would be able to make Eleanor happy at last.

As they turned to go, pausing by the heavy door with its surround of carven flowers and fruit, Eleanor sang under her breath old Madam's song.

'O the last that came a-courting was young Johnny Grove,
I loved him with a joyous love...'

Hand in hand, they went down the dark stairs. The house seemed to settle in contentment behind them, knowing they would come back.

The front doorbell sent its insistent jangling call through that other house, in St Leonard's Gate. Nobody answered. Belle, who was trimming a bonnet in her mother's parlour, slammed a bunch of artificial cherries down and stuck her needle crossly through one, before opening the door to shout, 'Aggie!'

No Aggie appeared, or any other servant. 'Drat her, she's gone deaf,' muttered Belle, and marched off to answer the door herself, though it was not the place of a young lady to do so.

'Yes?' she said sharply to the stranger who stood there, half seen against the dazzle of the setting sun reflecting back from window panes, turning grey stones to a flamingo pink. She was certainly not going to admit a strange man with her mother out.

'Yes?' she queried even more irritably, for he was standing there staring at her in a most impudent manner, she considered.

He raised his beaver hat. 'Dove?'

'No, I'm *not* Miss Dove, I'm Miss Belle, and I don't think I know you.'

He laughed, and turned his face so that the rosy sunlight lit his hair to a curling golden fleece, and gilded his skin, dark brown as a Spaniard's, and he was the handsomest man she had ever set eyes on in all her impressionable life.

'Have I changed so much?' he asked. 'I'm George Dilworth.'

Belle stared, and gasped, feeling extremely foolish. She made several false starts before asking him to come in, which he did with alacrity.

'I'm sorry,' she said, 'Dove is out, and so is Mother. I expect you came to see her — Dove, that is. If you would like to wait…'

'Very much.' She led him into the small parlour, conscious of its untidiness, of her untrimmed bonnet and sewing materials littered all over the table, and of her own merino day dress, one she disliked and only wore when no company was expected. A tress of hair broke loose from its moorings and trailed across her eyes; she swept it back impatiently.

'Well,' George said, sitting very much at ease, one long elegant leg flung over the other, 'I must indeed have changed, not to be recognised.'

'Oh, you have,' she said lamely. Even his voice was different, the northern tinge almost gone from it, a new lightness of intonation brought by travel among people of many tongues. It matched his new assurance, the old puppyish eagerness and bounce replaced by a high confidence. He seemed even to have grown; she could not remember him being so tall, or so broad in the shoulders. The once plumpish boy's face had fined down to show the structure beneath, high cheekbones, a commanding nose, a mouth with a firm line to it, and the bluest eyes that she had ever seen, a sailor's eyes, far-sighted, taking their colour from tropical seas, all the more vivid for the sun-darkened skin.

Yes, George had certainly changed.

He was saying that she had, too. 'Not a day older, of course, but … well, there's something it's hard for a man to put into words; as though you were now grown up, Belle.'

I begin to wonder if I ever shall, she was thinking. Aloud she said, 'I was very ill last year. Mother says it has altered my looks.'

'For the better, if possible,' George said gallantly. He was an expert by now on the right compliment to pay at the right moment, and had practised his expertise on a great number of ladies, white, black, brown, and of various delicate shades of coffee-cream. He had escaped marriage once, had not escaped fatherhood at least twice, had honoured his obligations to the mothers with generous gifts, and was eminently qualified to put at ease a slightly dishevelled and embarrassed Lancaster miss.

This he proceeded to do, chatting airily on about his voyages, ports of call, strange sights seen, until Belle began to feel almost natural with him again, though he was still a stranger, mysterious and violently attractive. She was almost sorry when she heard her mother and Dove come home, though at first she had wondered how to sustain the conversation until they did so.

The meeting with his former betrothed went off calmly. Mary greeted him with a warm kiss, Dove with a proffered hand over which he bowed. He was so composed in manner that it was impossible for them to be stiff with him. No reference was made to the broken engagement. Dove wondered why she had ever thought it necessary to delay her own marriage until she had had a serious talk with George, a tendering of explanation and apology. It was very clear that no such talk was needed. Never had a young man seemed less heartbroken. She saw that her mother shared her relief.

George took the weight of any embarrassment that might yet linger by mentioning Dove's new engagement.

'I'm most happy to hear of it. May I?' and he kissed her cheek, as lightly as though he and she had never been more to one another than childhood friends. 'Joe's a capital fellow. Mama told me of his successful lawsuit. What a corker, to get the better of those old witch doctors! Give him my best congratulations.'

'But you must stay and see him yourself,' Mary said, all doubts now dispelled that this might be a bad thing. 'He will be so pleased, and so will Ephraim. George, I never saw such a change in anybody as in you. You went away quite a boy, you know, and you've returned a man.'

'I hope so,' George said modestly. He knew, thankfully, that Dove had hardly noticed any change, wrapped up as she was in her love for Joe; and knew equally that Belle had hardly taken her lovely eyes off him since his arrival. They were, indeed, lovely, like the rest of her. Dove was still girlish, of fairy-like delicate beauty, but Belle had taken on womanhood, and with it a strong allure, for all that her hair was coming down and her frock an old one. He had a sudden vision of her dressed like a West Indian belle, her fairness dazzling under a tall glittering headdress, many-coloured skirts revealing legs that he knew were beautiful.

The women exclaimed over the presents he had brought them: three gorgeous silk shawls, a brown-skinned doll in festival attire (just as he had imagined Belle), a string of ivory carved beads.

'But George,' Mary said, 'however did you remember us all — for I suppose your mother and sisters have presents as well?'

'I could never forget any of you, Aunt Mary. And now that I see you again,' he added gallantly, 'I know why.'

'Silly boy!' Mary was actually flirting with him.

'I think,' Belle said suddenly, 'I shall go and change my dress. Pray excuse me.'

Her mother's gaze followed her exit speculatively.

Only three weeks later, George presented himself to Ephraim and Mary with a formal request for Belle's hand in marriage.

CHAPTER TWENTY-THREE

'Are you sure?' Mary asked her daughter, not for the first time.

'Quite sure, Mother.'

'But there was Uncle — there was Will. You were so set on him, and so determined you'd never marry anybody else. What became of that?'

Belle looked out of the window. 'How can I explain, when I don't know? I thought he was the one for me. I wanted someone older, I think … but you were right, he was *too* old, and I realised it … in time.' She had never told her mother of her escapade, only that she had changed her mind about marrying Will, even when he was free.

'If you want an older man,' Mary persisted, 'why are you for marrying George, who's only twenty-four? I do beg you to think about it, child.'

'I *have* thought, Mother. Don't you see that George is much older than me, in every way but years? He's travelled, he knows the world, he's very wise. He can teach me so much. It isn't just a fancy, please believe me.'

'And does George indeed care for you?' It was in Mary's mind that George had returned to England very far from the innocent who had left it. It was not ladylike to voice such thoughts, and perhaps she was even more old-fashioned than most mothers in these matters. She was feminine enough to sense George's new sexuality, his charm for women. Arabella, when consulted, had been no help, saying only that the lad had become quite a dasher, and she and Jack thought he would do very well with Belle, who had always been the on-coming one of the twins, always supposing she could entertain herself during his absences abroad.

Mary ventured to tell Ephraim of her doubts that Belle would entertain herself altogether respectably during such absences, and got a reproachful, 'Mother, Mother. Give the child some credit for good sense and virtue. Marriage will change her, that I promise.'

It was too much for Mary, embroiled as she was in other matters — Dove's wedding preparations among other things. She asked no more questions about the betrothal of Belle and George, which appeared to make both of them, and everybody else concerned, extremely happy.

Heaviest on her mind lay her coming meeting with Eleanor. Very tactfully, in league with Jesse and Shem, Ephraim had persuaded her to receive her sister, now staying near Eagle Hall during the drastic renovations taking place there. It was hard for her to agree. More than twenty years lay between Eleanor's flight and the present, yet still she felt remembered bitter resentment against the giddy girl who had brought shame on the family, added to the misery of Margaret's disappearance, and had contributed to the death of their mother and their father's slow fading-out from life.

Ephraim knew better than to reason with her about it. They were too close; he had heard too much from her in the past and used all his arguments. It was Margaret, quietly summoned by him, who faced Mary with a cannonade of common sense.

'It was a very long time ago and we are all different people now. You remember the idea Mother had, that everybody changes completely, every seven years, hair, skin, blood, all parts of the body? It may be an old wives' tale, I don't know enough of medicine to say. But we *do* change, Mary. I am not the girl who ran away with the players. You are not the girl who wouldn't marry Ephraim because of some sort of silly pride. Don't you think Eleanor has changed, too?'

'Has she?' The question was forced out of Mary; she had meant to maintain a dignified silence, asking nothing.

'Yes. Come now, you must know I've seen and talked with her. Many times, in fact. She and Jesse have visited me, and I have been to see the old house at Downham. She loves it so much, Mary; poor Eleanor, who has no children, loves it like a child. As for Jesse — if you think they'll come flaunting adultery about Lancaster, you're very much mistaken. They are simply a middle-aged pair who might as well have been married twenty years ago for all the difference it makes to them or anyone else. Jesse's made himself a promising career in politics, and is still young as politicians go, they tell me. I've no worries for Jesse. But Eleanor — do you think she can be completely happy, Mary, even with her house to care for, when her family still rejects her?'

Mary said, floundering for reasons, 'She wrote a silly letter, one that angered me very much … something about the Prince Regent and a firework fête…'

'The Prince Regent became King seventeen years ago, and has been in his grave for seven more. He has vanished like the fireworks, and like Eleanor's letter, which I'll wager you burnt, didn't you? I thought as much. Your daughters, who were babies then, are women grown, about to marry. Don't you think it very hard-hearted to keep our sister out in the cold, all for nothing?'

Mary made no reply, but ran out of the room, her handkerchief to her eyes. Margaret knew she had won.

Eleanor came to St Leonard's Gate in the mid-morning: a nice sensible time, thought Margaret, who accompanied her, with less danger of high emotions than later in the day. Jesse was not with them. One encounter was enough, Margaret had decided. Everyone else was out of the way, Dove and Belle out wedding shopping. Aggie, at Margaret's suggestion, had prepared a dainty tray of tea served in the prettiest Coalport china; tea was always so soothing to the nerves, and yet cheering.

Mary was sitting not in her own cosy parlour, but in the morning room from which she had once banished Will Raven. She wore her best day dress, a sombre dark blue poplin with a deeply pointed bodice and impressive balloon sleeves; she felt it made her appear slimmer.

Ellen Casson tapped at the door, and announced very quietly (Aggie had instructed her not to sound too excited), 'Miss Margaret and Mrs Bradshaw.'

Mary remained seated for a moment, gathering her strength to confront this strange person who had entered with Margaret. Tallish, slender to emaciation, she was someone who had been very pretty at one time, until cares had drawn little spidery lines on her delicate skin. The hair framed by the high spoon bonnet was fair not entirely by nature, Mary could tell, inexperienced as she was in such artifices; the dark grey dress was demure as a Quaker's. Only the faintest look remained of Eleanor Bateman of Highriggs.

Mary rose, and held out her hand formally. 'Well, Eleanor,' she said.

The hand in hers was trembling. 'Mary,' Eleanor faltered.

Margaret sailed into action. 'We had such an uncommon dusty journey — I declare the traffic gets worse every day. The more they carry on the railways the better it will be. Do you think we might have some tea, Mary dear? I feel quite parched and I'm sure Eleanor does. Shall I ring?'

'Yes, do. Won't you sit down? And ... Eleanor.' But she could not yet quite believe that this *was* Eleanor. And so it was all the easier to fall in with Margaret's deliberately light conversation, especially when the tea arrived.

'We are really quite exhausted, my dear,' Margaret said. 'Just look at my hands. The workmen have reached a stage when we can actually get at the ground-floor rooms to measure for curtains and carpets, and the dust is unbelievable.' She spread immaculate white fingers for inspection.

'Tell me about the house, Eleanor,' Mary said, merely for something to say, and because she dared not allow herself to become emotional. It was easy for Eleanor to tell her about the house, forgetting the strained situation in rapturous description of its age and charm, of the decorations they proposed for it, the Elizabethan knot garden at the foot of the terrace, the restoration of Jesse's grandmother's special room to exactly what it had been when they first saw it. Before long they were talking like cordial acquaintances without a pause in the chatter.

Margaret nodded in silent satisfaction. The hurdle had been jumped, nobody had flown into a passion and nobody had cried. There would be tears before long, but she proposed to retire before that on the excuse of inspecting the twins' trousseaux.

It was an immense relief to be back in Eagle Hall. Eleanor subsided on her favourite sofa, drinking chocolate prepared by her maid. The servants from Bryanston Street were coming north, one by one, as more and more of the house was made habitable. Jesse, now back in London, was looked after by a manservant and a housekeeper, but, to judge by his letters, was so often away from home that their duties were extremely light.

She re-read his last letter. It told her of his success in the Buckinghamshire by-election and his delight in once more being a Member of Parliament.

By a strange coincidence our old friend Ben Disraeli lives but a few miles away, or rather his learned papa does. We encountered each other at one of Ly. Blessington's salons (Gore House very splendid, better even than Seamore Place.) Talked with him at great length, and was deeply impressed by the increased maturity of the man since our paths last crossed. His novels gain wide notice and are indeed remarkable for a young man of his background (though not much to my taste) but I fancy his future lies in the sphere of politics, as I always prophesied.

He was good enough to travel back with me to Wendslake for the purpose of canvassing for me, a noble effort indeed which has put me much in his debt — morally, that is, for I fancy in the other sense he's in very low water. The gossip is that he and Ly. Henrietta parted over his discovery of her with another gentleman, and that he is now done with affaires du coeur *and determined to marry money.*

I find his views and political philosophy highly original and interesting. A Tory, yet opposed to the evils which we must acknowledge exist in our party...

Eleanor skipped the next passages until she came again upon Disraeli's name.

How would you fancy inviting him to Eagle Hall during summer recess, always supposing that the house is sufficiently renovated to entertain visitors? Company would, I think, do you good after your strenuous exertions of the past month. I recall that you used to find him amusing, and I would myself appreciate some leisure to talk with him at length.

Eleanor put the letter down, gazing into space, and saw in her mind's eye the likeness of the young lover who had enlivened her dullest days in London. She had not loved him truly; no. She had never loved anyone but Jesse, and he had subtly changed over the years into somebody quite different from the youth who had fought a duel with her husband and almost lost his life for her sake.

She cared less about that now. It was clear that Ben, too, was changing from the society butterfly he had once seemed to be. She went into her bedroom and opened her jewel box. In the lower tray of it, which opened with a secret drawer device, lay a piece of paper a little faded with time; the poem he had sent her.

Bright beauty, modest, wise, witty yet kind,
Where in one goddess may one so much find?

It was not a good poem, but it had made her very happy. A dried primrose lay beside it, one of the flowers which had come with the verse. Smiling, she put them back and locked the box. Yes, she would see him again, but if the meeting proved a disappointment she would not mind very much, just as she had ceased to mind Jesse's long absences. For now she lived for her house.

Over the weeks, as its wounds were healed, Eagle Hall came to life. All the damage caused by rot, rats and general decay was put right, the broad old floorboards were once more fit to bear the weight of people and furniture, the windows clean and shining, the roof intact. It became possible to look out of one without seeing a ladder and a workman going up or down it. The noise of hammering and sawing quietened, the smell of new plaster and the general miasma of beer and tobacco that surrounded the builders was mercifully fading.

The time had come for Eleanor to take over. How pleasant it was to have money! Jesse grudged her nothing in the fitting-out of the place. The best furniture arrived from London, elegant modern stuff, Shem kindly sent some fine old pieces from Bradshaw Hall, a Jacobean cupboard very like the one Eleanor remembered in his grandmother's parlour, a four-poster that had stood unused in a spare room since his mother's death, a table with extending leaves, some sturdy old chairs that suited the age of the house. Eleanor spent happy hours in the haberdashers' shops, choosing curtain materials, pretty old-fashioned patterns and materials, amusedly aware that the shopkeepers regarded her taste as strangely out of date for such a fashionable and obviously moneyed lady.

But the carpets must be grand, comforting the poor old floors, bare for so long. A rich red patterned Turkey clothed the stairs and landings, a magnificent Chinese square in delicate shades of blue and rose pink on white went into the drawing room; her own sitting-room floor was a charming riot of flowers, like a springtime wood. Still there were vacant places in the house to fill, wide mantelshelves, deep window seats. She remembered Lady Blessington's treasures. Alas, even with money one could not equal those.

'Why not consult Will Raven?' Ephraim suggested. 'He has a shop and a storeroom full of interesting stuff, and I think you'll find his taste faultless.' Ephraim's sorrow for his friend's disappointment in love demanded every possible reparation he could make; this was one of them.

Eleanor had barely known Will in the old days. He was glad to see her, struck with pleasant pain at her likeness to Belle, proud to show her his stock, bewildering in its range from, as he put it, thimbles to coffins. She chose a crateful of objects to be sent to the Hall: porcelain figures, shepherds and shepherdesses, deer browsing on foliage, cupids and Britannias; Bartolozzi prints for the walls, and an oil painting of a charming lady which had been sold to Will as a Romney. 'I knew 'twere nothing of the sort, but she were so bonny I bought her.'

She was enraptured by a set of tiny cups and saucers, eggshell thin, and chairs and tables in proportion, gilded, in the style of Louis XV.

'Oh! They remind me so much...' She looked round the small barn he now used as a storeroom. 'You haven't a dolls' house anywhere, I suppose?'

Will thought. 'No. And I don't know where there is one. They mostly get broken with rough handling, like these fancy little things.' He held up a delicate fairy cup, looking at the light through it. 'You don't want to let bairns have 'em too young, or it's good work wasted.'

'I don't want the dolls' house for children — I haven't any. Only ... for myself.'

His surprise was obvious, but he had often had odd requests from customers.

'You see,' she went on, 'when we first visited the house we own now, Eagle Hall, Jesse's grandmother lived there, and she had a dolls' house I very much admired, and small furniture. I've tried to put her room, her own parlour, back as she knew it, but the little house has gone. I've enquired round the district if anybody bought it or knows where it is, but in vain.'

'Well,' said Will after a moment's thought, 'I could make you one.'

'You? Could you, really? But of course — you were Francis's partner in the furniture business. How stupid of me to have forgotten.'

'Aye. He was the craftsman, but I learned a good bit from him. Could you draw it for me, what you want?'

Laboriously she sketched out the shape she remembered, the square front, the gables, nine windows, a canopied door. 'Something like that, after the style of Queen Anne.'

Will surveyed it. 'That'll do to go on with. I'll be pleased to do a bit of work with my hands again.' He flexed them. 'Big and rough-looking, you'd say, and they've happen lost their cunning. But I'll have a shot at it, for you.' More and more she reminded him of Belle, even to her mannerisms. He would put all his skill into the making of the tiny mansion.

She went back to Downham happy with her acquisitions, happy to have met Will, who was so pleasant and almost family. It helped to make up for the discomfort she still felt with Mary. A twenty-year breach is not filled easily, and pride dies hard. At that first visit Mary had certainly softened towards her, and her own emotion had led to a parting embrace warmer than she had expected. But she would never feel comfortable at St Leonard's Gate unless some great change happened there.

At Ephraim's hesitant suggestion, much against her own inclination, she went to see Roderick at Ashton Hall.

The sight of him shocked her deeply. Surely she could not be the wife of this old, shrunken, crippled man, unable to rise from his chair. The handsome soldier, the respected servant of the Duke of Hamilton, come to this! She could not bring herself to kiss him, or even go very near him. Her maid, who had come with her, remained outside the cottage; Eleanor was glad she was near at hand.

He peered at her under bushy white eyebrows for so long that she thought he could not know her. Nervously she said again, 'I'm Eleanor. Don't you remember me?'

'Aye.' His voice was rusty with disuse. 'I ken ye well.'

'It has been … a very long time. How are you, Roderick?'

'As I seem. You've aged.'

'We all have,' she returned sharply. 'I hope I am not too changed.' But compliments were not forthcoming from this moulting eagle of a man. He continued to stare disconcertingly at her, his one hand resting on the Bible open on the table before him. She very much wished she had not come, and her first feelings of pity for his decayed state were fading fast. Suddenly he said, 'You're living still in sin and whoredom, I'm told.'

Her cheeks crimsoned. 'Nothing of the kind! How can you be so coarse? I live with Jesse, yes — as his wife, since I'm still tied to you.'

The old man muttered, '…God's holy ordinance.' He was thumbing through the pages of his Bible, his lips silently working. Eleanor all but stamped.

'If you're looking for the appropriate text, pray don't bother. There was no ordinance about it, holy or otherwise, as you very well know — simply a runaway marriage between a very silly girl and a man with no notion how to treat women. It seems perfectly ridiculous to me that we should still be shackled together after all these years. I suppose you know that my nephew Joe recently obtained a divorce? Could you not bring yourself to take the same action against me? I would be quite prepared to pay; we have plenty of money.'

'Sixpence a day,' he murmured, 'sixpence a day…'

'What of it?'

'My wound pension. That, and what His Grace gave me. He's departed now, gone to the Lord's keeping…'

Eleanor sighed. 'So you won't consider divorcing me.'

He shook his head slowly. 'Ye must wait a while longer, till I'm gone. Ye've waited so long, a wheen more years won't hurt.'

Eleanor gathered up her wraps and pulled on her gloves, ripping a seam. 'I see we have nothing to say to each other. I only called on you to enquire after your health, not to engage in an argument. Goodbye, Roderick. Harrison, tell Brydges I am ready to leave now.'

She was fuming with temper, all her old resentment against Roderick seething up, annoyed that she had not maintained her dignity with him. All the way back to Downham she thought of things she might have said, cunning turns of reasoning which might have got through to his fogged mind. She would not wish him dead, that would be wicked. And in any case, she thought, as Eagle Hall came into view, it mattered very little whether she were married to Roderick or Jesse now, for here was her house, her all, smiling in the early spring sunshine, a grey, beautiful animal, basking, sending out to her a lazy welcome.

And there was a pleasant prospect to look forward to: the wedding of her nieces.

CHAPTER TWENTY-FOUR

There was never a wedding that went forward without some difference of opinion. This was no exception; indeed, it provoked more strife than most, involving as it did two brides.

Neither twin really wanted a joint wedding. Belle would have preferred to be the only star in the sky, Dove cared little about her own opportunity to be admired, knowing that Joe wanted above all things a quiet, even completely private wedding with only the immediate family present. Horrendous memories of the Bradhope scenes kept visiting him. Desperately he said to Dove, 'Could we not have the ceremony in the drawing room instead of in a church? It's often done, I believe.'

'Not in our circles, my darling, only in high society. In any case, the drawing room will be needed for the breakfast party.'

Joe shuddered. The strains of 'Grimshaw's Factory Fire' and 'The Bonny Gray' still rang in his ears, though common sense told him they would not be sung at any function organised by Aunt Mary. He understood why bridegrooms occasionally failed to turn up at the church and were later found many miles away, usually in a drunken condition. But he was helpless against petticoat power. Mary insisted that the girls share a joint ceremony, for what, she enquired illogically, was the use in having twins at all if they could not be married together? Nobody found any answer to this.

The question of the church then arose. Belle and George wanted the Priory Church, the biggest and most important in Lancaster, which would hold his many relations and friends, including the master and officers of the *Chloe*. Belle thought it would make a splendid setting, with opportunities for a procession with open carriages.

Dove proved unusually stubborn in rejecting the Priory Church. She wanted, she said, to be married in St John's, the small church just round the corner from St Leonard's Gate, where her uncle John had been vicar long ago.

'But you didn't even know Uncle John!' Belle accused her. 'He died before we were born, so what difference does it make, unless you think his ghost might like to give you away?'

Dove refused to argue, continuing to repeat that she wanted St John's. In the end, to Belle's annoyance, Mary gave in. The church was small and unimpressive, certainly, but it was so near that everybody could walk to it and return on foot for the wedding breakfast. This, of course, would be smaller than if they took the Assembly Rooms, but Mary was secretly quite relieved to have the prospect of cutting down the numbers of Dilworths and the young men of the *Chloe*, who might very well prove rowdy.

Then came the question of the bridesmaids. Suddenly a great number of young ladies appeared to consider themselves the very closest friends of one or other of the brides. Embarrassingly they dropped in with offers of help in choosing materials for the dresses, or with small gifts 'for luck'. Dove, not caring in the least what bridesmaids she had or if she had any at all, settled for two schoolfriends, Ellen Ashworth and Letty Chirnside, while Belle was to be attended by George's sisters, Amy and Sophy, two strapping young women with bright blue eyes and loud laughs. Dove felt that they ought to have been sailors themselves.

The groomsmen presented fewer problems, as George's elder brother Jack was a natural choice, and Joe flatly refused to have a groomsman at all. 'It seems to me a very silly old custom, and besides, with so many bridesmaids there'll hardly be an inch of room to spare. Jack can take charge of the rings for both of us, and kiss all the bridesmaids, if he chooses.'

The preparations seemed to both Joe and Ephraim to have been going on for years when the wedding eve came at last. Both men had kept out of the way as much as possible, with the house a maelstrom of dressmakers, flower arrangers, relatives, clergy — everyone, as Ephraim said but the mayor and the town crier. His sarcastic suggestion that they too be invited was ignored by Mary; he doubted if she even heard it, through the general din.

The two men, by tacit consent, spent the best part of their time at the office, glad to have it as a refuge. Their rooms were separate but the door was left open for company when they worked into the evening. Ephraim said, leafing his way through an intricate file of papers, 'Is this what you want, then?'

'What, Uncle?'

'This marriage.'

'Oh, yes. Above everything.'

'Your aunt said something to me about the dangers of cousins marrying.'

'And to me. She pointed out that Dove and I are double cousins, in a sense, your brother having married Aunt's sister to produce me. But I replied that we're all children of one family, if we go back to Adam and Eve. They say Princess Drina will marry a cousin when she comes to the throne, as there's no other royal person available. So we must equally take our chance.'

'I agree.' Ephraim went on making notes. 'And the future, Joe? Is law the answer?'

Joe put down his pen. 'No. I think you know that.'

'I gathered as much. And, without seeming to belittle the help you've given me, I feel you are right. Then what do you wish to do?'

Joe turned up the wick of the lamp, looking into its green translucent shade as though he sought the future there. 'If I have money enough to be independent ... shall I have enough?'

'A substantial sum will be left over from Bradshaw's damages and costs, which have now been paid, by the way, from his estate. I have taken only what I was owed for professional services, and Percy Blanchard and Counsel have their share. That leaves you comfortably provided for. When your aunt and I are dead (no, I must speak of it) the twins and you will have everything — you and Dove a double portion, of course. I doubt that you have any financial worries.'

'Then,' Joe said carefully, 'I should like to be manager of a mill again, but without a Whittingham or a Bradshaw over me. I should like full control of working conditions and the means to improve them to my standards. I don't like the look of England, Uncle. There seem to be — if it's not too fanciful to say so — dirty fingers of greed pulling at it and daubing it. Some evils have gone, like the hanging of children for petty theft, but I feel that others almost as bad are coming. I don't know what. Sometimes, when I can't sleep, I see formless things, like the devils in Aunt Margaret's old German Bible. I want to be able to fight them. I want to be just such a man as Anthony Ashley.'

'Your Christ Church friend.'

'Yes. I know now that I was wrong to think myself a mechanical genius. God knows I was never that. So I must work out my destiny on the philanthropic side, if I have the health, and the means. Do you think that sensible, Uncle?'

'Eminently.' In the soft light Ephraim's face was calm and relieved. 'I hoped you would say some such thing. I'm glad Dove's dowry will go towards such a future, Joe.'

On the eve of the wedding the twins were together in the bedroom they shared for the last time. Their hair was twisted into neat curl-papers for tomorrow's ringlets, their dresses, lingerie and shoes all in place for donning. The room smelt of scent, wax flowers, and fresh linen. Outside a March wind was blowing, bringing excitement and promise in its gusts.

'Poor room,' Dove said. 'Do you think it will miss us?'

'How could it?' Belle was patting lotion on to her face. 'Rooms don't feel anything. Do hurry up, I'm almost ready for bed and we shall look frights tomorrow if we don't get enough sleep.'

'Belle — are you truly, truly happy?'

'Of course I am, silly! How could I be anything else, or you either?'

'Oh, I am.' Dove said it softly, to herself, to Joe, who had been banished to the other end of the house so that there was no possibility of his glimpsing the wedding dress, the most unlucky thing a groom could do.

'But,' she persisted, 'do you really love George, enough never to want anybody else, even if you were to go away from us all and live in — oh, Iceland or somewhere?'

Belle turned from the mirror, laughing. 'Well, of course I do. How could you ever have let him go? He's so handsome, so good-humoured, so — everything I want. We shall be a perfect couple, I know that. Oh, and so will you and Joe, Dovekin,' she added magnanimously. 'You were always meant for each other. Do you remember the wager about the lilac gloves, and how you cried when I got him to flirt with me?'

354

'Yes. But ... Belle. It's not too late. What about Will? Have you really put him out of your heart? Please forgive me for asking, but nobody else will, now, and — you were so distressed when Mother forbade Will to see you.'

Belle smoothed her eyebrows, patted her cheeks, and pinched into shape the lace frill of her nightcap. 'People change. Let's not talk about sad things now. Shall I put out the light?'

Dove was already in bed. 'Yes.'

The room was dark, quiet but for the ruffling of the wind in the orchard trees. The girls lay, curled in their last virgin sheets, each thinking her own thoughts, until sleep overcame them.

The wedding day dawned bright and blustery, a brilliant blue sky with great white clouds tumbling across it. Breakfast was quite two hours earlier than usual, a scrambled affair to which nobody paid much heed, for the cold collation that was to follow the wedding was the real business of the day. The brides were invisible, attended in their room by all the other females concerned. The house was filled with a constant rushing up and downstairs, calls to one another to 'Pin me up, there's a dear!' nervous shrieks and giggles, and the constant pealing of the bell as flowers, food and visitors arrived. The ceremony was to be at eleven o'clock. Soon after ten the drawing room was full of close friends and relatives. Margaret, superbly dignified in watered silk of a rich shade of peacock blue, had brought the little teacher, Miss Jessie from Bradhope, herself betrothed to a curate and immensely excited. Eleanor and Jesse, an elegant Londonified pair, were early. Eleanor was relieved that Mary's motherly duties prevented any foregathering with her; she was still not wholly at ease in the house.

Will arrived, half an hour before. In the absence of the servants, all of whom were hectically engaged somewhere else, Ephraim let him in.

'I'm glad to see you, Will. We hoped you'd come, though we thought...' He changed what he had been going to say. 'We thought you might be busy.'

'Oh, I am, but not too busy.' He looked calm and cheerful, Ephraim noted with pleasure. Together they joined the waiting party in the drawing room, now increased by Arabella and Jack Dilworth, Arabella alternating between laughter and tears, as befitted the mother of a bridegroom.

Ephraim, an imposing figure in a finely cut frock coat and exquisitely pressed trousers, his face emerging from a snowy cravat, surveyed the company.

'I think the time has come for a slight nerve-strengthener,' he said, turning to the cabinet in which drinks were kept. Everyone gratefully received a glass of best sherry from the decanter, although Arabella declared it might well reduce her to hysterics. As they were drinking, Joe appeared. Ephraim, after a glance at his white face, conducted him to the cabinet and, unnoticed by the others, poured him a lavish glass of brandy. Joe drank it in one draught; a faint colour crept back to his cheeks. He spoke to nobody in the room, where Eleanor and Will were now chatting animatedly about the progress of the dolls' house — 'a fiddling job', as Will put it — and Margaret was conversing with Shem who had just arrived, and making him laugh.

'Will they ever be ready?' Joe whispered to Ephraim. 'Listen to them.' The sounds of preparation were indeed rising to such a crescendo that it seemed some terrible accident must have happened, judging by the screams and bumps.

'Nothing worse than girls' excitement,' Ephraim reassured him. 'That was a table going over. Thank goodness your aunt took an extra dose of drops this morning. Bear up, lad, it won't be long now.'

And indeed, at that moment the church bells began. At that sound everybody stopped talking and the noise in the house subsided. Ephraim and Joe went out into the hall. George was there, splendidly handsome but patently almost as nervous as his fellow bridegroom, and accompanied by Jack, his brother, surrounded by milling servants dressed in their best. Mary came downstairs, bustling through the throng into the drawing room, and clapped her hands.

'Come along, everybody, time we were in our places in church. Jack? Where's young Jack? Oh, there you are. Now you know where everybody's sitting, make sure you get it right, and you two bridegrooms, get along out of the way before the girls come down.' She shooed them all out of the house like so many hens, going out herself last of all. As she passed Ephraim he pulled her to him and gave her a kiss.

'Go easy, Mother, don't over-excite yourself. You look very fine.'

'You don't think this blue's too young for me?' she asked anxiously.

'Not a bit of it — charming. There, off you go.'

The bells pealed on, drawing spectators to the scene, all agog to see any pageantry that might be going. At five minutes to eleven by Ephraim's watch he left the house, a bride on each arm, the bridesmaids a quartet of beauty too awed now to giggle.

Within the church porch they paused. The bells stopped and the organ began a solemn yet joyous air as the father and his daughters appeared. Heads turned, a sigh of admiration went up, following their progress up the aisle. Both brides wore gauzy veils attached to the knot of hair on top of their heads, streaming behind, leaving their faces free to the view. Their dresses were of brocade, Dove's patterned in silver, Belle's in gold. Above their brows perched tiny wreaths of wax orange blossom and leaves; they carried posies of spring flowers. They had never looked more beautiful.

In those few moments all earlier memories of the church left the minds of Ephraim and Mary; memories of Joe's christening, and the girls', the death of John Atkinson in the pulpit and his funeral service in this, his own church. Nothing was real but the two fair brides, each now at the side of her groom, before the altar where stood the vicar, his book open at the wedding service.

Joe glanced sideways at Dove, barely taking in her loveliness. He had a dreadful irrational fear that at any moment she might turn into Rosie, and his freedom from that earlier marriage become only a dream. He felt he might do something mad — snatch Dove up and run out of the church with her, past them all, away into hiding and safety. She looked up at him, a long, expressive look that said *I know how you feel. Be calm, it will soon be over. I love you.*

The phantoms left him, exorcised by her strength. He turned to listen attentively to the opening words he had heard before; they meant so much more to him now.

'Dearly beloved, we are gathered together in the sight of God…'

It was over. The last morsel had been eaten, the last glass emptied with the last toast to the happy couples. Mary and Ephraim stood in the hall, one on each side, their faces stiff with smiling as they shook hands with the last of the departing guests. In the rooms behind them, exhausted servants and the men from the pastry cook's were clearing dishes with clatters and clashes.

Belle and George had already left on their wedding journey, which was no further than to Downham, where they were to be Eleanor's first guests at Eagle Hall. Dove was upstairs, changing out of her bridal dress; Joe was strolling in the garden, alone. Of the guests only Will remained.

Ephraim shut the door, thankfully. 'Well, heaven be praised,' he said, 'it all went off smoothly. You did wonders, Mother. Go and sit down now, and Ellen shall make us some tea.'

'I feel as if I could sit down for ever,' Mary said wearily. 'Dear me! What a crowd, and what a noise they did make — I thought my eardrums would burst. I don't remember anything like that at our wedding breakfast, do you, Father?'

'People were a good deal more sedate in those days — or perhaps we're frailer than we once were. Come along, Will. We'll have a quiet sit down and a talk, just we three.'

'You don't want me hanging about,' Will said reasonably. 'Just you go and have your rest. I'll wait here for Mr and Mrs Joe Atkinson. You see, me and Joe, we made a little arrangement. They wanted somewhere quiet to go, knowing what a to-do there'd be today, so I've got rooms for them at a little inn up above Kendal on Fellside, near where Joe was born.'

'You're a dark horse, Will!' Mary exclaimed. 'And so are they, sly creatures. They wouldn't say where they were going, no matter how I teased them to know.'

'Well, young newlyweds are like that, I'm told. I came in the trap, so as I could drive them. Joe looks fit to drop, like I thought he would.'

Ephraim clapped him on the shoulder. 'Will, you're a friend indeed. I congratulate you — no, I don't, we've heard enough congratulations today to last us for a bit. I thank you, and so does Mary, I'm sure.'

'That I do, Will. You're a real friend to our boy and girl, just as you've been to us.' The sorry past was forgotten as she kissed his cheek.

They all turned as Dove came downstairs, Aggie behind her. The old servant had for once given in to unrepressed emotion, and her face was red and swollen with tears. But Dove was calm, smiling, no longer a radiant bride but a beautiful young matron in a most becoming mantle of soft rose pink, and a bonnet of the same colour trimmed with white.

'Well, where's my husband?' she asked. 'Fetch him, Will, there's a dear, for if we leave much later it will be dark.'

The trap was brought round to the door. Will tactfully left Mary and Ephraim alone with the departing pair. They embraced and kissed, saying little, for they all felt much.

'We'll be back in a day or two,' Joe said. 'Cheer up. You're not losing a daughter, but gaining a son, remember.'

'We've always had a son,' Mary said.

The trap drew up at a turn of the winding road that led up from Kendal town. In the dusk Joe looked down to where he knew the house in Kirkland stood, and up towards the cottage of his birth. The air was quite still, a few stars prickling the spring sky, a moor-bird calling.

'You'll be a sight quieter here than they are at Downham,' Will observed. 'What with young George and our Belle, and a housewarming, it'll be like Bolton Wakes, if my guess is right. I'll be off now — it's been a long day. Good night to you both. Come and see me when you've nought else to do.'

They laughed, and waved him farewell. The small inn was warm and welcoming, a good supper waiting for them in a private parlour. They fell on it, having eaten very little at their own festivities.

Joe raised his glass and drank to his wife, first the glasses touching, then their lips. They had been talking quietly, like long-married folk, with no awkward pauses, utterly comfortable with each other.

'You're thinking of Belle,' he said.

'Yes. This is the first time we've been apart, but for the night she ran away.'

'Do you miss her very much?'

'Not at all.'

'Thank you, love.' He lifted her hand and kissed it, the tender palm, his new bright ring on her finger. 'Did you notice what Will said — "our Belle"? — as though he thought of himself as her uncle again. Do you think he's quite got over her? I can't believe it. If I had lost you … but I won't think about that.'

'I think,' she answered, 'Will has too tender a heart to heal easily.'

'Like yours; two of a kind… What can you see in your glass?'

She was swirling the remains of the wine round and round, making eddies and waves. 'Great things.'

'For whom?'

'For you. Your heart's desire, perhaps.'

His eyes held hers in a long look. 'I have that already. We've come a long way to this night, my little wife. Twenty-nine years ago I was born, up the lane, there; and now I'm home again, with you.'

He rose, taking her hand and raising her. They clung together in a wordless embrace, then went slowly, entwined, up the narrow stairs, gold head close to auburn head. The shadows took them and the firelight danced on in an empty room.

On the fells a fox barked, and was answered. But the little house was very still, as though waiting, hushed, for something quite new to begin.

CHAPTER TWENTY-FIVE

Will's prophecy that the wedding celebrations at Eagle House would be like Bolton Wakes was a fair enough guess. His notion of simple rustic merriment was, however, not quite what Eleanor had had in mind when she arranged the evening's entertainment. The marriage of George and Belle was to be one reason for rejoicing, the housewarming the other.

'Poor old place,' she said to Jesse, 'it's seen no fun for the best part of two hundred years, I daresay. Why not give it the evening of its life?'

'Up to you, m'dear.' Jesse privately had little confidence in the ability of houses to feel anything, and was fairly sure that what was planned was to be the evening of Eleanor's life, since she looked on the place as her child. The complicated arrangements for it certainly kept her busy and happy, writing notes of invitation, summoning tradesmen and extra domestic help from Clitheroe, measuring here and rearranging there, as though the imminent death of old King William had already happened and she were planning a coronation party for the young girl Victoria, waiting in Kensington Palace for the crown that was to be placed on her head.

'Do you think it will be dark enough?' she asked him anxiously. 'For lanterns in the gardens, and some portions of the rooms to be in complete shadow?'

'In late April? I suppose so — I never take much note of such things. Our northern weather ain't noted for its brilliance at this time of year.'

'Then that will be splendid. Dusk, and all the curtains pulled … oh, that will do very well. It will still be cool enough for fires, and we can have the candles out when —' she stopped short and giggled. 'But I mustn't tell even you; it's to be a surprise.'

It was a surprise, certainly, to the guests arriving from Lancaster when their carriages entered a drive hung with Chinese lanterns throwing out their soft glow from nine feet high in the air, evening moths clustering round them. And then, the house itself, when they reached it! There were gasps of delight when they saw it bathed in the light of gas lamps cunningly planted in the bushes in front.

'How extremely Gothic!' they cried, leaning out of the wound-down carriage windows. 'La, how pretty! Quite like a play!'

In front of the porch they scrambled out, the young Dilworths, Amy, Sophy and Jack, the two bridesmaids, Ellen Ashworth and Letty Chirnside, and friends of theirs who had been at the service and the wedding breakfast. Behind them other carriages unloaded guests, single horsemen cantered in from nearby houses, a whole coachload arrived from Clitheroe. Under the lamp in the porch stood Eleanor, radiant in a Paris-designed primrose dress of many flounces, diamonds round her neck, her face alight with welcome.

'Come in, my dears, come in, come in! Belle, how charming you look, and not at all tired from the fuss. George, give me a kiss as a good nephew-in-law should.'

George did, a lingering one, which he knew was expected. He and Belle had, in fact, slept most of the way from Lancaster, after the long-drawn-out speeches and toasts at St Leonard's Gate. Now they were perfectly fresh again, ready for whatever Eleanor had in mind for them.

Cloaks removed, they were ushered upstairs to the long, panelled drawing room, alight with wall-sconces. Gracious, exclaimed the young ladies, how old-fashioned! Why, Grandmama had had all those old panels taken out of *her* house and sold to the timber merchant, and surely a chandelier would have been smarter and shown up that quaint old plaster moulding on the ceiling. The furniture, too, was rather antique for today's tastes, but at least there were a gratifying number of little tables scattered among it, laden with dishes of nibbles, and neat-capped maids were advancing with trays of drinks. On every window seat and shelf were vases of spring flowers, even early roses, so scarce at this time of year.

In the wide inglenook fireplace burned a bright log fire that sent out its fragrant apple wood smoke to mingle with the perfumes of the guests. Jesse, looking on at the scene, thought with affectionate amusement that his fashionable wife had managed, unconsciously, to revive something of the air of the festivities that had been held in the old days at Highriggs, in her father's great farm kitchen. She was looking very handsome, years younger than her age. He toyed with the thought that he might make love to her tonight. They had grown into such a staid pair, these days. The sight of the pretty young girls, and of Belle and George close together on a sofa, excited him to feelings he had almost forgotten. It was years now since any of the charming bored ladies of Westminster had attracted him. He moved nearer to Eleanor, but she had darted to the middle of the hearthrug.

Clapping her hands, she called the chattering, laughing company to order. 'Now, have you all taken a glass of punch, and the gentlemen two? Good. Then we'll proceed to the evening's entertainment. Can you guess what it's to be?'

'Dancing,' cried someone. Someone else guessed an Italian singer.

'A marionette show. A sermon from Dr Badgett.' There was a general laugh at this, the clergyman concerned being a notorious sleep-inducer.

'Wrong, wrong. Something much more amusing. Very well, since you can't guess — charades!'

A general shriek of delight went up from the ladies, not echoed by the gentlemen. The party game that consisted of acting out the syllables of a word, then acting the full word and inviting the audience to guess it, involved a lot of dressing-up and foolery that was all very well for girls, but beneath the dignity of fellows. They glanced at each other in embarrassment over their high collars.

'Come along, now.' Eleanor was marshalling them into two ranks. 'I want some people to act and the rest to guess. Amy and Sophy, I won't have you, because you'll giggle too much and spoil it. Mrs Lacey, you must certainly not exert yourself, my dear, but Mr Lacey may take part. Belle shall come on our side, and George must rest.' A general laugh went up at the bridegroom's expense, to which that sophisticated young gentleman returned a knowing smile. At last Eleanor had organised ten guests to be players, the others to arrange themselves as an audience.

While they waited, the talented Miss Jane Barley, known in her own circles as the Polyhymnia of Downham, kindly agreed to render her best pieces on the piano for their benefit. Her roulades and glissandos were heard only faintly in the anterooms where Eleanor was busily superintending the dressing-up of the performers from the heap of costumes she had ready.

'Of course it will fit, Letty, they are all loose enough to fit anybody. Miss Alice, you'll pull the button off if you wrench at it like that — have some patience. I see Mr Lacey is in difficulties with his mask — just help each other, now, while I fit him.' And she rushed across to the gentlemen's dressing room, where Mr Lacey was indeed in difficulties, and growing purple in the face. In an astonishingly short time she had stage-managed everyone into the right costumes, checked the properties, silenced the squeaks and giggles, assured the gentlemen that they would hardly have to do any acting at all, only stand about in graceful poses, and arranged the setting.

The performance was to take place in a curtained-off alcove at the end of the room, from which the two anterooms led off on each side, each with a door communicating with the landing. It might have been designed for theatricals, though in fact it had probably been a food serving area in the old days: the curtains had been added by Eleanor. Now they were drawn, hiding the acting space from the audience, and the first scene was set up behind them. Eleanor, in the ladies' anteroom, gave three loud raps on the wall, the signal for Miss Barley to end her Mozartian tinklings and break into some stirring chords from the overture to that popular opera *Der Freischutz*.

The audience chatter ceased as the curtains parted. A voice announced, 'First syllable.'

In the centre of the stage a table was arranged as a shop counter, displaying boxes of jewellery — none of Eleanor's best pieces, but what she thought of as baubles from her poorer days. Behind it stood Jack Dilworth, thinly disguised as a shopkeeper in an apron borrowed from the kitchen. His goods were being examined by a couple who were obviously betrothed and about to choose the ring, judging by their ostentatious billing and cooing. There were some titters from the Lancaster faction in the audience, the girl being pretty Ellen Ashworth and the young man a neighbour known to be very sweet on her. Ring after ring was tried on and rejected, the shopman growing ever more and more despairing. No words were spoken, but the youth indicated in mime that for his sweetheart nothing but the biggest and best was suitable. He pointed to an invisible shelf at the rear of the counter. The shopman turned, peered through spectacles, reached up with back to them; at which the lover gave his lady a prodigious wink, both seized handfuls of gems, and with comical haste rushed off the stage, while the shopkeeper threw up his hands in horror.

The curtains closed. Assorted guesses at the syllable came from the audience: 'Rob. Steal. Ring. Flit.' As they argued, and Miss Barley played an interlude, frenzied activities were heard before the curtains parted again, and the announcement came: 'Second syllable.'

Belle, with a cloak of rags over her dress and her pretty feet shoeless in their white silk bridal stockings, was seated on a chair, demurely watching a young man wearing a crown of gilt paper trying a shining slipper on the feet of the two ladies seated beside her, each with heavy lines drawn on her face to produce an effect of extreme ugliness. If Eleanor expected a general recognition of the story of Cinderella, she was too ambitious. Only Londoners had seen the Italian opera *La Cenerentola,* whose plot was to find its way into the nurseries of Britain. But it was obvious that this princely or kingly person wanted to find the lady whose foot fitted the slipper. It would hardly go near the first ugly sister's extended foot. The second sister made a face of extreme agony as the prince attempted to squeeze it over her toes.

Success crowned the third attempt. Smoothly the slipper slid on to the tiny extended foot of Belle. The prince turned, gesturing triumph and cradling the foot in his hands, exhibiting its smallness proudly and pointing to the dainty toe, while the ugly sisters rubbed theirs in pain. Belle smirked, the audience clapped, the curtains closed, and speculation was rife.

'*Foot? Fit? Shoe?* Oh dear, I'll never get it. Why does she have to make them so difficult?'

For her musical prelude to the third tableau Miss Barley reverted to *Der Freischutz,* choosing a particularly dramatic passage. The scene revealed now brought a gasp from the watchers. Centre stage, standing on a footstool and looking immensely tall, was the figure of a man wrapped in a scarlet cloak. An animal mask hid his face, two curved horns rose from his brow, a long tail with a forked end was negligently draped over one arm. There were squeals from the more timid of the watching ladies, and apprehensive glances were cast towards Mrs Lacey, who was in an interesting condition.

Around the menacing form were grouped six ladies, each in a black cloak and a steeple hat. As Miss Barley played, they danced a slow and stately measure around their master, quickening until they were circling like a ring of whirling dervishes. When it seemed they could go no faster they stopped, suddenly, and with one accord swept him a deep bow, the crowns of their tall hats almost touching the ground. Loud applause, curtains, and excited guesses.

'The Pendle witches — of course. It must be *witch.*'

'Or goat — he was meant to be a goat, wasn't he?'

'Silly Amy, what sort of word ends in *goat?*'

Eleanor stepped out between the curtains. 'Has anyone guessed?' They flung speculations at her, to all of which she shook her head smilingly. 'Wrong, all of you. Every single one, wrong. Very well, we'll give you the whole — and if you don't guess *that*, you're a set of dunces. Miss Barley, if you please…?'

And Miss Barley played the first notes of the tune that gave the secret away. To its melancholy strains, the final scene disclosed four couples in their evening finery, dancing a stately measure very different from the wild cavortings of the witches. Belle, who had scrambled back into her wedding dress and orange-blossom wreath, swam gracefully in the arms of a handsome young man, unable to resist an occasional coquettish glance *(Don't you wish you were in his place?)* at George, who looked back somewhat grimly. The dance ended, the bride stepped coyly forward, her finger at her lips.

The audience knew the ballad backwards; it turned up at every Christmas festivity. Throughout the dancing they had been humming or singing:

'The mistletoe hangs in the castle hall,
The holly branch shines on the old oak wall,
And the baron's retainers so blithe and gay
Are keeping their Christmas holiday.
The baron beholds with a father's pride
His beautiful child, Lord Lovel's bride,
While, she, with her bright eyes seems to be
The star of the goodly company.'

Now, they knew, she was going to disappear.

"I'm weary of dancing now," she cried,
"Pray tarry a moment, I'll hide, I'll hide.
"But Lovel, be sure thou'rt the first to trace
"The clue to my secret hiding place."'

She was gone, blowing kisses, the bridegroom looking wistfully after her. Then faces began to wear anxious expressions, watches were consulted. The bridegroom was becoming frantic as one after another vanished in search of her, returned, shaking his head. He was searching desperately in imaginary cupboards, behind imaginary curtains and panels.

'In the highest, the lowest, the loneliest spot
Young Lovel sought wildly, but found her not.'

Before their eyes he began to shrivel, shoulders drooping, head heavy; a stick appeared in his hand, by which he helped himself about the stage, still looking, looking.

'And when Lovel appeared, the children cried,
"See! the old man weeps for his fairy bride."'

The scene on the stage grew darker; in the drawing room someone had unobtrusively blown a few candles out. The younger and more timid of the watchers were moving closer to each other, some holding hands.

'At length an oak chest that had long laid hid
Was found in the castle; they raised the lid…'

There was, indeed, the outline of a coffer at the back of the stage, though no one had seen it carried on behind the action. The music paused; the lid of the chest creaked slowly open, lifted: from within rose slowly and horribly a skeleton in the rags of a white dress, an orange-blossom wreath still crowning the skull. It stood, motionless, grinning at them, in a silence which suddenly erupted into screams.

Jesse, who had been stage-managing the lights, reflected that Eleanor had gone too far. He gave a hasty signal for the curtains to be closed, whispered to Miss Barley to play and sing the chorus, and joined in with his own full baritone voice: '*Oh, the mistletoe bough! Oh, the mistletoe bough!*' He pushed his way through the curtains and bumped into Eleanor. 'Get that nonsense off her and let them see it was all play-acting, or you'll have hysterics on your hands.'

In a moment, they had the skull mask off, the tatters removed to show a pretty pink evening frock and a pretty pink face above it, the face of Miss Matilda Bower, well known in the shops and lanes of Downham. The curtains were hurriedly pulled, revealing her to half-swooning ladies and pale-faced gentlemen.

'There, you see,' said Jesse heartily, 'just a clever piece of chicanery on my wife's part, nothing to be afraid of at all.' He drew Eleanor forward. 'Tell them yourself, my dear, it was only Miss Matilda and some stage properties.'

She opened her arms to them in charming appeal. 'Oh, forgive me, forgive me! I didn't mean to scare you *really*.' (Thank heaven, Mrs Lacey was looking calmly cheerful — she might easily have been confined on the spot.) 'With such a talented cast I couldn't resist my strongest effects. Had I thought anybody would be truly put in a fright I would not have *dreamed* of — of giving you anything so realistic.'

She was pink with excitement and at her most winning. Jesse knew that whatever she might say she was secretly gratified at the success of her *coup de théâtre,* and he, a connoisseur of theatrical speeches in the House, admired her for it, and felt a twinge of desire for her such as he had not felt for years.

'Now,' she was saying, 'let's put the horrors behind us. Who got the answers right?'

George was the spokesman. 'Nobody! It was the most deuced hard set of charades I've ever seen. What were the syllables, pray?'

'Why, simple,' said Eleanor, smiling sweetly. 'The first was *mizzle* — after they stole the jewels they mizzled from the shop. Perfectly clear.'

'Thieves' slang ain't allowed. And "mizzle" is two syllables, not one.'

'Oh, well,' Eleanor shrugged prettily. 'One has to cheat a little sometimes. You all got the other syllables, of course? *Toe* and *bough —bow*?'

They hadn't, and it was generally agreed that nobody could have been expected to. Jesse was going round refilling glasses from the punchbowl by the fire, to the considerable improvement of the company's spirits. Eleanor tinkled a small bell.

'Supper, everybody! Take your partners, please.'

Belle came forward and took George's arm. She had kept on the wedding dress, out of sentiment, and he was glad to see it, holding her more tightly than a supper partner need as they prepared to go downstairs. At the precise moment when all the company was grouped, Eleanor and Jesse leading the train, a maid appeared in the doorway and announced, 'Mr Benjamin Disraeli.'

He stood there, a picture surpassing all the stage pictures they had seen that night; a prince of dandies from shining black curls to shining patent leather slippers, and in between a rainbow of colours and a golden glitter of chains and rings. Smiling blandly, he surveyed the startled faces before him through an eyeglass, shaking back the fine lace cuff from his wrist.

Jesse saw Eleanor turn white, then scarlet, with a brighter blush than a woman of forty-nine should be able to summon. As she stepped forward, her hand outstretched and her mouth tremulous, he disliked his friend Disraeli very much.

'I really could not help myself,' Disraeli said, seated between them at supper. 'You were kind enough to invite me to visit in the summer recess, but knowing you to be at home in this divine season of spring, I took the plunge, and a coach, and — behold me.'

'You're very welcome, Ben, now or at any time,' Jesse said, wishing heartily that he had never mentioned the wedding and the housewarming. Eleanor was very quiet, only picking at her food, but her face was happy, calm and excited all at the same time.

'You missed our charades — what a pity,' she said.

'On the contrary, I saw, and marvelled. I was informed by your footman that they were in progress, and I took the liberty of mounting to the gallery that looks down on the drawing room. Mrs Bradshaw, may I say that you are a loss to Drury Lane? What an actor-manager we should have had in you!'

Eleanor blushed again. 'Oh, it was only foolery. I thought it would be an unusual sort of entertainment, but it seemed to get a little out of hand.'

'Just a little, perhaps. Will you take wine with me, ma'am?'

He raised his glass and touched it to hers, with a gesture that suggested a kiss. She asked him about his latest novel, *Venetia*. 'I have had so little time to read since I became a housewife, but I do keep up with the London journals. Tell me, is it a political novel?'

'Only in that politics, like cheerfulness in Dr Johnson's philosophic friend, will keep breaking in. I would say, broadly speaking, that it is a romantic novel.'

It would be, thought Jesse, listening to Disraeli discoursing in beautiful prose about Byron and Shelley and the darkest recesses of the heart. He had heard that Dizzy was between women, miffed over his last mistress's unfaithfulness and baffled by the unavailability of the dazzling and rich Mrs Wyndham Lewis, his present fancy. It was rumoured that Dizzy's glittering appearance belied his empty pockets and the debts his old father kept paying off for him. Eleanor was a rich woman. Jesse's earlier high spirits completely left him; he helped himself liberally from the port decanter. It was no consolation, when the eating was done, to see Disraeli circulating among the guests, charming and dazzling effortlessly, and quite eclipsing memories of the skeleton bride.

'I have put you in the tower room,' Eleanor told Disraeli later. 'I think you will like it, with your Gothic tastes. It's in the oldest part of the house — the staircase is very dark, I'm afraid.'

'I shall need no light but Beauty's eyes,' he said, his own holding hers with a look that set her heart beating fast. So long since they had met, and such a fancied coldness between them; and now this. Fate could be very kind when it pleased.

Chatter and excitement had broken out among the young people. 'Where's Belle? And George? Aren't we to have any ceremonies?' Some of them had come prepared for the jolly ribaldry of 'bedding the bride' which still went on in country districts when the couple had not gone away on a wedding journey. But Belle and George were nowhere to be seen. 'Another case of the mistletoe bough, only this bride has taken Lord Lovel with her,' someone observed.

General disappointment prevailed when it was made clear that the party must now break up, for carriages had been called to be in attendance at midnight. They left, all but those from Lancaster who were staying overnight, saying their goodbyes to the host and hostess and observing the custom of wishing the house well.

Eleanor was glad she had caught Belle's eye earlier, and whispered that they could leave unseen through one of the anterooms beside the stage recess, with no fuss or embarrassment. With satisfaction she saw them disappear through the curtains, George's arm round his bride's waist.

The newly wed pair had been given the best bedroom in Eagle House, decked with flowers, brightened by a fire which had been kept stoked all evening; the sheets glowed gently from the application of a warming pan. But Belle, startled and enchanted by the realities of matrimony, hardly noticed any of these kind attentions. She found herself nothing like as knowledgeable and worldly-wise as she had thought she was. Her pranks with young Gilbert, long ago, had hardly prepared her for a wedding night that proved to be as instructive as it was exciting. She had told her mother that George could teach her a lot; and he did.

Mary went from room to room of the house in St Leonard's Gate. Slowly, because the doctor said she was not to exert herself. To sit still was impossible. As soon as she tried to settle to sewing or reading, the ache came back to remind her that her daughters were gone.

She had never realised before how big the house was, how much room there was to fill, which now was only empty space. Furniture she had known all her married life had lost its familiar friendliness and become mere wood and upholstery.

There, in the drawing room, was the chair Dove had always sat in, a slender chair with a cane back and pink cushioned seat. There was the sofa, refurbished since the long-ago days when the two children had bounced on it, but still bringing back those days to Mary. Belle's window seat, the Broadwood piano on which the girls had sometimes played duets — Dove soft and correct, Belle dashing and inaccurate — the leg of the little games table which still bore the marks of Adam's teeth, made when the girls had brought the dog into the drawing room against express instructions. They had both been smacked for it; Mary wondered now how she could have been so cruel. If time would only turn back she would not smack them.

In the little parlour they had used there were still signs of pre-wedding frenzy: a scarf hung over a chair, a discarded cap on the floor; the servants had not had time to get round to this room. Mary opened the satinwood work table that had held their sewing. Inside was chaos: a muddle of silks, needle cases with the needles jabbed into them anyhow, scraps of material, artificial flowers, ribbons; it looked as though a kitten had been shut in to wreak havoc. Carefully Mary shut the lid and made her slow way upstairs.

Their bedroom was the worst thing she had to face. She had always been against their having separate beds, those two pretty muslin-draped beds that made this room so unmistakably, unalterably Belle's and Dove's. Mary set her lips. She would see that it *was* altered. One of the beds should go into the room Joe had used, and his less ornate one should be taken upstairs to the servants' floor. Perhaps Aggie would like it; it was more comfortable than hers, and she needed comfort now that she was an old woman.

Mary touched the coverlet of the bed that had been Belle's. Here her lovely girl had lain within inches of death from cholera, had convalesced, had been visited somewhat indiscreetly by Will Raven. Had it been right to discourage Will, to insist on that pathetic ring being given back to him? Wherever Mary looked in the past, there seemed cause for self-reproach. She hurried out of the bedroom, downstairs, ruthless in punishing herself by dwelling on the objects the girls had known, each one a mirror reflecting them in their mother's eyes.

Even the dining room hurt, though it was formal enough and had held so many people besides the twins in its pillared splendour. It had looked the same as long as she remembered it, furnished elegantly by Gillow's, twelve chairs ranged stiffly round the long table; it would take sixteen when the table was fully extended, for it was a 'bride's table', with four leaves that could be raised to extend it as the family grew. Three were up now. Mary's eyes filled; the tears spilled over.

It was there Ephraim found her. He had come home quickly from his office, anxious for her, so unnaturally quiet and composed had she been at breakfast. She was not in her parlour, where he usually found her in the evening, nor in their bedroom; nobody in the kitchen had seen her for an hour. With immense relief he saw her at last, her small plump figure shaking with sobs, leaning on the back of a dining chair.

'Why, Mother, what's all this? Come, now.' At his approach she turned to him, burying her face against his coat, weeping uncontrollably, unable to speak.

'Now, now, now,' he said. 'You know what the doctor said, not to upset yourself. Something's set you off, hasn't it. Try to stop crying, and tell me.'

'It will have to be … drawn in,' she sobbed. 'Too … too big now … for us.'

Ephraim caught her meaning with quick understanding. 'The table? Nonsense. Are we to have no more dinner parties now that the girls are married? On the contrary, we shall have more — plenty of friends to keep us amused and lively. Let's sit down and think of some names, and tomorrow you shall write the invitations.'

He pulled out a chair for himself, and sat Mary on his knee. She gasped out to him her misery, the emptiness of the house, her pilgrimage of grief from room to room, while he patted and soothed her, knowing it was good for her to talk it out. When she was calmer he said, 'There, that's better. My dear, don't you think I'm not feeling it, too? How can we help missing them? But you know, our girls are married, not buried, and we must be happy for them and happy for ourselves. As. for the things that make you sad to look at, remember that when our two brides have their own homes they'll be back to fetch all the furnishings we can spare — and the cradles from the garret before very long, I'll wager. Now, doesn't it cheer you to think that the fourth leaf of our old table will have to come up to seat the grandchilder?'

Whether it was the homely dialect word, or the vision of small people in high chairs ranged round that dignified board, Mary blew her nose and began to laugh. It was not, Ephraim noticed thankfully, the laughter of hysteria.

'Why, yes,' she said. 'Of course it will. What a silly thing I am.' Her train of thought sobered her again. 'Father.' She played with his cravat pin, twisting the gold fox-head round in her fingers. 'Do you think they're ... well ... happy? You know what I mean.' Her head was bent, but he did not need to see her face.

'Was your wedding night so fearful, Mary?' he asked gently.

She threw her arms round his neck and kissed him. 'You know better than that.'

'And they love their husbands just as you and I loved each other. Well, then. Can I see a smiling wife in her best cap at supper?'

The supper was an exceptionally good one, accompanied by one of Ephraim's best bottles of Madeira brought up from the cellar. Mary, cheerful again, looked round the room, remembering Ephraim's remark about the possessions the girls might need.

'When do you think they will be able to set up house?' she asked him. 'I know it was agreed they should not come back here, and quite right, but they can't remain in lodgings for ever. I should so like to think they would be not *too* far ... no, Father, I'm quite composed now, pray don't look at me with that warning eye. I merely meant...'

'I know what you meant, and be sure I would like to have them not too distant, though a little distance is a good thing when folk are first wed. Belle and George, I feel sure, will make do with lodgings at least until his next voyage is over. As to Dove — Joe is a rich man now, and could afford a handsome house, but I know he means to live where his work is, and that work is to be the founding of a model factory. So ... who knows? Wherever they make their homes, let's drink to them and their happiness.' He raised his glass. 'To Mrs George Dilworth and Mrs Joseph Atkinson, all joy and prosperity.'

CHAPTER TWENTY-SIX

The summer idyll was over. It had been a week long, but to Dove it seemed like the shortest of days, a time indescribably happy, for which her whole life beforehand had been but a preparation.

She paused at the door, looking back at the room they had shared under the eaves of the Kendal inn. She would never forget the slightest detail of it. The rough chair, which, apart from a hook on the door was the only place to put their clothes; Joe's usually finished up on the floor or mixed up with hers. His untidiness was only one of the endearing discoveries she had made about him.

The chest whose drawers stuck so obdurately that she and Joe had given up attempting to use them. Instead they carried their valuables about with them, for Kendal was a town of honest people, Joe said. The geranium in a pot on the windowsill, a splash of lovely pink in the drab room. Every day Dove had touched its petals caressingly, and watched bud after bud open into a flower, as though it sensed the love that filled the room and bloomed with it.

The bed. A simple, country-hewn bed covered with a faded patchwork quilt, its mattress of goose down, the pillows stuffed with dried lavender to bring sleep. She had given and received such happiness in it, a joy beyond joy, undreamed of before. In her arms Joe had forgotten the past and all its troubles; fulfilled and freed at last, he had been silently grateful to Rosie for all she had taught him; and Dove found depths of passion in herself which she had not known existed. When she knelt by the bed to pray, among her prayers was one that Joe's heart might never go from her, for hers would be his for always. Her first love, her first lover, her husband.

She took her last look at the room. 'Thank you,' she said, and closed the door on it.

They were to live in lodgings until Joe found the right place for a permanent home. The second floor of a tall house in Church Street, Lancaster, was to be their home for the time being. Ephraim had chosen it, and it was elegant, even luxurious compared with the humble room in Kendal, but Dove would never care for it as much. The landlady, a plump widow, took a keen interest in their newly married state; whenever they entered or left by the front door she would invariably pop out like a jack-in-the-box, some remark about the weather or the news tripping from her tongue. They tried ways of evading her, from tiptoeing in a thief-like manner to using a door at the back of the house which meant traversing the untidy bramble-grown garden, but she was alert to such tricks, apparently aware of their approach by some sixth sense.

It was her habit to bring in their breakfast herself, rather than entrust that delightful errand to a servant, letting herself in with only the sketchiest of knocks. 'One of these days,' Joe said, 'she *will* catch us in bed, and that will make her happy for life.'

So they moved a heavy chair to a position where the opening of the door would move it across the floorboards with a loud squeaking sound, giving Dove time to leap out of bed and put on a bedgown before Mrs Ledbury could get any nearer to her goal. It annoyed Dove that she was still unable to meet the landlady's searching eye without blushing.

Ephraim laughed when they told him of it. 'Don't deny the woman her simple pleasures,' he said. 'All the world loves a lover, and it does no harm. In any case, you'll not be there long, I'm sure. I have a client who travels a long way to consult me, and yesterday he breathed some information in my ear which interested me. He is investigating at present, so I may have news for you soon.'

'How far is a long way?' Dove asked suspiciously. 'I must be near enough to visit you and Mother.'

'Never fear. Sixty miles, perhaps. Possibly less. We shan't banish you to the ends of the earth, my dear, if only for your own sakes.'

Dove and Joe had not been reassured by their visit to St Leonard's Gate soon after their return to Lancaster. Ephraim had kindly kept from them Mary's crisis of grief after the weddings, merely saying that of course she had missed her girls but was as cheerful as ever now. It seemed that the sight of Dove, firmly and indisputably married, with her bright new ring and her hair curbed by a matronly little cap, brought back all the shock of parting.

Dove caught her mother's gaze fixed on her wistfully, and felt immediately guilty in her own self-satisfaction with her married state. Walking back to Church Street she said to Joe, 'Do you think we did the right thing, moving into lodgings? We *could* have stayed with Mother until we get our own house...'

'My darling, that would only have prolonged her sorrow. Having you living in the house again, she would feel that you'd come home for good, and the next parting would have been all the harder. No, we were right to stay away — even with Mrs Ledbury's eye at the keyhole.'

'Of course. You always see the sensible side of things, love. But poor Mother ... I do trust Belle's return will cheer her. She's alone so much, Father at his office and only the servants to talk to; and Aggie is growing so grumpy, quite a misery.'

Ephraim was increasingly concerned about his wife. She was visibly thinner, but her lessened weight seemed to do nothing for the palpitations she suffered at the least exertion. He tried to interest her in anything that might keep her from brooding: the public rejoicings for Princess Victoria's birthday, the dismissal of an unpopular town clerk, his own purchase of more railway shares. He even marked passages in the newspapers which might be worth pasting in her snippets book, gathering dust on a shelf. But to all these efforts she returned only a weary smile, and sometimes a gentle touch of the hand, as though she knew how earnestly he was trying to help her.

It was something at least that Belle was back from her honeymoon. Eagle House had been delightful, so much luxury and elegance, but Belle could not wait to be alone with George. In the small house near the quays which they had rented from a customs officer she drew the curtains close and devoted herself to him alone.

George, who had a wide experience of women but none of wives (of his own), was in a constant state of amazement at the ardour of his bride. The stories of bashfulness and blushes were quite untrue, obviously. But it was not his way to look a gift horse in the mouth. He matched warmth for warmth, kiss for kiss, was charmed, delighted, amused by his amorous wife, and pleased at the new beauty love had brought her. Pretty as she had been before, there was now a shining quality to her looks, a glow, a bloom that told of fulfilment. The fining-down of her features left by her illness was gone; she was almost childishly plump again. Men turned to look at her in the street, whistled, shouted compliments at her — some of them in doubtful taste — but Belle took them all in good part, for they were a kind of compliment to George.

Married life was certainly delightful, he thought. He had forgotten what the marriage service said it was intended for, but certainly nothing like this had been mentioned. Only, now and again, he felt a little sated, like one who has sat at a banquet too long. He missed the company and conversation of men; and far beyond the grey coils of the Lune, the blue sea beckoned.

They were still in bed one morning when the clang of the doorbell roused them from a protracted and involved embrace. 'Drat the thing,' said George, suppressing a stronger oath, 'who can that be? Some tradesman wanting payment, would you say? Let them wait.' He drew her down, but she struggled out of his arms.

'I *always* pay the bills promptly.' The bell rang again. 'It must be something important. Let go, do, there's a dear boy.'

She reached the door panting and dishevelled, her hair ruffled from the hurried removal of a nightcap, her lacy bedgown only just managing to conceal that she was wearing nothing underneath it.

'John! Good gracious. I, er, was not quite prepared...' But how ridiculous to apologise to her father's groom for her appearance. She smiled graciously upon the youth, who touched his cap.

'If you please, Mrs Dilworth, Mr Atkinson sent to say Mrs Atkinson's taken bad, and will you go round as soon as you can.' He tried to avert his eyes from the glimpse of charming bare leg disclosed by a waft of wind.

'My mother! Oh dear. Thank you, John — say I'll come at once. Is it very bad, do you know?'

'Can't say. I weren't told no more nor that. Doctor's there now.'

Some twenty minutes later she burst into the room where her father sat awaiting the doctor's descent from Mary's room.

'Oh, Father, what is it? John said he didn't know. Is she very ill? Is it one of her turns?'

Ephraim was pale and had obviously slept little, but she knew from his smile that things were not as serious as she had feared.

'There's no danger, my dear. I'm sorry John's call alarmed you; I'd have come myself but that I wanted to remain in the house to see the doctor. This is his second visit — we sent for him at four in the morning, poor man.'

Belle breathed a sigh of relief, both for the good news and the fact that her father had not called in person to find her in such extreme déshabillé. 'But what happened?' she asked. 'Was it a sudden attack?'

'In a sense, yes — the worse for being delayed, I think. We had a little trouble here last night: a visit from your aunt Eleanor.'

'Aunt Eleanor? Why, what's the matter with her?' Belle visualised her hostess of a few days before, all charm and flirtatiousness for the benefit of Mr Disraeli's harem eyes.

Ephraim told her, softening the more unpleasant details of the story. On the previous evening they had been surprised by the sudden appearance of Eleanor. Ephraim had known at first glance that she was disturbed, shaken, though the flippant manner she always put on in Mary's presence partly disguised it. She asked for tea, which was brought, and drank it thirstily, then told them, with a look that seemed to challenge them to criticise her: 'I was sent for to go to Ashton Hall.'

'Roderick!' Mary exclaimed.

'Yes, Roderick. I was told he was very ill and wished to see me. So I drove over immediately. Well, the first part of the story was quite true; he was clearly dying from some complaint of the chest. There was an old woman with him, a nurse, but she spoke so thickly I could hardly tell a word she said. I ... sat down by his bedside and asked him if he had any last wishes.'

Ephraim could see that Mary was growing distressed. He put his hand over hers, feeling it tremble. Wherever Eleanor was, there seemed to be trouble.

'And had he?' he asked.

'None that I could make out,' Eleanor said carelessly, 'he was rambling too much for any of it to be comprehensible. I might as well have saved the journey, for any comfort my presence brought him.'

'*Eleanor!*' Mary was deeply shocked. 'Your own husband!'

Eleanor tossed her head. 'A fine husband he was to me, I must say. Well, I sat there until it became clear that there was no hope for him, and when ... when he breathed his last, I gave the old woman some money for his burial. It seems he'd bought himself a plot in High Street Chapel graveyard, so I can at least see that they put up some kind of stone to him.'

'Yes, at least,' Ephraim said drily. 'And did he say nothing at all to you, after your graciousness in rushing to his deathbed?'

Eleanor looked him in the eye. 'No. Nothing.' He had seen that identical look in the eyes of persons in the witness box and in the dock, and they had all been lying. He could guess at the truth behind the lie; the last bitter words of a bitter man to the woman who had ruined his life, as he had in part ruined hers.

'And so you are free,' he said, and knew from her startled, angry look that his guess at Roderick Mackenzie's last words had been somewhere near the truth.

'Yes.' Her tone was indifferent.

'You will marry Jesse, I suppose, as soon as you come out of mourning.'

Eleanor's eyes flashed. 'Mourning? I shall not go into mourning. Mourn, for a man who did what he did to me? Because of him I've lived in sin all these years. Because of him I've gone without the children I should have had. Do you expect me to advertise a grief I don't feel? Besides,' she shrugged affectedly, 'black is so very unbecoming and puts one to so much trouble — it always seemed to me a silly old custom, and it seems even sillier on this occasion.'

Ephraim had been watching Mary's colour rise to a dark flush. He knew that all her long-held antagonism to Eleanor had come back, and he feared the effect of her anger on herself.

'Eleanor,' she said, 'I never thought to hear any woman, much less a sister of mine, utter such wicked words. Evidently you have no sense of decency — I never thought you had, mind — but at least you could put on some sort of show to save your face. I'm downright ashamed of you, and that's the truth.'

'Thank you for your good opinion!' Eleanor flashed back. 'You can keep your shame for your own family, when they deserve it — a lot you ever did for me, treating me like a leper in the wilderness and blackening my name to my own nieces. You're a cold-hearted, stubborn pig — there, and I'm glad to have said it to your face!'

Ephraim was frantically signalling her to be quiet. 'Eleanor, Eleanor! She doesn't mean a word of it, Mary...'

'Yes, she does!' Eleanor retorted, jumping to her feet and buttoning her gloves with frantic haste. 'She means it all, and she's leaving this house, with great thankfulness, that she came to expecting some sort of understanding, if not sympathy.

Good evening to you, ma'am, and pray don't ring to have me shown out.' With a flurry of skirt she swept past them and through the door, slamming it behind her violently and repeating the same process on the front door.

Mary sat trembling for a long time. To Ephraim's soothing words she only shook her head speechlessly. He tried to persuade her to go to bed, in vain, but when he brought her a strong dose of her special drops she took it obediently, and let him sit by her side with his arm round her.

'Mother, please try to think no more of it. There was not one grain of truth in anything Eleanor said. A little bitterness from the past, perhaps, but surely we can comprehend that, in the circumstances. And we must remember that she must have been far more affected by poor Roderick's death than she said; one cannot see someone die and remain unmoved. That was why she behaved as she did, unfortunate as it was.'

'Shameless,' Mary murmured.

'Yes, no doubt, but people sometimes behave shamelessly in a disturbed state. I recall a woman prisoner who became extremely agitated under cross-examination, and began — quite unconsciously, I'm sure — to unfasten her dress, button by button, to the alarm and consternation of the court.'

To his relief, Mary gave a faint giggle. 'Did she fasten it again?'

'At the express request of the judge, yes.'

He thought the crisis was over, but in the middle of the night Mary began to cry out with pain in her chest and left arm. The doctor was summoned to deal with the worst heart attack she had so far had.

When Belle went in to see her she was calm, though exhausted, propped up on pillows. Forewarned by Ephraim,

Belle lavished on her every endearment she could think of, promising to visit her every day and to bring George.

'He's home for six weeks more, isn't that delightful — the next sailing has been put off, and George says he may even take me with him!'

Mary surveyed her daughter. 'You're happy, I can see that.'

'Oh, so happy!'

The baggage, thought Mary fondly, *I'll warrant she is.*

'And Dove is wonderfully happy too, and I shall call on her this morning and say that she must come and see you as soon as she can. Now you're to take care, dearest Mother, not to excite yourself one little bit, or I'll ask the vicar to come and read a volume of sermons to you.'

Mary promised that she would not incur this dreadful penance.

Before leaving, Belle said to Ephraim, 'Father, I don't think Mother should be alone. Dove and Joe think so, too. Is there nobody who could come and be company for her when you're at your office?'

Ephraim shook his head. 'Not that I can think of — unless we were to advertise for a lady companion, and who knows what kind of person would apply? It troubles me very much, Belle.'

Eleanor returned late to Eagle House after her stormy meeting with Mary. She was still furious and shaken, ready to pour out her outraged feelings to Jesse. But Jesse had gone back to London, she was told. Annoyed, she asked the maid, 'He's taken Mr Disraeli with him, I suppose?'

'Oh no, madam. Mr Disraeli's in the smoking room.'

Eleanor began to feel better. She made an elaborate toilette, transforming herself from a tired, travel-stained woman into a vision in rose-pink muslin, a daring confection worn without stays so that it floated loosely round her figure. Thus improved, she swam gracefully into the smoking room.

Benjamin was seated by the fire in a comfortable wing chair, his Turkish-slippered feet extended before him on a footstool. He was smoking a hookah, a complicated Eastern pipe which he affected; it made curious bubbling sounds and gave off heavily scented smoke, which Eleanor sniffed appreciatively.

'My dear lady!' He leapt to his feet, abandoning the hookah, all in one flowing gesture. 'I'm more than honoured. I was told I should not enjoy your company tonight. Pray forgive the indulgence,' he waved towards the hookah, 'which you must find quite nauseating.'

'On the contrary, I like it. In any case, if a lady enters a smoking room she must expect to encounter smoke. Do sit down, Ben, and don't stand on ceremony with me. I feel like light, agreeable conversation, after such a day as I've had.' She shook herself like a cat shaking off rainwater. 'Lord! I wouldn't go through it again.'

'No personal disaster, I hope?'

'Not at all. A family visit. An old ... relative. Just enough to fray one's spirits.'

'I understand.' He did not, for in his Jewish society an old relative was as worthy of concern as a young one, if not more so. Eleanor would have been surprised to learn the extent of his knowledge about her situation, gathered from gossip, hints, a piece of information, an inspired guess. He would never know the full truth about the wretched scene in the cottage at Ashton Hall, but he remembered from his old acquaintance with Eleanor a remark of hers which suggested that her marriage to Jesse was a fiction, and his one brief visit to the Duke of Hamilton had given him the clue to the connection between the crippled dispatch rider who was a pensioner of His Grace's and the lady at Eagle House. He had seen Jesse go off that day in a pet and had drawn his own conclusions. Well, women — the enchanting creatures — were meant to be kept happy and amused. It would not be his fault if this one were otherwise.

'I trust I have not overstayed my welcome,' he said, knowing full well that he had not. 'Mr Bradshaw heard the call of duty, but I seem to have no particular business beyond pleasure, and that, in the modern Babylon, comes confoundedly expensive. Besides, my rooms in Park Street are the very obverse of what a man of luxurious tastes ought to occupy, and so well known to the debt collectors that I have to take the strangest means to avoid them. In the country, one may hide down a well; in town, there are fewer stratagems at one's disposal.' He described them, so extravagantly that Eleanor laughed heartily.

Before long a bottle of very good wine had appeared, brought by a servant concealing yawns, and they were sharing it. A glass or two later Eleanor was reclining on the hearthrug at his knee, her head back, contentedly having her hair stroked and played with by long, delicate white hands. It was not, he reflected, the sleek dark hair of his lost Henrietta, or the bright brown hair, spaniel-ringleted, of his wished-for Mary Anne, but it was very pretty of its kind, and so was her long, extended throat, that still had only a hint of middle-aged sag to it, and her fine-boned face.

'I'm too old for you,' she murmured sleepily. 'Forty-nine, you know.'

'Youth is a blunder.'

'Well, then, you funny person, we are behaving very badly.'

Man is only truly great when he acts from the passions.

She sat up, pointing at him. 'I do believe you're quoting your own works!'

'Of course. Whose better?'

'Oh! I give you up.'

'Don't do that.' He pulled the pins out of her hair and gathered up the mass of it, letting it trickle through his fingers. 'Take me up, instead. Up to my charming, isolated, utterly Gothic tower room.'

Eleanor scrambled up from the hearthrug, contemplated him with a mixture of amusement, satisfaction, gratitude and anticipation, all of which emotions he recognised and approved. She reached out her hands to him; he took them, and, embraced, they left the room. The hookah grew cold, its smoke dispersed as the fire in the grate sank and died.

Joe and Dove were on their way to Manchester. Dove's white brow was knotted with anxiety as she looked out of the carriage window.

'Are you *sure,* Joe? Aunt Margaret and I passed through Manchester on our way back home, and I recall it as a very dirty, spreading place. I should not like to live in a dirty town. Do you think Father's friend knows what we want?'

'I've no doubt of it, my love,' Joe returned equably. 'Uncle Ephraim is very experienced in the art of describing what we, or other people, want. I'm sure he will have made it plain, and from the map Uncle showed me the site looked extremely promising.'

He could see that she was still apprehensive, though moors and the distant Yorkshire hills reared themselves to the left of the road, in misty beauty, and small farms and cottages still appeared along the way. Ahead was a pall of smoke, lying low like a dark cloud over tall chimneys and high buildings. It was not like Lancaster, or London. Dove shrank nearer to him.

They were passing an inn, the Royal Oak, and close by it a maypole. 'Failsworth,' Joe told her. 'Almost in Manchester, yet things still look countrified. Look, over there you can see t'Owd Church.'

'What?'

'The collegiate church. They call it that from affection, I suppose.' He pointed to a square tower. 'We'll be up to it in a few minutes... Here's the Old Shambles, better looking than its name. That's the Sun Inn, where I used to take my dinner when I came here on errands for Whittingham. There's 'Change, the Royal Exchange, and there's the Market Cross. I forgot to tell you the river we crossed was the Irwell.'

'I feel sick,' said Dove very clearly. 'If this carriage doesn't stop soon I shall be sick.'

'Oh, my darling, pray don't! Shut your eyes, that sometimes helps. Here, have a tot of this.' He pulled out his pocket flask and filled its small silver cup with brandy. Dove drank it with a shudder, and settled against his shoulder, refusing to look at any more of the beauties, or otherwise, of Manchester. She had sunk into a kind of doze when she heard Joe's voice saying, 'Here we are. I said it wasn't far. Now, open your eyes and see if I've misled you.'

She opened them. The carriage had stopped in a small cobbled square, such as one might find in a country village. An ancient black and white inn dominated it, cottages and one or two prim houses clustered round. The air was very fresh and sweet, bringing the scents of fields and gardens; somewhere a cock was crowing. Dove, helped out by Joe, looked round in bewilderment.

'This isn't Manchester?'

'Just outside, to the south. We're near the River Mersey, in farm country. Are you stiff with sitting? We'll walk a little.'

He gave the coachman directions to change horses at the inn, and set off with Dove on his arm, across the round cobbles. She no longer felt sick as she breathed the strong air, and saw the sun glint on the bend of the river, across a meadow. It might have been a village beyond Lancaster, somewhere like Wray; any minute one might see Highriggs appear round a corner, and her grandfather Bateman leaning over the gate, smiling, waiting for her.

But the gate they were coming to was a dignified affair of wrought iron, with a touch of gilding on its curlicues and spears, and it stood between two carved stone posts. Joe opened it and ushered her through, into a neat drive with lawns on either side.

And there, in front of them, was the house. It was not large, as houses go, yet larger twice over than her father's, and it stood by itself, bowered in trees. A plain, comely house, with a face that almost smiled and windows that twinkled, a house built in old King George the Third's day, its grey stones mellowed by time, sun and river air. They came nearer to it; on each side of the front door, on built-out supports, sat, proud and straight, two stone lions.

'Well?' Joe's voice trembled a little.

She turned, her face alight. 'This ... is it ours?'

'If we want it. Ours.'

'The Lion House.' She bent to stroke one stone creature's head, fingering the curls of its mane.

'That's what they call it. How did you know?'

She shook her head. 'I seem to have known it always. Joe, am I dreaming?'

He kissed her, long and tenderly. 'Is that in your dream? Well, then. All quite real, my Dove.' He pointed to a high, many-windowed building almost hidden by trees, just where the river bent round. 'And there's my factory.'

Margaret joined Ephraim in his study. 'I'm glad you sent for me,' she said. He looked up from his work, startled.

'Mary's not worse?'

'No, no. But very low in her spirits. Glad of the news that Dove and Joe are settled, of course, and yet I know it saddens her to think of them so far away. "If anything were to happen," she keeps saying. I know she means that she might have another attack, this time fatal, without Dove being at hand. Or anyone else, for that matter, if you were out and the servants failed to hear her bell.'

Ephraim passed his hand wearily across his eyes. 'What can I do, Margaret? I can't neglect my work. These nurses the doctor suggests we might hire — how do we know but that we might get some drunken slut, or someone who would be cruel to Mary when my back was turned? One hears such tales. I'm at my wits' end, I can tell you. God knows what the answer is.'

She sat in the chair on the opposite side of the wide desk, very straight-backed and composed. 'I think God has already told you the answer, Ephraim, whether you were aware of His voice or not. I think he put it into your mind to send for me today.'

'You? Well … I knew it would please Mary to see you.'

'More than that. Who else, in our family, is a free agent? Who has no ties of husband or home? I have thought it all out, and I am quite resolved. Nobody can look after Mary better than her own sister. There's plenty of room here, and I shall be very comfortable. I shall come as soon as I can settle my affairs in Knott Green — if that's agreeable to you, of course.'

Ephraim stared, hardly able to believe his ears or credit this simple solution to the difficulty. 'But, Margaret, you *have* a home. How can you leave it — or your parish duties, or your writing? No, no, it's too great a sacrifice.'

She shrugged. 'I'm a middle-aged woman, Ephraim, with no domestic duties to occupy me — one house is much the same as another to me. As to parish work, I'm sure there is plenty here for me, and my writing can be done on any table, so long as I have books at hand.' She pushed to the back of her mind the image of her neat, elegant house, her well-trained servants, her beloved routine of morning work, afternoon visits, work again for an hour or two, then peaceful evenings of reading by her own fire; of the shelves of treasured books, the furniture and ornaments that reminded her pleasantly of Mrs Mortison, and her rescue of the poor short-sighted theatre drudge. These things were all Margaret had, husbandless and childless, and she loved them very dearly; but the time had come to give them up. She smiled brightly at Ephraim, completely deceiving him.

'So you see it's all but settled. When I move in all your troubles will be over — or so I hope. I can read to Mary — she loves that, you know — or talk to her or whatever she pleases; then when you come home perhaps I may go to my room and write. I can see it all falling into a pattern, so neatly.'

'But — your house?'

'Oh, I shall shut it up, all but two or three rooms, and my maid Jane Bryan can live in them and keep the place aired. No difficulty at all about it.'

There was just the least crack in her tone, enough to cause Ephraim to put on his spectacles and regard her shrewdly.

After a pause he said, 'I think you are doing a very noble thing, Margaret. I don't know how to begin to thank you.'

'Oh,' she said airily, 'I am only doing what is right, and to do that always benefits oneself, so in fact I am being quite selfish. Goodnight, dear Ephraim.' She kissed him lightly on the forehead and went out quickly.

It came into his mind that he had been visited by something very like an angel, disguised though she was in gold pince-nez.

CHAPTER TWENTY-SEVEN

Jesse Bradshaw was returning to London in no very sunny mood. He was annoyed by Disraeli's sudden appearance, which had distracted Eleanor's attention from himself and frustrated his intention to improve their relationship. It seemed that Eagle Hall was to be merely a social centre for her life, not a home for him. Hardly worth the long journey from London.

Perhaps he would give up the Bryanston Street house and take cheaper bachelor lodgings. There was nothing very inviting about sheeted furniture, dust-bagged chandeliers, and no woman in the house. Perhaps he could, like so many bachelors and husbands with country homes, find his recreation at Marguerite Blessington's.

He was displeased with himself for having left the north in such angry haste that he had not troubled to go up to Bradhope and visit Shem. His brother had not looked well at the wedding; Jesse had noticed him hurry out into the churchyard before the rest of the congregation as though he urgently needed fresh air. Poor old Shem, alone up there in Bradshaw Hall — as alone as he would be in London.

He had chosen to travel by stage, rather than hire a carriage for the long journey. The coach was crowded and stuffy, the roads full of traffic. By the time the Highflyer reached the Midlands he was heartily sick of travelling. When it stopped to change horses at St Neots, still many miles short of London, sudden impulse made him reclaim his luggage and take a coach departing from the same inn, going westwards to Buckingham. He would go and visit his constituency.

It was a relief to his spirits to find himself in the pleasant little market town in good time for dinner at an inn. He decided against the most notable ones, the Swan and Castle and the White Hart, and made his way, slowly because of the bag he carried, down a steep cobbled street to the Red Horse, that stood near the edge of the town and looked towards open country.

He had stayed there before, always enjoying the quiet of the situation and the cleanliness of its rooms. Fastidious Jesse had a violent dislike of the bugs which almost invariably emerged at some time of the night, to render the traveller's night sleepless and leave him with red itching bumps all over. Some people took them as a matter of course, even entertained them in their homes: not so Jesse. He knew that old Mother Burslem, the landlady of the Red Horse, had a short way with the creatures that involved a lot of hard work and many journeys upstairs with hot water by her handmaids.

The public room was on the full side, he found, and he elected to take his evening dinner in one of the private parlours, a small flagged room with a good fire and one comfortable chair. Stretched out in it with his boots off and wearing a clean neckcloth, he felt the irritation and stress of the past twelve hours dropping away from him. The smell of cooking drifting in from the kitchens made him realise how healthily hungry he was.

At last his meal was served. He remembered a slightly crippled oldish man who had waited on him last time, and talked of Waterloo and Salamanca. Tonight the tray was brought in by a young woman who gave him a shy greeting in an accent tinged with rural Buckinghamshire. He reflected that Mother Burslem must insist on as high a standard of cleanliness and neatness in her staff as she did in her bedding.

It was disagreeable to have one's food served by dirty sluts; this girl looked as clean as a new pin.

'What's become of Tom?' he asked her.

'Died, sir. Three months since. The doctors said 'twas a bullet lodged in him that killed him.'

'Indeed! So many years after the wars. How strange.'

He watched her as she laid out dishes and cutlery on the table, placed a pan on the hob by the fire, laid out a napkin crackling with starch. There was something soothing about her presence; he asked, to make her stay a little longer, 'Are you from these parts?'

He noticed that she kept her eyes cast down as she answered, obviously trained not to encounter the bold eyes of gentlemen more than was necessary. 'No, sir, from Wendslake. Near on ten miles away.'

'I know it well: it happens to be my parliamentary constituency.'

The eyes were raised suddenly. They were of a soft, deep blue, the blue of forget-me-nots, and they held flattering admiration. 'Why, be you our Member for Parliament, sir?'

'Happily, I am.'

'There, now.' Evidently she was not a talker, but there was no question that she was deeply impressed, and for some reason Jesse felt gratified. It was ridiculous, he knew, to care about a servant-girl's admiration; he might as well have worn a placard round his neck advertising his status, and gained the applause of the whole town. He smiled at the silly thought, and saw a smile touch the girl's face. But she indicated the soup tureen, saying, 'It'll get cold,' and vanished.

The soup, a rich beef broth, was delicious. He could not remember when he had enjoyed anything more. The roast duckling that followed was equally delicious, and the fillet of fish which preceded it. He asked the girl, 'How do you come to have fresh fish, so far from the sea?'

The eyes were modestly cast down again now. 'Madam has an ice-house, sir. It serves very well.' She placed the pudding on the table, covered it with a steel dish, and was gone before he could extend the conversation. Now she would not come back except to clear away the dishes. On impulse, he jangled the bell. She answered it swiftly.

'This ale is excellent. A local brew, I fancy? Will you fetch me another tankard of it?'

By now he had had the chance of taking in her appearance fully. She was of medium height, very neatly made, with a slender waist and delicate wrists and ankles, these last displayed in white cotton stockings and bound with the ribbons of her little black slippers. The skirt of her dark blue dress was short and full, the bodice long-sleeved and low-cut in the present fashion, showing a good deal of creamy shoulders and bosom. Round her neck she wore a black ribbon, simply knotted. Her cap was a becoming wisp of net that sat lightly on brown hair parted in the centre. Her face was not beautiful — not even very pretty, perhaps — but there was something about its smooth youthfulness and gravity which Jesse found infinitely pleasant; a face to gaze at, and never want to look away.

When the ale came he showed her the substantial remains of the pudding. 'Excellent, but far too much for me after such a meal. Won't you take some yourself?'

'Oh no, thank you, sir.' Her expression said, *It'd be as much as my place is worth.*

'I wish you would.'

'I get plenty of food, thank you, sir.'

Yes, she had nothing of the starved look he was used to among the peasantry. 'Are you of a farming family?' he asked, fearing to scare her away by questions yet avid for more information about her.

'No, sir. My father was curate at Wendslake. He left mother with seven of us to bring up.'

'Ah, yes. It all proves the point I am constantly making...' In time, fortunately, he realised that he had begun to embark on yet another exposition of the Malthusian theory of population control. Eleanor often told him it was an unsuitable subject for female ears, and it would certainly have frightened away this shy bird. Yes, she made him think of a bird, a young thrush, perhaps: bright-eyed, soft, defenceless. He noticed the dimples in the hands that held the pudding dish; dimples where hard knuckles would be in an older person. They were curiously alluring to him.

'Tell me your name,' he said. There was a pause before she answered.

'Sally. Sally Winterslow.'

'Then, Sally, I'll be much obliged if you'll bring me a draught of mulled ale at ten o'clock or thereabouts. I find it conducive to sleep even at this pleasant time of the year.' He glanced out towards the inn garden, where late May blossom was still pink on the trees, and a young moon showed.

'Yes, sir. Shall I bring a lamp, sir?' She glanced at the book he had by him.

'If you'll be so kind.' Damn it, would she say no more than five words at a time or so? When the lamp came he opened the book, a political treatise with which he violently disagreed and which normally would have kept him stimulated with annoyance, but it failed to hold his interest. His mind constantly wandered away, until he shut the book and went to look out at the darkening garden. He could think of nothing but Sally, and of no reason why it should be so. A man

403

accustomed to assessing facts and figures, not given to self-analysis, it did not consciously occur to him that he was missing his wife's love, suffering from a sense of being cheated, middle-aged, growing stouter and balder (though still very presentable), in need of reassurance and emotional sustenance. It was a kind of sunset with him; he must enjoy its glow while it lasted. All this lingered far beyond his thoughts, in some region he was not used to exploring.

When she knocked with his drink of mulled ale he asked her to sit down. She shook her head at first, then, accustomed to obeying her betters, took the chair by the table and seated herself stiffly on the edge of it, her hands in her lap.

'Sally,' he said, 'I am very lonely. Won't you talk to me?' He was surprised to hear himself saying it. Lonely? How odd a state for a man of his wide acquaintance, yet it was true, he was as lonely as Shem among his money boxes and figures.

She raised her eyes, and this time they sent him a message: *I am afraid of you, I have only my reputation and this humble work. Please leave me alone.* He thought of the miserably underpaid farm labourers whom he and others tried continually to help, of the small people of England still subject to savage penalties and punishing hours of work, and he was ashamed for a moment. Then he said, 'Well?'

'I'm not accustomed to talking, sir. Madam will be wanting me.' She got up with a rush and was out of the room before he could woo her further. It was the strangest wooing he had ever engaged in.

He stayed at the Red Horse for three more days, seeing her, noting how she avoided him when she could, falling into an ever deeper infatuation with her. On the afternoon of the third day he saw her gathering vegetables in the garden on the edge of the orchard, and hurried to join her. She paused at his voice, stood up, her apron full of young green pea pods. There were wooden pattens on her feet to keep her slippers from the soil, and a cotton sun bonnet over her hair. She looked up at him with something like an animal's resignation in her eyes.

'Sally,' he said, and no more; he who could talk for an hour in the House.

'Yes, sir.'

'Sally, I love you.'

'No, you don't, sir. It's just the way ... you feel.'

'What do you know about how I feel? Tell me this, do you like me at all?'

'Yes, sir.'

'Well, how? As a man you'd marry, if things were different?'

'I can't say. You're a grand gentleman from London, I don't know more nor that.'

He found himself babbling, pleading with her, promising and believing his own promises. She should have a better place than the Red Horse, fine clothes, education if she wanted it, anything, if only she would be kind to him. If it had been possible for him to go down on his knees in the field, he would have done it, but between narrow rows of peas trained on sticks it was not. He trusted to his own eloquence and the near despair he felt. When she had heard him out she turned her face away; he read trouble in it, and was angry with himself, but would not have taken back a word.

'I must get on,' she said. 'Let me think, sir.'

He drank more that night than he should have done, the more because she did not wait on him and he thought she had taken flight. At last he extinguished the lamp an ill-favoured elderly woman had brought him, and flung off to bed, determined to leave in the morning. It was time he showed his face in London. These were bad times for the poor, for people like Sally and her family; there were problems of unemployment for politicians to deal with, troubles worse than his own hankering for a servant-maid. He would take in Wendslake on his way (the town he now knew she had been born in), talk to farm labourers and the oppressed, who needed him as she did not.

It was quite dark, the house quiet, when the wooden latch of his bedroom door was softly lifted. As he sat up, startled, she crept in. She was wrapped in some long dark garment, and carried no light. Her face was a faint glimmer, no more.

'Sally?'

She murmured something, he could not hear what. He saw her take off the dark cloak, which fell to her feet, showing her in what he guessed to be her white nightshift. He hastily lit the candle at his bedside, but she cried, 'No!' He extinguished it, and made room for her in the wide, old-fashioned bed, then drew the dark red curtains round them, so that the only light came through the window, where the moon now shone bright through the clouds, showing him her frightened young face, her white skin, as he gently, inch by inch, took off the coarse nightgown.

He thought, he knew, he made her happy that night. For all his burning need he was gentle, tender, thinking of her always as the little bird, the soft-feathered creature fallen from the nest into his cherishing hands. And she, though she cried, afterwards began to talk quite merrily, almost as though to an equal, telling him quaint little stories, giving him her own profound reflections on life, charming him, though his passion was sated now that she was a woman, no longer a tormenting, inaccessible vestal virgin, her mystery discovered, her secret revealed.

When she left him he gave her a handful of guineas, and she took them calmly, as a matter of course. 'I shall see you again soon,' he said.

She echoed 'Soon.'

He heard no more of her progress back to her garret on the floor above than he would have heard of a mouse's.

Two days after Jesse's departure from Eagle Hall a letter arrived for Disraeli by the earliest post. Eleanor scanned the envelope curiously, wondering who, among his friends, could possibly write such an unseemly hand, a scrawl slanting from bottom left to top right of the paper. It was taken up to him with his breakfast chocolate, so that she could not see his reaction to it. But later that morning he appeared immaculately dressed, pomaded and perfumed, bent reverently over her hand, and announced that sudden business commanded him back to London.

'Oh. So soon? I thought you had very little to occupy you there?'

'These things come up. Who can order them? I am quite devastated to tear myself away from your charming company and your immensely *intrigante* palace, but it must be. And now, if one of your people would be so kind as to drive me to the nearest town where I may take coach for the capital — I think it was Clitheroe...'

Their farewell was hasty, disappointed on her part, absent-minded on his. Ah well, she thought, so much for the pleasures of adultery, fleeting like all others. She took the trouble to go up to the tower room to see whether he had torn up the letter and thrown away the pieces, but there was no trace. It came into her mind that such a wild scrawl could only have been a woman's hand. She wished Jesse had not left so abruptly, knowing it was her fault that he had done so, her fault and Ben's. Ben was not for her, never would be. To try to keep him would be like hanging on to the tail of a comet or capturing the rainbow he sartorially resembled.

She had, in fact, been a fool. Bored and irritated by herself, the guestless house, the servants' humdrum enquiries about food and duties. She would drive to Lancaster. Not to Mary's — never again, after the last upsetting scene (though she would rather have liked to drive past the windows in an open carriage, showing off her new street dress of watered green silk and its accompanying bonnet with feathers dyed gold). No, she would drop in on Belle. They had always got on well; Eleanor felt she could have enjoyed such a daughter, had fate been kinder. Some cheerful, possibly catty conversation, a cup of tea, a good laugh. These were just what she wanted, and one could always be sure of them with Belle.

There was no answer to her knock at the door of the house by the quay. She repeated it, then turned the knob. The door was not locked; she walked into the narrow hallway.

The sound of noisy, uncontrolled sobbing filled her ears. She opened a door at random, and found herself in a cramped little sitting room cluttered with furniture. The portrait in oils of a naval gentleman glared down from above the mantelshelf strewn with seashells and objects which were obviously souvenirs from foreign parts, including one which looked suspiciously like a very small mummified skull. Eleanor hoped it was a monkey's.

Belle lay face down across the battered sofa, weeping with such abandon that she did not turn at the opening of the door. Eleanor ran to her.

'Belle, Belle! What is it, child? Gracious, how you cry! Pray don't distress yourself so. Come, now.' With pats and strokes and consolatory words she gradually induced her niece to sit up, showing a scarlet face and eyelids so swollen they were almost shut. She pushed back the damp, tangled hair from her cheeks and regarded Eleanor with a look of dumb wretchedness.

'Won't you tell me what it is? Is it George? Some accident?'

A shake of the head.

'Then ... your mother?' Eleanor disliked having to ask about Mary, but it was just a possibility that her nasty temper had carried her off suddenly.

'No,' Belle muttered. 'Nobody's ill.'

Eleanor sought about for other reasons for such lamentation. 'You're behind with the rent?' she hazarded. 'In which case there's no difficulty at all — I have plenty of money with me, look.'

But Belle was shaking her curls again like a wet spaniel. 'It's ... me,' she got out. 'I ... I'm...' A flood of further tears stopped her words. She wept for quite a minute, while Eleanor stared helplessly on, then raised her head and said in sepulchral tones: 'I'm in a ... condition. I'm expecting a b-baby. There.'

'Well!' Eleanor gasped. 'How very delightful. I do congratulate you, my dear. And so soon...'

'So soon!' Belle blazed out, now dry-eyed. 'When we've only been married a few weeks, and ... and George had got permission to take me out with him to the B-Bahamas. Oh!'

'Oh, pray don't go off again, there's a good girl. You mean that ... you would not be safe at sea, in such a state.'

'George says not,' Belle said sullenly. 'He says there'd be no surgeon aboard capable of looking after women, and there'd be no proper care when we got there, to Nassau that is, because they're all savages or something, which I don't believe for one *moment*. I've been all over the *Chloe* and she's as comfortable as a house, at least George's quarters are, and I've looked up the Bahamas in a dictionary and it says they're a British possession … not that it matters, for I'm sure having a baby is much the same wherever one is.'

'I believe so,' Eleanor murmured. 'However, George doubtless knows best…'

'He doesn't! He doesn't! He *wants* to leave me behind to get fat and ugly and have to nurse a horrid little brat when I'd much rather have a kitten, as I'd meant to have on board — because of the rats, you know.'

Eleanor was very much inclined to laugh, but she suppressed the desire, and sat quietly patting Belle's hand. It seemed that ladies were being deserted right and left at the moment, herself by Jesse and Ben, Belle by George. There was not much she could say, except to suggest tea, which Belle made very carelessly before the water was quite boiled, and which tasted horrible. Delicately picking the tea leaves out of her mouth, she said, 'I have the trap at the door. Would it do you good to come for a little drive?'

'Yes, it would, Aunt. Perhaps we can go on some nice rough roads, and shake this … this *creature* up a bit.'

'Belle! Really, child. You will feel quite differently before long.'

'No, I won't. You'll see, I'll feel just the same.'

'Do your parents know of this?'

'No. I've only been sure myself for a few days. I shan't tell them until later.' Her face brightened. 'After all, it *might* pass off…'

Eleanor reflected wryly how happy she would have been to find herself in Belle's situation, and how the last wish in her mind would have been for it to pass off. Life dealt out its cards very oddly, to be sure.

Another month had gone before Belle brought herself to tell her parents the news, and was disappointed at their totally unsympathetic reaction. Both were delighted at the prospect of a grandchild so soon, then pained and shocked by Belle's attitude.

'I don't understand you,' Mary said flatly. 'To think that any young woman in your fortunate circumstances shouldn't welcome her own child. Why, when I knew I was to have you I thought it a kind of miracle. Girls must have changed since my time.'

Belle had gone pink, but said indifferently, 'Perhaps they have, Mother.'

'"Mother"! I suppose that word on the lips of your infant won't sound sweet to you, then?'

'I hadn't thought of it.'

Ephraim broke in. 'Belle, your mother and I have all the patience in the world towards you, but your coldness in this case tries it considerably. We can only be charitable and put it down to a disturbance of the mind which often affects women in your condition … and perhaps ill health as well.'

Belle met her father's stern look boldly. 'I am perfectly well — never better — and if my mind's disturbed you'd better have me committed to the asylum, hadn't you? Except that it wouldn't suit you to have your precious grandchild brought up there, would it?'

Ephraim rose and walked out of the room. They heard him go upstairs and shut his study door. Belle was overcome with guilt. She knew she had behaved badly, hurt her father very much, and angered her mother, who was glowering at her in a way that suggested an impending attack. It was time to haul down her colours. Almost timidly she said, 'Perhaps Father's right, and I am not quite myself.'

'I should hope not.'

'Don't upset yourself, Mother. I wish I had told you some other way. It's only … I am so bitterly disappointed that I can't sail with George. Don't you understand? We've been together such a short time. It's too soon to be separated by a … a stranger, which is what a baby really is, if one is to be frank and not sentimental?'

Mary said, 'I think you'd better go home to your husband and let him talk some sense into you.'

George was quite prepared to talk sense, though not the sense Belle longed to hear from him. He was pleased that he was to become a father again. He was very fond of the parti-coloured daughter and son he already had by different mothers, pretty, jolly children with curly black mops of hair and teeth as white as melon seeds; it would be interesting to have a blonde one as well, and he was quite sure it would be handsome. He was as attracted to Belle as ever, and felt a twinge of regret that he would not be able to show off her English beauty to his friends in the West Indies, dressed as fine as the governor's lady.

But he knew himself well enough to realise that he needed to get away from her, away to other scenes and activities, as a tree needs to have the ivy pruned away from it. And he was certainly glad not to have to face another six months or so of Belle's moping.

'After all, my love, I shan't be away long. The last voyage was exceptional, because our cargo was of different varieties. You'll hardly notice I've gone before I'm back, just you see.'

'You know I shall. Besides, I shall be alone when the — when it's born.'

George laughed. 'Alone? That you won't. What with your mother and my mother, and Dove and the girls, and your friends, you won't have a moment to yourself.'

'But I don't care for them, I want you,' she said.

The last nights before his going were the most miserable yet the most passion-filled she had ever spent. The strength of her embraces made him fear for her and the child, filled him with a pity tinged with impatience. Had she been able to take it lightly it would have been so much easier and pleasanter. George liked things just so; violent emotions alarmed him.

With a coward's heart, he crept from their bed in the small hours of the summer morning when the *Chloe* was to set sail, wind and tide allowing. His luggage was already packed and waiting in the hall. Silently he dressed, glancing continually towards the huddled form in the bed. She had cried herself to sleep.

In a few minutes he was at the quay. He sent a sailor for the bags, giving him the key, so that he need not have to disturb Belle. Until the man came back he waited in high anxiety. If they could not sail at that time, it would all have to be gone through again. But he and the *Chloe* were lucky: within an hour, the anchor was raised, the sails rattled and crackled in the breeze; they were moving. His heart lifted, he felt as light as one of the seagulls wheeling overhead; he blew a kiss towards the shore.

A watchman slowly passed down the street, beneath Belle's window, crying solemnly, 'Five o'clock and all's well.' But she did not hear him. Merciful sleep still held her from the empty place at her side.

In another bedroom, many miles to the south, Dove woke in the faint light of early morning. She stretched herself, blissfully comfortable. Beside her Joe slept in complete silence. In the first weeks of their marriage he had wakened her with bad dreams. Now that was all changed. He was calmer, more cheerful, than she had ever seen him; he had come into his own at last, a husband and householder, no longer 'Young Mr Atkinson' in Ephraim's shadow, but Mr Atkinson in his own right.

Husband, householder — and next year to be a father. She stroked her own still-slender body. She was counting the weeks until her child should awaken and stir. There had never been such joy, such excitement in life as now.

A sudden thought of Belle came into her mind, unsummoned, and with it faint uneasiness. Belle didn't even know about the coming baby. It was not easy to find time to write, with so much to do in the new house. Dove would tell her when she went up to Lancaster on the visit she had promised herself soon. Poor Belle... but why should she think of her sister so?

She drifted off to sleep again.

CHAPTER TWENTY-EIGHT

That same morning, June 20, as the sun began to show through the mists of leafy Kensington, a carriage bowled up to the lodge of the old red-brick palace. The gates were shut, the porter asleep, but the errand of the eminent gentlemen in the carriage was an urgent one. Soon the gates were opened for the Archbishop of Canterbury, the Lord Chamberlain and the royal physician to be admitted to the presence of a girl with her hair flowing down her back, over the dressing gown she had hastily put on.

She was just eighteen. A few hours ago she had been the Princess Alexandrina Victoria. Now her uncle, old King William, lay dead at last, and she was Queen. The British nation had become Victorians.

Jesse Bradshaw, back in London, was plunged into activity along with his parliamentary *confrères*. Parliament was dissolved, as always on the death of a monarch, and a general election impended. The new Queen had made it clear that she wished Lord Melbourne, the Whig leader, to remain at the head of affairs with the rest of his colleagues in the Ministry. She was known to favour the Whigs strongly; if the country followed her, as was likely, so wildly popular was the succession of this pure young girl after the weary old monarchs who had gone before, the tide might turn against Tories such as Jesse. He would have to fight to keep his constituency.

He was not too perturbed, for he knew his own principles to lie in the direction of democracy. He had seen enough of the condition of the people, whether in field or factory, from his youth onwards, and without flattering himself he could honestly say that he was not angling for a knighthood or political leadership, but for what he felt to be a better way of life for England. The change of monarchy filled him with hope. Year by year, he had seen improvements in his lifetime: fewer and fewer hangings, lighter punishments except for the most extreme crimes, a Poor Law which was not in itself a good one but must lead to better things. Times were changing — perhaps the coming of a queen to the throne would turn the wheels of change faster.

Something of his ideas and ideals had come, he knew, from Ben Disraeli; he must be thankful to his friend for that. Now, in the excitement of the campaign, he no longer cared very much about the silly situation that had come about at Eagle Hall. The place, and Eleanor, seemed very far away. Not so Disraeli, who was embarking upon a tussle for Maidstone, whose Tory seat had been won two years earlier by Wyndham Lewis, husband of the lady who held Ben's susceptible heart. Backed by his influential friends Lord Lyndhurst and Lord Chandos, and enthusiastically canvassed for by Mary Anne herself in bouncing ringlets and a startling gown of electric blue, Ben was enjoying himself immensely. He was not available, as he had been before, to help Jesse with his influence in Buckinghamshire. Jesse's solitary campaign was waged against an elderly Whig who had lost a certain amount of popularity in the borough. Had his opponent been a Radical, matters might have been very different. As it was, his views were so broad in comparison with the Whig's, so aware of the high prices of food, the low wages of labourers, and the changes that were coming as railway building went on, that his position was strong.

Tirelessly he spoke on public platforms, visited constituents, waged small personal wars to remedy hard cases of want. In early July he reaped his rewards: a victory for Jesse Bradshaw, Esquire, over Augustus Elphinstone, Esquire. He would be back in Parliament when it sat again.

In all this he had not had a moment to go back to the Red Horse. Sally came into his dreams often, into his thoughts sometimes, particularly when he was very weary.

He would take up a letter from Eleanor, full of light gossip about doings at Downham, and suddenly the writing would blur before his eyes, replaced by a clear, sharp vision of Sally's face as he had seen it first, by his dinner table, grave and composed. Somehow he never saw her in his mind's eye in that low-beamed quiet bedroom. But other matters came up; it was four months before he travelled the ten miles from Wendslake to Buckingham.

The Red Horse had not changed at all — why should it? Only he had changed from the restless creature he had been in May to a busy, fulfilled politician. He was glad to be back, at leisure for a few hours. He looked up appreciatively at the twisted old chimneys above the low gables, the diamond-paned windows set in intricate patterns of timbering. Eleanor would appreciate its picturesqueness — he must bring her here sometime, he thought, and then was struck by the unsuitability of doing any such thing.

He dined in the public room, rather to his disappointment; he had envisaged himself in the small parlour again, waited on by the same dimpled hands. Two waiters attended, in fact, both men he could not remember to have seen before. He was surprised to find, as the meal went on, how little he was enjoying it, and how much he felt the want of Sally's presence. He hoped she had not been degraded to the kitchens or to a chambermaid's duties. But upstairs, when he unpacked his valise and rang for more coal for the fire, it was a completely strange woman who answered. Perhaps the ownership and staff had changed. He asked the woman, 'Is Mrs Burslem still landlady?'

'Yes, sir.'

'Where is she now, do you know?'

'In 'er parlour, I'd say, sir.'

He went downstairs to the small room off the corridor that led to the stable-yard door. Mrs Burslem was indeed there, a large spreading figure, knitting in a chair which was entirely hidden by her voluminous skirts. Jesse made some light conversation with her before asking casually, 'The girl who waited on me last time I stayed here — what was her name? Sally, I believe. I haven't seen her about the house.'

'You won't. She's gone.'

'Gone?'

'Left. Been dismissed her place.'

'But … may I know why?'

Mother Burslem regarded him coldly over tiny steel spectacles. 'I'd rather not say, sir.' Her tone implied that it was none of his business.

He sought about for a legitimate reason to question her further. 'She … the girl was one of my constituents, in fact. Her family live in Wendslake. I take quite an interest in them. The father, you know, was a curate — a very worthy sort of man.'

'Pity his daughter didn't take after him, then, isn't it.' Her needles clashed together inexorably.

Jesse was quite used to getting answers out of reluctant people. 'I feel in part responsible for this family, ma'am. I should take it kindly if you'd give me the reasons for the girl's dismissal. If her sisters and brothers are in want because of it, I may be able to relieve them.'

The woman laid down her knitting. 'Very well, if you must know, she disgraced herself. Got into trouble.'

Jesse gasped. 'She...? I find that hard to believe.'

A curious glance was directed at him. 'Knew her well, did you, sir?'

'No. I ... a general impression.' He gulped.

The knitting was resumed. 'Three months gone she was, when it was found out, and packed off immediate with a week's wages.'

The room seemed to be spinning round Jesse. He took hold of the back of a chair, feeling himself turn hot and cold with a terrible suspicion. 'Where is she?' he managed to ask.

'How should I know? With her people, most likely. If you know 'em, go and ask.' With which the sharpest-tongued landlady in Buckinghamshire bent to her work.

Jesse went to his room and sat on the bed, his head in his hands. Ironically, it was the room he had briefly shared with Sally, on that night when he had disastrously forgotten Malthus's *Essay on the Principle of Population.*

December snow lay thick and untouched on the leaking thatch roof of the cottage at Wendslake, lending its shabbiness a certain false prettiness. The woman who opened the door to Jesse, and said she was Sally's mother, might well have been her grandmother, grey-haired and lacking teeth as she was. The room he entered was hardly furnished at all, the floor, of earth, ran with damp. An overgrown boy sat huddled by the fire, coughing, obviously very ill; Jesse had seen the symptoms too often before. He wondered whether Mrs Winterslow was slightly wanting in the head, so slow and vague were her answers to his questions. But, looking at her skeletal face and neck, as thin as the boy's, he guessed her ailment to be malnutrition, which starved the brain as well as the body.

No, she said, their Sally wasn't at home. They hadn't seen her since she looked in, oh, a long time since, to say she was changing her place.

'How long ago?'

Her mother couldn't remember. Before it turned winter, that was sure. Before the youngest died, her brother Johnny, and that was after harvest. A poor, thin harvest it had been, no profit for anybody. And after all there'd never been another word from Sally, or a penny of wages, which they'd counted on. The eldest girl next to her had gone to a hiring fair with her brothers only last week. It might be they'd send something, if they'd not been hired too far off... She gave Jesse a wincing, painful smile.

He was shivering, not only with the cold in the miserable room.

'But have you no idea where she might be?' he asked her desperately. 'With other relatives — your late husband's? Or some clergyman, perhaps? Do please try to think, Mrs Winterslow. I — I knew Sally and thought well of her. There might be something I could do — some employment I could get her. I have a good deal of influence in this part of the country.'

The woman only shook her head, not even sadly, he thought, but in utter resignation. 'Can't say, sir. Only that she don't write or send.'

He searched through his pockets, finding only banknotes, besides a few coins, and held out the paper money to her. 'Take these to your vicar, or your doctor, and he will tell you how you can spend them. I'll send someone to you as soon as I can.'

She nodded, putting the notes away carefully in the pocket of her torn skirt, but he doubted that she had taken in his words. He remembered the guineas he had given Sally. How long had they lasted?

He was thankful to get out of the cottage and rush across the snow to his tethered horse. His thoughts were turmoil, disaster uppermost in them.

Ironically, it was time to go north for Christmas. Eleanor looked at him curiously a few times, but seemed to think nothing in particular of his distracted condition after he had explained that parliamentary pressures lay heavy on him, taking his mind off everything else. He had no idea what they ate for the Christmas dinner, what guests came or what garlands decked Eagle Hall. Fortunately he was struck down by a violent cold which kept him in bed, away from the merry-makers, free to think what he could possibly do to find Sally.

At the first opportunity he returned south. Then began a weary round of journeys, interviews with unhelpful people, postmen, housekeepers, vicars, parish workers. He wished he had Margaret Bateman at his side, to help him by her experience. He had thought himself knowledgeable, influential; now his knowledge and influence were nothing, in the search for one lost girl. Sometimes the thought came to him that he was being foolish — that some other man than himself had betrayed Sally; but in his heart he knew it was not so.

It took him two months to find her. At a workhouse many miles from Wendslake, in Northamptonshire, on the edge of black industrial country, he was shown into the office of a matron who was civil, friendly and ladylike, compared with some he had met. She looked up her books. 'Yes, we admitted a young woman of that name, some six weeks ago.'

Jesse felt relief overpower him. Then something in her look struck to his heart. 'Is she here now?' he asked hurriedly. 'Is she well? Tell me, please. It has taken so long...'

The matron was slowly tapping her fingers on the back of the ledger. 'She was very ill when admitted. She had travelled a long way, and the weather was bad. We did our best for her, Mr ... I fear I didn't catch your name.' At the sight of his face she bent forward, anxious. 'But you're not well. I'll get you some water.'

'No. No. I'm ... well enough.'

Tactfully she busied herself with a file of bills until she saw that he was able to speak again.

'When did she die?' he asked.

'Two weeks ago. The twelfth of February. The birth was early — only a very strong woman could have survived it.'

'The ... birth.' Somehow he had forgotten the child; how could he have forgotten? So it was dead too, there was nothing of Sally left.

'Fortunately,' the matron went on, 'the baby was very lusty, and flourished with the good nurse we found. Would you like to see the little girl, Mr —' she looked down at his visiting card — 'Mr Bradshaw?'

He must have said yes, or nodded, for he found himself with her in a big, bare room full of cots and crying infants. The baby she produced from what was little more than a wooden box was not crying, but asleep. It was very tiny; it looked as if it would break at a finger's touch. Even more helpless a small bird than Sally. The matron watched him, understanding, silent.

'What,' he said carefully, 'what would happen to a child like this?'

'Well, we should rear it among other orphans until it was of an age to work, then find it suitable employment. You know the details of the recent Poor Law, I expect. Its future would lie with the parish overseer.'

He knew, very well. Small chimney sweeps, skivvies, drudges of all kinds, were what such children became. Suddenly he was strong again, knowing what he must and wanted to do.

'I will take her,' he said. 'I am her father.'

A respectable young woman, not one of the workhouse inmates, was found to accompany the child and Jesse on their journey. With money he gave her she bought some tiny clothes to replace the yellowed blanket the baby had been wrapped in. It was explained to Jesse that a wet-nurse must be found as soon as they reached their destination, and that the young woman, Mrs Park, would find one, such searches being her speciality.

Before they left Jesse asked to be shown Sally's grave. It was in the female paupers' burying ground, where no memorials marked the last resting places. But fresh-turned earth, lightly sprinkled with snow, showed where Sally lay.

Jesse looked at the mound for a long time. 'I will send for the coffin soon,' he said. 'She shall lie somewhere better than this.' He turned away, without looking back, from the grave of his last love.

The carriage drew up to the workhouse door. Mrs Park entered it, a swathed bundle in her arms. Jesse followed, and they set off through bleak February rain for Eagle Hall.

He had never seen rage like Eleanor's. Though he had tried to break the news to her gradually that he had brought home his illegitimate child, in the hope that she would bring it up, she hardly heard him out before her hand closed on a heavy ornament beside her. She hurled it at him, barely missing his head, then went off into a tempest of fury.

'You! You, who denied me my own children, to bring me your bastard, got on a servant-girl! Oh, you've never been faithful to me, I know that. I never accused you, did I? I put up with everything and said not a word.'

He said, 'You were not exactly chaste Lucretia yourself, my dear.'

'That's right, throw my flirtations in my face. If ever a woman had an excuse for flirting, I had. But I never shamed you as you've shamed me. Don't you suppose the servants know about it by now, and the whole of the village? Don't you suppose they'll all point, and stare, and whisper, at the barren woman who let her husband lay his brat on her doorstep and expect her to pick it up?'

'I've been very careful,' said poor Jesse. 'Mrs Park took it — her — into the housekeeper's room with a story we prepared. Nobody will talk, nobody at all. My dear, do please think about this...'

'Think? Is this a time for thinking? No, Jesse Bradshaw, my mind's made up. That foundling goes out of this door — back to the workhouse, if they'll have it, or the river if they won't.' Her breast was heaving, her eyes flashing; she looked like a handsome Fury.

'Eleanor, I beg you. I know it is a great deal to ask of you. I suppose I acted without thinking, but I was very distressed. Won't you try, at least, to understand?'

Instead, she dropped into a chair, lay back, and fell into the first fit of hysterics he had ever seen. Scream after scream was followed by wild laughter, bringing servants running from all over the house. Jesse left them gathering round her in alarm.

For a long time he stayed in his own room, thinking. Then he went down to where Mrs Park sat placidly, the baby on her knee, singing to it. 'I'll go out to enquire for a nurse as soon as she's asleep, sir,' she said. 'Look, how good she is, and so pretty a child. Who'd ever think she came from such a place?'

'Who, indeed?' he said absently. 'Mrs Park, I have some domestic problems. My wife is … unwell. I am going to my brother's for the night. Will you take charge, and use your own good sense, until I come back?' He had told her something of the story, which she seemed to comprehend perfectly; cottagers did not find such things shocking, particularly when the gentleman behaved as honourably as this one was doing towards a poor child that hadn't asked to come into the world.

Shem Bradshaw was very ill. He received Jesse in his bedroom, propped up high with pillows, gasping for breath. A nurse was there, not pleased to have her patient disturbed, but Shem waved her out of the room.

'I'm sorry to see you so poorly,' Jesse said. 'I wouldn't trouble you, but it's a matter of life and death.' He reflected, then said, 'Yes, that's true. It is.'

'Any matter of death concerns me closely,' Shem replied with a choking laugh.

Quickly, concisely, Jesse explained. There was no time to elaborate on his feelings for Sally and her daughter, but he knew his brother's sharp sensibilities. Much talk was not needed.

'So, you see, I have nobody to turn to but you. To cast the child out is unthinkable. I won't let it into the hands of some wretched baby-farmer who might let it die. I'm asking you, Shem, will you give my daughter house room, and her nurse, as long as she needs it? I promise I'll look after all the arrangements and see that you're not troubled.'

'I ... shan't be troubled with anything long,' Shem whispered. 'Will you reach me that?' He pointed to a covered bowl on a table, from which steam was rising. Jesse gave it to him; he uncovered it and breathed deeply of its vapours. 'Only way I can take breath at all.'

'Oh, Shem! Forget it all. Rest yourself. I'll find some way.'

The sick man waved a thin hand. 'No, no. Do what you like; bring the bairn here and make a nursery for her. Two nurseries. As many as you like. This house will be yours when I'm gone. Hers, if you like. I'll send for the attorney and have it written into my will. Tonight. Not much time.'

Jesse's eyes were full of tears; he was almost as speechless as his dying brother.

Moonlight streamed through the old many-paned windows of Eleanor's room, touching her as she lay on the chaise-longue at the foot of her bed. The room smelt strongly of the eau de cologne with which she had been bathing her face. She had taken frequent sniffs of her smelling salts, which had quite cured the headache caused by violent weeping, and the hoarseness of her throat had subsided.

Satisfaction filled her. She had shot all the bolts in her power. Jesse had been driven out of the house, obviously, and would not return that night; much she cared, she told herself. After the worst of her afternoon tantrum was over she had gone to Jesse's study and written him a long letter couched in the most vituperative terms she could summon. Once again she told him what she thought of his conduct: *If I was a Catholic it might well drive me to a convent, but I hope I have more sense.* She suggested that, as Eagle House appeared not to interest him in any case, he should remove all his belongings from it and live entirely in London, *where you may dispose of any* encumbrances *of yours as you please.* Eagle House had been bequeathed as much to her as to him; she defied him to get her out of it. As for the *being* he had so vilely introduced that day, he might remove it by noon tomorrow, or it and its attendant would be put out into the street. Finally, she wished him as much success in his parliamentary career as he deserved. She was rather proud of this last shot.

The letter had been left on his study desk, where he could not fail to see it. She hoped it would lacerate his feelings as hers had been lacerated.

Now, late at night, she felt strangely floating and airy, almost light-headed. She had taken no food or drink since midday, except for a glass of brandy and water that her maid had pressed on her. She got up and walked about, her feet hardly seeming to touch the ground. If it were not impossible in the circumstances she would have said she felt happy. All the resentment she had felt over the years for the situation Jesse's way of life had put her in had been worked off in a highly satisfying drama.

The curious lightness that possessed her sent her out of her room to roam the quiet house. She looked up the staircase that led to the tower room, only vaguely aware that something significant to her had once happened there. Along the dark corridors she went, the faces of portraits glimmering out at her from the panelling, the scent of the pot-pourri she kept all over the house spicy and fresh. A great white moth had blundered in through an open window; she watched it beating its wings against the glass, and on impulse opened the casement to let it out.

Without any particular design, she found herself on the first floor, near the head of the stone stairs leading to the hall. She was drawn to the heavy door with an iron ring for a door handle, the first room she had ever entered in that house. It opened, squeaking.

She was in the long, low room whose walls and ceiling were little changed since the time of the Tudors. Its one-time shabbiness had been replaced by tasteful decoration and furnishing in the old style; Eleanor was proud of it.

The silver light from a full moon was almost as strong as daylight. People said that if you stood in it long enough, you went mad. Eleanor smiled, wondering if she were not a little mad already. There was something odd about the air in the room. The pot-pourri scent was not noticeable here. Instead, she was inhaling a faint, sweet perfume of dried roses, the perfume she associated with this room. She had meant to make it up herself from the roses in the garden, but there had been so much to do that it had got overlooked.

A voice in her head said clearly: *Infusion of Roses. Take a small handful of Rose Leaves, Boiling Water, one pint, Dilute Sulphuric Acid, a teaspoonful and a half. Macerate for one Hour.*

Yes, of course. She knew that. But somehow the recipe had sounded quaint, as though it were not herself remembering it, but someone else. She was looking towards the great carved fireplace. Even in the moonlight its details were not clear, a trifle misty. Then she realised that she was seeing it through something; what? It looked like a collection of coloured shadows as much as anything else. The dolls' house Will Raven had made for her was visible through it, too, standing on the floor by the hearth.

The shadows joined up and made a shape. She was looking at a tiny figure in old-style dress, panniered skirts, cobweb lace, silk rosebuds and bows, a 'head' of powdered hair, feather-topped. The face was invisible; she sensed rather than saw a smile, just as she sensed rather than heard a voice.

'So it seems we're to be alone here, Nell, my doll, just you and I? No more husband, a naughty man as he is. Ain't it a sad thing, now, after all your high hopes. Ah me, these men... Yet he was never unkind — now, confess it — only this once in fetching the child to you, and then 'twas because you'd been unkind to him and driven him to a warm wench. Ain't that so?'

Eleanor stood very still; she could not have moved if she tried. She was not so much frightened as fascinated, like a person under a spell. The voice in her head went on. It seemed to come from far away, though she knew it was the figure by the fireplace that spoke.

'All these years and never a babe to bless you, oh deary me. A husband for the bed and no babby for the cradle... But 'tis too late now, ain't it, Nell? Your bosom as empty as your arms, no heart left to be a mama. Since you won't take it, this maid-child will die, you must know that from me. Then I can't tell you what will become of it, for 'tis not allowed to tell, not allowed...' The voice faded, then came back. 'The daughter I'd have cherished, poor creature, the daughter you'd have cherished too in your time, Nell. But too late ... too late...'

The faint, reedy tones had died away, the coloured shadows were fading, until the carved figures on the fireplace were sharp and clear again. The rose scent had gone, too, leaving only a blend of pot-pourri and beeswax polish in the air. Eleanor began to shiver.

'No! No!' she cried aloud, and rushed out of the room, banging the door, hurtling down the stone stairs like someone in a nightmare, and downstairs again to the basement.

Jesse came back the next day to pack his belongings. Without having read Eleanor's letter, he had already decided to leave Eagle House. The maid who admitted him wore a curious expression, as though she knew something she longed to say but dared not. Jesse was irritated; things were bad enough without servants making faces at him.

'Well?' he snapped.

'Please, sir, you're to go up to mistress's parlour, not to the study.'

'I was not going to the study, as it happens. Very well.'

Nerving himself to another awful scene, he entered the room overlooking the new rose garden which Eleanor kept for her own use, and almost fainted with shock at what he saw there. Eleanor was sitting by the window, clad from head to foot in a frilled and starched pinafore. At her side was an antique cradle — he remembered seeing it in the attics — polished and filled with white woollens; and in her arms was his daughter.

'Don't ask me,' Eleanor said hurriedly before he could speak. 'Just don't ask me, Jesse. I can't explain. Only that I'm very, very sorry for all that I said yesterday, and I blame myself for everything, not you. I think I must have been mad. This child is ours now — I shall bring her up as if I'd borne her.'

The stunned Jesse could only say, 'But … but you said… Are you not afraid you might…'

'Come to hate her? Never. Not now. I *wish* I could tell you what happened, but you wouldn't believe me. I'm not even sure it did happen. Never mind. Come and see how comfortable she is.'

She held up the baby towards Jesse. Its tiny face was framed in a delicate, fluffy shawl, its dark blue eyes regarded him thoughtfully. He took one of its fragile curled hands in his, looking with wonder on it.

'What shall we call her?' he asked, knowing Eleanor would have the answer.

'Lucetta,' she said promptly. 'It will be Lucy, of course, but she must be christened Lucetta.'

Jesse's memory was not good. 'Why?'

'After your grandmother, of course.'

Belle's son was born on a windy April morning at the house in St Leonard's Gate, up in the nursery she had known as a baby. She had wailed a good deal when they brought her from the house by the quay, complained about George's absence, and prophesied her own death to such an extent that Ephraim had made Mary go to her own room, afraid she might have one of her attacks. Yet the strong, heavy boy had arrived in the world with no trouble or fuss, changing his mother's attitude a good deal. No new mama could have been prouder or more radiant than Belle, surrounded, as George had prophesied, by every available member of her family and a large number of friends, in a new nightgown seething with frills and her hair down.

Ephraim was, if anything, prouder. For so much of his life he had conditioned himself to be without heirs. Then the twins had come along, and now this large, calm grandson, who was the fulfilment of his hopes and Mary's. She could hardly bear to be away from the baby's side, continually exclaiming that she thanked God she had lived to see the day.

'You'll live to see more grandchildren yet, Mother,' Ephraim told her, knowing that he erred on the side of optimism, by the doctor's opinion. Yet he, too, was thankful she had this.

Dove was not at her sister's bedside, for only an hour before George's son entered the world, her own had blinked and cried at the light reflected from the Mersey and the noise around him. His had not been an easy birth. Joe hovered anxiously round Dove, watching her come back to life and animation, after giving him and her nurse a few bad moments. When she could speak, she asked, 'Is he — healthy?'

The nurse stared. 'Aye, the Lord be thanked. What else should he be?'

But Joe remembered his first-cousinship with Dove, and carefully he examined his crimson, wrinkled son, waved a hand before his eyes, even pinched him, very gently. The child responded with indignant speed. He was, if anything, slightly ahead of his hours in promise.

'He's very healthy, love,' he assured Dove. She smiled and fell asleep.

Lucetta Bradshaw was christened in St John's Church at the same time as the two babies only a little younger than herself: Dove's son Edwin and Belle's son Laurence. Both Atkinson and Dilworth grandmamas protested against these outlandish names being introduced, but the parents were firm. It was time to put away the old names, son always called after father. Their children should have fine, melodious, romantic names befitting this new, exciting Victorian age. Belle, after all her earlier vapourings, impressed everyone at the christening by her extraordinary fondness towards Laurence, whom she would hardly let out of her arms long enough to be held by his godfather, Jack Dilworth. She seemed not at all worried that George was still abroad.

Dove, so happy in her own marriage, had already begun to matchmake for others. Speculatively she looked from one baby to another, the already-handsome blond Edwin to the already-pretty Lucy, as they called her now, a thatch of soft brown hair showing under her lace bonnet. Wouldn't it be strange if...? After all, Lucy was no relation, only the orphan child of one of Jesse's constituents, whom he and Eleanor had so kindly and so unexpectedly adopted. How fortunate she and Belle had been, first in their husbands, now in their children.

They came out of the church, the proud procession of Atkinsons, Bradshaws and Dilworths, a flutter of silks, pretty bonnets, well-cut suits and snowy neckcloths. There were daffodils on Shem's new-made grave, but that was not too sorrowful to contemplate, for by his wish he had been godfather to Lucy by proxy a few weeks after his death. The sun shone on the babies, as it had on their mothers when brides.

It was spring, 1838, the Atkinson fortunes were in the ascendant, and they saw only joy ahead.

A NOTE TO THE READER

If you have enjoyed this novel enough to leave a review on **Amazon** and **Goodreads**, then we would be truly grateful.

Sapere Books

Sapere Books is an exciting new publisher of brilliant fiction and popular history.

To find out more about our latest releases and our monthly bargain books visit our website: **saperebooks.com**